By the Same Author

Novels

Life Before Death

Are You Mine?

Licorice

Snap

Short Stories

Fruit of the Month

Polly's Ghost

A Novel

Abby Frucht

Scribner

SCRIBNER
1230 Avenue of the Americas
New York, NY 10020

SCRIBNER and design are trademarks of Macmillan
Library Reference USA, Inc., used under license
by Simon & Schuster, the publisher of this work.

Designed by Brooke Zimmer
Set in Adobe Garamond
Manufactured in the United States of America

1   3   5   7   9   10   8   6   4   2

Library of Congress Cataloging-in-Publication Data
Frucht, Abby.
Polly's ghost: a novel/Abby Frucht.
p.   cm.
I. Title.
PS3556. R767P65   2000
813'.54—dc21   99-35883
CIP

ISBN 0-684-83589-4

For Don

Acknowledgments

Thanks to Deborah Schneider for her invaluable insight, and to Jane Rosenman for her care, her insistence, her eye, her advice. Diana Madison, for our friendship, our late nights, our great talks, your thoughtful reading of this book. Buzz Inderdahl, for your stories and your talent for telling them. Alex, for being Alex. Jess, for being Jess. Mom and Dad, for your generosity, your intelligence, your friendship, your curiosity, your avoidance of judgment, your open minds, your love.

With thanks as well to the Vermont College MFA in Writing Program, for its support and for all I have learned there.

And to the National Endowment for the Arts, which provided much-appreciated assistance during the writing of *Polly's Ghost*.

Contents

Prologue

I

I never intended for Tom Bane's airplane to fall out of the sky.

I only intended for *something* to fall.

A meteorite, maybe, lost soul of a comet, trailing its echo of sparks past the island the size of the tree on the night my son and his new friend, nine years old, sat at their campfire there.

Or better yet a brown pelican, more thunk than plummet, making the boys quit teasing the flames and cock their heads at the water, thinking maybe Chicken Little was right all along.

Hailstone, maybe.

High-jumping, back-flipping carp.

I'd heard of cows falling out of the sky in places, buckets of money, whole school buses dropped from great heights onto soy fields. Jack once knew a man who heard some banging on his roof and climbed a ladder to find . . . I couldn't remember. Still, not knowing my limits, I thought I ought to start small and respectful. Lost box kite or maybe an acorn, just enough of an impudent thwock to make the boys jerk their heads up in unison and be friends for life, and love and admire and pursue happiness together in sickness and in health, and sit under the tree that grew on the island to break bread and be twins and protect each other.

That's not much for a ghost to ask, I whispered modestly into the Night's broad shoulder, trying hard to sound wifely and not so pleading, so weary, so sick of this dance when it was only just beginning, nine years after it started. I knew a good dance partner when I was swept up by one, but the Night had outwaltzed me already, had outtrotted and outpirouetted me, my face pressed dizzily into Its black tuxedo, when all I wanted was a chair and a tumbler of Pepsi, to fan myself a minute with the Night's soft cuff, pull just a trinket out of Its handkerchief pocket and let it drop past the island—thwack! and splash!—to teach my son and his new friend the value of two heads watching a thing come down.

But just as I did when the babies were born, not Tip but his brothers and sisters before him, I found myself fumbling, losing my grip, my fingers demanding the babies or nothing—not wood, not paper, not ladle or pot lid, rag rug or vegetable peeler. We ate ordered-in pizza those nights, though I hated the grease on the puddles of melted cheese, and we didn't make love, or I didn't anyway; Jack called our reckless attempts at postpartum lovemaking a one-horse town though not entirely inhospitable. But how clumsy I was, those first shocked days after every unlikely twin birth, as if to touch a single object other than the crease of a baby's cry was the source of all confusion in the universe. After David and Dennis were born, I dropped the car keys in a storm sewer outside the post office and, when I'd managed to retrieve them with a dry-cleaner hanger, drove off with the stamped bills overdue on the roof of the car. When Drew and Douggie were born, I spilled the contents of my handbag—the atomizer of Yardley perfume, a pair of extra kid's undies in case of toilet-training mishaps—into Sheila Horn's cabbage-scooped bowl of Finnish potato salad at the city council picnic, and after Jenna and Becka were safe in their swaddling blankets I once left their diaper pails behind our front door and stood on the front stoop myself in a rain shower waiting to be picked up by the diaper service to be exchanged for clean ones. But with both twins within reach—one at a bottle, one at the breast, and then the other at the bottle and the other at the breast, the plaid sleeper always zippered on one and the sleeper with the tugboats always on the other—I never so much as pricked the pad of my thumb with a diaper pin or skipped a beat in my rocking. I could have moved the world then, I remember thinking, and bit a thin, sharp sliver off each of Jenna's fingernails so she wouldn't scratch her eyelids, and sucked an errant drop of milk from the down-turned corners of Becka's mouth, and called to David and Dennis to start doing their homework or help Douggie and Drew with their games while I settled the girls in their cradles. Then I said to myself, Let the world be so moved once a day and even heaven will be better off than it is already. A cradle was what I wanted for Tip that night on the island, better finally than never, one with dowels for him to wrap his tight fingers around so I might pry them away at bath time, but neither a ghost nor a mother can make cradles fall out of the sky.

Nor airplanes either, I would have preferred to believe.

The boys' houses sat close to the edge of the lake, where the current was bewildered by the jetty. There were other houses, too, on that lip of the road, but none of them mattered at all, for not far across the serenity of the bay sat the island no bigger than the canopy of the stunted oak on top of it, which seemed to belong only to Tip and Johnny. First the island was Tip's, but after he motored out there one evening to find Johnny already hunkered over Johnny's own stash of magazines, to read and then to burn in Johnny's own campfire, the tiny island became Johnny's, too. Johnny was nine years old, like Tip, and must have thought he had enough wits and gumption to venture alone onto the glistening ink of the bay. Tip was wounded by Johnny's presumption, a wound I felt like a snag in my hem that first night I at last whirled past him. Like a merry-go-round, the Night's relentless maneuvers, and me clinging to the slippery mane. My first glimpse of my son since the day he was born was that night he was nine—nine! at night!—on the island, but I could barely stop for long enough to tickle him under the chin or get down on my knees to tuck in his shirt. I don't actually *have* knees, I reminded myself. Funny having no knees after all of that scuffing and dancing, all that decade's chafe and ache, the sweat on my thighs nothing more than a rise in the evening's humidity causing Tip's blue jeans to take too long drying from when he'd waded the rocky slope between the tiny island and where the boat was anchored. Knees, elbows, wrists, thighs, nape, crook, bend, crease—my whole ghost of a body a fluke in the day's barometrics, the air pressure dipping and swelling, a spiral of leaves on an eddy of exhaustion. At least I still have my dress on, I said to myself, smoothing the tired excuse for a pleat. We ghosts have our modesty. Nakedness is one thing, nothingness another. Tip had his eye on an oak leaf trapped in a backwash of current. Which part of me was that? Maybe the small of my back? I wondered, longing for how the flat of Jack's hand used to occupy that fleshy hollow like wind in a curtain. The Night wasn't nearly so tender when It whisked me into another spin. I reached for the gold ring, caught hold of a little of what Tip was thinking. There wasn't supposed to be another boy like Tip anywhere, certainly not in his own neighborhood. Johnny's small family—just Johnny and his parents—had lived in the house next to Tip's all along, though despite Gwen's prodding and hoping, the two boys had only solemnly disregarded each other from opposite goals during neighborhood games of stick hockey or from opposite sidewalks during water-gun wars. Johnny had fat shoulders and a crease between his eyebrows from worrying, so Tip didn't force him to leave the island. For some months he'd been prepared for the night he might discover a trespasser. In Tip's fantasy, he waited for the boy to fall asleep at the campfire before towing the boy's empty boat across the bay to the wrong dock. In the morning the trespasser had to swim home. Since Tip's fantasies often came true but not exactly the way he'd imagined, he dismissed the idea of making Johnny swim home and instead selected a spot that would be Johnny's on the island, under the branch of the tree that was most likely, by Tip's reckoning, to shed sap and inchworms. The boys could be partners as long as Tip was better at climbing the tree, and as long as Johnny knew Tip didn't have a mother.

"I don't have a mother," Tip confessed, peeling off his wet blue jeans, wringing them out, and oozing them back on.

Johnny's silly brown pants were still soaked through and clung to his puckery thighs. Small puddles of ash fizzed and popped in the campfire, which held a charred sugar fragrance of marshmallows from the fire before.

"I know," Johnny answered.

Tip was disappointed. All the kids in the neighborhood thought they knew, but they couldn't possibly.

"She died the second I was born," he added.

"She did?" Johnny leaned back for a bigger look.

"I never got to see her. She never even got to tell me she loved me."

"Then how do you know she did?" asked Johnny, scrunching his eyebrows while trying to imagine the two parts of a second big enough for giving birth and dying both to happen in it. Because Johnny didn't blink when he scrunched up his eyebrows, Tip blinked on purpose, and felt the same awed repulsion as when a kid in the school yard wiggled his ears—glad he couldn't scrunch eyebrows himself. But Tip could curl his tongue and arch his neck in the rain to fashion the curled tongue into a funnel and suck the cold drops into the back of his throat. So he ignored Johnny's comment and let it drift with the smoke before the words had a chance to settle. No use being enemies if they were going to be friends. Johnny wasn't allowed to spend the night in a sleeping bag on the island, like Tip was. Instead he had to be home in two hours and not a splitting second later, his mother had admonished, confusing seconds with headaches as usual, even though she never got them. Gwen could see the island from the window in her kitchen where she stood washing dishes, could make out the dark oblongs of the anchored boats, the spastic shadows of the boys above the orange glow of campfire. For the first time in years we had something in common, Gwen and me, because she couldn't smell the burnt sugar toast of the marshmallows either, or touch the shallow damp V between her son's shoulder blades, or even catch him if he lost his chubby balance and slid off the mossy roots of the island. If she called to him now, from across the dark bay, he wouldn't hear her, just as Tip couldn't hear me. Both Gwen and I inaudible, our small sons untouchable, stubborn in their skins.

"I'm sorry I didn't stick around for another cup of coffee all those years back," I whispered quick as I could to Gwen. "Our friendship was barely beginning when I wigged out on you. We were hardly anything but neighbors yet, really. But we were two pees in a pot," I fumbled.

Gwen glanced at the kitchen clock, wiped the itch off her nose on a dish towel, and drew in a hard breath of air. Across the bay the smoky presence of the tree made the sky appear milky on top of its darkness. She dumped tomorrow's green beans into a colander, sprayed them clean with the nozzle, selected tomorrow's groceries out of the pantry, lined them up on the counter, and reached for a steel wool pad. Scrubbing the stove top, she imagined herself a helicopter hovering over the too quiet, too solitary geography of her kitchen, eyes peeled for some commotion of crumb or smear that might require her to stir up the atmosphere. Why she and Polly used to laugh at the paisley contact paper in the cupboard she couldn't exactly remember. But she was envious of the boys' shadows commingling on the island the way hers and Polly's might still commingle in the kitchen if only Polly hadn't died, sharing the ironing side by side as the boys' boats skimmed past the smocking in the water. She'd never learned how to swim, after all. She would need to take lessons now that she lived on the water, she'd declared on the day she moved into the neighborhood. She'd been pregnant with Johnny, her first and only child, that year. And Polly pregnant with Tip, her seventh. "If you swim when you're pregnant, you're buoyed on top of the water," was one of the first things Polly ever told her. "You paddle yourself like a raft. But after the baby you sink like a brick. Mother Nature reeling you back in, I guess."

Gwen placed the steel wool in its green-rimmed saucer and imagined learning to dive like a child, arching her body over a broom handle, the saggy cloth of a swimsuit not quite hiding the spread of her hips. Were Polly alive it wouldn't be necessary to pretend to be so busy in the kitchen, Gwen often regretted, bending to see what was kicked under the oven aside from her husband's peace-sign tie clip, which she'd long ago decided not to sweep up until he noticed it was missing from his things. When there was no longer a war going on, peace wasn't so needful of representation. John needed no symbol anyway. He found his peace in all things, even in Gwen when she was most frustrated, most at odds with herself, and most angry at him for not knowing.

Had Polly still been alive, the women would have passed back and forth a pair of binoculars to keep watch on the boys while spritzing John's shirt and smoothing Jack's cute boxers. Between sips of decaffeinated coffee laced with Gwen's health-nut soy milk, they'd discuss ways to unnerve John—steal his wallet, steal the car, join the army. But John was unflappable; he must find his peace at work, in bottles and vials, in the translucent insides of gelatin capsules. An anesthesiologist, John made a living doling out sleep. What was to stop him from tossing a few sweet dreams under his own pillow? Gwen should feel lucky he was so amiable. Maybe tonight the way to knock him off balance would be to tell him she let Johnny take the boat to the island. The reason was that Tip was taking *his* boat, and the reason Tip was allowed to take his boat was because he didn't have a mother to say no.

"You miss your mom?" asked Johnny.

"How could I miss her if I never even knew her?" scoffed Tip.

"Do you realize her molecules are still in the air?" Johnny encouraged.

"What, like a dinosaur?" asked Tip, insulted.

Johnny's logic was the kind of which the twists and turns of hypothesis and experiment could be mapped by how high up his eyebrows went when an idea first came to him and by how fixed his gaze became as the idea was contemplated. Speculation turned either to certainty or doubt on Johnny's face. Tip took a shallow breath of the invisible molecules and then, worried that Johnny had seen him do it, began hyperventilating, hoping to make himself dizzy enough to fall down.

"Want me to write a top forty hit about whatever you want?" Johnny offered.

Tip quit his deep breathing, embarrassed to be so entranced by his new friend, whose eyes turned to pinpoints with the earnestness of his queries.

"If someone shimmied to the end of that branch," Johnny pointed, "and jumped into the water, do you think they'd break their neck, or be okay?"

"Break their neck if it was you, be okay if it was me," Tip gladly answered, and was up the tree before he'd even sat down at the fire. Even Johnny's hair, which grew in tight, rusty curls pressed close to his skull, appeared to coil more damply with curiosity. Just to wait for those squashed springs to pop made Tip more restless than usual. Last summer, he'd let go of that branch and got cut-up feet and a bruised butt to show for it. The lake was more swollen this summer than last, and the branch reached farther over the lap of the water, stopping just above the place where the boats knocked together, drifted apart, and knocked together again. Johnny's was red, Tip's blue. In the twilight the hulls blended to purple. Really Tip enjoyed roasting hot dogs and marshmallows from up on that branch, his eager body flush with the tree's knots and kinks as he lowered the speared food over the tips of the flames. There was never a second when Tip didn't feel his own heartbeat, I furtively observed as the Night spun me past, the way a new mother sneaks looks at her infant's toes, memorizing every plump knuckle. He wrapped his hands around the branch and let his feet tread air above the shimmer of water, his fingers ablaze with the comfortable scratch of the bark. Tip was built like a chimp. Broad chested, X shaped, and a bottom so compact no mother could have brought herself to spank it anyway, though how I wished I could if only for a minute, throw him over my knee if only I had one and nuzzle him looking for tics, and *thwack,* and *smooch,* gentle as an ape whenever I laid eyes on something burrowing that didn't belong. Slow down, ease up, I begged flirtatiously of the Night, my voice yawning like a shadow in the overhanging branches of the oak, a space between leaves Tip could have put his hand through except he didn't care that it was there. He took another deep breath, knowing Johnny's mother had forbidden Johnny to ever hyperventilate. I had a discomfiting thought. Over the coming years, between the boys, it would be me who got the credit for being the best of their mothers, by being dead, thus permitting Tip to do whatever he wished. Already as much man as boy, he was; and the newborn still fisted inside him where, if only I could reach it, I might tweak its bottom and sing "Rock-a-bye" into its ear. Johnny'll sing to him instead, I comforted myself. Johnny and all his top forty hits in the making. Maybe two hailstones would be enough. Maybe a mussel shell dropped from the beak of a gull would startle them enough to secure their friendship.

From where Tip swung in the tree, his and Johnny's outboards appeared primed for a fight like bullies in a school yard, their blunt noses do-si-doing as they rallied and sparred. Around them the water rings backed up in circles to watch. A rising moon gave the water a faint tinge, yellow as a spreading bruise. The boats knocked and drifted, drifted and knocked, but so erratically it wasn't safe to try jumping into the ribbon of water between them. Tip realized he might snap his arm on the gunnel, or slice too close to the blades, or come up trapped under the hulls where the water turned suddenly deep. He was reckless but he wasn't careless, and since he tended to his own body with far more scrutiny than anyone else did, he was strict with it as if it were his own pet dog, likely to get itself in trouble if he didn't leash it in. So he hoisted himself back up on the branch, grunting deep in his belly. "Hey, move it!" he yelled to Johnny while shimmying backward toward land. "Move it, kid!"

Johnny gaped, then quickly gave up the root he was sitting on for a knobbier one. It wasn't nonchalance that let Tip drop so casually practically into the campfire, but a stubborn respect for the absolute rightness of certain opportunities that presented themselves to him. After he made himself comfortable, the boys began setting fire to one copy of each magazine they had in common, scooting so close to the flames that their pants began to steam. Tip took hold of one page of the doomed magazine, Johnny of another, then they tore the pages off the spine as competitively as if vying for the longer part of a wishbone. Tip wished he were alone on the island, Johnny wished for adoration from this squat, wild boy who chased every moment as if it were his own mischief and stubbornness and impetuosity trying to get away from him.

Too soon, years later, both wishes would be sorrowfully granted.

There was a story I wished I remembered.

That poor girl with red shoes, dancing and waltzing.

The shoes wouldn't stop, the floor spun underneath them, her arms flailing so crazily she couldn't reach her shocked fingers to undo the buckles, the laces, the clinch of the heels, whatever keeps a shoe in place; how fondly I recollected them, shoes.

But the rest of the story . . . I must have heard it off one of the twins' 45s, when I was alive. The younger twins liked to hide in the walk-in closet to listen, their heads poking the hems of Jack's shirttails, or tunneling into my empty pressed skirts as if squirreling in a forest of soft, hollow trees. Back and forth past the closet I used to hear bits and pieces. Laundry to fold, and that poor girl still dancing. Phone call to catch, and her blisters beginning to form. Calendar to mark, doorbell to answer, package to open, and the blisters past popping, the girl's head going loose on her shoulders, her eyes closing in spite of her whirling. Nap time to see to, the sheets turned back in the rooms of twin beds, the washer snagged on a blanket in the basement, knocking and whining. Somehow I must have missed it, the end of the story. I heard the one about the dog with its eyes big as platters, the one about the top in love with the ball. But how did the girl stop dancing? How did she manage to lie down to rest? How did she pull herself free of the music, the heels tapping and swiveling, the scuffed toes leaping to carry her off? I never liked being led, while dancing, but that was the grace of the thing, I recall. Submit to the partner, lean into his inclinations, take him where he thinks he's making you go. But the Night wouldn't have it, the Night pulled me hither and pushed me yon. My six older children were safe in their twinships, but Tip was there on the island with Johnny, neither boy knowing enough to need the other, and me in the swept-up arms of the Night, and around and around I must go and go.

2

Across town in his office in the basement of the Catholic church on Eagle Street, the same priest who at forty-one had been responsible for Tip's arrival in the world was turning fifty years old. For his birthday the congregation had presented him with a racquetball racquet (fiberglass and aluminum instead of the graphite he preferred, but oversized the way he liked it) whose grip exactly matched the spread of his fingers, along with a set of eye goggles he would never wear. They were the fourth set of goggles that people had given him over the years, all offered in the same spirit of rebukeful pleading with which he himself sometimes addressed God. Being a priest, praying for the impossible was the closest he ever came to humiliation. To ask for a thing that would not be forthcoming had always seemed to incur the most satisfying of defeats. So when Polly Baymiller had confessed to him nine years earlier that according to her doctors she would hemorrhage and die if she had her seventh baby—and she did say *baby,* not *babies*—the priest counseled her to continue to bear the child.

"Or children," he added, shifting his posture on the failing upholstery of God's allotment of bench. Sometimes he wished he didn't recognize his parishioners when they came to confession, but this wasn't one of those times. He could hear Polly crossing her legs in their nylon stockings, hear the tocking of her shoe against the wood as she jiggled her foot. She was a slender thing, Polly Baymiller, even with her pregnancy gently cinched under her pastel dresses. Auburn haired, sociable, she had a zeal for dancing, but only with Jack, her husband, and for breaking into contagious fits of laughter while chaperoning Pre-teen Night, and for the never surprising bursts of temper that accompanied her loyalty to her rambunctious pairs of children. The most famous was the time she removed her high-heeled sandal and hammered it into somebody's cake at a rummage sale when a lady at the same table accused David and Dennis of having superglued shut half the mailboxes in town. *Of course* David and Dennis were the vandals, thank God, Polly had argued, determined to raise them to be as hot blooded as Jack. The shoe in the cake was her gesture of proud indignation. "What practically teenage boys with half the imagination required to grow into men *wouldn't* glue mailboxes shut if the mailboxes were all lined up waiting for them to do it?" Polly seethed, then stomped past with one shoe half off amid a spattering trail of white frosting.

Let Polly Baymiller make it safely through the births, the priest had murmured in his prayers again and again, convinced, as was everyone else except Polly, that having beaten all odds by having borne twins three times already, she'd bear twins again. *Let her not bleed to death upon delivering these babies. Please, let the children grow up with a mother who in defense of their distaste for history class will clap together two blackboard erasers directly above the nun's wimple. Let Polly not mellow with age. Let her husband persist in bumping her ass much too persistently while in line for the Eucharist. Let her sing to herself as she drives down the street all the rock and roll songs the kids are forbidden to quote on the playground.*

Prayers like that. Heavy with irony, certain of God's deflection. Knowing Polly would die no matter how vehemently he pleaded for her to live, had the priest ever spoken those prayers aloud? Or had he only imagined their whispered cadence? Perhaps he heard them in the echoing thud of the racquetball ricocheting on court, the sudden dead sound of an out-of-play ball. When Polly died he felt chastened by the unanswered weight of them. Later, embarrassed, he recalled what he'd said to her in confession. "Don't ever tell those babies you came here to ask me if you should bear them or not," he'd insisted, forgetting she wouldn't be able to tell them anything at all.

"Baby, not babies." Polly corrected the high-voiced priest in as husky a voice as she could muster. The priest didn't catch the mockery, noted only a whisper of wrist against sleeve when she folded her arms.

Tip's birth proved her right; no beating the odds this time, just one baby. One mouth, two hands, and only one set of eyes that couldn't find their match when they roamed the room, searching. Compared to his paired-up brothers and sisters, Tip looked more alone in the world than an escaped pram on a slope of bare sidewalk. The priest found himself eager to christen the boy. But there wasn't a name. Jack didn't want the baby in the house, wanted only for the baby to have been selfless enough to have been born a girl so he could name her for her dead mother before sending her away. Jack had numerous sisters and brothers in town, but the baby was christened north in Sturgeon Bay, where he'd been taken by one of Jack's nieces, who managed a cherry orchard. Jack couldn't stand for the baby to be in town because he couldn't stand to hold it, but neither could he stand *that*, his own lack of simple, fatherly courage, the way he gritted his teeth when the telephone rang on Saturday mornings—his niece, calling to tell him what his son was doing new. Were it not for Jack's easygoing, perspicacious niece, the baby, Tipper, might have grown into toddlerhood never having been cuddled or plunked ankle deep in his very own cherry bucket of soothing pink water on sweltering days. When Tip's second summer ended and Jack arrived unannounced to reclaim him, the dappled shadows of the shade tree could be seen on Tip's face at all hours of the day, fixed there by the hours of sunlight. Jack left behind the bottles, the stacks of crib quilts, and piles of stuffed, jingling toys. The boy would grow up a bit less leisurely than most, agreed the ladies at church, who had admired Polly despite the shoe in the cake and her habit of slamming the brakes if their husbands were tailing too close in their cars. Now that Polly was dead, it was her left-behind husband for whom the ladies were most protective. Jack Baymiller! A man alone with toddler daughters and four skinny-dipping boys so well hung his own family jewels could only be imagined. A man with a heat you could fry an egg on if only you could get him to lie down on top of you the way Polly had done.

But nobody else could even get close to that skillet.

Bless me, Father, for I have not sinned with Jack Baymiller, the priest imagined all the women lining up to say.

"He can drink pop from a straw just like anyone else," Jack was rumored to have reassured his niece in Sturgeon Bay, then reached for the toddler's cherry-stained hand with surprising tenderness, glad to see Tip was so steady on his feet. "I want you to know I don't hold the boy responsible," Jack was said to have added curiously, pausing to straighten a crease in his linen trousers. The niece admired Jack's black hair, which hadn't shown up in other members of the family. He was a well-dressed man. Widowed, he cut a heart-stopping figure—tough as nails, though you could see he wasn't sleeping as much as he needed. Why hadn't his hair turned gray with the sadness that showed in his eyes? That would be his stubbornness. She knew he was too proud to dye it. Would he ever remarry? The niece had a feeling no, though he'd likely take up with a suitable woman when close to retirement, to prove to himself that he still had some Baymiller in him. Before then he wouldn't turn bitter, only far more successful in business than he even was already. He kicked a stray cherry pit off his shoe, then caught himself admiring the sturdy set of his little boy's shoulders before concluding, "He can't help what he did to his mother."

In the sky on the night of the priest's birthday, far above where the two boys sat hunkered on their island, Tom Bane was so suddenly aware of a lurching in the larboard wings of his biplane that it was as if his awareness caused it to happen. His fingers slid from the controls, then gathered again around an uncommon stiffness cramping his rib cage. Either the plane or the moon was on fire. The biplane tumbled like a stunt plane. What was a falling dervish? Tom's wife would know the answer, even though she didn't know Tom owned an airplane or even was licenced to fly. Whenever he headed out for the airport he told her only that he was visiting one seed or equipment warehouse or another, then staying to chat with the other guys buying seeds or equipment. This way he'd avoided even mentioning the plane, fearing that Angie, worried, might persuade him to stop flying, or worse, that she'd insist on coming along. Also it pleased Tom to exist in some arena of which Angie knew nothing, given that she was smarter than he was. Thankfully she didn't flaunt her intelligence. Only if one of the other graduate students called her at night when they were frustrated at Scrabble, or early in the morning while composing Dear John letters, might Angie, who knew all the truest meanings of words, rescue from disuse some small, rusty piece of neglected vocabulary. "Try *baleful*," he'd once come upon her saying in their bedroom, except that the phone was not at her ear. She was turned toward the window, the phone on the nightstand, untouched. Through the window Tom could see his ladder propped in the orchard, where he'd left it to come in for breakfast, and it was to the bare rungs of the ladder that Angie spoke, and to the unripened globes of fruit.

"Say, *It's too tiresome an imposition to have to pretend that I don't notice your baleful looks anymore*," Angie had continued, her words forming only the slightest of fogs on the glass.

But there'd been no hint of malice in Angie's voice. She was too pure for malice, hopeful as mown grass. When she told Tom she was ready for a change, he thought she meant for him to plant more sunflowers, or stop growing the stringier varieties of squash. Really she'd meant she wanted to leave the claustrophobia of the farm among the wetlands and move to San Francisco. Also, she was pregnant.

San Francisco, pregnant? he'd wondered, thinking maybe the words had a metaphorical significance of which he was ignorant. Before his eyes, she'd positioned herself at the mirror and cut off her hair, snipped away the cascade of bronze dangling ringlets so the baby's fingers wouldn't get knotted and pinched. But the haircut didn't make Angie look any more practical minded than before, Tom regretted. Nor did it make her appear, in particular, motherly. It made her look . . . unpredictable, he feared. The obstinate highlights made her look like Joan of Arc, eager for disarray. If she dozed in her rocker, her hair seemed to shock her impatiently awake, her lashes shooting open under the clamorous mutiny of shorn tufts.

Or perhaps it was the notion of leaving the farm, rather than the unruly hair, that made Angie resemble a scarecrow full of starlings. Tonight, alone inside the whirling dervish of his biplane, Tom was chagrined to have ignored that possibility. Then maybe he could have done something about the resemblance, even forbidden it. At the very least he might have given in and told her about the plane, so he would be, in her eyes, less boring and less deserving of her impatience. In the third trimester of pregnancy, Angie spent hours at a stretch without rising from her chair, in which she was far, he feared, from content. Her rocking was ironical, a relentless percussion marked by the exclamations she jotted in the margins of her notes for her graduate thesis. In more relaxed moments, she'd be tearing the papery husks off a bushel of tomatillos, or searching for names for the baby, although never in a book designed for that purpose. At last she'd discovered the name in a cookbook. *Honey* if the baby was girl, she declared, the dusk glowing providentially above Tom's forty acres as if exulting in her decision. But tonight the sky shuddered and spun rebukefully around the nose of the biplane, while on the glassy, tilting surface of the lake a bonfire danced like Angie's uncombed hair.

Out of control, the night a torrent of disobedient sparks.

Tom could feel them burning in his chest and in the tumbling sky and in the smashed-apart blackness of the lake when it rose to claim him.

3

"Someone's dead," Johnny remarked. "A falling star means somebody hopped the twig."

"Means they *what?*" Tip demanded, incredulous. A bug darted into Tip's mouth. He clamped his lips closed around it and let it bat from cheek to cheek before spitting it into the fire.

Johnny knew enough not to answer.

"Hopped the twig!" Tip shouted.

Don't be mean, I scolded fiercely, leaning as close to his ear as I could as the Night whisked me past, blisters forming on my heels though I had no heels. Bills to pay, letters to answer, water to boil, and the girl's head wobbly with sleep on her shoulders, though I had no shoulders. The Night's deep pocket was empty now, I was chagrined to discover. What was it I'd plucked from the linty darkness and flicked off the foggy tips of my fingers? An acorn might have been enough, a pebble dropped by a tern, to make the boys be still and regard each other.

You've got your older brothers to teach you how to say things, I scolded my son. Johnny's got no one. Only you.

Tip didn't hear me. Either that or he chose not to listen. Motherhood, ghosthood, know one and you've known the other, I said to myself. Not a voice but a skitter of leaves on a threshold, my dancing gloves settling with a fluttery whisper onto the dusty top of a side table. The Night had set me free for a waltz or two, exchanged me for the moment with another soul, allowing me to rest my tired footsteps for long enough to remember a movie I'd seen. *Marathon,* I seemed to think it was called. Some young people dancing collar to collar. Thirty, fifty hours at a stretch they danced, to raise money for some long-ago war, the girls' dresses limp on their frowzy, bruised bodies, the boys' shirtsleeves dangling sweat. I remember a girl with her hair in her eyes, drinking chocolate-covered raisins out of a crumpled box. Let me slip into something more comfortable, I must have tittered against the Night's cool shoulder, hoping for a break in the music. Ladies' room. Freshen up. Drinks time, I tittered, wishing I remembered what it was like to be thirsty. But then, once the Night set me down, what a wallflower I was on the island, just another dizzy flicker among the breezes in the tree. The two boys sat quiet as chairs at the fire, hands on their knees, not knowing quite how to look at each other. The extra magazines had all been dutifully burnt, the duplicates heaped unread in a hollow of tree root. Alone, there was nothing at all embarrassing about sitting near a fire not speaking. But with somebody there, Tip found his own silence downright excruciating. No harmonica to play like in an old Western, no crook they were running away from, and no need to stanch telltale flames. Not even a bear they were hunting. Nothing to prove they were boys together growing into men the way I intended. Johnny wasn't embarrassed by the quiet of the flames, only worried he'd have to start back home before anything happened but a sissy falling star. A few raindrops might have been more than enough, I scolded myself unsteadily. A limb dropping off the tree might have caught Tip and Johnny off guard and pulled them closer together.

Tip found a last page of crumpled magazine and poked it into the fire, sorry to see it shrivel up and blacken. Now they would need to read the ones that were left—*Wisconsin Boy, Outboard, Duck Season.* Tip thought there was something dreadful about two people reading side by side the way he'd watched his aunts and uncles do in their studies in the evenings. All Jack's side of the family were readers; Jack read alone with the TV on. There was something too much in agreement about the aunts' and uncles' pages turning at the same time or not, their heads bent just so.

Tip decided he wouldn't read quite yet. Instead he'd climb the tree again and piss in the water between the two boats. The back of his neck felt massive in the warm breeze, bigger around than his coffee can of matches, when the boys caught sight of the cartwheeling flames again in the distance, only closer than before and faster. A smell of oil teased the insides of their noses. Across the bay in her kitchen, Gwen didn't notice the tumbling airplane or smell the faint, speedy friction of it, for the lake was too big, fifty miles end to end and twelve miles across, for her to care about what happened even just past the mouth of the bay. Besides, she'd taken everything out of the pantry and was sponging the can lids with dishwashing liquid. She did miss Polly's company. Gossiping with a neighbor once darkness had fallen was one of the few things that made a day officially full enough to be over, Gwen had long ago decided, and in search of another way to tighten a day's loose ends had once toyed with the notion of making evening visits to her dead friend's grave. Riverside Cemetery rested in deep grass along a mile of the river that ran between the big lake and the small, and somewhere within those acres lay Polly's grave, beneath a spreading elm or in the shade of some ornate mausoleum whose pillars threw their shade across her stone like the rays of the sun through the vertical blinds in Gwen's living room, blinds that hadn't existed before Polly died. Gwen had never seen the grave, had not attended the burial, had rushed home from the church service to ready Jack's house for the guests—laying out platters of food amid fans of paper napkins and plastic forks. "Like a picnic, my funeral," she'd imagined Polly saying. "That must be why there are so many aunts." Since then, Polly always seemed just near enough—her sly humor slipping in and out of sight like the joker in a deck of cards—that a visit to her grave struck Gwen as, finally, irrelevant, for how would a stone, a plot of earth, do justice to her lively friend? Jack probably felt the same way, so he didn't much go there either, and the boy twins might not think to visit, Gwen reasoned, but surely Jenna and Becka must ride to their mother's grave on their bikes, bearing small rakes and trowels for tending and planting.

Gwen snatched a jar of apple butter ready to roll off the counter, and thus didn't catch sight of the last spiraling tumble of fireworks over the lake.

"What *is* that thing?" Johnny exclaimed.

"What the hell *was* that thing?" Tip shouted.

Both boys leaped to the shore of the island, where the branches overhung the sheen of the lake. Tip couldn't stop himself this time. He moved according to his own laws of gravity, yanking his body toward whatever captured his attention. He stretched his sweatshirt up over his head, tossed it behind him too close to the campfire, and splashed toward the gentle ripples made by the rocking, slapping boats.

"It's a UFO! It's a UFO! We'll never make it that far frigging out!" he cried ecstatically, galloping past the boats as if he might swim to the place on the lake where the falling bright spiral had vanished, nearly a half mile away.

Johnny had made a promise to his mother not to swim that night. But in the boat, he could follow Tip for as far as they needed to go. Gingerly stepping among roots and rocks, at last he reached the outboards, climbed into his own, and was about to start the motor when Tip reared up from beneath the blades, spitting fans of water before thrashing in the direction of the backward pull of the island. Nothing could stop Tip's excitement, even though he appeared to have forgotten the cause. Tip and the rest of the world were polar opposites, Johnny observed, his pale hand going slack on the motor. No matter where Tip was, there was something against which he needed to push and pull in order to stay in one place.

Soon Tip sat dripping by the fire and held up the singed cuff of his sweatshirt. A thin haze of campfire smoke wafted out of the cloth, as if to join a blacker, acrid smoke farther off in the humid darkness, the faint perfume of oil merging already with the smell of the woodfire. Meanwhile, the darkness made it nearly impossible to tell the sky from the lake, the tree from the surrounding blanket of air, the night itself from the crickety pulse of the island.

"I couldn't see nothing out there even if I ever did get there!" Tip was still grinning happily. "No way on earth we'd be able to find where that thing went down. But anyway it wasn't a falling star. It was frigging goddamn falling airplane."

You couldn't see *anything*, I corrected his grammar, though who was I to fuss with grammar when I'd just thrown an airplane out of the sky and killed a man?

Johnny drew his eyebrows closer together. Tip counted six seconds before his new friend's face relaxed into its usual, not quite so worried expression. The Night circled nearer, ready to sweep me back up. Soon the halls would start spinning, the chandeliers dimming, the polished walls a long aisle of faces and tasks to be spun through and wandered one year to the next before I'd ever be at peace. A ghost can't just *be*, I whispered to Tip. Just like a mother can't lie on the couch all morning. There's too much to do, so much to take care of, and every so often mistakes to undo, like now. Any mother who can just *be* isn't the kind of mother you'd want me to be . . . or ghost, I tried to explain.

There was a nearly impenetrable moment of perplexed, bewildered silence.

"Then someone really is dead," both boys exclaimed in awe, already determined to keep the downed plane their secret, their vow.

Part *One*

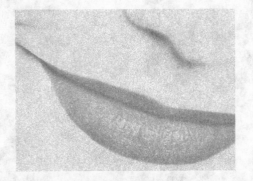

1

Polly's Journey

Rain made a kind of veil, I remember. Jack used to stand in the open garage and look out at the blur it made of the pavement and of the houses across the street, or he would stand proprietarily in the patio doorway and watch the drops turn to mist on the lake as if he'd bought tickets to see it. He was a possessive man, Jack. All he needed to do to lay claim to a thing was hold it in his eyes for longer than if he didn't. He could have bought and sold me anytime he wanted, provided it was to and from himself, I used to tease. He wore a knitted shirt open at the collar, washed and ironed to fit snug across the span of his chest and tight belly. Cinched trousers, always a belt. Clothing gave itself to him, and rain wouldn't dare dishevel him. Fog brought out the natural astringency of him. You're fresh, I used to joke, I always like a man fresh. But he was not an easy man, Jack. Romantic, yes. And as savvy with me as he was in business. He didn't open the restaurants until after I died. He was in salvage, excavation, had an eye for restoration. The restaurants came out of that, I suppose—the perfect salvaged view from a refinished table at the perfect salvaged window in a warehouse ready to be reborn. A hungry mix of investors, and add to that the banker's son just out of cook school and Jack with only the string of housekeepers he called "the help" in the kitchen at home. Jack was opportunistic, what he called "optimistic with style." But easy, no. If I was angry or fed up, if we had argued over how to discipline Dennis or David for having forgotten to lock the gate at the salvage yard, or if Jack had brought home for dinner another round of business contacts without checking first with me, then I swished my hips in the kitchen planning how next time he brought guests unannounced I'd whip a stack of TV dinners from the freezer and serve them bubbling in their compartmentalized trays.

I did it, too.

Polished the silver, laid out proper linen napkins, fixed a centerpiece of yellow tapers, put on Jack's favorite Tijuana Brass (I hated that pretentious fake bullfight music, but Jack never knew), then ushered the cluster of city council members to the table, where they chose between Swanson fried chicken or Banquet Salisbury steak. Has anyone ever seen a drumstick from a real chicken as miniature as the ones they fit in those trays? Midget chickens, apple brown Bettys two bites across, but Jack poured the wine like Niagara on a honeymoon and everyone hopped in the barrel and went smashing. Tipsiness suited me fine on certain occasions, I remember. Giddiness, too. I remember how mischievous it made me knowing when I was sixty Jack would call me his girl. After supper he rolled up his sleeves, sudsed those aluminum trays, rinsed them, dried them with a tea towel, set them on the plate stands in the china cabinet, locked the door, and dropped the key in his pocket, told me if I ever pulled a stunt like that again he'd sleep on the couch for as many nights as there were bones in a TV dinner chicken's body.

Jack would have kept his word. However many bones there are in a chicken would have been too many nights for me. Loneliness was never a charm on my bracelet unless Jack was doing something he wanted, hunting, maybe, and when he got home he'd be shivering with all the cold he'd stored up in that tree stand waiting to come home and get dunked in a warm bath. I only went four times to the cabin on the family hunting land. There was wild turkey dung on the outhouse floor. Anyway, the longer I managed to stay away from Jack, the quicker he'd come back.

Any woman worth the high heels she topples to and fro on knows that.

Also, Hansel and Gretel, the blind witch pinching the

chicken bone. I should have read to the children every night, three sets of books for the three sets of twins, me with an open book on my lap and a twin half asleep in the crook of each elbow. From what I gather these days of the children, only Becka and Tip are likely to pick up a book, Tip more than Becka. Funny, since of course I never had a chance to read to Tip at all. Magazines I used to skim if I had a few moments. Cookbooks, barely. Books weren't my style, I suppose. I always felt a million things pulling me away from a page. If a book was an anchor, it couldn't hold my boat. The reason I chaperoned church ice-skating socials wasn't to keep the pre-teens in line, either. I enjoyed the admiration of the girls. I liked to imagine what figure I might cut when Dennis and David were too old for Teen Nights and Drew and Douggie came instead. Becka and Jenna, too, although I see now I would have been a hindrance to the girls, the comparison not in their favor. I had a perfect posture when I was alive. When I was dead and, after so many years of being waltzed and fox-trotted, got plunked near Becka and Jenna's postures, it was when they were sunbathing in their stretched-out one-piece bathing suits with the feet of their lounge chairs tipped higher than the heads so the tips of their toes burned pink in the sun. Made me feel like I had company up here. Not beholden to gravity, I mean; Becka's goggly contortions, Jenna's long neck curved like a goose's. Oh well. Really I have no claim on the girls. They were two years old when they last laid eyes on me. I gave them each a small push as if on a swing, set them in motion, the blue sky rocking above them. One evening I said—because they were my girls, if tomboys, their abandoned dolls dun headed in the sidelines of their Wiffle ball games—I said take care of your new, younger brother, knowing he'd be a boy, knowing he might help them grow into their girlhood, needing his nose wiped, needing his shoelaces tied on the back cement steps. Becka especially would need help growing into her girlhood, though tucked in bed the girls didn't hear me, their heads pressed so insistently into their pillows I had to shake out the dents every morning, punch the pillows back in shape until my last day on earth, knowing no one would do so when I was gone. If Douggie, Drew, Dennis, David, and Jenna had a way of missing me through Jack, attaching themselves to his stoicism like taut, bright kites to a brooding sky, Becka loped either ahead or behind, attracted by hunkered things lost in the grass. But my ghostliness was powerless to touch any of the twins, who weren't my business anymore apparently, and for that I had already yielded my regrets, folded them like tears in a crumpled tissue. Even when I was alive, Jack's and my debates about our ornery pairs of children had a way of escaping me. Jack was a smart-ass—not a word I would have spoken when I could be heard!—when he was trying to distract me from keeping him from doing what he wanted. He wanted David and Dennis to have to stay late at the salvage yard stripping crown moldings every night for two weeks in retaliation for forgetting to padlock the gate. I said no boys of mine'll have to miss two weeks of the too few summer nights of their too brief boyhoods for acting only as responsibly as any boys their age could be expected to act. Jack said how would I feel if the yard were vandalized, the tarps spray-painted with dirty jokes about twins, the leaded windows sledgehammered, the racks full of ornate doors knocked over, and the power tools left running? I said certainly David and Dennis couldn't be blamed for all that, and Jack said how would I feel if I were some other boy's mother and *he* had snuck into the unlocked salvage yard and chopped off his own head with a power saw? I said don't be ridiculous. Jack said the punishment for any act should weigh up against all the bad things that could possibly come of it. I said in that case, two weeks of stripping crown molding past bedtime wouldn't be nearly enough for having caused some hapless boy to get his head chopped off.

"Hatless," said Jack. "Not hapless."

Which I regretted laughing at, the second I started, of course. Jack had gotten the better of me again. David and Dennis were punished with two and a half weeks of sanding, brushing, buffing, and staining crown moldings.

I loved all my sons for being as smart as their father.

But I love Tip for being smarter. Tip's a whip.

I only wish I ever had the chance to hug and kiss him, teach him his letters and numbers, the colors and shapes, the animal sounds, all the starts of the ways of the world that accompany a person through life like rocks in a hard stream, put there as if for crossing. Really there's practically nothing I ever saw or heard or did of which I can't remember the slippery balance, the last-second leap to the next mossy foothold. Pink Cadillac. Ethel Merman's face. The names of my primary-school teachers. What goes in turkey stuffing. How to fasten a brassiere. How to kiss. How to make the tires squeal at the corner when someone who deserves a minor heart attack is waiting to cross. How to pretend badminton is your favorite form of entertainment, not to mention croquet. Card games. Flowers. Mrs. Carney, Mrs. Trainer, Miss Higgans, Mr. Harris, dahlias, salvias, marigold, aster, hearts, spit, slapjack, poker. I never did learn sheepshead. The clincher is I don't miss any of it, not even standing in the doorway with Jack in the rain, sharing one of his cigarettes. Rain was the only time I ever smoked. If it rained and Jack was smoking and I wasn't, then we were separate. But if I smoked, too, then we blended. Together, rain and cigarettes balanced our differences. The slight ticking of the smoke, the mist of the smell of ash, the moist drift and clatter of sulfur and burnt thunder, that mixture was our perfect cocktail. Three quarters Jack, one quarter Polly, or three quarters Polly, one quarter Jack, depending on who was in the friskier mood, together in a cup that would be sipped from as much by one of us as it was sipped by the other. But nor do I miss even Jack. All I miss is Tip, who I never kissed, or knew, or held for just a second in my dead arms. When a baby is stillborn, sometimes the grieving parents are permitted a few moments to rock the child deeper into sleep, calm the troubled creases from its forehead, sing lullabies into the translucent cones of its ears, nuzzle its name into its dry, open mouth. But when it's the mother who's dead, they cover her with the bedsheet and whisk her away, zip her up like a spent change purse, belly empty, fingers clenching not a penny. If only they had put him to my breast for a moment, I might still be able to conjure Tip's groping. And if they had held him once to my lips, I might remember the smell of him. Every baby is different, every baby's push is different from another one's pull. I used to lie on my back now and then during my babies' nap times, let them drape their limbs over my chest, could feel gravity reach through me like a rope through deep water to keep them in place. Douggie and Drew were rigid as bundles of dirty laundry, Becka and Jenna scaly as lizards, David and Dennis prickly as fresh-picked flowers. When at last the Night danced me within whispering distance of Tip, he was nine years old on the island with his new friend, Johnny, but right away I could fancy what it might have been like to hold him. Him like two crossed sticks of dynamite, the fuses lit but not blowing, stubborn as ever but always about to blast himself right out of my arms.

The reason it took me nine years to get to Tip was, simply, because it does. Take a while. To get back. To find whomever. Not even the Night, my capricious dance partner vain in Its black tuxedo, knows quite where to lead, for the halls are all mirrors, the dangling prisms of starlight yellowed. Uncertain as I, still Its hand prodded the small of my back, our dance over the years growing never dull but languid, our bodies flush together although we had no bodies. And then at once It'd set me down and take up another partner, another pair of pale arms although there were no arms. I sat stiffly those first few times between dances, like someone mousy at a social, clutching her clutch, waiting to know what to do and say, whose evening to influence and whose morning to leave alone. Tip was my unfinished business, of course, but as usual there were errands to be run along the way before the Night might snatch me up again, my respite only temporary, transient as dust lifting up and then settling back down. Ghosts don't know how to be ghosts right away. We have to find our own methods, unfurl our own maps, unwind, one way or another, the routes that might lead us to rest. Knowing this, even so I still need to reassure myself that when I finally came upon Tip with Johnny on the island, I didn't mean to invite Tom Bane's airplane to pull half the sky's constellations into the lake. I didn't mean for it to be a plane at all that fell out of the sky. I meant for it to be a falling star.

Or rain.

I meant only for the two boys to look up in unison to see something earthbound, a thing hurtling toward them out of their reach and control.

I wanted them to notice the big world around them and feel themselves small and necessarily kindred in the middle of it.

I wanted to accustom them to the idea that they must look out for each other.

Rain might have been best, I say to myself with hindsight. A falling star has too many irrelevant connotations. A fishing bird is likely to be as silly as a pelican, the acorn too big a deal out of nothing even if it landed in the campfire between them and popped and sizzled. But at the time I said, Enough contemplating, anything falling will be satisfactory as long as the boys see it together and be twins for life and protect each other. It was then that the plane began its first cartwheel, and ever since it hit the water, Tom Bane has slept on my name like a reel of foreign language played through a pillow of sand. *Polly Baymiller, Polly Baymiller,* he doesn't know what it means, but it both spurs him on and soothes him. Confuses him, too. He believes he is my adversary. Because he can't reach me directly, he'll try to punish Tip instead. If my sallying to and fro is meant to tame Tip's sorrows, then Tom means to compel them, means to draw the sorrows forth. If I intend to bring Tip happiness, Tom intends to thwart me. If I intend to bring Tip love, Tom means to confuse him. But the Night didn't care. It only picked me up, twirled me, and put me back down. Pretty casual on the uptake, aren't you? I said, and huffed off to the ladies' room to powder my nose, although I had no nose. Drummed my fingers on the side table and tried not to look worried, although I had no fingers. Finally stalked off home, although it turned out I *was* my home. My own threshold, my own door, the skittered leaves unswept from my dusty hallway. How disheveled I was, and miffed at my date, not even to have been driven home and given a kiss good-bye. The cad, I declared, though I set about doing just what the fickle Night wanted of me. Cleaning the house. Wiping, dusting, mopping, and swabbing, the Night stern at my window whenever It came back to fetch me. Clean this, clean that. Is this your house, or mine, anyway? I asked and, miffed, clutched the broom too fiercely, swished the dust cloth like skirts in an arrogant tango. On my private, ghostly dresser, Tip and Johnny turned to static, the tiny island became a blip on my radio, half the state of Wisconsin slid past my dial, all at once I ended up within whispering distance of some other dead wife and mother's rightful husband, Lysle, and son, Gem, who missed her so much I wanted to *be* her.

Drive slower, I found myself whispering contentiously to Lysle as if already accustomed to this new man's fondness for belligerence, my words thumping inside his too rubbery ears, only to blend with the purring of the highway under the eighteen wheels of the semi. Never having sat next to such a wiry truck driver before, and never once having sat in the cab of a semi, I supposed I had to trust in the Night's intuition and be not only concordant with wherever the Night plunked me, but sensible as well. All predicaments have purpose when one is a ghost, I figured, so I secured myself within the high, speeding perch of the surprising truck and waited to make sense of why on earth I'd been put there. Had I been not a ghost but a mortal I might never again have set foot in a normal car, which from the cab looked like toys with no room for humans inside them. Squashable as bugs, and less important. In the trailer behind me sat forty thousand pounds of jalapeño poppers, whatever that was, which Lysle could practically smell the steam rising off between him and his wife, where she'd set the plate between them at ten o'clock of the last morning they spent together, the TV on since the morning before, and the morning before that, too. The shows didn't matter to Lysle as long as his wife fell asleep in the armchair next to his at bedtime, dressed in her day clothes, and woke up next morning, same chair, wearing her nightgown, a yellow brushed flannel as soft as her name. Violet. Skinny as a stem, too, no matter how many times she ate "one of them poppers, now I know why they call them that," Lysle imagined her saying. His ears were pink as ham; if she wanted to rib him about something, she gave them a tweak, but that was as pissed off as she ever got. *Pissed off.* I never heard that term before Lysle used it, his whole manner of speaking knocking against me like moths at a window. Such a tranquil woman, Lysle's wife, Violet. A heart softer than pussy, Lysle thought in my head, shocking me so much I could have died all over again if such a thing were possible, his words jumping around in my head as if *he* were the ghost, haunting *me.* I could feel him banging doors in the house the Night had made of me, the thunk of Lysle's beer can when he set it on the table next to the poppers, the habit he had, while sitting, of lifting both legs at once and plunking his feet down square on the cat-smelling carpet, his boots never off unless he was taking a shower, but always untied. The TV on to a movie no one knew the name of, the mangy cockatiel pecking its calcium stick in the cage in the living room, the blinds open at night to a sandy view of pines, and open in the morning, too, the light glinting on Violet's glittery toenail polish she bought for ten percent off from her Mary Kay representative, who was the next teller over at the bank Violet worked at, which blew up one day from a gas leak underneath it, the fuckers, the goddamn stupid shit-ass fuckers, I had to listen to Lysle thinking over and over, which is the closest probably anyone ever came to blushing when they were vapor, like me, thinner even than the steam that gathered on the windshield of the truck.

But I forgave Lysle his language. His grief was more substantial than I was, and anyway he didn't know I was there.

So, I was stuck with the wrong man knocking around inside me. A rude awakening, Lysle, for someone learning what it's like to be a ghost. A real plate smasher, Lysle, all my cupboard doors swinging half cocked on their hinges. I thought if I didn't get back to the tiny island that second and let Tip step over my threshold and let me hold him, I'd . . . I'd what? Die?

It was then I caught sight of Gem, who was dwarfed by the passenger seat, his untrimmed bangs like rows of crooked W's.

Don't forget to wash that peanut butter out of your eyebrows when your daddy pulls in at the next truck stop, I whispered to Gem, after which I heard all his ideas, too, as if I were the hallway and they were the footsteps, only Gem's footsteps were harder to follow than his father's because Gem didn't quite know how to talk yet even though he was five years old. Gem's eyes were so dark brown the black dot in the middle was like a tunnel with no end. But he remembered every runnel of chocolate sauce in every ice cream sundae his mother had ever made him, and every spoon she made him lick so clean he could see his pursed lips in it, and every time she urged him not to squeeze the new guinea pigs too hard. The guinea pigs were left at home in a cardboard box with their mother, lucky things, but Gem's mother's slippers were right where she'd last stepped out of them, under the dining room table with the bowl of drippy peaches on it. After three days of driving, the inside of Gem's elbow smelled to him like a puppy. No it doesn't. Yes it does. No it doesn't. Yes it does. Gem shook his head no and nodded yes. He was such a tiny thing, Gem, half swallowed up by the passenger seat of the semi with nothing to sit on but his own cowboy boots to see out the windshield. He was up on his knees even with the seat cranked high as it would go, craning his neck at all the motorcycles his father pointed out to him. Gem knew motorcycles like other children his age knew the letters of the alphabet. His father caromed right past the next couple of truck stops. Gem wet his pants. A whole day went by before his father thought to give him clean clothes. With a dry paper towel he rubbed the peanut butter so deep into Gem's eyebrows it couldn't be seen. Violet would have taken a damp dish towel to him, a gentle spiral starting at the tip of his nose and ending round and round the creases of his neck. Gem felt like the genie's bottle when his mother washed his face, like the genie might pop out of him and give her a Harley, but still the only place she ever wanted to go was home with Gem. Now she must have changed her mind. No she didn't. Yes she did. Gem clapped his hands over his ears in a rhythmic way so the sound of his father's truck was like the custom-made gurrr of his mother's new Harley starting up and shutting off again every time she remembered she hadn't said good-bye. Gem had never ridden in his dad's truck before, had only sat in it nights when it was parked near their house with the engine running so the poppers wouldn't spoil. Twice-baked potatoes were better than poppers if you were as hungry as Gem was, so at the truck stop his father bought him a hot dog.

Get him some milk, I whispered to Lysle, then gave a hasty swirl of the dust rag across the dial of my radio, trying to get back to Tip. But I just skimmed past him, heard just the timbre of Tip's laughter before sliding helplessly into range of Lysle again.

"Go get you one of them straws," Lysle said to Gem so Gem could blow milk bubbles when Lysle left him in the truck outside the tavern Lysle always stopped at en route to St. Louis. It wouldn't do to bring a five-year-old into the bar, especially when he had to tell all the truckers about what happened to Violet. Yes it fucking would, you don't protect a five-year-old from his own mother getting blown to pieces when she was counting other people's money, her and twenty thousand dollars turned to fairy dust in the same second. You can't protect a kid from something like that, Lysle debated back and forth between my ears. Yes you fucking did, especially when every trucker in the tavern was going to buy you a shot. How much money did Violet take out of the bank when she rode off on her Harley? Enough to buy heaven, I whispered to Lysle even though there was no such place, exactly. Heaven for me was for one split second seeing Jack at his desk in one of the restaurants writing a check to one of the charities (just because Jack was possessive didn't mean he wasn't generous, too), and when I lost sight of Jack and couldn't find Tip no matter how fiercely the Night bid me dust, I felt heavenly enough watching Gem eat his supper and drift off to sleep like a good boy. I had to be happy, simply because the idea of being a sad ghost instead of a glad one was too redundant. Dead is dead, but glad's more resourceful. Not even glad ghosts know how to be ghosts right away, however. We take hold of whatever catches us, and reach for what doesn't. Hell was nothing more than the opposite of heaven, like feeling Lysle twist inside me like a wet towel when another trucker in the bar joked how his girlfriends got too many headaches. The other men shushed the man, but Lysle was already gasping with indignation, his ears pinker than ever, his anger slapping my insides like a wet towel swatting the walls.

"At least your girlfriend had her head still attached to her body. At least you get the whole lady. Me, I don't even get my wife in my own wife's coffin. I get confetti. I'll give you an ache to think about, you don't get down on your knees this minute and thank God your lady's alive. Get down! Get down!"

Lysle's bootlaces snapping like whips every time he brought his foot down. The trucker raised himself off his bar stool. I'd never been hit by anyone. No one ever even slapped me. Certainly Jack would sooner die himself than even pinch my arm to bring me back to life. But now Lysle was all fists and kicks around the wrung-out pleats of the dress Jack buried me in. Appliquéd daisies. Not my favorite dress at all even back when we women pretended to like such clothing, but I didn't bat an eye when they prodded and poked me into it, although who would have imagined going sleeveless into eternity? Heaven was Gem's breath ruffling the daisy petals, dreaming about the front door of his house in Wisconsin with the light that blinked on by itself when anyone got close to it. Hell was Lysle spitting shots down my throat after the other truckers held him and the offender apart. Whiskey didn't faze me and though I'd never liked the odor except on New Year's, I'd give anything to be able to smell it now. That and sweat puppies. *Sweat puppies* was Lysle's way of talking about the smell in the creases of Gem's elbows. Glug glug. When Lysle drank I felt like the bottle with the whiskey going in backward. I'd never thought how glad I was Jack wasn't a drinker. A social drinker, yes, but so was I a little.

Still, Lysle wore whiskey quite naturally. He just missed being dapper, with a shot in his hand. His muscles were all skin and bone, Lysle's. He was built like a ranch hand, all wire and denim. There was something raw about him when he wasn't drinking. Then, cooked.

Gem, take the keys out of the ignition, I whispered maternally, when his father was still in the tavern. I was frightened of the notion of a drunken Lysle behind the wheel.

Being a ghost, I couldn't hear my own voice, but I could feel a breeze in Gem's ears.

Gem kept sleeping.

Gem, get hold of those keys and pull them out of the ignition, I whispered again.

Gem's sleep was like water tunneling through pipes. His dream of the front door light blinking on by itself was like an attic I didn't know I had in me. He would haunt me forever if I couldn't make him live past age five and a half. In the bar, Lysle was getting ready to leave, the roar of the truck already a promise to him. He was putting on his jacket even though he hadn't taken it off. How a man can get his ears snagged in a zipper is a puzzle only alcohol can solve. He was determined to drive very fast with his eyes shut so when he woke in the morning he'd be where he was going even though he didn't quite remember where he meant to get to anymore.

Gem, you can drive your dad's truck, Gem, I whispered to Gem's tousled hair, the top of his head squared off willy-nilly like his pet guinea pigs thirsting for water back home in their box of wood shavings.

Gem's nose whistled in sleep. There were dots on his face, I couldn't tell if they were freckles or dirt. If I were Violet I'd leave them there, even if they were dirt. He was such a cute boy, Gem, so tiny in his black T-shirt and black jeans and his cowboy boots.

Gem, just think, you could be the first five-year-old ever to drive a semi full of jalapeño poppers, I whispered. I didn't know what poppers were. I'd never heard of anything like that when I was alive. Wake up, Gem. I pleaded. Take out the keys.

Gem stirred and woke up. He wasn't wearing his seat belt. The door of the tavern banged open. Out stumbled Lysle all wired to get on the road. That was Lysle's word, too. I didn't know *wired.* I wondered if Jack did, or if he knew *jalapeños.* Sounded like a dance step. Lysle lurched toward the truck. Gem climbed on his knees so he'd be able to see out the windshield. His tousled head just an inch or two clear of the glass.

For a moment, just a moment, I was angry with Violet for leaving me to look after her child. Not to mention her husband.

But then—*Poor Violet,* I said to myself, like *Poor me,* knowing how much I wanted to be with Tip. Like me, Violet was drifting, spun by the Night, then jilted, left standing on a doorstep or crossing a threshold into the outskirts of some other dead woman's family with the object of easing their troubles, polishing their edges, unsnarling, if not their hungers, at least their hair. Being dead, I thought, is not unlike being in a kitchen with the door shut, the new dishwasher humming so nobody knows what you're doing in there, what you're thinking or feeling, what they're getting to eat. I used to stomp my foot in my kitchen, bang pots and pans, throw a wet sponge if I was angry at Jack, mix a batch of biscuits maybe, pour grape juice into Popsicle molds, burn my knuckles in the freezer finding a steak for tomorrow, lay it thunk on a plate, unwrap the crisp heavy white paper, no one knew, no one heard. All the tenderness, frustration, and mischief that happens in a kitchen happens in private, then vanishes the second they stab it with their forks. I used to think the only men familiar with the waxy crispness of butcher paper are the butchers, the only men who know the gritty pop of a can opener are the die-hard midnight snackers intent on a tuna fish sandwich. And Jack a restaurateur these days! In my kitchen, before I died, before he found entire restaurants reflected in the curve of every salvaged spoon and platter, Jack didn't even know where to find the bread and butter. I remember the time he asked, "Where do we keep the toast?" and how he used to read the newspaper after dinner in his armchair next to mine, but my chair would be empty, I'd be printing the twins' names on lunch bags, next day they'd never notice when I'd spelled all their names incorrectly on purpose, even packed Jack a bag marked *Lilian* once, he never noticed, he'd have choked with embarrassment to discover he was eating some dainty lady's sandwich.

Lysle stopped short in the middle of the parking lot, appearing troubled. After a moment he did something I'd never seen a man do in a public place. Jack would hang himself before he peed in a parking lot in the presence of a lady even if he didn't know she was there. I never even saw Jack pee in the bathroom. My own husband. And he never saw me either, though sometimes we chatted through the cracked-open door. Lysle's pee splashed against the dark of the pavement. He wasn't thinking about doing it, just doing it, so I didn't feel it on the floors of my house. I was a house, he was peeing, everything happening naturally. Gem caught sight of the truck keys hanging from the dash. He touched them, they swung, Lysle zipped up still looking troubled, I could feel his confusion like a jug of milk turning sour in the fridge. Gem grasped the key and tried to turn it. His hand was so tiny the key stayed as it was. The curve of the windshield was big enough to represent everything he'd need to pass through to get from life to death. And Lysle drunk as a skunk, ready to stink up Gem's chance at a good, long life. Put your weight on the key, I whispered into Gem's guinea pig hair. You can do it, I whispered across the span of his chest, a chest so narrow I could have kissed both nipples at once, though of course I'd never dreamed of touching a child's nipples. Not a body part I was ever terribly aware of. Bottles had nipples. That's all. Rinse the nipples, brush the nipples, boil the nipples, buy new nipples, that's all. Kiss the nipples, I whispered to Gem by mistake. Gem gazed down at his narrow wedge of T-shirt, where the picture of a cowgirl lassoed a motorcycle with a coiled purple snake. Never had I even caught sight of such a T-shirt when I was alive, buying T-shirts for my boys. I bought white ones, so I could have the pleasure of keeping them white. Spotless. Ironed. There was a whole stack of hand-me-down snap-sided T-shirts waiting for Tip to be born, white as they'd been in our first layette. There is something I regret, something I could have done that I didn't, after the priest told me to give birth and die. Knowing I'd never have the chance to dress Tip, still, I could have played with those shirts like a girl with a doll, snapped them, smoothed the white cotton under my fingers, even spilled a little milk on them, washed them, ironed them all over again, folded them just for the pleasure, as if Tip were born already and I was doing it for him. I had a feeling from the start he wouldn't be twins like the others, he'd have twice as many T-shirts as the rest of them but no partner like the others—the way they held each other's hands while climbing the steps, the way they learned their pairs of names as if both names belonged to each of them, so David was *David and Dennis,* and Dennis was *David and Dennis,* too—but I didn't say as much to Jack, how Tip would be alone with his pile of too many shirts.

Back and forth the keys swung. Gem gave the key a good, hard twist. Already he'd pressed the buttons, pulled the knobs. The wipers swished, the radio blared, the turn signal blinked. Gem's baby teeth showed crooked when the engine roared. Lysle lunged for the truck, nearly fell on his face, threw himself over Gem, yanked the keys from the dash, and with a drunken yell threw them as far as he could, past the noses of the other parked trucks.

Just as I'd planned.

Bingo, Lysle, I whispered.

They made no noise when they landed, the keys. They might not ever have landed at all. Who could have heard them anyway? What'd ya do that for? What'd ya do that for? Lysle screaming at Gem, the words ricocheting like pool balls inside me. But Gem was unfazed. He was accustomed to his father's flailing, his father's hullabaloos. He decided the keys hadn't fallen. Hadn't landed. Were still skimming and careening.

"Bingo," he said.

After he slept off his drink, Lysle spent forty minutes kicking the grass in search of the keys, then gave up and dug through the glove compartment for the trucking firm's phone number to call in for new ones. By then the morning heat had turned to foil on the top of the trailer bisecting the small dirt lot, the truck's nose in one patch of shade and the rear fender in another, but everything in between square in the sun. Under the trailer, where Gem crawled looking for fishing lures and parts of old pocketknives, there gathered a slippery smell like the inside of an empty popper box when he stuck his nose in it looking for the last poppers to spread in rows on the cookie sheet for his parents. His mother was dead. The tavern was closed on Mondays. The pay phone was outside the door, but his father kept losing his quarter. Three facts, like three drawers Gem opened and closed inside me to see if the contents snuck from drawer to drawer when he wasn't looking. Every so often the pay phone rang two and a half times for no reason, after which the trilling of the insects in the grass became more pronounced. Finally his father's quarter clinked the right way, but no one answered the phone at the trucking company, so finally Lysle phoned his sister, Carol, in the pinewoods outside of Iola, Wisconsin, and asked if there was anyone who felt like driving the four hundred and fifty miles south to come get him. It wasn't just being stuck that made Lysle so homesick all of a sudden. It was what he'd found out. He never should've hit the road so soon after Violet got blown up. Deep down, he must have hoped to come upon her hitching a ride on the highway, but now that he understood that this wouldn't be so, he longed at least to have a cry on the shoulder of Iola, where he had grown up, not far from the pinewoods he'd kept home in with Violet, their beach chairs sunk in a bed of pine needles around a giant fire pit for parties in the clearing outside their built-on trailor. Iola sat in the skirts of the kettle moraines on the edge of dairy country. Dawn smelled of milk, noon of clover.

"Sid'll do it," Carol answered Lysle right away. "He's on his way back from wherever."

Lysle guffawed, relieved to have something to snort at in the midst of his yearning for a double-decker cone from the ice cream gazebo near the water reservoir in Iola. No one had seen Sid in years. *Wherever* was jail, most likely. In any case Sid Haarstad, Lysle and Carol's older brother, who'd spent ten years in the navy before kayaking ninety miles of the Mekong River, only to be arrested upon return in Honolulu for packing a hilt full of opium, was the last person in the world, twice married and twice divorced notwithstanding, who upon acquittal and release from jail would choose to spend a summer watching home movies of spilled ice cream cones melting on the sidewalks of Mainstreet, U.S.A., even if he was desperate to recoup. But now he was on his way east to Wisconsin. Sid must be feeling unstrung, Carol confided to Lysle. *Unstrung.* The funny word plunked inside me, but everything else about Sid was as legible to me as print on paper, a book on my shelf that I wouldn't have so much as flipped through if I were alive. Dead, I was required to play a role in it, somehow, it being not Lysle's but Sid's story between the lines of which the Night had so trickily slipped me. And so there I was, reading Sid Haarstad inside out as if for some test to which the Night was preparing to put me. In all the phone calls Sid had ever made from jail, he claimed not to know how the opium had ended up in the hilt of the sword. He'd traded his kayak for the sword at the close of the Mekong River trip. It was a World War I sword, but the farmer who traded it used the weapon to gut pumpkins. For supper on the day Sid climbed the terraced slope to the village for a case of the bitter, beerish liquor they made in those parts, the farmer placed a wobbly pumpkin between Sid's feet, pulled the sword from the sheath, and lifted the blade over both their heads as reverently as if waiting for God to say which of the three round objects—Sid's head, the farmer's head, or the pumpkin—should prepare to meet its demise. For a long moment the sword stayed horizontal with the sky, and the look of concentration on the farmer's face intensified, as did the tautness of the muscles in his arms, but when the blade arced onto the pumpkin it made only a wet thwacking sound that did nothing but dent the rind. The farmer burst out laughing at his favorite joke, then grew more and more hilarious as he hacked at the pumpkin like he did every evening, thumping and sawing, the blade of the sword dull as mud, the orange pulp flying. Finally the farmer's bent-shouldered wife scooped out the meat and stewed it with chilies and basil while Sid wondered in English whether the sword had ever killed anyone in a war. The farmer raised his eyebrows, then poured more beer into Sid's mug from a standing height the way the waiters poured tea in the fancy Asian restaurants, the arc of liquid spanning the table without a splash. At sundown Sid was due back at the river with a case of the sour beer. He offered the farmer first some money and then his wristwatch in exchange for the heavy curved sword, then sign-talked the man into accompanying him to where the kayak waited with the other boats. The upswept shape of the sword resembled the curve of the kayak, making the trade seem inevitable to Sid, who lived his whole life anyway trading one event for another in an unending chain of adventure of which the opium stuffed in rolled bags in the hilt of the sword was the link that finally didn't seem to lead anywhere but back to Iola. That was where the Book of Sid ended, so far, the brittle pages edged with gold because that's what Sid's heart was made of even if nobody knew it but me. Many years had gone by since his family had laid eyes on him, except for a formal navy portrait of someone who looked like a Gettysburg militiaman time-warped to the wrong war. At family gatherings the photo was passed hand to hand, the droopy handlebar mustache commented upon and examined until some consensus was reached as to whether the portrait was really of Sid, and if so, then for what act of heroism was there a Purple Heart pinned above the National Defense ribbon on the breast pocket of his uniform?

"Couldn't be his head he lost," one of the family always remarked, meaning Sid had lost his head long before going to Vietnam. But aside from the women, Sid was the smartest of the family.

Carol said to Lysle, "Tell me the number of where you are and how to get there, and Sid'll swing by and pick you and Gem up. You know Sid. He'll do anything once."

"Forget it," said Lysle, reading Carol the phone number anyway. "Like I'm gonna wait three weeks for some disappearing brother who ain't showing up before he goes somewhere else on the way. Gem!" Lysle shouted, pressing the receiver against the crook of his shoulder, "You ain't found them keys, you shouldn't be sitting there playing with that fishing lure!" Gem wrapped the parts of the pocketknife in a dandelion leaf, then crawled back under the truck in search of shade. He couldn't search for the keys because he knew he wouldn't find them. They were safe in heaven in his mother's blue jean pocket or swinging in the sparkly wind, a thousand colors trapped in the strands of Gem's mother's long dishwater hair. Every time Violet used to say her hair was *dishwater,* Gem imagined soapy lather in a jelly jar cup. Instead of searching for the keys as his father had told him, Gem searched for the grasshopper he'd noticed earlier perched secretively in one of the tire treads. When he spotted it flexing its legs on the slope of a matchbook and had caught the pale insect in his cupped hand, careful not to crush the helmet or twist the strawlike feet backward, he shimmied on his belly through the dirt into sunlight, leaving the matchbook behind so he could look for it later.

Lysle hung up the phone, wondering if it might be acceptable for a stranded man with a hungry son to break the tavern window in hopes of honey-roasted peanuts, soft drinks, jerky, and beer.

No more beer, I advised. The grasshopper butted against Gem's folded palm.

Lysle hunted for the best way to kick open the tavern. The front door was too thick, the windows nearly too narrow but not quite too high. He found a rock propping up a loose drainpipe, took off his T-shirt, then on second thought put it on again and ushered Gem over.

"Take your shirt off quick, it's dirtier than mine," he said.

"What for?" asked Gem.

"To get in the window," said Lysle.

Gem wondered how a T-shirt could climb in a window. Anyway, if he tried to take off his, the grasshopper would escape. But then he would find out how a T-shirt could climb in a window. He took off his shirt. The grasshopper plummeted upside down to the ground, where it wiggled its feet like someone pumping a bicycle. The telephone rang two and a half times and stopped. Lysle wrapped his hand inside the T-shirt and picked up the rock with it before climbing on top of three stacked bricks.

Tell your son to move away and shut his eyes, I whispered fierce as I could, for it dawned on me finally that I could be heard, my words a skitter of dust but their message conveyed.

"Move away and shut your eyes," obeyed Lysle, whose eyes glazed a moment with the start of a sneeze.

Gem stepped back a distance and shielded his eyes, peeking between his fingers. Smack smack smack. Every time the wrapped-up rock broke glass, Gem's toes curled in his boots.

Head or feet first? Lysle pondered back and forth inside me, making me think of dancing on the moonlit pontoon knotted to the end of the dock. Even nights I was pregnant with Tip, Jack and I danced on that boat, knowing we probably wouldn't have another summer to dance through. Now I was glad Jack didn't know what I know—that my death would be a dance in the arms of the Night, who stepped in to steal me and Jack from each other. But those nights on the dock, the lake air smelled of lake flies and citronella while the lily pad blossoms gave no fragrance at all. The music was tinny where it drifted off the dock, like a hotel band under distant palm trees away from which we'd snuck to a private cove. I wanted a thatched umbrella, those nights, and a torch with an open flame, and someone crossing the house with towels folded over their forearm, heading for our bedroom to turn back the sheet and lay wrapped mints on starched pillowcases. Wrought iron, plaster of Paris, brass polish, varnish, steel wool, and sawdust. Those were Jack's smells, that summer I was pregnant with Tip, but I couldn't smell them now if we were stepping on each other's toes. Nor cigarettes. Smoking, Jack held the cigarette backward so the lit end hid in the curve of his palm. His wrist swiveled when he inhaled. Side to side on the dock, dancing with Jack, pregnant for the last time, I kissed the cigarette pack under the hem of his shirt pocket. I kissed the crease of the collar and rubbed the tip of my nose around the shaved spot below his ear. I had a theory I told only Gwen, when we were starting to be friends, when she was pregnant with Johnny, when the neighborhood was new. Jack was tight with the developer and made sure every house had a view of the lake, or if not, a piece of the channel. He still called them his houses years after other families had been paying them off. Gwen and I liked to spy on him surveying the lawn, evenings when John, Gwen's husband, was still at work at the hospital, rallying for peace. "Married to an anesthesiologist." That's why she fought herself instead of him, it was less frustrating. Gwen used to sigh. What good was peace without struggle, negotiation, truce, capitulation, or surrender? What good was peace when you could pop it along with a tranquilizer? Had I lived a little longer I might have drummed up the gumption to ask if she thought she might coax John to seek some help for his drug use—I saw him at the hospital once, when I stopped there on some errand, he was gliding around on those black Chinese slippers—but instead I only told her I knew how it went, and that Jack's and my battles were all tongue-in-cheek, no pun intended, I said. And that I had a theory. I told her love isn't a state of mind, the way a lot of people think it is. It's a method of behaving, there's nothing abstract about it, it's like electrons in a wire, you need to flip a switch for the light to come on; love is cause and effect, first the act, then the feeling, first the kiss, then the forgiveness, first you iron the damn trousers and then you love the way he looks in them, and so on.

Gwen said, So that's why they call it making love.

Even dancing on the pontoon, I knew Jack wouldn't be able to adore Tip the way I wanted him to. Side to side on the wood slats, I knew this and hated Jack for it, and nuzzled his pocket and hated him, and watched the moon slip between some clouds and hated him, and leaned my head into the crook of his arm and hated, yet forgave, and hated, yet forgave.

Lysle shook the glass from Gem's T-shirt before giving it back. The larger shards of window lay heavy in the brittle grass and didn't shatter when Gem stomped them with his heels.

"Gem," said Lysle.

Gem quit stomping, flapped the shirt even harder than Lysle had flapped it to try to shake off the parking lot dirt and reveal again the picture of the cowgirl lassoing the motorcycle, and said to his father, "Not me."

"You don't even know what I asked you yet," said Lysle.

"So what. I ain't doin' it." Gem's smudged face lifted as if into the sky reflected in his eyes. Brown marbles swimming under willful flecks of clouds.

Not *ain't*, I amended. *Not.* I'm *not* doing it.

He ain't doing it, Lysle thought with a shake of his head, wanting a beer more than anything. He stepped back up onto the three stacked bricks and gripped his hands around the smoothest-looking part of the windowsill and jumped and pulled, but the window was narrower than it appeared or else his belt loop was stuck on a nail. "God fucking piss on a fucking stick!" He struggled. "Fucking horseshit goddamn piss on a fucking haystack." Lysle yanked and shoved, it didn't matter which way, the window was too narrow and his belt loop was snagged on a nail, too. Both. At once. And the sunken floor inside was lower than the ground outside the wall. He was stuck like water in ice.

Just as I'd intended.

"Pull my ankles!" he yelled.

Gem couldn't reach. Even standing on the stacked bricks he could do nothing but unlace his father's boots by mistake. The telephone rang three and a half rings. "Shut the dickface up!" Lysle yelled, knowing how all the truckers would make fun of him tomorrow night before they unstuck him. He knew they'd feed Gem a hamburger but feed Lysle salted peanuts by tossing them from a distance into his mouth while keeping score on the blackboard. Home versus visitors. Whichever team won would get to give him a shave. He'd need a shave by then, all right. He'd need a cry, too, stuck in a window with no Violet giggling gently at the sight of his jammed backside the way she used to titter if he left his fly unzipped. His nose itched no matter which way he rubbed. As for me, I was laughing so hard all my memories shook inside me, which made me cry instead. Now that I knew I could make myself heard, I was all the more impatient to try it on Tip. Tip was growing up without me; the years were flitting by, and I couldn't catch them from where I was, stuck in Lysle's life and Lysle in the window. How I wanted to get near Tip, he'd sneeze, or almost. I couldn't wait to see him tilt back his head and wince. Alive, I used to play a game with David and Douggie, Dennis and Drew—stop their sneezes midsniff just by placing my pinkie finger against their nostrils and saying *gesundheit* before it was time.

"I want a drink," Gem announced from the far side of the wall, interrupting my reverie—the sight of Drew's nose twitching like a mouse's, but Douggie's as disdainful as a cat's.

Lysle's voice was muffled when it came through the window.

"You don't want it half as much as I will soon enough," he said. The phone rang again with a kind of a flutter, more like a bird than a phone.

"Catch it!" said Gem. He ran for it, blissful.

"Who dare?" he blurted into the receiver.

"I do," said the gruff-voiced man at the other end. "Who dis?"

"Me," said Gem.

"Me who?" said the man. "Me Gem?"

There was a nodding silence.

"Well, Gem, so happens I'm just a hundred miles down the road," said the man. "Want to get rescued by your uncle Sid?"

"Who dat?" said Gem.

Tell him to hurry, I whispered, for though I didn't know yet why I needed Sid, I knew he could help me, steal me out of the fickle whirl of the Night, settle my nerves, and tell me not to despair, though there was so much Tip was doing that I couldn't see or stop, wiping my eyes although I had no eyes, preparing me for what as yet unknotted grief my tears could possibly be made of.

2

Tip and Johnny

One midsummer weekend, when Tip and Johnny were seventeen, Johnny's girlfriend's parents decided to go camping on Lake Superior. The campground would have no phone, so first Rhonda's mother and then her father and then both together took a detour from their packing to pull Rhonda aside and say how much they trusted her not to take advantage of their absence. None of them knew what to make of this plea. Rhonda's parents already recognized the awkwardness of being lustful, free-spirited parents to a daughter as restrained as they were exuberant, while Rhonda knew her prudishness disappointed her mother and father. Perhaps Rhonda's stiffness was a response to her mother's liquidity, or in retaliation for her father's playful Jewish charm. Maybe her parents ought to leave her alone, under the influence of her more adventurous friends, her parents must have decided one night in their bedroom, after making love. Maybe, were she left in an empty house for a few steamy mid-July days, Rhonda would pull off her high-necked nightgown and loosen up a little; maybe her best friend, Cindy, along with Cindy's new boyfriend, Tip, would provide some inspiration. After all, Tip was one of the Baymiller boys, while Cindy exhibited that big-boned blend of languor and impatience; she never yawned without reaching for a tube of lipstick or body buffing cream with which to pamper herself, never sighed without flexing her neck and toes. Rhonda, on the other hand, was endlessly practical, always bound to some penitential sewing project that made her parents feel, especially on Sundays, as if they were visiting their daughter in a convent. There was Rhonda with her hair in her eyes embroidering a recipe for vanilla fudge on someone else's denim jacket, there was Rhonda with a cold sore calculating a half-size increase in length of a sweater she was knitting, there she was on her knees—yes, her knees—searching for a dropped thimble. Her parents were chagrined by the way she tacked closed, with neat star-shaped stitches, the slits in her skirts. "She's like the girls who died virgins in the Triangle Shirtwaist fire. One sacrifice piled on top of another," Rhonda's father enjoyed saying with horrified indulgence. Rhonda's boyfriend, Johnny, whose father was the anesthesiologist who'd helped care for Rhonda's dying grandmother, was a polite boy who seemed to be considering, from beneath a veneer of worried reserve, at least the possibility of engaging in what Rhonda's mother hopefully termed "ordinary teenage experimentation." But Rhonda, so far, hadn't coaxed the boy's buried impulses into the open.

"I just don't want her to grow up to be the kind of woman who always does the *appropriate thing*," Rhonda's mother confided in her husband.

To Rhonda her mother added, "Now, Rhonda, when we're away, when we're home, too, but especially when we're away, just because we don't want you to take advantage of our absence doesn't mean we don't want you to have fun."

"I *am* having fun," Rhonda answered truthfully. She lifted the cooler into the trunk of her parents' car, rescued the family puppy from where it had tumbled behind the duffel, then squatted on the lawn with the floppy ball of fur, teasing its ears with a dandelion. Years later, when Rhonda looked back on this girlhood moment, she saw in her posture—the kneeling, the flower in her hand—a blurred forecast of how what happened to Johnny finally cemented her modesty, making of her virtue a statue on a lawn that she would tend when its alternative weighed too heavily on her—but for now there was only the puppy, the house blissfully empty, her friends not to arrive till nightfall.

"I'm going to house-train you if I have to tear the house down in order to do it," she whispered into the animal's moist brown eyes, tired of her mother's affectionate scolding of the puppy, her father's amusement at each morning's soiled newspapers stinking up the corners of the rooms. As her parents drove off, Rhonda waved good-bye with the puppy's paw in a flirtatious way. But she was a skinny girl who seemed not to care that when she nodded, laughed, stood up, or waved, her tights sagged yet further around her ankles. That night when Johnny kissed her she bent over so far backward that he felt like the pole in a game of limbo. The unwitting flare of her upside-down nostrils excited him by offering just a shadowed glimpse of inside her body. The nostrils were so clean they sparkled, so silky he wanted to slide in his tongue.

What would they taste like, Rhonda's prayerfully flaring nostrils? Johnny imagined something pungent yet fresh, like the cubes of honeydew his mother dipped in sweetened soy sauce for backyard parties.

He imagined the glossy tunnels tapering like the curved insides of seashells.

He speculated on whether one of Rhonda's nostrils might be different from the other, as perceived by the quivering tip of his tongue, or if the subtle asymmetry of his view of them was only an illusion.

His brow furrowed more deeply with every new spin on every new question. Was there a difference between a boy who slid his tongue into his girlfriend's ear and a boy who even momentarily fantasized about licking the inside of her nose? he wondered. What if she told her friends, and he then became the boy at whom the girls stifled shrieks in the hallways at school? The other boys would come up to him and say, "Johnny, how ya doin? Snot so bad, eh?"

But did he care what the other boys said to him, not including Tip?

Or did he care more about the salty crevices that might pro-

vide the only doorway ever to lead him inside his girlfriend's
body?

She had bidden him, as she led him to her room, to please
forgive the mess, but he saw at once that her room was cleaner
than the rest of the house. Instead of smelling of dog shit on wet
newspaper, it smelled of shorn grass from the open windows.
Neatly spread on the floor lay a sewing pattern weighted with
steel bobbins, two spools of bright thread, and an arrangement
of zippers and measuring tapes. Upon the bed lay a smooth fold
of minty-colored fabric under a glint of scissors. Tonight's dress
was for her sister's graduation. Rhonda had shown him the pattern envelope, on which the sketch showed a girl wrapped in a
giant anklet. Maybe Johnny wouldn't mind if while they talked,
she pinned.

Johnny recalled that Rhonda's fingertips often bore the scars
of penetration, and was suddenly empathic to all needles and
pins that had managed to stick themselves at least that far into
her. Never had he even put his finger in anyone's ear. Aside from
kissing and holding hands, not a single part of him had ever been
surrounded by part of anyone else.

Was Rhonda even his girlfriend, then?

Or was she only some too skinny girl practicing back bends
the way girls used to do during recess? What did that make
him, to be the person who, if he lost his grip on her back bend
while they were kissing, would cause her to collapse on the floor?

Meanwhile her upside-down nostrils appeared to harbor their
own expectations and secretive misdemeanors. Perhaps Rhonda's
nose would do what she wouldn't, perhaps it would receive him.
Except that then Rhonda reached for the box full of pins and
held it outward as if introducing him to a rival. Maybe Tip was
right when he suggested Johnny simply picked the wrong girls,
girls to whom Johnny was attracted for the very things—their
coy indecision, their sudden fits of platonic snuggling, their hot,
grinding refusals—that most tantalizingly refused him. Still, Tip
never flaunted whatever it was that made sex come as naturally
to Tip as math did to Johnny. Tip was a genius in bed, and bed
was everywhere Tip went. All the hardest places in town—the

resinous, splintery docks, the plank floor of the lakeside gazebo, the loading docks of Tip's dad's Jack of Steaks restaurants, even the tables themselves—seemed designed to yield to the shape of a girl's body when it was Tip who lowered her onto it, and all the softest places in town seemed actually to breathe when it was Tip who whispered his appreciation into some girl's half-closed eyes. Tip never bragged when he talked about sex, he let the girl's contented ravishment get the word around, and then appeared not to hear it. Gratefully he reveled in his own appetite and its satiation, his own incredulous delight in all the different ways of doing the same thing in different places and different positions with different girls. There were so many ways to make a girl feel good that made him feel good, too. Tip was beholden to the reciprocity of sex, which made it the exact good twin of fighting. You hit a boy, he hits you in return, you hunker down between a girl's legs, she hunkers down between yours. Fighting was what you did with boys because you'd die before you kissed one, even one of your own brothers. Sex was what you did with girls because you'd despise yourself forever and suffocate in hell if you ever raised a hand to one, including one of your sisters, even Becka. Between the two—boys and girls, punching and screwing—Tip swung as if on a rope swing, his voice raw from shouting. Maybe Johnny was too tentative, too cautious, too polite. Maybe being like Tip was the solution, yet no one could be like Tip, completely, for when Tip was at his most enthusiastic, that was when he reached, somehow, his complementary, most introspective nadir, which girls saw if they were smart enough and didn't if they weren't; it didn't matter to Tip, who only laughed all the harder in order to preserve it, that dark, low swirl that Johnny knew enough about to know he didn't have one himself. Maybe Johnny had to stop wondering, stop hoping to solve everything before it even became a problem. Just do it. He wrapped his arms softly around Rhonda's back bend, clenched shut his eyes, sought the ridge of her nostril with the emboldened tip of his tongue.

Rhonda screamed in three parts like three separate scandalized girls, dropping her box full of pins.

*   *   *

On the fireplace mantel in Rhonda's parents' living room sat a cup and saucer, an unopened bottle of California wine, a stuffed Horton the Elephant doll, and the floppy-eared puppy. Cindy wondered which of these things had been put there on purpose and which had been left there by accident. You never knew with Rhonda's parents. The puppy seemed nervous about finding a way down, but was distracted by a handful of pretzels in the teacup. A blanket had been spread out already on the couch, as if to dare Tip to discover the fake nose and eyeglasses hidden underneath it. A lot of boys, most boys, *all boys not including Tip,* Cindy decided, would have put on the mask for a minute, trying to be hip and break the ice before kissing her, but Tip didn't need to be hip, for there was never any ice to be broken. He pushed the glasses between the cushions along with Cindy's panties. He left her bra fastened but with the straps pulled just to the insides of her elbows, then sucked on the blanket where he'd draped it over her nipples. How he managed to become naked without her having touched his clothing, Cindy never could fig-ure out. "It's like he was born naked," she once said to Rhonda, and had since decided it really *was* like that, Tip was born naked again and again, every night between her legs or somebody else's, hers if she had anything to say about it, but she wouldn't, after tonight, because like the other nights in the weeks they'd been trying—frantically, pensively—to make love, their attempts were in vain. Either he was too big or she was too small, and now they were bruised and smarting. Tip wondered if despite what every-body else knew about Cindy, she was as scared as Rhonda, but he was gentle in the face of this speculation, touched by her body's stubborn unavailability to both their pleasures. Cindy'd already hunted through Rhonda's bathroom for body oil, and then, fail-ing that, and not wanting to interrupt Rhonda and Johnny upstairs, she pulled herself away from the nubby friction of the couch to search the kitchen for cooking oil. *Extra Virgin* she found. Maybe all the other boys before this were only playing doctor. Tip was the only one who knew what he was doing, if only her smart aleck body would cooperate with the rest of her and let him. Underneath him, the sofa turned feverish. Cindy's sex glistened with olive oil but still threatened to break like a snagged zipper. Tip bit his lip. He bit *hers,* then combed her eyebrows with two slow swipes of the tongue. He wasn't patient, exactly. Only determined to ride Cindy out one way or another without causing her harm. Already he was accustomed to holding himself back and waiting for girls to be ready, and then waiting for them to orgasm before he did. His older brother Drew had advised him in this art when Tip was fifteen.

"You keep them coming, they keep coming," Drew laughed. Tip didn't see the humor. And it wasn't a bribe when Tip let the girls come first. For he wasn't conniving or sly. He had no reason to be.

"Come on, baby. Oh baby, come on," Tip would say, and take a lock of their hair and wrap it around his knuckles to draw the sighs from their throats like undulating pink ribbons. Then he'd whisper his pleading into their hand before sucking just one of their fingers into his mouth, or pressing his forehead flush against theirs with a solemnity that belied all their bucking and moaning as if to pay respect to the thought that at their very centers all girls were inaccessible even to Tip. Like trees the girls were, with concentric rings at their cores. Tip's family kept hunting land north in Peshtigo, a cabin crowded with dusty blankets on sagging cots, the slanting kitchen cabinets scuffed up by mismatched cookware. Assorted moth-eaten couches and chairs faced a portrait of the family painted before Tip was born— brown-haired Polly, black-haired Jack, and the three sets of blondish twins—beside a stone fireplace hung with shotguns and camouflage gear. From the rear of the cabin stretched acres of marsh and woods, in which Tip and his brothers and father had each laid claim to their own tree within sight of the shaved miles under the power line. On the frost-shrouded mornings of hunting season, when Tip was up in his tree stand keeping his eyes peeled for movement at the foggy margins of the woods, he heard the big, columnar silence of the tree reveal itself to him in a hymn of groans and harsh, snapping creaks, insubstantial in the face of the tree's greater, massive stillness. His heart sped. The rules of the woods were rock solid. All the moist expanse of land that he could see from his tree stand was his territory. All the willowy blond grass across which Tip's arrow might fly, the ragged banks of the stream turning spongy at the shifting edges of the marsh, the brittle reaches of the woods, belonged to his arrow. So if a deer—even frightened by another hunter a mile away—if that deer appeared, then it was Tip's and he could hold his breath and go for it. He was all tendon while drawing the bow, the deer standing stock-still as if to wait for the arrow or darting crazily around or leaping into the woods to escape it. Tip threw down the bow, then clambered from the tree, not feeling the rungs of the ladder, then chased the frightened clatter of the deer to see if he'd hit it, swearing so excitedly everyone rushed over to make him shut up, his brothers' pants soaked with mud, his father's hands raw with dew, their gustiness no match for his even if he hadn't hit it, even if the deer were chased for an hour and then the arrow found west of the tree stand upside down in a clump of sumac. No matter what, the silence was bigger than the noise. For there was silence in the vesicles of the trees, the churning innards of the animals, the banging of the coffeepot against the scarred sink, and in the girl whose clothing he so tenderly, so tumultuously removed from her body. But there was no silence ever in Tip, or if there was, no one heard it. Well, maybe Johnny. Who was clever enough not to say. Tip was the shout in whose aftermath the silence was greater than before. He had no choice but to be. Sometimes he wondered what bade him act as he did, shout, yell, think, throw, do what he did. For instance, even after he'd given up on him and Cindy, his erection didn't die, just stood there, guarding itself against its own composure. Cindy's clenched knuckles trembled against his balls. There was something Tip wasn't divulging, she felt, some thought he was thinking, some vigil he was keeping that she'd never know. Sex wouldn't have divulged it, anyway. She felt sore all along her chafed, oiled body, pummeled by desire and its disappointment. Sex was a better education than school. Life would be filled with lessons like this, when she wanted a thing yet needed to refuse it, yet couldn't make herself push it away. She arched her back under Tip, pulling closer again. He was so broad, so compact. Menstruation had nothing to do with turning a girl into a woman, Cindy speculated. Neither did loss of virginity. To be wrapped in the arms of a man rather than a boy, *that* was what did it.

"Forget it, okay?" Tip whispered, meaning he didn't hold it against her and he wouldn't tell anyone, either. Years later when Cindy looked back on this moment, she imagined Tip had been clearing small injustices out of the way in order to do obeisance to the insurmountable injustice of what would soon happen to Johnny, but tonight she only saw how he yanked on his jeans, threw on his T-shirt, left his sneakers untied so they clumped past the slate entryway of Rhonda's house. It was then that, upstairs, Rhonda screamed three screams in a row. Tip bounded outside, slamming the door.

"Write a song about it, Johnny!" Tip gladly yelled, believing Johnny had finally scored, even though Rhonda wasn't exactly top forty hit material. "She's the Boobless Booby Prize" would be the name of the song. Tip gave another yell as he skidded toward the car, savoring the throaty pitch of his voice. He loved the bad muffler of Johnny's car when he backed it out, honking so Johnny would know he would need to walk home; he loved the stillness the big car left in its wake, Cindy throbbing with unhappiness on the tossed-apart couch, the fake nose and eyeglasses peering through chinks of lamplight.

Upstairs Rhonda felt cold all over, certain she'd never allow any male human being to touch her again. No two people ever want the same thing from each other at the same time, she was learning. Life would be filled with times like this, when she imagined she was doing what the other person wanted, until they turned out to want something nobody wanted unless they were out of their minds. She'd been prepared to ask Johnny to spend the whole night kissing. But he wanted to lick snot. Three screams weren't enough. Even Johnny was shocked by his misbehavior. Rhonda busied herself scooping up pins with two pieces of facing. At last she made a funnel of the empty square, tilting the full one to make a river of pins cascade into the pin box. Earlier in the day, when she'd decided to allow Johnny to spend the night the way her parents had barely stopped short of encouraging, she'd imagined he might lie against her, cool as a sheet, clean as a pillow. Johnny's heart wouldn't thump. It would slide through the minutes like a clock on a night table, aligning itself to the flow of shared time.

Judging from Tip's celebratory honk of the horn, Cindy and Tip must at last have been able to make love. Good for Cindy, Rhonda thought a little enviously. Palming the carpet for the sting of pins, she'd begun to feel annoyed by her own squeamishness. Maybe Johnny hadn't meant to stick his tongue in her nose, or maybe other people stuck their tongues in each other's noses every day but were too uptight to talk about it. Besides, Johnny looked so distraught that not to forgive him seemed corrupt. Rhonda felt around on her bedside table for Cindy's blue eyeliner, considered doing her eyelids, instead drew a vertical line along Johnny's forehead where the crease was deepest.

"You can't even tell that I drew anything there," she assessed when she was done. "The crease is the same as always. Let's just lie down, okay?"

"I don't want Tip getting drunk and driving my car," Johnny answered.

"Tip'll get drunk and drive *somebody's* car if not yours, and then you won't know what he's doing next."

At Rhonda's urging, Johnny stretched out on his back. Why did Rhonda think he was more worried about Tip than he was about the car? In Johnny's mind he saw the car crumpled around a telephone pole and Tip's head smashed against the shattered windshield. Johnny could get a new car, but Tip was irreplaceable. Nothing that could sit still for long enough to be duplicated could be a duplicate of Tip. Maybe Johnny's car was parked at Harry's Pub already, maybe it was cruising out past the motor vehicle bureau, checking out the secluded lawns from where it was possible to spy on rich people fighting in their houses, maybe it was parked near the boardwalk on Lake Butte des Morts, where Tip would drink a Pepsi while perched on the lookout tower, maybe it was parked in Johnny's driveway, from where Tip would have snuck in through Johnny's bedroom window, borrowed a couple of Johnny's tapes, and snuck out through the window again before climbing the ladder propped on the grass between the two boys' houses. The ladder made it easy for the friends to go from one of their bedrooms to the other without having to depend on ordinary methods. Johnny's bedroom was on the ground floor of *his* house, Tip's bedroom, next door, on the second floor of Tip's. The ladder rose from the strip of lawn to Tip's window. Some mornings Johnny woke to find that Tip had descended the ladder during the night, to sleep on the rag rug near Johnny's bed, or to sit in Johnny's kitchen, sharing breakfast cereal with Johnny's parents, or to take a shower in Johnny's bathroom because Tip's brothers had used up the hot water at home. The ladder bestowed, on each visit, a stealth and palpable devotion. Rhonda was right, it wasn't the car that mattered to Johnny. What mattered was where it was cruising, speeding, idling, parking—with his friend inside it.

"You look so serious lying down," Rhonda was saying, wetting her lips with a sip of water. Her mouth looked crooked and surprised as she lowered it toward the zipper of Johnny's khakis, her natural pallor shot through with a lavender tinge that made Johnny think it best to shut his eyes. Through a haze he heard her turn off the light at the bedside, then turn it on again.

"Where are those scissors?" she asked, having forgotten before now to take them off the bed.

He could feel the line she had drawn on his forehead bisect the whole rest of him like a road up a hill. Yes, he looked like he was taking the SATs, Rhonda said to herself, thrusting her tongue past the teeth of his zipper. Johnny clenched his fist as if around a pencil. His studiousness was worthy of all the mock conversations Rhonda and Cindy had ever staged about it.

"How was your day, Johnny?" one of the girls would ask the other.

"Oh, you have to measure it from all angles," the other would say.

"What would you like for a snack, Johnny?"

"Pi, please."

"What's your phone number, Johnny?"

Cindy would print his number on a slip of paper, then read it off. "Two million, three hundred thirty-one thousand, nine hundred and two."

But just because Johnny was adorable didn't mean Rhonda had to do what her parents wanted her to, Rhonda supposed, pausing to swallow more water. She could feel the tidy rush on the back of her throat, the cold drink cleansing itself inside her. She would do as she pleased. Johnny would do as she pleased, as well. *Everyone,* from now on, would. She would lather her hands, dry them, brush her teeth, then sit very still in her bedroom until she felt back to normal, then smooth the yards of sugary green fabric on the floor and pin the dress pattern to it, and cut, and sew, and clothe herself, but first, make Johnny go home.

2

"We'll drive out to that intersection where we bought the coffee, with the fir trees around the picnic tables, where the old man was worried he stepped on a praying mantis, which is impossible, there's so few praying mantises left anymore, well, maybe because people kept stepping on them, and call Rhonda from there. I'm sure they have a phone at that place. They have a pinball machine," said Rhonda's mother inside the tent, where the drifting marinade smoke from other people's campfires had already become enamored of her husband's beard. Delicious. She loved that smell. It made her feel young. Upon her husband's chest, too, the fragrance of barbecue and ashes, the stirred flames of hair.

"I just don't know what you're going to ask her," Rhonda's father protested. "She's not going to tell you what she's doing, anyway. You wouldn't *want* her to tell you. Rhonda's a teenager . . . Rhonda's our daughter!" At this he grew distracted for a moment, as he often did when he heard himself using the word *daughter.* "She's not supposed to tell us what she's doing.

She's supposed to do the opposite of what we want her to do. Remember?"

"Sometimes," replied Rhonda's mother, watching the play of her fingers along the parts of her husband's body that were showing his age, the small pockets of fat below his armpits, the filled-in hollow beneath his rib cage. "But I could sort of figure things out just from listening to what she does or doesn't say, maybe," she went on. "Also maybe we'll spot a moose on the road on the way to the gas station. Darling, by the way, don't you know that those girls who died in the Triangle Shirtwaist fire were real girls? It doesn't matter how many years ago it happened. They were real, they had parents, they were someone's flesh and blood. *They* were daughters, too. You sound like you don't realize that . . . not that you're heartless, but when you make those little comments about them . . . It's thoughtless. Okay?"

"Deep down I've been waiting for you to tell me that," agreed Rhonda's father.

3

Tip bought a six-pack of Pepsi at the Kwik Trip. In case he fell asleep that night on the lookout tower, he intended to wake up as clearheaded for Sunday fishing as if he'd stayed up all night and watched the day appear. Rumor had it the walleye were biting north of Asylum Point. Tip would bicycle there with his waders rolled tight, coast the grounds of the nuthouse feeling how glad he was not to be one of the nuts, then wade the shoreline until he reached his fishing spot. If the sun was strong, he might take off his shirt in hopes that his pneumothorax scar might turn more pink against the increasing brown of his skin. The nurses had promised the scar would fade, but Tip wasn't eager for the raised line to vanish from where it measured the space between one rib and another, for it was a marker from four months earlier, a souvenir of the biggest insult his father had ever done him.

Sump pump was what the pneumothora tube had been called

by the doctors the week it was in him, Tip explained to the several grown women to whom years later he told what happened to Johnny.

Tip swallowed the last of a bottle of Pepsi, leaning forward from where he perched at the end of the boardwalk to take aim at the headlights traversing the bridge above where the river flowed into the lake, nearly a quarter mile away. No matter with what force Tip threw the bottle, there wasn't a chance he'd come close to striking a car on the bridge. He knew this absolutely. What he didn't know was whether, had the bridge been close enough to hit, he would have thrown the bottle anyway. Sometimes he wondered how many temptations he would need to overcome in order to apologize for having caused the death of his mother. Tip's father, Jack, who'd escaped to the waiting room during the births of the three sets of twins, had steeled himself hard for the birth of this first solitary baby, had watched Polly's blood follow Tip all the way out of her body. When Tip was born and Polly died, Polly had been only thirty-one years old. Since then she'd been in heaven, Jack taught them—dressed as she was in the belted dress in the framed photograph on the wall of Jack's office at the Jack of Steaks on Ohio Street, or in the leopard-print jacket she wore in the photo on the wall of Jack's office in the Jack of Steaks on Route 21, or in the blouse and plaid Bermudas she wore at Jack's office at the salvage yard. The dress had giant round flat buttons from collar to hem. "Dresses had their heyday when your mother put them on," Jack once let himself say to the twins, who sometimes repeated the line to one another but never in earshot of Jack. In all the photos, Polly wore the same high-heeled sandals. Her dark hair curled at the shoulders, her fingers having just coaxed, or preparing to coax, the stiffness from the bangs. How did Polly walk on clouds in heels sharp as golf tees? The unanswerable question only made heaven yet more ulterior; higher up, farther off, a befitting inconvenience since Tip never expected to get there anyway. It was the world at large—all the places and things bereft of her—to which he owed his apology. His mother already forgave him her death, was even, sometimes, grateful for his having taken her place. Why Tip thought this, he didn't know. Only, he believed in her forgiveness the way some people might believe in ghosts, a little afraid, not of the ghosts but of the amount of faith required to sustain such belief. Tip feared he had too little. His mother's conciliation of him would turn to oblivion if he let the faith go, the way balloons disappeared as they rose. The sky above the highway taunted him with this fear every time he climbed the lookout tower on the boardwalk, which was why he spent so many nights there. Jack seemed to know of Tip's stubborn hold on his mother's forgiveness, and was as jealous as if it *were* her ghost Tip kept hidden from him.

Tip flexed his muscles, throwing out another bottle after running it gently over his scar. The pneumothorax just proved how cockeyed Tip was inside. The air escaping from the punctured lung, the pressure in the chest cavity making the esophagus, as well as the aorta, crooked, the initial burst alveoli resulting from a congenital weakness, though not inherited from Jack, Jack illogically pointed out on the night of Tip's homecoming after the stay at the hospital.

"You mean to say I'm not your kid," Tip had had the quickness of mind to retort.

In the middle of the bridge, the headlights of two cars appeared to collide, then sped heedlessly apart. The launched Pepsi bottle struck another bottle floating on the matted grasses clogging the lip of the river. A large shape flapped up from among the reeds near the shattering bottles. Tip grabbed another, unopened, and sent the full weight flying toward the heron. There was a thump and squawk. For an hour the bird flailed clumsily in the sedge, then sunk resignedly into the muck. "Mind over pain," Tip whispered to it. His father's motto, which Jack had once stapled his own finger in order to prove. Bravery wasn't the issue. Only force of will. A few months ago, when Tip woke one Saturday morning with a pain like a dart in a bull's eye, was the only time such determination failed him. All morning the dart worked its way in deeper, breathing back when he tried to suck in air. Tip doubled over while taking inventory at the salvage yard but completed all the lower rows of plumbing fixtures on two aisles of Peg-Board before beginning to moan. The salvage yard was Jack's hobby after the Jack of Steaks got under way, but Jack still treated the salvaged stuff like his livelihood depended on it. Jack said to price the fireplace grates, after which he'd drive Tip home, except that a bike ride was the best cure for a crybaby. It was the tears that sent Jack over. Tip never cried. Jack grabbed Tip's shirt and tore at the pocket emblazoned with the Jack of Steaks playing card logo, saying anyone who left work for a stomachache didn't belong in the business. Tip had chained his bike in the lot behind the salvage yard, where a set of church doors propped on a truck bed were flung open to the view of the train tracks beyond. A pink bathtub lay neglected in a puddle of shavings smelling of Rust-Oleum. Tip's brother Drew made fun of him trying to swing his leg over the bike, but it was Drew's idea to slice the tire with a straight razor he found in the bathtub so Tip's bike would have a flat, so their father wouldn't blame him for walking instead of riding. All the rest of the day Tip howled in bed while one of the string of housekeepers fed him Pepto-Bismol his father called "pink for the girl." Near midnight Tip started to hack and gurgle until Douglas, who'd moved out of the house but came by to do laundry, rushed him to Emergency. The lung had begun to deflate, the escaped air halfway to his brain already, so Tip couldn't be held accountable for what he said to the housekeeper all week in the hospital.

"Get your skin and bones off my bed," he complained upon waking, then fell to tossing and turning.

"What did he say? He's delirious," consoled a squeaky-shoed nurse.

"Skin and bones. Get them off. Ugly bitch. Fake hair. Twiddle cunt," Tip leveled at the housekeeper. She was young, Finnish, engaged to be married. Her skin was like milk, for she had never liked sweets. Already she and Tip had discovered this small thing they had in common, enough to allow her to hope she might make herself last with the Baymillers until her wedding day. A demanding household, all the older, bachelor brothers dropping socks in the hallways and leaving paper cups of milk souring on the chair arms even this summer when they'd started moving out one after another, and now Jack up in arms about Tip's disobedient illness. She looked around the room in search of some way to vent her compassion for this only untwinned offspring, who looked always alone, self-possessed in the company of his paired-up siblings. Tip couldn't see her makeup, a deception because he knew she wore it. Not even the lipstick was apparent. Any girl who wore her makeup like that he adored.

Finally she pulled the curtain separating Tip's bed from the empty one.

"You're not my mother! You're an impostor twat!" Tip yelled triumphantly.

"He could have died," said Becka from behind the pulled curtain, where she'd been sitting invisibly in one of the visitors' chairs. She and her twin, Jenna, were the tallest in the family, and though Jenna enjoyed being, as Jenna put it, statuesque, Becka wore flat-soles. She visited each day bearing Tip's homework, which she completed herself after pulling from her pencil case a message from Johnny, who would be outside the hospital that night as on the others with some friends. The girlfriends all wanted to sneak up on the elevator, but since no one could get in after visiting hours, they'd be joining all the healthy boys on the docks to commiserate over Tip's absence. Late the previous night, from his third-floor window, trapped in his stitches and hospital gown, Tip had watched the girl's heads bob seductively under the lamplight as they crossed to the shore, where fishing docks narrow as love seats jutted over the lapping water.

"No wonder he's delirious, he could have died, Johnny's father said if Drew and Douggie didn't rush him over he would have had a disrupted nervous system," declared Becka from her chair behind the curtain, her pencil scratching against Tip's notebook as she bent above the pages like a giant fishhook. Her forgery of Tip's headstrong penmanship was exacting. Though Jenna called herself "an adult woman," Becka was still a tomboy, her way of not caring about looking like a boy, anyway. She would have styled her hair with a jigsaw if only it grew enough to cut in the first place, was one of the family jokes. Now she

dotted an *i* in just Tip's fashion, so the dot wasn't properly cen-
tered, and drew one of Tip's doodles in the margin of his homework—big tits camouflaged to resemble spectacles worn by a
man with a goatee.

"Here, Tip, let's change the washcloth," said the housekeeper,
her white-knuckled fingers lifting the damp cloth she'd laid
across his brow to mop up the delirium.

"Don't say my name! Don't think you know shit about me!
You're an impostor twat," Tip repeated. The housekeeper closed
her eyes, never blaming Tip for mocking her attempts to show she
cared. None of Jack's other children mocked the housekeepers
like Tip did, but that was because they weren't as smart. The
housekeeper was right about this, to a point. Really the three pairs
of twins *did* see through her feeble attempts to behave motherly
even toward the older boys, who were older than she herself was.
On the far side of her face was the face of their real mother, Polly,
squinting mischievously at them the way Polly had used to, tilting
her gaze backward over her shoulder through her mirrored leather
compact, then darting out a hand to—quick—pat some powder
on their noses. But when Tip saw through one of the housekeepers' maternal pretenses, it wasn't Polly he saw but a skeptical sky
across which his mother's forgiveness too often vanished while on
its way toward him.

Tip wouldn't leave even a camouflaged doodle in the margins
of his homework, Becka reflected, peering past the curtain to
watch him pretend to lose consciousness. He was too protective
of his girlfriends to reveal them to a teacher. When she'd crossed
out the doodle, there was nothing but a lozenge of pencil lead
that sent up a small cloud of glittery dust when she blew on it.
Tip needed Becka, the way Becka's mother had told her he
would. This was Becka's only secret, one she only skirted past in
the diary she kept hidden in her underwear drawer in her and
Jenna's room at Jack's. Becka didn't remember her mother as did
Jenna and the other twins, but she remembered, as Jenna didn't,
the evening her pregnant mother had sat between the two girls
and described to them how they might help look after the baby.
They were only two years old. Their mother's request soothed

Becka. If Tip fell off the swing they were to comfort him. If he was taunted by his brothers they were to shield him. Growing up, Jenna had no recollection of this agreement, and Tip no appreciation for it. At nineteen, Becka felt she'd remained invisible to her brother, *not counted,* somehow, no matter how diligently she tried to keep her promise to her mother and watch over him. In her diary she touched on this subject only indirectly, then slipped the book back in her underwear drawer, where it was wrapped in a yellow chiffon scarf inside a cosmetics case. Becka had made Jenna promise not to tell anyone it was there, but even though Jenna didn't always keep her promises, none of Jenna's friends had ever tried to read it. *Tomorrow I'll go to Mom's grave,* Becka sometimes wrote in her diary, and while writing the next day's entry, didn't trouble to explain why she hadn't gone, after all. She had never once been. The grave was polished red granite under an elm tree, Becka knew from Jenna, who had never been there either because Becka wouldn't accompany her. The elm's pale leaves would darken were Becka and Jenna to approach it without Tip between them, Tip being off on his bicycle or out with his friends. Jack went often to the grave, Becka comforted herself by imagining, though he never said when, preferring, she imagined, to go by himself. She imagined his sturdy shoulders reflected in the red granite, his black hair the more glossy the closer he knelt, the plucked weeds quivering between his fingers.

When the hole in Tip's lung had healed and the sump pump had emptied every last bubble of escaped air from his chest cavity, Tip was brought home from the hospital to find himself facing his father from over a newspaper folded stiff as a paddle. Jack's pants had been expertly ironed. We're restaurateurs, not construction workers, Jack liked to say even when he and the boys were on site during restoration. The thing that other businessmen didn't know about Jack was that he was superstitious, and the thing that Jack didn't know was that Tip was, too. There was a Jack of Steaks at the site of the town's oldest fire station, and another where a granary had been restored. But the town's first hospital Jack wouldn't touch, and though he salvaged pews and doorways from dilapidated churches, he wouldn't want to eat where people had once been laid out in their coffins. He smelled of resin and batter-fried onions, of turpentine, pine sawdust, and sautéed mushrooms, but wore these outlandish blends as if they were dapper colognes. The handsome black-haired Jack on the playing card logo on the pockets of the shirts worn by all his hundreds of employees was designed to resemble him.

"Glad to see you home," Jack had said to Tip when Tip arrived from the hospital, Jack rising for the first handshake they would ever have shared.

But Tip could think only of how much his father wanted to hit him. Tip's guts steaming on the carpet, Jack lording himself over the tangy smell of them the way he'd always wanted.

"*Sucks* to see *you*," Tip answered.

Jack reddened.

Tip shoved the ottoman into Jack's shins, then kicked him just high enough to miss his balls. But Jack didn't strike back, wouldn't even raise the paddle of folded newspaper, which flopped lazily open to a page of women's fashions. Jack's gaze lingered on a photo of hats. Ignore the pain and it will go away, he'd said, unwilling to fight Tip for having been born. Tonight on the boardwalk at Lake Butte des Morts, Tip was still smarting. To be his own essence wasn't enough. The July night was misty and rumbling; through the haze over the marshland the surrounding houses cast an aura on the slats of the overgrown boardwalk. Cindy had run the tip of her tongue along the scar on his rib cage, the raised line like a lock on a strongbox, but Johnny was by far the closest to cracking Tip's combination. Tip and Johnny were like dogs that had grown up together, sniffing around, wagging their tails, one dog maybe just a little slower on the uptake than the other, but that was okay because which dog was which depended on what they were doing. The ladder Tip kept propped beneath his bedroom window was their vow of loyalty to the prospect of shared misadventure.

He drove home finishing the last of the Pepsi's fizzy rush. Because the wet reeds rose high between the slats of the sagging boardwalk, his boots had a pleasant, damp, squelching weight that would mimic the pull of gravity against the upward heft of the ladder. He parked in the apron of Johnny's driveway and was crossing the margin of lawn between their two houses when a white nightgown rose in the breeze of his approach, just where the light from his front door turned to blackness among the pruned shrubbery.

Tip was inhesitant but curious. Girls often approached him across darkened lawns.

Tonight it was Rhonda, Johnny's girlfriend, looking skinnier than ever in a dress that fit like the paper sleeve on a drinking straw.

There were two kinds of girls, Tip realized. There was the kind who called to a boy from a distance and by the time she got near was breathless from having said something the boy couldn't make out because she'd been too far away when she'd said it, and there were the ones whose mouths softened into wordless smiles as they approached him so close that the velvety stuff on the thighs of their blue jeans brushed up against the velvety stuff on Tip's blue jeans, and then they poked a finger at a button on his shirt and said, "Hey."

Rhonda was neither. She stopped at arm's reach and said, "There's something I don't know if I should tell you or not. But maybe really I should." She was stroking a mouse in the palm of her hand, then poking its nose between her knuckles. Tip felt light-headed. Rhonda swung the mouse desultorily by its tail. Just because Rhonda wasn't one of the two kinds of girls, the kind that exclaimed from afar and the kind that got close and said, "Hey," didn't mean that there were more than two kinds, he decided. It meant Rhonda was the exception proving the rule. Even Johnny knew that. Sometimes Johnny said, "That's what I like about her. She doesn't want to fit right in with everybody, you know?" but other times he exclaimed, "The girl is *ignorant.*"

"Johnny left because I felt like sewing, at least that's kind of why, except he didn't really go. He stayed," Rhonda began, swiveling to show Tip the pins in the armholes where the sleeves would be attached to her dress, and the fringe of the unsewn hem. At three in the morning she'd gone downstairs for the iron.

She didn't want the board, she preferred to iron on a bath towel spread on her bedroom floor. Why was she telling Tip this? Tip pursed his lips in the gesture of patience he practiced on girls who told him things he didn't want to know. At lunchtime in school people bit off the ends of the paper sleeves of drinking straws before blowing the sleeves across the table. Rhonda looked like the straw that would be left over. *Once* (this was a joke he'd heard, which came into his head to save him from laughing at Rhonda's dress) *a man walking on a beach came upon a woman lying in the sand. He nodded to her and she nodded at him. The woman was all right–looking except she had no arms or legs. Above the crash of the waves, she called out to the man, "Please, stop and talk to me a minute. You see, I have no arms or legs. I'm happy but there's one thing I want. All my life, I've never been kissed. If you would only stop to kiss me, then I'd have everything I ever needed. So the man shut his eyes so he wouldn't have to look at her missing arms and legs, and he bent over and kissed her, then started walking again. But over the crashing waves, she called out to him, "Please, stop a minute longer. You see, I have no arms or legs. I'm happy, but there's one thing I want. All my life, no man has ever fondled my breasts. If only you would fondle my breasts, then I'd have everything I needed. So the man shut his eyes and gritted his teeth and got down on his knees and fondled the woman's breasts, then went on his way. But over the sound of the crashing waves, she called out to him, "Please, stop, there's one more thing! All my life I've wondered what it's like to be fucked. Please, please fuck me!" So the man shut his eyes and gritted his teeth and picked her up and threw her as far as he could into the pounding surf of the ocean and said, "Okay lady, you're fucked."*

Tip's grin suppressed his usual burst of laughter. In fact he didn't like the joke this time as much as he had before. Poor lady, he thought now, stuck in low tide only to be rescued by a moron. Rhonda raised the hand holding the terrified mouse to her face. Was she going to kiss it, or swallow it? The mouse had no whiskers. Probably this after-hours visit was some kind of girl test, Tip supposed, cooked up by Cindy and Rhonda to see if he might say something to Rhonda that would indicate whether or not Johnny had serious feelings for Rhonda or was only using her. Using! What did girls mean by that? he scoffed. Everybody used everybody anyway, for something! Probably Cindy was crouching in the bushes reading Tip's expression. Incorrectly. Girls always made the simplest things complicated.

"So I went up the front stairs instead of the kitchen steps, so I could turn off the light in the front hall. So . . ." Here Rhonda paused, not for drama but to swat the mouse at a mosquito. "So, I had to go through the living room."

Yeah, so? thought Tip, the suppressed joke still making him a little ashamed.

"Past the couch," Rhonda continued, the darkness turning to moisture between the strands of her hair.

"Yeah, and?" said Tip. He knew she was going to tell him Cindy was crying. Big news. He hadn't wanted to hurt Cindy. That's why he'd left her. Didn't girls know that?

"Johnny and Cindy were making it on the couch," Rhonda finished. She opened her hand. The mouse wasn't a mouse, but a rabbit's foot flattened from squeezing. "That's what I don't know if I should tell you or not," said Rhonda.

Too late now, Tip thought.

"Making what?" he asked, knowing what a stupid question it was, of course. Dishonorable, too. Tip didn't often talk about girls behind their backs, no matter what they had done to deserve it. Still, he awaited Rhonda's answer. "How would you know?" he suddenly asked.

"I'm not going to get into a big description how she had her legs jiggling around Johnny's bare-naked backside," said Rhonda. "You can either believe me or not. They weren't under the blanket, anyway. The blanket fell off."

4

"Rhonda saw us in bed," Cindy finally let herself whisper to Johnny, having waited until he had got his breath and was sliding the bangle bracelets between her elbow and her wrist as if she were a problem to be solved on an abacus. His eyelids flickered but remained closed in honor of the hundreds of sensations introducing themselves to the tips of his fingers. He'd never touched another person blindly before, nor done anything blindly on purpose that he could remember. What did Cindy mean when she said Tip had seen them in bed? They weren't in bed. They were on a couch. In Rhonda's living room. The cushions were lumps of tweedy pellets, but the throw was smooth. Everything Johnny touched was at once comfortingly strange and mesmerizingly familiar; the beveled slope of each bangle, the down of her arm, the soft clacks of the bracelets like those of a girl's footsteps along the hallway at school, only closer, so close he could smell them. Maybe the scent of the sound of a girl's footsteps would be the subject of the first top forty hit for which he wrote actual lyrics. Morning light was beginning to filter through the nubbly curtains. *Day one of the beginning of the end for Cindy and Rhonda,* intoned Cindy in her head. United boys against divided girls. She and Rhonda would make a show of forgiveness, but then they'd forget—each other. Tip and Johnny would practically disembowel each other only to stitch each other up again after exchanging yet a few more drops of brotherly blood—if one of them was type A and the other type B, they'd both be buried in the same crypt by now. *Romeo and Romeo,* Cindy said to herself, closing her lips gently around Johnny's eyebrow. Briefly, she imagined it was Tip she was kissing, Tip who had slid so naturally in and out of her. Probably it would always be this easy to float from one man to another as if on a boat from shore to shore. Years later, looking back on this moment knowing what happened to Johnny, the thought still dismayed her. It was too fatalistic. Too old for a young person to have. Too much a product of experience rather than of speculation. She wasn't ready just yet for such thoughts, she realized whenever she had them, better to grow heedlessly into them. Meanwhile she bristled at the thought of being lumped together with Rhonda in Johnny and Tip's boisterously shared account of their boisterously shared history—two more girls that the boys got the better of. Suddenly, nearly everything about Rhonda was irksome. A mantelpiece was no place for a stuffed Horton the

Elephant. The devotion of two hours to learning how to stitch darts was an inappropriate sewing project for a flat-chested person. Cindy wished she and Rhonda could skip the forgiveness and start forgetting each other right now. She would rather be forgotten than forgiven for having drunk too much booze in her soon-to-be-no-longer-best-friend's house. She would rather be forgotten than forgiven for having been unable to fit her own boyfriend's giant cock inside her and so having had to fit in Rhonda's boyfriend's normal-sized cock instead. She didn't want to be forgiven for having burst into tears just when Johnny came down from upstairs, or for saying, when Johnny asked if he could help, "If you need to ask, probably not."

"Forget me," Cindy said to herself to Rhonda, jumping at the ringing of the phone. No memories, no regrets, she said to herself. Who else but Rhonda's mother would call at three o'clock in the morning wanting to talk to Rhonda?

"I don't think she's home right this minute," said Cindy, watching the puppy squat on the mantel.

"Not home!"

"I mean, she's sleeping. I don't think I should wake her."

"Oh, but you can."

"Or maybe she's in the shower." Three steaming puppy turds dropped into the teacup. The puppy sniffed under its tail, jumped comfortably off the mantel onto the back of a chair, and rolled with a gentle thump to the floor.

"So, bye," Cindy said.

"Thank you, Cindy," said Rhonda's mother.

Johnny raised himself on one elbow, took hold of a lock of Cindy's long hair so sleek it looked wet, and began threading it under and over the row of bracelets. Aware that for the first time in years his brow was unfurrowed, he encouraged himself to indulge each smooth, unworried moment. He let go of the woven strand of Cindy's hair to slide his fingers along her bare hip into a damp hollow of thigh. Her shiny blouse lay open; her nipples were like other buttons. Her skin was cool in places, warm in others, dusky with an ancient perfume of olive oil. He spread her legs "to a fifty-five-degree angle," Cindy imagined telling Rhonda when the girls had made up and were pretending to be friends, before they dropped out of each other's lives.

"Rhonda went to tell Tip what we're doing," Cindy told Johnny. "Right now, Tip's probably on his way over here ready to drive your car through the chimney and run over that poor puppy."

5

But Tip didn't have it in for the puppy. Instead he found his sleeping bag in his closet, tossed the bag out the second-floor window, and climbed down the ladder after it. Becka could see Tip's ladder from her window if she craned her head, her twin sister, Jenna, sleeping in the bed beside hers, dressed in a spaghetti-strap nightgown, dreaming of boxes of jujubes that could be dialed like one of the new push-button telephones whenever Jenna needed to make social engagements. The skinny girl on the lawn in the unhemmed tube dress had driven off without glancing up at Becka. Tip hid in the backseat of Johnny's car all zipped in the sleeping bag thinking nobody knew he was there. Johnny rushed home in his flapping khakis too eager to escape Tip's punishment to notice Becka watching him. He threw himself into the driver's seat, where Tip had left the keys in the ignition like always, and drove off with a bang and a sputter. Becka's fingers tightened on the sill. She pressed her nose against the glass for nearly half an hour, waiting for the newspaper boy to ride past on his rickety bicycle and toss the paper clumsily in her direction.

6

"What did Rhonda confess?" inquired Rhonda's father after he and Rhonda's mother had finished their campsite breakfast. Greedy eaters, they'd cooked scrambled eggs, bacon, hash browns, and had filled two halves of cantaloupe with scoops of canned fruit cocktail. Their coffee had been brewed in a three-part pot that got flipped right side up when the water boiled, allowing the water to filter through the coffee grounds trapped in the middle section. The first time they flipped the pot over, somebody, though Rhonda's father wasn't saying who, had apparently forgotten to put in the coffee. The second time, the same someone had flipped the pot upside down without realizing that the water had already brewed and gone through; coffee gushed through the spout and stanched the flame on the Sterno. But the third try was perfect, and they'd remembered to pack their favorite mugs from home. With his mug upraised, Rhonda's father waited for his wife's answer. She was scrubbing the fry pan. For hours, after she'd hung up the phone and returned to the car at the gas station, he'd feigned disinterest in her and Rhonda's conversation. Rhonda's life was Rhonda's own, it was none of his business. But now that he'd asked, he felt only that he had been infinitely, respectfully patient. He tipped the mug at his lips, always surprised, when they were camping, by the domesticity of the act of drinking coffee, which calmed his nerves. He liked the idea of camping better than he liked the practice.

Rhonda's mother balanced the soapy fry pan on a scrap of two-by-four on the ground, then loaded in the utensils to soak.

"She told us to stop bugging her," she lied to her husband. "She said if we thought she was grown-up enough to be left alone, then we should let her be. I said she was right, and I apologized for being such nosy parents. I can't believed we used all our fruit the first day."

They'd been nowhere near a moose while driving to and from the gas station, but several days later they would just miss catching sight of one, a baby, its head too big for its knobbly legs, venturing into a cranberry bog.

7

Years later, if Tip was telling the story of him and Johnny to another man, he might describe the way, from inside the sleeping bag on the floor in the back of Johnny's car, he smelled not Cindy's hair, exactly, but her skin when her long, thick hair had blanketed it and he lifted it out of the way in order to kiss her arm, maybe, or her breast, or the back of her neck. Also, olive oil. Every lover's smell was different from any other lover's smell, and any memory of smell was more potent than the original. Tip barely noticed a woman's smell when he had his nose buried in it, a smell of which the essence evaded him when he was in the act of penetrating it, a smell that when mixed with the other smells of foreplay surrendered itself to Tip's ragged panting and the sweeter, Pepsier smell of the deeper breath that was trying to get out of him. Even grown up, he never really noticed a woman's essential scent until it had rubbed off onto his own skin, when he was no longer beside her, when he was alone, not thinking about her.

But if Tip was telling this story to a woman, he was careful to avoid the subject of Cindy's smell, just as he was careful to respect the privacy of Johnny's desire to someday write songs. Not even his sisters tolerated his accounts of another woman's perfume. To tell a lover about another woman's fragrance, the fragrance of her person, not from a bottle necessarily but maybe bottled up inside her, that emerged with her pleasure—to tell a lover about *that,* when the lover was in his arms, which is where the lovers always were when Tip told them Johnny's story, would be like telling them, "Someday I'm going to remember your fragrance, too, when I'm alone in my house with the telephone off the hook so you can't call me and I can watch TV in peace, goddamn it."

Instead he might explain to the women, years later, "Johnny wasn't poured out of as big a mold as I was, exactly. So he was just, you know, taking advantage of my disadvantage. What I mean, he could fit his cock in Cindy. I couldn't."

Mostly, Tip's lovers accepted this information as delicately as Tip delivered it. Of the whole world of men there were only a few whose entire natures swelled into their cocks when they were making love, like Tip's did. Those women who'd been around for a while knew this absolutely. Some, who'd been around only a little so far, suspected it, and the ones who had been sheltered or embarrassed would never be sheltered or embarrassed again.

If not for the fragrance of Cindy's slight sunburn, Tip might not have been able to breathe inside the sleeping bag in the rear of Johnny's car. The only oxygen he could make sense of while burrowed in the checkered cotton musk of the bag was wrapped up in that echo of her. Had the recollected fragrance—along with his memory of having left her alone on the couch—not been so satisfying, he would've needed to inch his head closer to the opening and sneak big gulping breaths, which Johnny might have heard and done a U-turn over the median and sped home and rushed inside before Tip could catch him.

Johnny had cousins and an aunt and uncle living in Minneapolis. Tip could tell he and Johnny were driving northwest. It would be necessary to get to Johnny before Johnny could get to his macho cousins.

Midmorning, Johnny pulled into a rest area somewhere outside Eau Claire. Tip poked his head from the sleeping bag when Johnny got out of the car, noting at once that the squat, louvered building housing the bathrooms was too derelict a setting to house as well the kind of fair play this fight was bound to require. There would be no honor in the gritty floors, the mess of wadded filthy paper, the sharp stink of ammonia, the abbreviated toilet stalls.

But the scrappy woods behind the low building were noosed-up with vines, buzzing with Tip's expectation even before he got there. He took off his sneakers, made his way past the tight brick corner of the building where the paved walk led to a jumble of chained-together Ditch-Witches. Passing under the louvered windows, Tip could hear the low humming Johnny made in his throat instead of talking to himself, the notes nervous but whole and too big for the space they were in, like people bravely singing rounds in a tornado cellar. Johnny was taking too long in the bathroom. It seemed he meant to stay there the rest of his life, which might not last much longer if he ever came out. Not once during the drive across Wisconsin had Johnny quite relaxed, for there had been, in the close air of the moving car, a whispery sensation all down his spine suggesting that Tip was on the floor behind him, but still Johnny hadn't been certain enough to stop to look and sacrifice the faint relief of uncertainty.

At last, when he emerged from the rest room and snagged his shirt on a rusty spring on the screen door, when he was pulling the weave of the T-shirt free and blinking the glare from his eyes, that's when he saw the rear door of his car wide open to reveal Tip's sleeping bag.

For a moment Johnny thought he'd stay where he was. Tip wouldn't hit a person stuck to a door, would he?

There was no one else around, just cars on the road, some bugs in dry grass, the heat full on the backs of some cows grazing a distant ridge.

Johnny couldn't fight to save his life or liberty.

Tip could compromise anyone's pursuit of happiness who was careless enough to move him to do so.

Both of them knew these things as well as they knew their own names. Between them, the pipes in the low brick building clanked and sputtered, while in the rangy stretch of forest, the steep banks of the gully carrying runoff to the Mississippi River were ablur with the vibrating wings of dragonflies suspended in an ether of airborne pollen. Half out of the creek where some vines lay tangled against the eddies stood the upright wheel of a semi, and that's where Tip sat waiting for Johnny, who would find him sooner or later. Now Johnny circled the building, knowing Tip could jump him in a heartbeat.

There was a path he hadn't noticed, the grass bent under the shadow of somebody's passing, a clump of dry sumac still shifting and settling. Tip might have eaten a few of the tart red berries. And he had taken off his sneakers; Johnny had seen them in the runnels of the sleeping bag. So Tip would fight thirsty and barefooted amid the brambles in the gully, broken glass all around, bumblebees, frog scum, pop-tops, cracked-open robins' eggs, nettles. But the soles of Tip's feet were more resilient than leather. Johnny's shoes would blister before Tip's bare feet showed even a scratch.

Both of them knew this, too.

Along the slowly vanishing path to the gully, the dry air crackled at the edges of the leaves and at the tips of the husks poking out of the undergrowth. The sky was so roastingly bright

Johnny didn't see Tip sitting on the wheel of the semi thinking what a good place this was for a fight, the kind of gully where you could scare the hell out of someone but stop short of throwing them over the edge. Johnny, who worried too much and did everything too deliberately, needed a scare. Tip imagined his friend would have more fun if he got the sense knocked out of him now and again. Anyway, Johnny deserved it, and Tip had no choice but to be the one to do it to him. Not that he minded, really, about Cindy and Johnny going to bed. Consensual adult sex was one of the few incorruptible activities left on earth. A woman was always most herself and most like other women when a man was making love to her, as he was most himself and most like other men.

Even so, there were codes. Declarations to be made. Tip picked a bit of gravel from the rubbery tread of the wheel of the semi and dropped it into the eddy. His friendship with Johnny was to be strengthened by their encounter. The second piece of gravel he flicked into a swifter current. The third, into the eddy again. By the time Johnny got close enough for Tip to leap onto the bank and grab Johnny's shirt collar before Johnny knew what hit him, Tip had nearly forgotten what the fight was supposed to be about.

"And the sucker pulled my arm out of the socket," Tip would say to the women years later when he got to the part of the story that made him most proud. "He had a big square head, I never noticed how square, I got him down in the weeds but he lunged at me and butted my stomach and pitched me over the edge of the gully. He didn't know what he was doing, he just did it, he grabbed for me and yanked my arm out of the socket!" Tip exclaimed to the women years later, his eyes already wistful before the excitement went out of his voice.

"And then what?" the women would ask.

"First we fixed the arm. You hang a weight from it. Jesus. Then we wiped the dirt off our faces with Pepsi, then we drove for hours. Before we went home we drove to Cindy's house and broke up with her. Both of us. We were like one guy limping to her door, telling her . . . whatever . . . she was distraught, that was messy, being broken up with by two guys at once who couldn't even hardly stumble away from her door."

"Then what happened?" asked Mary Anne.

"Not that day. Later that summer," Tip would answer.

"But what?" asked Patty.

And Eileen.

Patty could only begin to imagine Tip as a boy. But Mary Anne would have seen his family album and the photo of the baby in the cherry bucket grinning toothlessly into the camera. Eileen and a couple of others who had grown up in the same town might remember the day Tip climbed a tree in the school yard and got stuck hanging too high, yelling and kicking, looking more motherless somehow than he looked with his feet on the ground, so it all made sense, his bruising kisses, the way he made love instinctually as if suckling.

"And then but how did it *happen?*" the women would insist, hoping to remain in Tip's X-shaped embrace a while longer before he sprang onto the balls of his feet to sing in the kitchen while scrubbing away all evidence of the dinner he'd hunted and prepared—venison roast, or pheasant, or walleye, and some spicy potatoes baked in foil.

8

Had the bicycle been parked, unlocked, in the bike rack near the kiddy train tracks that encircled the paddleboat lagoon, or had it been lying unexpectedly on the gravel slope leading to the docks where the sailboats passed on their way into harbor, then somebody more impulsive than Johnny, like Tip, or one of Tip's pairs of brothers, or a couple of boys who wanted to be *like* Tip and Tip's brothers, might have been the ones to hit on the idea of riding it off the edge of the dock. Jealous yet relieved, the one who didn't get to go first would watch the other pedal madly down the dock to fly over the end where the water was deep enough to sink and drift awhile, his windy hair turning sentient in the sluggish current. To ride a bike off the end of the dock on an August evening in the throngs of a party—that would be a perfectly ordinary thing for any number of boys to do, but today the harbor was sedate and inky. A green bloom of algae dissolved under the linty surface. Some kids thought the algae was mold and that people allergic to penicillin shouldn't swim in it.

Or maybe the boys would've waited for nightfall and hoisted the entire bike rack with its row of locked bikes off the end of the dock in a half-moon of teenage reverie, cheering the violet dark of the harbor.

Probably that was how the bicycle, a serpentine glint barely visible in the water, had ended up under the dock to begin with. Since Johnny was more shy than other boys, and more focused in his attention, and since he still worried, and liked asking experimental questions in order to better understand the things around him, it was Johnny who scrunched his eyes to peer between the slats, put spoke and glint together, and discovered a bicycle wedged in the green translucence.

Which was not an outlandish thing. Surely there were bikes underwater everywhere, stolen and ditched or just plain forgotten.

So there would be no glory attached to being the boy who found the bike unless he pulled it from the lake and kept it, and since it wasn't right to steal anyone's bike no matter how careless they must have been to lose it, he decided not to call attention to his discovery. The front wheel, free of the stones and debris against which the rear wheel was wedged, appeared to be turning, but the spinning was only a trick of the light. *Trick of the light* would be a good refrain for one of his future top forty hits. So would *Spoke and glint,* though too Joni Mitchell. Johnny decided he'd tell Tip about the sunken bike later, after the party had cleared away. Tip would take the bike home, Johnny would share the fun but be burdened by none of the crime. The crime wouldn't be Tip's burden, either. Taking the bike, Tip would be doing a blameless thing. Tip was naturally blameless, so the crime would be canceled.

One of the girls climbing the pyramid of teenage boys' shoulders on the dock nearly lost the top of her bathing suit, but since she was the same girl who nearly lost the top of her bathing suit

all the other evenings, too, the pyramid began to wobble only
after someone else's foot was bitten by a mosquito, by which
time an object other than the sunken bicycle claimed Johnny's
eye. He stepped to the edge of the dock to look, his khaki shorts
loose around chunky thighs, the crease in his forehead relaxing.
Since the night he'd spent with Cindy on Rhonda's couch, he'd
noticed that elation erased his accustomed flutter of philosophical debate, and that even the flavor of fried chicken, or the way
he sometimes found himself humming a made-up tune, laid
themselves coolly between his eyebrows to smooth out the
worry.

Now it was the sight of a little girl with her mother on the
pathway on the adjacent shore of the lake that so absorbed him.
The mother strolled, the daughter glided and flailed. When they
reached the gazebo the mother sat long legged on the step, flipping open a paperback as the girl performed a flapping dance
along the sidewalk like a stunned seagull. Both mother and
daughter wore plain white T-shirts with slim brown jeans, and it
seemed to Johnny that they'd chosen to dress alike in such unremarkable fashion in order to impress upon the rest of the world
that they weren't beholden to it. They were a private club. The
club included a third member Johnny imagined, a girl on her
way to becoming a woman, or a woman still remembering what
it was like to be a girl, invisible between them.

Johnny could nearly see this third girl through his wet lashes
after he'd slid off the edge of the dock, dived underneath for an
experimental grab at the bike, and come up again. He'd dove in
order to impress her, the invisible girl, even though everyone
knew he wasn't the type to jump fully clothed into the lake. The
bike came free of the rocks the instant he closed his fingers
around the handlebars. It wheeled easily out from under the
dock. He stood alongside it, uncertain and dripping, not even
waist deep in water. What to do now? He blinked the water
from his eyes to look between mother and daughter at the girl he
imagined. She would soon grow out of the young girl's awkward
grace, but would have no need of the woman's graceful awkwardness. Johnny wiped his eyes again to coax her into focus. Her

invisibility made her seem indifferent to him, as who wouldn't be, for he was only a boy hip deep in water, the bike balanced beside him as if, having pedaled to the crest of a hill, he'd paused to admire the scenery. The purple bike wasn't rusted. When he pinched them, the tires remained solid between his fingers.

Watch me make a fool of myself for you: another top forty hit Johnny wished he could sing to the girl he imagined. Then he wheeled the bike shoreward onto the ramp and positioned himself at the start of the dock. Having twice collapsed, the pyramid of teens had regrouped around a snuck-in jug of wine, and when they saw Johnny racing toward them, parted only at the last minute to let him pass. Airborne, the bike soared less grandly than he had anticipated, then pulled him flat underwater. A little bruised, a little scraped, still he was contented as a fish. He might hold his breath forever, keeping his eyes wide open. Against the mud floor of the lagoon where it met the sandier region of the harbor, the pilings appeared only as looming shadows, falsely threatening, cowardly even, a dark blur here, a sudden, stark, jutting albino shape there. And then suddenly ordinary, just dock posts amid clusters of slippery rock. Tendrils of soft weeds waved their crisp bubbles around them.

The second ride was better, the third even better than that. Along the length of the dock his friends made fake grabs at his dripping khakis but always let him race by, and then came Tip's laughter, the boys stomping the dock as if to cheer Johnny on. After four jumps, the water turned chilly, and on the sixth jump the bike slid sideways and pinned him. A ringing sound bruised his ears like a hungry cry. The front wheel came gently to rest on his shoulder, the rear wheel swiveled under his leg.

I can't get up, he realized in the next, panicky moment, the hungry cry growing dizzily nearer.

Above where he lay pinned, and where he felt so alone, so terribly unaccompanied, the giant playing field lights surrounding the softball diamond opposite the boat landings were switched on as they were every evening. From the dock, under the buzzing spotlights the water appeared black as oil. Across the channel the rocky island on which the seagulls nested soon became silhouetted by the dusky sky beyond it. A boat motored in from between the buoys, slow and purposeful. Night was beginning, day over and done. The summer was nearly over, too, for it was nearly September, and everyone who tipped their head back for a sip of wine on the dock was aware of this without letting themselves be glum about it. Tip was especially flamboyant tonight in his muscle shirt. No matter what the joke, Tip's laughter was the punch line.

"So I was up there laughing, when Johnny was down there drowning," Tip said years later into the sympathetic curve of Eileen's neck.

Into the elegant arch of Patty's neck.

Into the unfortunately affectionate tremor of Mary Anne's neck.

There were many more kinds of women than there were kinds of girls, Tip had discovered.

"We were just kids, just seventeen years old. I was with him when they pulled him out and brought him to the emergency room, but he was already dead," Tip always concluded in wonder, the wonder always unexpected, always the thing that lifted him off his couch into his kitchen, away from whichever kind of woman was lying there and whatever fresh temptation she offered. He slid the roasting pan into the sink, sponged the counter, blipped past the channels with the remote. If he thought of his mother's forgiveness of him at this moment, he blipped the thought resentfully out of his mind.

"Bitch," he muttered.

"What?" The woman lifted her head from the place on the couch where Tip's shoulder had slid away.

"I went crazy. I tore the place apart. I threw the EKG in the sink," Tip recalled more loudly than necessary, as if from across a great distance.

3

Even Birds
Knew More than Polly

Even the heron, stunned by Tip's bottle, knew more than I. Even the redwings harvesting wild rice in the marshes. Even Cindy's round bangles, Rhonda's addle-brained parents, the creek bed, the walleye, knew more than I. I didn't know yet that Johnny was dead, didn't know Tom Bane was more than a pesky annoyance. Johnny hadn't slaked Tom's irascible thirst, but I didn't know that, either, the wild rice on the water like rice at my wedding, the years thrown like confetti around me, a ballroom of dancers dusting my floors with their hems. A year was a minute, a minute the Night's flip side of a decade. Lysle's bottom in the window, Gem asleep in the truck, and all the while even Honey knew more than I did, knew, deep down, where she didn't know she knew it, that Tom Bane's blindest, sorest eye was fixed on her. Along with the sound of Tip's laughter on the dock, the girl drew the knowledge of her ghost of a father down too far to reach, and didn't think of it at all as she drew it inside—that deep breath turned warning, turned intuition. Meanwhile Tip's laughter caused Honey's hair to give off sparks every time anything anywhere caught her attention.

4

Tom Bane's Daughter

Not long after Tom Bane's biplane tumbled into the lake, when Tip and Johnny, nine years old, still tingled with their recollection of the cartwheeling flames, Tom's wife, Angie, neared the end of her pregnancy. The plane still lay in pieces undiscovered on the floor of the shallow lake, among the shadows of moss-covered rocks and the hulking sturgeon poking for food among drifts of weed and algae. Above one of the control levers around which Tom's wire-rimmed eyeglasses had come to a lopsided mooring, droves of carp roiled at the surface of the water, but Tom was far from the place where the carp were jumping. His body rested beyond a sandbar, away from the wreckage, in a dip in the lake floor where grass grew high and colorless, where every blade was so distinct from the ones around it that between them could be seen other distant blades of grass like a tall, bleached-green, thin person reflected in a hall of mirrors.

Though much of the Dacron had melted from around the tubing of the wings of the biplane, Tom himself hadn't burned, but over the weeks his clothing had turned to translucent tatters while the strap of his seat belt no longer held him quite securely in the seat, which also had come undone. The seat bobbed lumpishly against his backside as it carried him away from the shadows of the rocks and brought him to rest in the siltier, softer region. To anyone who found him, the seat might appear to be rocking Tom rather than the other way around, but so far neither fisherman nor swimmer had parted the curtains of mirrored grass to stumble on Tom's bed of sand. The same habit of privacy that once masked itself as Tom's desire to subsist on the small farm rather than find work in Milwaukee, where Angie was enrolled in graduate school, had forbidden him not only to tell Angie of the plane but to file a flight plan or register his air space, and now was responsible for this long spell of watery solitude aggravated by an immense tangle of fishing line knotting him tightly against his parody of a rocking chair. Not even years later would the tiniest bones of his fingers and toes escape the confounding embrace of the fishing line. Not even his soul would pull free of the secret he kept from Angie—the speedy roar of the plane and the silence in which it plunged him. Thus Tom would remain bound to himself forever, which wasn't what he'd once imagined of death, at all. Secretly, while flying, because flying set him free to imagine himself a flexible being, he'd imagined that his air of reserve, his measured, eked-out days, his simple need to dominate his plot of land would fall away and be replaced by a lighter way of being, making him into someone maybe even a little amiably sociable who'd frequent the kind of mirth-infested party he'd always avoided, no matter how many evenings Angie tried to coax him out to one. Being by nature lean in spirit, as if his soul were strung too tight against the tautness of his body, he'd hoped that in death the tightest strings of him might snap, making him into a more liberal, joking sort who swore during card games interrupted by raucous stories about . . . about what? Tom used to wonder, the plane dipping underneath him, the fleetness of his heart giving way to the need to master the instrument panel.

Directly after the crash, tangled in the yards of fishing line, Tom would likely never know the answer. Anyway, he was dead, without worry or hope, his ghost still napping.

2

Knowing nothing about the airplane or about Tom's surreptitious flights, Angie had no reason to imagine her husband was at the bottom of a lake. The discovery and eventual return of his car from the lot at the Milwaukee airport only made her imagine that there had indeed been *something* about Tom of which she'd been unaware, a notion that made her sometimes happy, for him, and sometimes sad, for her, and always, always puzzled. If occasionally she imagined something awful had become of him, she distracted herself by diligently wondering if he might have decided to resettle in the neighborhood in Ohio in which he'd been raised, a neighborhood of houses and picket fences that the zoning laws demanded all be painted white, with weather vanes of blue or green if the owner was inclined to be flamboyant. Tom was a puritan, at least he wished he was, at least that's what Angie's wish to understand him made her suppose. Even in bed there had been something of the moral purist about him. He didn't like to lose control, and if Angie grew excited, Tom made certain he knew how he was causing her excitement so as not to make it happen again unless he meant to, which he didn't very often because her cries and clenching fingers made her look like a sparrow being captured and eaten by a hawk. After sex, exhausted and dismayed, he lay back with his eyeglasses askew on his face, and in the middle of the night sometimes woke with such a start that the mattress wobbled, as if in sleep he'd forgotten their shared bed and its uncomfortable claim on him. Then he always sat up, took a sip of water, and raised the blinds on the window opposite the headboard, from which could be seen the moonlit orchard of pear and apple trees, beyond which stretched the careful rows of crops, the farm a diagram of order and efficiency all laid out as if no shape but rectangles remained in the world. He didn't sell any food, but what he grew was parceled through the winter and lasted the two of them fine. He'd bought the land with part of an inheritance, and worked the farm alone while Angie commuted to the university. She was soon to start on her dissertation, for which she'd already purchased, on sale at an office supply store, a ten-ream carton of typing paper, of which, if she wrote three drafts, there'd be enough left over for her to type the required copies rather than pay for the Xerox or endure the smudge of carbon paper. She and Tom lived frugally off her loan money, their small investment income, and the harvest, and went early to bed, and got up early, too, like old people, Angie sometimes joked, but Tom assured her they were just old-fashioned the way they wanted to be, otherwise why wouldn't they own a computer, and he would gesture upstairs where Angie's clattery typewriter sat on a desk made of bricks and a door. He wasn't gruff or unkind, Angie often felt compelled to remind herself, it was only that his kindness was Germanic, as if all daily chores were themselves acts of kindness in which case any other kindness would be redundant and therefore sinful. So when Tom sliced the carrots into wedges for freezing, or reset the clocks for daylight saving, these were his ways of rescuing from uncivil disobedience the parts of the universe, including Angie, that were in his hands. On the second long night he didn't come home, Angie rocked in her chair and, refusing the sneaking suspicion that something more terrible had happened, reasoned that maybe his having snuck off on a jet was meant to be rescue, too—Tom's visit to Ohio, which she'd been spared, her shocked muteness at his unspoken departure, the contradiction between her memories of unsatisfactory sex and this satisfying baby rolling politely inside her—yes, maybe this was kindness, too, she reasoned, hugging herself, maybe he meant to teach her the civility and obedience required of a mother, soon after which he'd return and be a husband again.

Tom had a hobby—carving duck decoys—which had kept him busy the long winters in an upstairs room, where a lamp spotlighted the changing hunk of wood, a box of carving tools and paints, and a book of Audubon waterfowl. The finished decoys he posed on a bookshelf above the table on which they'd been carved. Motionless, their heads cocked too precisely, their carved feathers meticulously ruffled, the ducks appeared to Angie woefully perplexed, as if pondering the difference between being a chunk of wood and being a duck, just as Tom, unbe-knownst to his wife until she thought of it just this minute, might have pondered the difference between being a responsible husband and being freed. Standing in the doorway of the decoy room on the third night he didn't come home, Angie speculated she was most likely wrong about Tom having run off to Ohio, and that probably he'd had the kind of urge she'd secretly wished he was capable of having—something extravagant, like escaping to Hawaii and strolling the nightlife of Waikiki on the arm of a prostitute dressed in strips of leather thong. Why wouldn't *any* man have harbored such an urge to take a breather from the rig-orous monkishness of his days, allowing himself a little playful-ness before the baby was born?

After the first week Tom failed to come home, his three pairs of shoes, lined up in pairs near the kitchen door where he'd left them, were like three messengers bringing bad news but refusing to divulge it. If they knew where Tom was or what on earth he thought he was accomplishing, they weren't telling. Eight and a half months pregnant, grasping the kitchen counter for support, Angie kicked Tom's shoes in an unmessengerlike heap, wishing she had something more satisfying against which to throw the weight of her bewilderment. But there was nothing to fight against, nothing even to *do* except to plunk herself down in her chair and rock, dizzy with the baby's snuggly kicks. Maybe Tom wouldn't be back at all. Maybe he thought she and the baby would be better off without him, Angie said to herself, perturbed that such an idea might be comforting as long as it saved her from thinking maybe he was dead. Tom couldn't be dead. How could he be dead when he'd never allowed himself to be really alive? Perhaps that was Tom's plan—freeing their baby of having to love and admire the dry soul of its father, whom Angie must have married out of nothing but pity. Maybe someday he'd con-tact Angie, asking her to give him another try. Which she didn't think she'd do. She had called the police once, then twice, but what could cops tell her, other than that Tom wasn't the first ass-hole in the world who walked out on his pregnant wife? Angie filled a pink bowl with ice cream, rocked while she licked the bowl and spoon clean, then stacked the bowl in the sink with the others. Tom didn't approve of ice cream, even vanilla. Nor of dirty dishes. The fewer Angie dirtied, the less compelled she was to wash, the more they piled in the sink. In the second week, she discovered she liked her impulsive disarray far more than she had ever felt comfortable in Tom's compulsive neatness, discovered, too, that she liked not always having to be poised for the sound of Tom switching on the vacuum cleaner while she flipped through her index cards in search of some note that might help with her final exams if she found the note in time. She decided that once the baby was born, she'd set the cluttered, sour-milk-smelling playpen near her desk while she worked on her thesis, a rattle in one hand, a book in the other, although somehow even now, before the baby was born, the exact configuration of the question she'd set out to ask in her thesis, which had to do with fairy tales, had begun to elude her. For some time she'd been chipping away at it, changing the focus, the methodology. At first *simpletons,* then *stepmothers,* then *poisons* became the objects of her analysis. Now she considered *double-crossings, betrayals,* out-and-out *lies.* Maybe Tom had intended to leave all along, bored with her bronze hair, her self-absorbed habit of flipping through pages in moldering books, pausing to waste time on the pictures. An irrefutable gesture, his leaving, she thought, balancing an index card on one finger.

An act of careless selfishness.

For which she ought to be angry. So, why wasn't she? The index card wavered, then fell to her belly. Angie tapped her belly with her pen, lightly drumming the delicate ears of her child. Never again would she come upon her husband realigning the hammers on their hooks on the Peg-Board in the garage, or sprinkling mothballs in his clothing trunk in which some nested baseball caps filled the only space not taken by neatly folded sweaters. Maybe he hadn't been bored with her. Maybe he'd figured out how silly she thought he was, she realized with a start. Surely she hadn't intended to wound him. Nearly nine months pregnant, she propped herself on the front stoop of their silent house, watching the glow of daytime turn to a regretful dusk among the twisting branches of the orchard, wondering if she would rather he appear on the road or preferred that the road remain empty. Really, she wanted to stare into his eyeglasses and press her chin against the cleft of his day-old stubble the way she did sometimes if she managed to catch him before he shaved, and promise him she hadn't meant to hurt his feelings, and say she was sorry, and hear him say it back to her. Surely he'd come back at least for that, and then they could decide what was best for them to do in light of their surprise at what would seem to the two of them, together again, a discomfiting turn of events. Hadn't Tom mentioned something about a surprise, come to think of it, in the weeks before he'd vanished? He was going to surprise her with something, he'd said, a remark that had annoyed her, she guiltily recalled. He always told her in advance he was going to surprise her. Then, if she pressed for details, he was silent, and if she didn't, he dropped too many hints.

The breeze from the fields smelled of new shoots of garlic. To keep her devil of a husband from trying to convince her to take him back. But then she noticed Tom's camp trunk in the corner of the room. Baby clothes. Maybe that was what it was taking him so long to bring her, and if she wasn't surprised, at least she'd be ready. Soon she'd emptied the trunk, tucking his stacked sweaters on a shelf in the closet where a mousetrap had sprung on nothing. She sweetened the trunk with a potpourri bag, and sat in her rocker to wait. Night turned to dawn. No one came down the road. When Angie woke, it was only to the sight of the coffee table, on which several pamphlets about the cultivation of rhubarb were arranged alphabetically by author in a neat diagonal. Poor Tom couldn't help who he was. That was the beauty of him, just as it was the beauty of everyone else in the world being helplessly *them*selves. She laid her hand on her stomach, wondering what kind of person, with what kind of peculiar, troubling beauty, their baby would be. Hopefully not the kind of baby prone to arranging mixed vegetables according to meaningful classification systems upon the tray of its high chair. Really Angie wished she could at least speak to Tom long enough to confront him for having tricked her all these years by lining up the magazines before doing something so out of line as to—but Angie didn't finish the sentence. Her confusion of anger, giddyness, sadness, and relief caused the rocker to rock so hard that she did not notice her first contraction.

Nor her second.

Nor her third.

3

Close to the time of Angie's fifth contraction, just a few short weeks after Tip and Johnny had watched the plane go down from their place on the tiny island, a clump of lily pad stems dismembered by the blade of a power boat completed its brief pilgrimage across the lake by becoming entwined around the control knob on which Tom's glasses placidly bobbed. The wire-rims were knocked free and drifted awhile without touching down, like a nearsighted ghost looking for someone to haunt.

Tom wasn't awake enough yet to appreciate the image. Groggy, he didn't know he was a ghost. He was thinking, *I am a Sleep,* the way he once had thought, *I am a farmer.* There was nothing he needed to do, to be a Sleep. He didn't need to plan the harvest in order to relax his breathing, or contemplate methods of irrigation while curled into a fetal position to better indulge the ache in his back, or take a last sip of water while listening to the weather forecast. He didn't even need to close his eyes.

The lake in which Tom's plane had cartwheeled was only ninety miles north of the farm, but now it seemed like a whole other climate away. Tom had even forgotten about the fountain pen, the purpose of his journey, custom-designed by a cloisonné artist in Pine River. The pen hadn't been ready, as it was supposed to be, for him to surprise Angie with it in time for the birth of the baby. Certainly a pen was an impractical gift on such an occasion, but that's why Tom had chosen to give it. Angie would be charmed. She didn't know he had it in him to do anything fanciful. Truth was, he really didn't have it in him, he only wanted to try. Or even only to pretend. The pen would be festooned with tiny images of gold coins of the sort often foolishly traded by careless sons and daughters in fairy tales. Coins, poison apples, fishes, the only things from fairy tales small enough to enamel onto the cylinder of a fountain pen, all against a black glaze meant to fire Angie up to keep writing her dissertation. While Angie wrote, Tom would carry the baby upstairs to the duck room and set it in a bassinet, where it would watch him overlap the feathers of his decoys. A feather was a thoroughly organized mechanism, which the baby would quietly admire, by looking closely and not fussing too much to pay careful enough attention. Then, if its hands were clean and not clumsy, the baby might run its fingertips over the delicately carved barbules and distal shafts.

Tom would have his hobby and be a good father at the same time, he commended himself while following the cloisonné artist around the counter of the showroom to see the progress she'd made on Angie's pen. How put out he'd been to be told that the pen wasn't ready, and then to be led into the artist's workshop as if the pots of colored shards and powders might reassure him. Still, he'd done his best not to give in to a show of annoyance. After all, he was soon to be a father. To a baby! A baby wouldn't know a promise from a falsehood if its next swallow of milk depended on it. Not everything could go as Tom wanted, and though he wasn't often able to accept that, he thought maybe he'd better force himself to be a little more flexible. Angie would laugh if she heard him say that, *force himself to be flexible.* He gave the cloisonné artist another week. Only as he left the studio and headed back for the airstrip did he realize that to fly back to Pine River in a week might cause him to miss Angie's labor.

For which Angie wouldn't blame him.

Because of the beautiful pen.

Banking, gliding, he thought of the coppery colors of Angie's hair as she reached for the pen. And then of coins and poison apples, the clusters of stars above the dark of the lake as he flew toward the farm, disburdened. The unwashed baby, the greasy pink cord, the white stuff like paste on the grimace of the baby, but Tom would be in the plane, flying, when the baby was born, he wouldn't get the sticky white paste on his fingers, he wouldn't be asked to sever the umbilicus, he'd be trying, or just pretending, to become a freer soul.

He felt the tightening in his chest, then the release, then the tightening again. The plane whirled like a dervish. The lake tilted underneath him, pulling him nearer to the island the size of a tree, on which a small, jeweled campfire dizzy with heat came so close he felt the burn.

4

At the time of Angie's first contractions, when the heat of evening was beginning at least to move in minute spirals instead of lying like a smoldering blanket, still none of the fishermen unloading their boats off the dock near the car ponds had spotted the tubular wing of Tom's biplane wedged among some boulders beneath an overhanging willow on the banks of the Winnebago Mental Health Institute grounds. A bit of white Dacron still clung to the aluminum frame but was too sodden to flap around and get attention even after a branch knocked the crushed wing free. Minnows swam in the folds of cloth as if in a drifting tide pool. None of the fishermen noticed, though one of their girlfriends watched in luxurious, smoky silence as what she thought was an inside-out beach chair floated past on the sunset-hued water. Clouds massed on the distant side of the lake, obscuring the cliffs and the silos. When the wind picked up, so did the current. Soon the wing of the biplane was nearly submerged by the newly slapping waves. Each time the cloth bobbed under another small whitecap, another cluster of minnows swam out of the darkening folds. Ninety miles to the south, Angie decided she'd rather give birth in the hospital than in her rocking chair at home. She wrote a note to Tom, declaring that she'd left for the hospital without him, and pinned it to the door. Halfway to the hospital she decided the note was too snotty and made a U-turn, knowing if any cops stopped her, they'd make allowances. At home, she rewrote the note, trying for a less accusatory tone. Probably Tom only meant to escape being present at the messy birth of the baby. How fastidious Tom was. He couldn't help it.

Bygones be bygones, Angie hurriedly printed on a fresh scrap of paper.

She pinned it to the door just as her water broke, splashing the slats of the porch.

Several times during the night, the wing of Tom's biplane was smashed against the breakwater that kept people's houses from being washed into the lake, but it didn't break apart, nor did it stop traveling. By daylight the wing had swung past the public moorings at the park, then followed the shoreline along the cove that led beneath the railroad trestle and into the river. Before dawn the trestle swung shut twice for trains, but the wing of the plane passed under the bridge to wash up on a strip of dirty sand at the edge of a vacant lot adjoining the Department of Natural Resources office building. From there, the tangle of cloth and tubing was spotted by the Fisheries biologist, who decided to walk over to see if somebody's wayward canoe had lost its tether. She plunked down on her knees for a closer look. The object wasn't a canoe. Nor was it kayak or sail. Whenever the Fisheries biologist knelt down even to scrub the floor in her rather large bathroom in the apartment she found too spacious for just one person, especially herself, she was reminded of the time, nearly twenty years ago, when at five years old she played Romeo in a school production. The words *Name what part I am for, and proceed* came into her mind every time she knelt down, even though they were lines from another Shakespearean play.

Name what part I am for, and proceed, she said to herself, reaching for the stiffened cloth where it lay bleaching in the sunlight, then pulling it farther onto the mucky beach and hurrying off to phone Search and Rescue. Ninety miles south, the bronze tufts of Angie's hair had darkened with sweat, while the shadowy smudges of her fingerprints arrayed themselves on the nurse's white sleeves. Angie had discovered that she could make the labor pains go away by imagining that the reason behind Tom's abandonment wasn't because he was scared to attend the birth of the baby but because he had fallen out of love with her. Then when she could no longer stand the pain of Tom no longer loving her, she had only to give in to the contractions again, like riding a seesaw with a partner who kept trying to bump her off. One pain overshadowed the other.

Angie gripped the nurse's sleeve. The nurse never startled. She only glanced at her watch, fearing another long labor. Ninety miles away, the Search and Rescue helicopter began making passes over the lake, while the speedboat depth finders scanned the floor for more debris, though no pilots had been reported missing. Even had the lake been serene instead of choppy, the warble of the biplane's emergency location transmitter signal wouldn't have been detectable underwater. The coast guard canceled its search the following nightfall. Ninety miles south, Angie had entirely forgotten the day, months past, when she'd searched cookbooks for a name for her daughter, but after kissing the child's bald head for a while and wondering if it was the baldness that made the child so sweet, or the sweetness that made the baldness so delectable, she decided on the name Honey. The name was smooth on her tongue, the color of amber, as if it might preserve all the hard knocks and satisfactions that had been part of its making.

In the years following Honey's birth, Angie neither wrote her dissertation nor earned her Ph.D., but was able to find a job teaching English composition at a community college close enough to the farm that she might at least pick the uninfested fruit off the trees along with tending a few short rows of the snap peas Honey loved. The rest of the farm grew in on itself, a tangle of vines amid the dried-out shells of crops. When a strong wind blew, the seeds rattled inside the squash, and when the moon was high, the pumpkin rinds glowed like lanterns. Soon the orderly plots relinquished their borders to thistles, and to the unpredictable appearance of sunflowers. By her willful daughter, Angie was sometimes mistaken for a sunflower herself. At dusk, when Angie sat on Tom's rusting tractor, her slender neck erect, a beer at one hand and a stack of student papers at the other, Angie's just-washed hair stuck out in blunt orange petals as if vying for a better glimpse of the wood duck decoy that inhabited the scooped-out swamp of a rangy maple grove. Tom would have chopped down the saplings of those maples before the roots were flooded by rain. Some days, Angie was furious with Tom for having left her to confront the obstinate vegetation, but other days she was smug with the idea that the maples were hers to do with whatever she wanted. Mainly, just let them be.

Once during the first year and once during the third, Angie phoned Tom's estranged brother in Ohio. The first time, Tom's brother feigned worry, the second time he was only defensive when Angie told him she hadn't seen her husband since before Honey's birth. A third and a fourth time she called the police but hung up before they answered, fearing whatever it was they might say, or not say. All this time, the wood duck spun more slowly than the dragonflies atop its small pond among the rotting trunks of the maples. In winter when the swamp froze, the duck sat as serenely as ever, even though its bright colors had molted away. Ducks mated for life, but none of Tom's other decoys had lasted in the maples; they'd either split in half or swelled up like moss-covered sponges. It had been Honey's idea to plunk the carved ducks in the woods, and despite their ruin Angie wasn't sorry to have given in. Sometimes she glimpsed the surviving wood duck decoy from her seat on the lopsided tractor, in which the corroded key had become wedded to the glommed ignition, and supposed if there was something to be learned from the decoy's stoically fervent posture, it was to nurture a hope that she might someday be as dignified.

Only once in a while did Angie feel dread. The dread greeted her when she was opening or closing the blinds at the windows, while Honey was sleeping, when the just-born or just-dying light of the day muted the acres of neglected land. The plowed rectangles gone, anyway, in the dimness. The neat promise of the compost heap unkept but unremarkable in the shadows. The staked tomato plants sunken into the loam but the loam into the gloom. At such moments Angie found no more sign of Tom's abandonment than of his return, no more sign of his loyalty than of his betrayal. Night fell or day began as if Tom had never been, and never would be. Always, the rebuke of the dying orchard made Angie rear back from the glaze of the window, as if a crow had come from nowhere and slammed into the glass. But there was never a thump, and no ball of feathers crumpled on the ground outside. So, no crow. So, the dread passed and the day came or went.

Ninety miles north, when Honey wasn't quite eight years old, a team of divers began searching for a drowned ice fisherman, whose body had drifted all winter beneath the tire tracks crisscrossing the snowy surface of the ice, finally to be trapped within an intricate pattern of fissures, white and feathered, lying deep in an amethyst sheen. In April the black ice groaned with the thaw, a low bellyache of sound ascending to an agitated clatter. The white fissures broke apart. The divers pulled up the fisherman by the cuff of a sleeve, catching sight, as they rose, of the wrecked fuselage of Tom's plane, his lost eyeglasses winking sleepily amid the debris.

5

It was Honey who answered the telephone call from the coast guard, whose salvage of the fuselage and reading of the Identaplate allowed them to trace the downed plane's owner. And it was Tom they asked to speak with, having found no remains of a body and no reports that he was missing.

"I'm-Sorry-There's-No-Such-Person-At-This-Number," replied Honey, who had heard her mother answer calls in this manner so many times that the words were strung together like those of the national anthem. Just as her mother did while speaking those words, Honey tapped one sneakered foot impatiently, drumming her fingers, admiring the percussion of her glitter nail polish along the countertop. Her mother didn't encourage cosmetics, and never wore polish, but Honey had bought seven half-full bottles at a yard sale with thirty-five cents of allowance savings, and already had turned the investment around by doing other girls' nails during recess at school, two girls per appointed slot, because the second one had to dry before the bell rang to go inside.

"Is your mother there?" the caller asked.

"She's on the tractor," said Honey, although she guessed that the day was too cold for Angie to be outside.

"Can I speak to her, please?"

Honey laid the phone on the counter, crossed the lawn to the tractor, confirmed her guess, then went back to the house and yelled for her mother from the foot of the stairs. Angie picked up the phone in her study, enabling Honey to listen in at the phone in the kitchen. Honey didn't mean to be sneaky. She meant only to wait for a pause in the conversation to ask her mother what she could eat for snack. By the time the pause came, after Angie told the caller she hadn't heard from her husband in eight years but that anyway he didn't own a plane, Honey had nearly forgotten her hunger.

"But you always tell me to say you don't *have* a husband," Honey finally blurted into the phone, standing on her toes to run a blast of cold water over her wrists at the sink. One of her friends' older sisters did this to stay cool during arguments.

"I *don't* have a husband," said Angie. "And he didn't have a plane."

The caller remained quiet.

"Then how did they find his eyeglasses at the bottom of a lake?" asked Honey.

The upstairs line clicked off. Honey was alone with the man from the coast guard.

"How did they?" she repeated.

"A lot of people like wire-rimmed eyeglasses," the man answered gently. "Your father isn't the only one who wears them. Besides, we don't know if your father was even flying his plane. We haven't found . . . there hasn't been . . . there isn't—"

"I don't have a father," Honey interrupted, for this was another thing her mother had taught her, though Honey suspected her mother might be mistaken, for she'd discovered a sort of message in the bottom of the camp trunk in which she kept her clothing. The message read only:

Chicago Cubs
Cincinnati Reds
Houston Astros
Milwaukee Brewers (YES!)
Pittsburgh Pirates
St. Louis Cardinals

As messages went, it wasn't much, but the yellow legal-sized paper signaled importance, and though Honey was perplexed by the boxy precision of the handwriting, she found it disturbingly fatherly. The day the telephone call came from the coast guard was the first day Honey began to distrust her mother's interpretation of things and feel sorry for her at the same time. Angie was upstairs in the bathroom dry-retching over the toilet, a red marking pen clutched in one hand. Since giving birth to Honey, she'd developed a lovely full round stomach that made her look like a raindrop elongating during its slide down a window pane. Or like a flame on a candle burning too high. She was always going up or coming down, reaching and clinging. Until signing off with the man from the coast guard, Honey had found her mother to be the most soothing of women, the most dependable, the most enviable of mothers. But today there was something questionable about Angie's posture, as if she might collapse or float unreliably away.

"That man said the eyeglasses might not be my father's," Honey declared from the bathroom threshold, too subdued by her mother's retching to take a bite of the cookie she'd chosen for snack. Instead she lipped the dark icing, then nibbled the edge of the graham cracker circle under the marshmallow cushion, waiting for her mother to answer. *Of course the eyeglasses aren't your father's. You don't have a father,* she hoped Angie would say. But Angie only doubled closer over the toilet, pressing a hand to her belly as if to force out the blasts of bitter air. Her eyes watered. She shook her head so vigorously the drops flew side to side. When the icing was scalloped all around Honey's cookie, Honey gummed the rest into her mouth and pulled her father's Houston Astros cap off her mother's head. Angie was too sick to notice.

"The man told me a lot of people wear wire-rimmed glasses and just because they're rectangles doesn't mean they're my father's," Honey repeated, turning the cap backward on her own head. "He said nobody knows if my father was even flying the plane. You told me I don't have a—"

Angie threw the red marking pen into the toilet, slammed the lid, and flushed. "Maybe he had a plane, maybe he didn't. Maybe they're his glasses. Maybe not. Of course you have a father. How do you think you got here? Honey. Darling," she said. Then she opened the lid of the toilet again, to see the red marking pen still at the bottom. Pens in toilets didn't matter. Things that didn't matter were a luxury. They should be taken advantage off, appreciated for all their lack of worth. She sat down and peed on it.

"He might have had a parachute, your father," Angie suggested over and over to Honey in the days that followed. "He might have had a life raft he could have carried down and inflated with one pull when he got there."

"And paddled to shore," added Honey.

"And paddled to shore," her mother echoed.

"So, why didn't he come home?" Honey asked, then answered, "Because he couldn't see where he was going because he lost his glasses."

"Yes. Because his glasses were still underwater. And his road map."

"And anyway, he didn't have a car, because it already had been towed to our house," said Honey, who knew the script exactly, they'd been through it so many times, each believing they were humoring the other. "But why didn't he call us on the telephone? Because he didn't have the change. Because it costs a lot of money to call someone up long distance, and that's where he went, because he was afraid I wouldn't like him."

"Yes," said Angie.

"But why didn't he think I would like him?" Honey hadn't asked this particular question before.

"Because it wasn't very nice of him to leave without saying good-bye, was it?" asked Angie. Over the years of meeting with her composition students, whose papers she vigorously marked up before forgetting every word, she'd developed a talent for improvisation, now honed by her daughter's talent for mimicry. If only Tom could see and hear them, acting out the drama he'd produced for them. Angie imagined being onstage with Honey and glancing at the audience to see Tom dripping lake water, squinting because he wasn't wearing glasses, one arm around the bare shoulder of his Waikiki prostitute. Most likely she was a perfectly nice person, the prostitute. Probably she was just another single mother like Angie trying to prove to the man who had been stupid enough to dump her that she could get by without him. A prostitute can't be held responsible for some lustful jerk falling in love with her. But Tom wasn't lustful, at least he certainly hadn't been when he was living with Angie. And he wouldn't have had a life raft, if the reason he kept the plane secret was because he was more reckless than he made himself out to be. The life raft, the parachute, were things Angie had invented, to make Honey believe Tom might still be alive. Because if Honey believed he might be alive, Angie might go on believing it, too. Problem was, it wasn't working.

"If we ever see him again, I'll tell him I still like him anyway," Honey suggested.

Angie didn't answer. She was standing at the window. Outside in the late spring weather, where no sunflowers would grow for four months longer, the maple swamp suddenly appeared negotiable. Angie could leave it. Behind. Forever. Sell it. Get money. Get out of here. Relinquish all her bewildered denial and start fresh with actual grief. She resolved to turn this idea over in her mind for a week or so, in the town at the edge of the lake in which his plane had been found.

Deep down, while packing their bags, Angie must have realized she and Honey would be gone for longer than a week, for she folded their sets of winter thermals even though it wasn't close to winter, then untethered the wood duck from its home in the swamp and packed it with Honey's favorite possessions—the bottles of nail polish, the kid-sized purple Walkman with the yellow flower decals—in an extra duffel. The drive north was peaceful, and took them past a pig farm bathed in tendrils of lavender fog. It felt strange to be seeing new things. For a moment Angie thought she might turn right around and return to the farm at an earlier time, the scrappy maples shrunk back into their winged seeds as the withered rinds of squash turned plump and yellow, the rows and plots restored to their flawless rectangularity, and do the long years over, grieving from the beginning. Maybe, then, she would have been finished by now with grieving and would have shared Honey's humor in the lined-up rears of pigs feeding at a trough. But she kept on driving, and within a few hours of reaching town had rented an apartment down the road from the giant lake. Every evening she and Honey strolled the same paved trail that followed the shoreline for several curved miles between the garishly illuminated yellow bricks of the hospital and a distant spit of land where people sat fishing on chunks of concrete. Teenagers gathered on docks in the harbor. Boom boxes played. The smell of bratwurst rose from grills. Again and again off the end of a dock, one of the teenage boys kept riding a purple bicycle. Angie envied his wild arc above the water, and wondered if there was similiar recklessness in her having descended upon this town.

She sat down on the steps of a gazebo while Honey skidded around on the imaginary ball bearings of her nonexistent skates, her bronze hair sparkling with haughty bliss. Honey liked this town. There was water almost everywhere. Flocks of white birds rose above the shopping centers. Whole gardens of petunias blossomed in painted rowboats stranded on the grass islands at the intersections of the streets. The lake was bigger around than all of Milwaukee. Maybe her father had worn a wedding ring. Maybe the ring had slipped off his finger when he'd crashed into the water. Maybe it had been washed ashore where Honey would skate by it, the ring a token as much of his life as of his death. If Honey finally understood that her father was dead, she understood as well that he had once been alive. She was as glad that he had once been alive as she was glad he was no longer. She liked life with her mother just as it was. On nights all the dishes were dirty in the sink, they set the one remaining plate in the middle of the table and ate with two forks like people sharing dessert in a restaurant. They had never been forced by a man to go golfing, she and her mother, or take tennis lessons, or get used to some shadowy figure smoking cigarettes on the screened-in porch or having one of his bad moods in public. Honey knew about fathers. Her friends had them. She couldn't imagine the sound of his voice, but she could imitate exactly the kinds of commotions her friends with fathers needed to put up with, like, "Okay, girls, out on the porch!" as her friend Susan's father scolded when they were playing in the living room. And she could say, "Sweet Jesus, tell me that bastard didn't do it again!" and slam her hand on the couch, the way her friend Jenessa's father did when watching football.

Honey shifted her weight from one skate to another, round and round the gazebo. Ahead on the trail, a cluster of geese pecked argumentatively at some bright object lying at the edge of a puddle. Honey was certain it was a ring. The closer she came, the more certain she was it would prove to be the mate to her mother's, the two names entwined inside the sculpted whorls of gold. Sometimes her mother wore the ring. Other times she kept it in the silverware drawer. Angie had no other jewelry.

The bright object at the edge of the puddle really was a ring, but from a gumball machine, and too small for Honey's finger. A tuft of orange fuzz sprouted out the top.

"Okay, girls! Out on the porch!" Honey said, tossing the trinket back to the geese, which had dispersed at her approach, then regrouped atop a grassy mound. From the steps of the gazebo, Angie kept half an eye on her daughter while thumbing her paperback book and toying with the black ribbon laces of her sandals, but really she was watching the boy on the bike, embarrassed by the way he was looking at her. And at Honey, for that matter. He wasn't gawking, at least, only admiring, blinking at their bright T-shirts in the dim evening light, and at Angie's gaze riveted by the view of the darkening lake, and at Honey's arms outstretched for balance, and at Angie's cropped bonfire of hair

once she removed her baseball cap and laid it on the gazebo railing. Then he wheeled his bike back out of the water, and sped
again off the dock, the spokes ablur with spray. The other teens
parted to let him through, then stacked themselves into another
pyramid. Another of the boys gave a burst of laughter throaty as
a song, and the spotlights blinked on in the baseball diamond
with a steady buzz. In an inlet several miles from the entrance to
the harbor, on a sandy dip of lake floor, in a tangle of fishing line,
Tom Bane was no longer a sleep. But neither was he exactly
entirely awake. He was the current under the water, he said to
himself. Ever since the ice fisherman had stepped so incautiously
out of his shack, Tom had been a little nervous about what he
could do, if it really was him who was doing it. He believed it
was. Their ears rang, they came. Drowned seagulls, drowned
mayflies, and now this boy with the nerve to ogle Tom's wife and
daughter. Tom's stripped ribs warbled with surprise and anxiety
to see Honey and Angie so close, Honey not long for being a
child but a long way from being a woman. When a terrible commotion arose on the dock full of teenagers, Angie had already left
the gazebo and started walking again, so it wasn't for days that
she learned what had happened to the boy on the bike. Honey
didn't notice, either. "Sweet Jesus, girls!" she shouted, the soles of
her sneakers fluid as wheels on the asphalt as she swiped the St.
Louis Cardinals cap off the gazebo railing and stuffed it under
her shirt. At home, she'd brush the band clean with baking soda
and secure it in her camp trunk along with the other. "Turn
down that music! Turn up the set! Tell me the bastard didn't do it
again!"

5

Polly Had Never Been Fond of Tea, but This Honey Was Different

Another story I wished I remembered, the one I just told. But Angie and Honey were nothing but words floating out of my mind, the curtains open in my windows, the Night fondling the radio dials. I remember when I used to dance with Jack, my hands on his chest, how I'd bid the day's anxieties away from me; small things, usually, things I never told to Jack. Why trouble a man, when I'd already got things fixed—the missing twin (Drew, I remember) discovered hiding in a cupboard, the Joneses' bowling ball returned, the snake unperturbed on the car seat, the bucket of rinsed peas sucked down the drain in the bathtub— really, why amuse a man with that kind of story when you can ask him his own, instead? So away it would drift, the day's mixture of phone calls, stubbed toes, and adrenaline, till there was only me and Jack, and he didn't burden me until I asked him to, at which time it wasn't a burden, anyway.

Across the parking lot of the tavern where Lysle's skinny bottom hung like a gibbous moon in the smashed-apart glint above the windowsill, a shower of crab apples plummeted onto the brittle grass as if to call me to attention. A dragonfly big as a helicopter toyed with the tops of some fence posts as if the evening really ought to last forever. "Tell your uncle to hurry," I'd whispered to Gem, but the child only nodded experimentally at the telephone as if at his own face in my mirror. The phone didn't respond, Gem noticed; Sid's voice at the other end didn't turn into an actual uncle. What would Sid smell like? Sweet soap and shaving cream, scrubbed fingernails with the dirt still inked in the creases, snug jeans, and a tarnished buckle, like an uncle should. Finally Gem let the receiver slip from his fingers and poked off in Lysle's direction. Everything went up and down and back and forth. Whole years, high and low, full moons, rising moons, half truths, and nose-diving airplanes. I hadn't intended for it to be Tom Bane's airplane that cartwheeled into the lake, but still, ever since, Tip and Johnny were like two dogs on a single endless leash, that much I'd inferred from the pieces and bits the Night doled out to me, the two of them horsing around on the dock all those fine summer nights of their boyhood together. Horsing around. Dogs. Black Beauty, Mr. Ed, Lassie, Toto, Spot, palomino, Appaloosa, Afghan, Old Red. I wasn't keen on dogs and horses when I was alive, but still I remembered their names. Tip's laughter made everyone within half a mile stop what they were thinking just in order to hear the hard edge smacking against the mirth of it, though even the bubbles escaping from the thawing fisherman's shirt cuff heard more than I did. Tip, in his cutoffs. My son. Happiest when he was saddest and vice versa, so he'd fashioned a knot between the two feelings no one could untie, except maybe Johnny, by being nervous and determined at the same time as usual, sunning himself on a spread-out beach towel with his belt still threaded through the loops of his khakis, all buckled up and as casual as an intense person could be, except that one evening something caught Johnny's eye, caused him to lift himself onto his elbow to gaze at the paved trail tracing the curve of the harbor. Mother and daughter were walking there, their ghost of husband and father stinging my eyes, although I had no eyes. Angie's steps soothed the tarmac, and Honey's pretend skates made mirages fluttering over the heat of the pavement, and between them walked a girl that Johnny imagined, neither woman nor child but tossing her hair and, so as not to be mistaken for some flirt, her body and T-shirt and the surrounding breezes all clinging to one another equally instead of being nothing but too tight clothing on an ordinary teenage girl.

Tip noticed nothing. His hair too long in his eyes. I might

have stolen a better glimpse of the blunt, canny lines of his face if only I'd been there long enough to gape at it—not elegant like Jack's face but with the illusion of some imperfection that the more you looked for the imperfection, the less of it you saw. I wanted to tell him . . . I wanted to whisper . . . something . . . but even the purple bike knew more than I did and all I could think of were horses and dogs before the static began—the Night's harsh scold—and I was in Its arms, skimming again, dizzily, back to the tavern where Lysle's skinny blue-jeaned butt crack—Gem's term, not mine—still stuck out the window.

Somehow Gem's uncle Sid had been clever enough about the habits of small children to remind Gem not to hang up the phone before Gem went to fetch his father. Gem had forgotten his father was stuck in the window, but when he saw Lysle squirming around in the too narrow frame, he forgot about Uncle Sid, instead. Soon Gem climbed into the semi and pretended to drive. He was such a squirmy nub that when he pressed his chin against the steering wheel, I was able to slip into the seat beneath him and rearrange him on my lap without him noticing anything but an urge to sneeze. I was sad, missing Tip, and Tip untouchable to me, and Violet's wriggling nugget of boy on my lap, comforting me. Being five years old, today was the very first time Gem ever felt a sneeze turn back up his nose and go back where it came from. He felt tickled all through. When he arched his back, I could see the peanut butter smeared under his chin but I couldn't smell it. Done with dancing for a while, though soon to be swept up again, I had put down my mop, snuck a dust rag along the Night's crammed shelves, and reopened the Book of Sid. After the navy and the Mekong River kayaking trip, but before the arrest for the drugs in the sword, he was married twelve months to the owner of a chocolate shop in Sydney, Australia, who refused to sell any truffles in heart-shaped boxes because the shape of the heart and thus the very idea of love had been trivialized and distorted by capitalism. Somehow twelve months sounded longer than a year, to Sid, in retrospect but not when it was happening. His second marriage. The first, before the navy, lasted about the same. Now Sid believed he'd never be in love again and if he was, he'd be deceiving himself or settling for less than he wanted. Needed, really. Every time Sid had to wait on line at an airport or in the mess hall in jail or on the other end of a phone, he felt like he was waiting for love all over again forever. Maybe he was too picky. Maybe women were too picky. Maybe love itself was picky. The world was a giant place. Love couldn't possibly be everywhere at once. Everyone said love happened when it was least expected. Certainly Sid had observed this to be true, especially since love was unlikely and therefore always unexpected. For several years he'd been stationed on a gunship in Hong Kong harbor surrounded by hundreds of floating junks whose inhabitants appeared never to touch solid ground, who fetched their supplies from cargo ships, who gardened on small floating plots and raised chickens in floating coops and shopped in markets and shops on the streets of the junks and who seemed to do everything afloat except maybe get thrown overboard once in a while for fun or transgression. One night on the forecastle of the *St. Paul,* Sid squinted at the thousands of lights on the floating, tethered junks and believed he could see in the darkness where love had settled unexpectedly for the night. There. And there.

On that junk.

And that.

A few needles of lamplight poking through thatch. A cook fire drifting about on a raft. Never more than two or three places at once, love, and the whole world teeming around it, and children being made and born and raised in the absence of it. Next night the cook fire had been stanched and the leaky thatch repaired, so Sid would have to scan the blinking, bobbing, drifting lights again, but never expecting, never even really exactly quite hoping, to find what he was looking for. He flicked a cigarette ash onto the yellow water sixty feet below him and waited. He could make out half a dozen separate tunes playing on different radios within a mile or so of his high lookout on the harbor, but above them he heard the faint kissing sounds of cheap aluminum oars parting the oil slicks in the water. A raft was approaching. The book was quite clear about the *St. Paul* being a giant ship with Sid perched sixty feet high like a swallow on a mast, able to see nothing of the raft but the bright, combed part in a woman's hair and her thin arms when she raised them upward for a five-inch shell casing, which a sailor on the lower deck of the *St. Paul* held out to her but didn't let go. Brass was of great value on Hong Kong harbor. Withheld, the burnished casing of the five-inch cast a halo between them.

"Eight hundred dollars," Sid heard the sailor say.

"Fuck you, GI," the woman shouted back.

"Seven fifty," amended the sailor.

"Fuck you!"

"Seven. That's it. That's it!"

The woman nodded. Her thin arms vanished a second when Sid struck a match to another cigarette.

"Money first," said the sailor.

"Fuck you, GI!" But the woman's hands sunk into darkness, then reappeared holding a wallet of folded cloth. The exchange was made. The woman nearly dropped the shell onto the thin floor of the junk, but then crouched and laid it gingerly on a pallet. A five-inch weighed three pounds and was nearly the length of the women's arm. Why it was named for its smallest circumference might have had something to do with the size of the hole it would make when it hit someone, before it blew them apart. Sid smoked on. There was tension in the air even before the sailor shouted, "We agreed seven hundred!"

"Fuck you, GI!" shouted the woman, already taking up her oar and starting to paddle away.

"I want the other four hundred," ordered the sailor evenly.

"Fuck you, GI!" She sounded terribly young. There was a tremor of fear in her voice that seemed to shimmer around the lip of her oar as she paddled. The sailor hoisted another stolen casing over the gunwale of the lower deck and threw it nose first onto the floor of the raft. The woman wailed. Beneath her shrieks the floor splintered and yawned apart. The oar flip-flopped onto its last kiss. A wire cage of yellow songbirds tilted off the shattered raft and floated perversely away.

Whenever Sid stood in line to wait for anything, he imagined he might have jumped the sixty feet off the ship and rescued the woman if only he was sure she would have rescued him in return. Love or death, love or death, and all the waiting in between was just a race to the finish, whichever came first, Sid guessed. He could hear the gentle swing of the telephone receiver outside the tavern. Still, Lysle didn't come. There was only muffled yelling and a muffled thump of boards. Sid never guessed his brother's skinny butt was stuck in a window. At last he hung up his end of the phone. Hours later when Sid's car purred into the lot, Gem was fast asleep in the driver's seat of the semi and a bird had crapped on Lysle's backside where he'd given up straining to pull free of the window. The bird poop was my doing. I thought it might crack Lysle up a little, no pun intended, let him see some humor in the situation. Boys will be boys. Men will be boys, too. Sid found his carpentry tools in his trunk, popped the window frame out, and slid Lysle affectionately to the ground, then climbed in himself, for a couple of beers and a big draft of root beer for Gem. Sid was broader than Lysle but more acrobatic. All night in the car on the way to Iola, Wisconsin, the two men argued about money. Lysle said when Violet blew up along with twenty thousand dollars, he learned the true value of money: zero. Sid argued that if Violet had had twenty thousand dollars of her own, she wouldn't have been working in the bank in the first place, and would still be alive to spend it. Soon the brothers were old friends again. Gem slept on Sid's lap, because the back of the small car was loaded up, so there was little room for me. I thanked Sid for his question and made it my own, supposing his question was all I required. Where has love gone this evening? Where has love settled? I practiced the words, determined to make them my question to Tip and then point out the answer, Here, and there. Still, swept up in the Night's pushy waltz, I found myself, dust rag in hand, touring the scenery in Iola; a circle of picnic tables near the ice cream parlor, the ski jump rickety over the summery slope of the mountain. Where is love hiding? I was frantic to whisper to Tip, knowing a lane might camouflage a year, a hillside a decade. Funny that a person might accumulate greater regret while dead than she did while alive. Who can count the uncountable ways I might have managed to stop Johnny's drowning? Warned he was cold and the bicycle could wait. Commanded Tip to quit horsing around and fix his eyes on the slippery end of the dock. But no. The Night had me making breezes, blowing flirty seeds of dandelions under the ski jump. Where has love flown this lovely morning? I teased, and watched the small ghosts precede me along a maze of green ski trails. When finally I managed to make my way back to Tip, he was seventeen years old and had lost his best friend for all time. The first thing I noticed was the kitchen light off in Johnny's house next door, and Gwen not washing dishes, and not scouring rust spots before they appeared in the sink. I didn't know yet Johnny was dead. Tom Bane was nothing more than a swattable, pesky annoyance, I still ignorantly believed and would go on believing. Even Gem's praying mantis knew more than I did. Even Tip's frayed cutoffs were smarter than I. "Thank God that woman's finally got herself out of the kitchen. Maybe Gwen *did* take up swimming," I whispered stupidly to a tree, and felt the tree shudder inside me as a leaf dropped too quietly onto the lawn.

Part *Two*

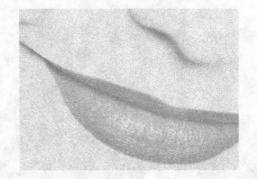

6

A Questionnaire

I

To be the father of twins was like having two legs. Because a man's legs mirror each other, because they act with one purpose, which serves not themselves but a higher, single will—yes, it's right that a man has two legs subject to his inclination, just as Jack had so many pairs of children, who by being so similar to each other were also subject to his will.

Thus they were part of Jack, the three sets of twins—their duplicate faces and complementary natures servants to the larger, cohesive symmetry of his life. David and Dennis, Drew and Douggie, Jenna and Becka: growing up, they belonged to Jack as if parts of his house and body, although he never quite put it that way. Except for Jenna, a travel agent in Green Bay, they all intended to remain in the restaurant business, and even though, except for Becka, they'd recently moved out of the house, the grown twins still belonged, their proper balance holding Jack so buoyantly aloft that he barely felt the ground under his feet some days, for the ground moved so smoothly, so uncomplainingly when he needed to get from one place to another. He was like a man passing through a set of French doors to sit in a chair with a footstool under his feet—he didn't think about the legs of the chair, the legs of the footstool, the two halves of the door swinging open to let him through. No, he only thought of himself walking, then relaxing under the fabric of his robe, and how the things with which a man surrounds himself become his mode of expression, the way the waves lapping against a rock become the rock itself, and a dragonfly alighting on top of it becomes part of the larger display of time and endurance. A philosopher? Jack Baymiller? Not on your life. Too namby-pamby. But still, if a man were a rock, he would also be the froth exploding around it, and he would be all the dragonflies that had ever . . . Jack had tried to explain this to John, next door, after John's son, Johnny, had drowned, pinned under a purple bicycle. By way of offering condolence, Jack had tried to explain that soon it would be autumn, the house shifting gears, the grooves in the wood floor tightening themselves against winter, the new screens on the gutters keeping them empty of leaves . . . but John appeared not to understand or even to need such consolation. He looked untidy, but not undone. Unshaven, his face wasn't coarse or neglected, only bathed in its own dusky retreat. An anesthesiologist, John likely drew solace from other quarters; a milligram of this, Jack supposed, a megagram of that. Then again, Jack couldn't console himself, either, with mere words. That was why he was so glad to be soothed by his house instead, the doors closing gently after him, the plates empty on the shelves awaiting Jack's hunger, the rolled newspapers patient on the front stoop or in the vending machines near the bank, for Jack sometimes bought them there. Polly had died years ago in winter. Nothing was left of her. For this reason he never visited her grave. There were only her bones in a moldering dress beneath a chunk of polished granite and no soul, no spirit, no voice or caress above it. Winter nights, when Jack heard the hum of the refrigerator, he didn't let himself imagine Polly's ghost humming saucily to herself behind the door of the kitchen while stirring something in a pot or wiping her hands on her apron with the same swift, downward motion with which she smoothed her hands over her skirt, when she had pulled the skirt back over her hips, when he and she were finished, for the time being, with the reason for the skirt having been lifted above her hips to begin with. Do other women have hips? Jack regretted the question. It had a bitter, unsociable taste of which he was ashamed. Besides, the answer depended on what one considered hips to be. Yes, other women have hips, of course, but Polly had a chicken pox scar on one of hers. Years after she was gone, when Jack sat reading in his study with the TV on, the newspaper seeming to vibrate slightly with the noise from the dishwasher, he didn't let himself wait for Polly to emerge furiously from the kitchen and reclaim him with a swipe of her rubber glove amid a frothy gust of detergent, but still the newspaper consoled him, the TV, the dishwasher, the hum of the refrigerator consoled him. Dead was dead. That's why he couldn't bring himself to visit the grave all these years, after the elm trees all had vanished from the otherwise verdant sweep of the cemetery, leaving the sky so empty, so unreadable all of a sudden, for there had once been an elm tree over her grave, and now it was gone, which only proved it. How dead dead was. If Jack set his hopes on heaven, then heaven wouldn't be there, but if he didn't expect to, maybe he'd see her again, in whatever way there was to see and be seen, except Jack had standards, certain requirements—if it wasn't her whole face, he wouldn't be satisfied, and if he couldn't embrace her, then heaven wouldn't pass muster, for what good would the stupid golden gates be if he couldn't so much as touch her after he passed through them? As for the grave, though the twins felt the same as their father, Jack suspected Tip snuck there on some of his lone nights out, brushed the snow from the glassy red granite in winter, clipped the weeds in summer—BELOVED WIFE, BELOVED MOTHER, and an engraving of her likeness that Jack regretted, the flared dress more pious than mirthful, less fetching than demure. What disturbed Jack as much as his failure to visit the grave was the abstract question, Did his wife still belong to him after she'd been taken away and buried? Alive, Polly had been Jack's in a more mysterious, more savory way than the twins were, because she was the woman he loved, she was astonishingly herself, Polly, yet she had given herself to him while remaining her own, the way the salt in the chicken soup she made was his, the way the cup of black coffee was his but the cup of coffee with cream in it was hers. "Sugar wasn't sweeter when your mother was alive, but cream was creamier," Jack once let himself say to Douggie, who repeated it to Drew later on when they were mixing ice cream sodas.

Polly had been pregnant with the first set of twins when Jack drew up the plans for their house, which included a bedroom spacious enough for each of the three pairs of children, as if the house knew what was coming before he and Polly did. There was Dennis and David's room with the ceiling and walls still spotted from the time they'd inserted a gunpowder bomb between the axles of a remote-control racing car, for which Jack had punished them by forbidding them to paint over the walls or replace the charred curtains. And there was Becka and Jenna's room, which Jack had insisted be decorated with pink-and-yellow checked flounces and two dressing tables, even though his tomboy daughters never sat before their mirrors except to do their homework or paint fake blood on their faces on Halloween, and there was Drew and Douggie's room, which was perfect, with its rows of sporting trophies arrayed on the shelves, and above the glass gun case the mounted head of the boys' buck, thankfully smaller than Jack's buck mounted between the bookshelves in the study.

Then there was the kitchen, Polly's room, which was as steamy and moist and mysterious to Jack as the cooking that once went on there, which nevertheless seemed to belong to him as much as it did to Polly when he zipped up the back of her dress or brushed her hair for a moment after she'd washed it, when it was wet and sweet smelling, when she'd have to brush it again by herself, laughing at him for having parted it the wrong way. Even her comb, a version of Jack's, was slimmer than his and more decorative, and the ornate handle of Polly's brush, adorned with cast silver roses, was like an accessory to Jack's elegant, simple, fluted silver brush, just as Eve's rib had been a smaller, more decorative version of Adam's. Even the books the children were given to read at school appeared to be versions of the books Jack kept in his study—the print larger and more widely spaced than in his books, the stories abridged, the histories and biographies condensed and lavishly illustrated. It was almost as if, by having read his own books, Jack had caused them to give rise to the children's books, and though he never quite allowed himself to think in these terms, it was the same way with the boy's knitted shirts, which appeared to be the progeny of Jack's shirts, and it was same way with Becka and Jenna's cookies, for even though Becka and Jenna were girls, the cookies they baked always melted together in one glob on the cookie sheet just like Jack's cookies might have melted together if he'd tried to bake some. On one of his bookshelves was a history of science describing the homunculus curled up in a drop of sperm as if in a raindrop, a miniature, perfectly made, fully formed being, and though Jack didn't think in these terms, that was what the objects in his house seemed to be—homunculi of all the things they represented, which Jack had cast about simply by possessing bigger or sturdier things just like them. The children's school-work was the offspring of Jack's paperwork, the children's mistakes were bred of those he had made as a boy, and the stitches in Polly's driving gloves were more tender than the stitches in his own. Jack still kept Polly's driving gloves in his desk drawer, where the help wouldn't come across them. His fingers didn't fit in those of Polly's gloves, but when he laid them across his palm and traced the paths of the stitches, he felt like a river defined by its banks, the banks astringent with the smell of pine needles, comforting him. Which he had tried, but failed, to explain to his neighbor John.

On some nights Tip came barging into the study to stand solidly at the bookshelves while choosing a true crime or a mystery or an adventure, startling Jack because Tip wasn't part of the symmetry of the household, and seemed not to be truly of Jack's surroundings. Aside from Becka, Tip was the only offspring still living full time at home. Not even Tip's Jack of Steaks shirts, which were white, like Jack's, and had the restaurant logo embroidered on the pocket but with Tip's name below it instead of Drew's or Douggie's or Dennis's or David's, appeared related to Jack's shirts. Even when Tip was a baby just home from the cherry orchard, Jack wondered, Who is this X-shaped person who has his very own bedroom, meant to be the sewing room even though nobody sews, which seems not to be part of the house?

Jack was a more slender X shape than Tip. Polly's legs had been slender and straight like the twins', except for Becka and Jenna, who were taller than the boys and chunkier at the ankles. Other women's legs—did other women have legs?—were pale blue, dimpled, triangular. Even when Tip was still a baby in a cherry bucket, his legs resembled Jack's, but still Tip's were like the legs of a person Jack might notice from a distance on a golf course, poised with Tip's purpose and concentration, which had nothing to do with Jack's game, Jack's ball, Jack's swing, or Jack's score.

"What are you looking for?" Jack asked Tip when Tip scanned the bookshelves, but Jack didn't mean, *Which book are you looking for?* Jack meant, *What are you hoping to find, in my house, in my life, where you don't belong?*

"Escape," Tip punned, running his fingers along the books' spines as if the wall might spring open under his touch. Tip always knew exactly what his father meant, and sometimes came into the study just for the pleasure of hearing his father unable to say it. He slipped a book into the pocket of his robe, a hand-me-down of Douggie's. The robe had a softer, more natural drape on Tip than when Douggie had worn it, and seemed to vanish from Jack's study as if on legs of its own, a living robe, a stowaway in Jack's house, a scrap of flannel on a gust of wind that should be outside, not in, that should never have got past the door.

Jack crossed his ankles again on his footstool, checking his watch against the date on the wall calendar. But the date didn't help, because he still didn't know. How old Tip was. How many years. If he knew how old Tip was, then he would know how long Polly was dead. If Tip was zero years old, Polly wouldn't be dead, she might spring from Tip's head if Jack parted Tip's hair with a hatchet. Sometimes Jack believed the only reason he didn't get Tip with a hatchet was because he was afraid it wouldn't work. But really it was Tip who kept Jack alive after Polly was dead, Jack occasionally realized, surprised this was true. Tip kept Jack's dander up. Just because Polly would have hated being called an angel didn't mean she hadn't been a most passionate one, underneath her tempestuous halo, and when she was dead and irreplaceable, Jack needed a demon to struggle against that wasn't his own. Tip was shorter than Jack, stockier than the twins, his center of gravity so near to the ground that the study ceiling trembled when he reached his bedroom upstairs. Some nights, Tip sang out loud like someone taking a shower, and in the mornings it was always with some comment that Tip threw off the covers, some daily exclamation Jack dreaded the flamboyant sound of, that shouldn't have been in Jack's house, that made it impossible for Jack to dream at night, which was a good thing, for Jack's dreams would have filled him with sorrow.

"If not for me, he'd be mush, and he knows it," Tip muttered as he went upstairs. The sash of his bathrobe was loosely knotted, his boxers showed between the flaps. The steps quaked as if he were bounding on purpose, but he wasn't, he was only flat-footed like his father. It wasn't merely a book he had taken from the shelf in the study and slipped into his bathrobe pocket, for inside it would be one of the letters his father had written to his mother while on business in Indiana, years and years ago. Jack's letters to Polly were all alike. Wouldn't she please hop a plane to Indianapolis and surprise him the way he always hoped she would, show up at his door in the motel hallway wearing the wings of her new sunglasses as if their sudden, rhinestoned flutter had deposited her there? The glasses were a gift from Jack. The choker necklace mentioned in another of the letters was also a gift from Jack. The clutch mentioned in yet another of the letters mystified Tip until he asked one of his girlfriends what was a clutch. The first girlfriend had no answer, the second opened the clasps of two evening purses, thrust Tip's hands between the satin linings, and said, "You're in my clutches," which made Tip feel so trapped he broke up with her then and there. Jack had addressed the envelopes to Mrs. Jack Baymiller, and Polly had cut them open with pinking shears. Tip ran his chin along the zigzag margins of tonight's envelope, pleased to have come into ownership of more evidence of his father's humiliation in the face of Polly's refusal to so much as share a cocktail in Indianapolis. Tip had found the letters years before in a Keds box, and not wanting to read them all at once, had hidden them inside Jack's books himself, in order to dole them out to himself over the years as if he were a sleuth in one of the mysteries, as if his mother's ghost had put them there knowing Jack read only newspapers now. Had Jack known his pleading letters still existed, he would have held a match to them until after the flame singed his knuckles. Or maybe, because Polly herself had read them, had caressed the pinked edges . . . perhaps Jack would have hoarded the bundle of velvety envelopes in the desk drawer where he hoarded Polly's driving gloves with the clover leaves stamped out of lambskin. Unlike his father, Tip never tried to fit those gloves on his own hands, or traced the fingers stitch to stitch, but had secretly appreciated the look and suppleness of the leather, such a strong, soft lady his mother must have been and so different from any lady Tip was bound to ever know because gloves were no longer in fashion except in winter. Maybe someday he'd meet a woman in gloves, indoors. Tip set this notion before him as one of his fantasies. Then maybe it would really come to pass, as his fantasies usually did, only always slightly altered. *Please come to Indianapolis, as long as I'm stuck in this motel, we'll have a second honeymoon in the swimming pool,* Jack had written to Polly over and over, making a fool of himself. What elegant, soft, strong lady in her right mind would join her husband in Indianapolis for a second honeymoon in a motel swimming pool messed up with other guests' lost Band-Aids? Observing the playful vacillation of Polly's pinking shears, which seemed to grow sharper with every one of her rejections, Tip decided he would never ask any woman to join him in Indianapolis or anywhere else for that matter, and slid tonight's letter unread into his bathrobe pocket. He meant to savor it awhile, open it only later. The other letters—its partners in Jack's embarrassment—were kept in plain sight among the other borrowed books between the cowboy-shaped bookends on Tip's nightstand. There was nothing on earth to stop Jack from coming in and discovering the letters, except that Jack never came into Tip's bedroom. Although Polly hadn't been the one to hide the letters in the books, still Tip was the one to find them. They were her message to him, and he believed absolutely what he thought she was trying to tell him. The more you craved a person's company, the less of it you'd get. The more you needed a person, the less they needed of you, like Johnny these days. The more you loved, the further away you were compelled to remain, like Tip from Johnny even as Johnny was drowning.

Behind the letters in the bookends stood a flask of crème de menthe, also borrowed from Jack's library. Tonight Tip intended to get drunk enough to do something even stupider than he had done the nights before—stupider than toilet-papering the skimpy corner lot of the funeral home where Johnny, Tip's coconspirator, lay mischievously inside in the casket, stupider than the time he'd snuck into Johnny's bedroom and found the folded clean T-shirts stacked neatly on the shelf in Johnny's closet and taken them home to wear them. He got them damp and smelly as if Johnny weren't dead, as if Johnny had worn them himself to strike out in baseball. Then he smuggled the grass-smeared, sweat-soaked, fly-spotted shirts back to Johnny's closet and tossed them in the empty laundry basket.

What could Tip do tonight that would be stupider and yet more personal than that? The toilet paper could have been anyone, some grade school kids or a sleepwalking loner, the flimsy streamers dangling mute in the trees and Johnny not telling who did it. Tip uncorked the cut-glass decanter, tonguing the syrupy lip. Too sweet, as expected. Last week he'd got lost in the cemetery, of all scary places. In search of Johnny's grave. He'd intended to spread his jacket across it and stab his pocketknife through the hem into the relaid sod like the guy in the story who dies of a heart attack thinking he's been grabbed by the corpse. Instead, disoriented by the balmy mist of the night, Tip followed the river away from the cemetery and climbed a utility ladder onto the roof of the microbrewery. He hadn't dreamt about Johnny at all, up there. Instead of mourning for his friend, he dreamt of a girl in white gloves cleaning fresh-caught fish, ornamenting her gloves with the glittery blue scales. Around him the

odor of yeast made a yellow sigh in the blackness, but the giant
vesicles of the brewery stayed quiet. No lurching. No steaming.
Beyond the cylindrical shapes of the pipes, the mist had stalled at
the elbow of the river, but the river appeared to be motionless,
too. Nothing moved as far as Tip could see, except for Tip himself. He slid closer to the edge of the roof for a better look. No.
The river probably never would move, under the motionless fog.
Tip's stomach flexed with its dream of fish scales. He was moving
all the time, every inch of him noisy with motion even while sitting most still. What made him sit still? he'd wanted to know.
What influenced him to like it up there on the brewery roof,
where he was the only moving thing, everything else blindsided
by silence? The private, sweet, stolen smell of brewer's yeast—
trapped by the weight of the sky. The vastness of sky beyond the
gleaming twists of pipe—trapped by the larger press of the universe. Even Johnny in his coffin lay underground forever, but Tip
could jump off the brewery roof into the river if he wanted, or
shimmy to the tops of the pipes if he wanted, or just lie flat on
his back and congratulate himself aloud about the strength of his
will, his voice imposing itself on the view of the river. There was
a game he played Sundays in church, when he whispered, *Don't
think of a white rhinoceros goring the priest from behind.* At which
point, despite what everyone said was expected to happen when
you told yourself not to think of a white rhinoceros, that is, that
you *did* think of one, Tip didn't. Instead he thought of his father
drinking orange juice at the open door of the refrigerator in the
kitchen at home. The priest wore a green robe. The high pitch of
the priest's voice embarrassed some people and made others
imagine he must be extra chaste. How could a person be extra
chaste? Tip was glad not to know. He said to himself, Don't
think of a white rhinoceros strolling up to the refrigerator and
snorting all Jack's orange juice out of the pitcher, so he didn't.
Instead he thought of the time Jenna dropped her hot dog on an
escalator. Behind the pitifully high-pitched intonations of the
priest, the door to the sacristy was always slightly ajar. Directly
under the sacristy in the church basement was a tunnel for the

storage of folding chairs and tables, and if Tip told himself not to think about a rhinoceros hurtling though the tunnel, he didn't.

The variation of this game created by Tip that night on the brewery roof had nothing to do with a rhinoceros but was the same idea. *Don't think about Johnny riding his bicycle in his khaki pants with the bungee cord around his ankle so his pants won't get stuck in the gears, humming a few bars from one of his made-up top forty hits,* Tip had said to himself, at which point he *didn't* think of Johnny, he saw the priest in white robes, white being the color priests wore at funerals, and the door to the sacristy firmly, uncommonly closed.

The crème de menthe turned Tip's feet a sickly yellow when he looked at them through the faceted decanter, and left sweet sticky rings on the bedside table, where he played with the cork so contentedly he worried he might fall asleep if he didn't hurry up and do something stupid. But what? Something persuasive. The toilet paper had been crude, the sweaty T-shirts unrefined. There was an accident Jack liked to tell dinner guests about, that Tip and his brothers and sisters had heard so many times it didn't sound like an accident but like Jack had done it on purpose. The accident was, Jack had walked out a set of sliding glass doors assuming there was a balcony on the other side, but there wasn't, so he'd fallen to the balcony a floor below and landed in a crate of grapefruits, which broke his fall and kept him from breaking any bones, except that several months later, when Jack demonstrated this event to some people in another house, he walked out another set of sliding doors, assuming there was a balcony on the other side, but there wasn't, so he fell into a snowdrift, sprained his ankle, and went skiing the next day anyway, which was the point of the story and would have been the point of the accident if Jack had stepped into midair on purpose, for the skiing proved Jack's theory that the way to make pain, sickness, and injury go away was to ignore them.

Tip swung his feet over the edge of the mattress, knowing at last what prank the night had in store. He had decided to climb out the wrong window of his bedroom. The window next to

Becka and Jenna's room was the one with the ladder propped against the sill, but the other window, closer to David and Dennis's room, dropped one storey to the lawn below. He would climb out that window as if by mistake, and fall all the way down and drowse in the damp grass. Whenever Tip did anything noisy after midnight, that became the moment in which the brief night ended and the longer, sleepy lapse into morning began.

He slid backward out the window one-handed, still holding the bottle. The ladder was there, where it didn't belong, against the wrong sill. He had moved it himself, earlier that day, away from a puddle of sprinkler water.

So he climbed instead of fell. He was nothing if not adaptable. Besides, on the opposite side of the river of grass between their two houses, Johnny's room was still dark, Johnny's book of math puzzles untouched on the desk, and the compass stuck in the dartboard where Johnny had kept it so he wouldn't prick himself on it when he reached in his desk for a pencil.

It wasn't right, Tip believed, that the compass should still be buoyed in the dartboard where Johnny had stuck it, a dumb thing, the compass, with no understanding of what had happened to the person who'd flung it there. The idea that a room should be left as the dead person left it insulted that person.

Tip crossed the lawn to Johnny's sill and pressed the end of the ruler they kept under the screen for a lever. The screen squeaked raggedly upward. Johnny's solar-system mobile, stalled in its corner of ceiling, bobbed its greeting when Tip gave a light tap to Mars before the planets resumed their orbits around the Styrofoam sun. For years, Johnny had kept his planets obsessively aligned, climbing up on his desk if he needed to untangle Jupiter's moons, even dusting Saturn's rings with a corner of washcloth. Beneath the mobile Johnny's math book lay closed on the blotter, but since Tip wasn't going to allow things to remain as Johnny had left them, he turned back the cover and let the pages fall open as if Johnny himself had done it, switching on the desk lamp to make a circle of light as if Johnny were sitting puzzled by one of the brainteasers. This was the quietest Tip had ever been, he believed. And the saddest. Before now,

he'd thought of Johnny's death only from his own selfish perspective—how he'd never see his friend again, or hear his voice,
and how much he already missed, and would go on missing,
him. But now suddenly Tip wanted to understand how awful it
would be to be Johnny, trapped by the purple bicycle under the
dock, unable to breathe and hearing the muffled laughter from
above on the dock—Tip's laughter!—and then to be forever
trapped in the coffin, blind, deaf, dumb, and never to touch
another girl or write a song to be someday played on the radio
or forget to unwrap the bungee from his ankle so his pants
looked like bloomers. Tip couldn't fathom any of this. No matter how strong willed, no matter how insistently he closed his
eyes, he wouldn't stay blind or deaf for eternity. He could hear a
passing car, and the lake water lapping, and he could practically
see the faint electric glow of Johnny's clock.

Because Johnny had left the clock plugged in, Tip unplugged
it. He wiped a few blades of grass off his bare feet onto the rug,
made a knot like a fist in the sash of his robe so as not to be inde-
cent when he lay in Johnny's bed, and stood the crème de
menthe beside the bed, on the floor. The pillow was too thin for
Tip's liking, but Johnny preferred it that way. Tip intended to lie
there only a minute or two before reading Jack's letter to Polly,
which was still in his pocket. He had nearly finished savoring its
saw-toothed, ripening presence. Also, he'd forgotten to take his
pocketknife. *Don't think about stabbing your jacket into a grave so
it feels like a dead person grabbing you,* he said to himself, closing
his eyes.

So he didn't.

2

Of the infinite number of things that might be done with a
child's room when the child has died, leaving it alone was the
cruelest, Gwen thought when she couldn't help but think about
it, which was nearly all the time that autumn except in moments
of watery cool submersion when her head was a bubble of
empty air. Cruel not to the child, because Johnny wouldn't

know that the objects in his room had been left as he had left them. And cruel not to the parents, who steered clear of the room as if their chests might explode if they didn't. Cruel not to anything, really, but just a small, harmless mirror of a larger, endless cruel indifference. The world didn't know that a child had died. Trees didn't grow backward into the earth as if in acknowledgment. Cans didn't fill back up with soup, and rain didn't rise back into the clouds.

Cruel, because the universe was cruel, Gwen concluded, peeling off her cotton underpants to step into her tank suit, then hanging her clothes on the hooks in the metal locker, where someone's tube of orange lipstick lay forgotten. The owner of the lipstick hadn't died, but still her makeup lay untouched where it had fallen. Gwen didn't wear lipstick except to the cocktail parties that had once been frequent among the other doctors and their husbands or wives, and to which she and John weren't to be invited anymore until someone decided a decent amount of time had elapsed. Never, Gwen commanded. The straps of her bras had turned gray. Her underpants resembled a failed parachute where they hung in the locker.

Johnny had been a Flying Fish when he stopped taking lessons from Gwen's colleagues at the YMCA. After Flying Fish, Shark. After Shark, Porpoise, Barracuda, and Stingray. Which designation might have stopped him from riding a bicycle off the dock? He wasn't a reckless boy. He didn't act, then think. To a fault, he did the opposite. Of what had he been thinking as he pedaled the bicycle along what might have resembled a runway? Gwen couldn't guess, but the pool made it easier to be in the dark. Swimming, she was none of the animals listed above. She was a squid. A single eye, a cloud of ink, she billowed away. Who could have imagined? The kickboards, the flippers, the paddles strapped to the children's hands, the twenty minutes of treading, the half-hour back floats, the endless wet slap of the butterfly— all had made Johnny too sure of himself, the pull of a breast-stroke as natural to him as the way he didn't swing his arms when he walked on land. Who could forgive the swimming instructors for teaching him he was a flying fish? Gwen could forgive them.

It was the lifeguard she wouldn't forgive. Gwen was the lifeguard. Wouldn't Polly be surprised? Gwen had taken up swimming when Tip and Johnny were ten, and now look where it had gotten her. The night Johnny rode the bicycle into the lake was *Jumpin Jelly Beans Night* at the YMCA. *Lap Swimmers! Guess how many Jelly Beans are in the Special Jar. The Lucky Winner takes home an End of Summer Basket. Place your bid with the Lifeguard on Duty,* read the sign near the chair between the shallow pool and the deep one. Gwen must have read it a thousand times between looking from one swimming pool to the other. Also, she counted the colorful rows of beans. Vertical, horizontal, diagonal. It wasn't good for lifeguards to stare at the water the way people thought they should. Staring makes a lifeguard space out. Every lifeguard knows that. That's why they so often appear not to be paying good enough attention. Seven prisoners were in the two pools that evening. One swam laps in the far lane of the deep one. Two threw a ball. The rest were harder to keep track of, aimless, indecisive, impulsive even in a swimming pool. For good behavior they were bussed once a week from the correctional facility. Their skin more sallow than grubs. Their flimsy swimsuits transparent where the wet cloth clung to their thighs. The ones not overweight were scrawny, and all were more polite than they needed to be. Bashfully, they offered Gwen their guesses as to how many jelly beans were in the jar, then knocked elbows on the way to the hot tub. All the prisoners knew how poorly they swam. A few kept their faces out of the water, and one, his hands. Their suits were knotted with fraying drawstrings. Which of their drawstrings would come undone this evening as usual? Gwen wondered. The man with the acne scars on his jawline? The one wearing the necklace of human teeth? Why did the prisoners all look like prisoners? she often asked herself, perplexed. Had they looked like prisoners before they got caught for committing their crimes, or only after?

Had Gwen ever looked like a lifeguard? she asked herself now. Or did lifeguards look like lifeguards only after they'd saved somebody? And what if they failed? What did they look like then?

And why couldn't even the lap-swimming prisoner swim a decent lap before joining the others huddling and lunging? All the prisoners' hair needed cutting, all their teeth needed fixing, all their postures required attention, their very fingernails appeared bereft of care. Where were these boys' mothers when they'd got themselves in trouble? Gwen didn't know, anymore, which questions had come before and which after Johnny's death, or how long ago she had seen the boy with the tennis racquet walking New York Avenue at midnight. She and John had been driving home from her mother-in-law's. The car windows were open, the breezy night warm, the lights on in the eccentric third-floor rooms of the elaborately cantilevered houses. The boy wore a white shirt, white tennis shoes. The dark trees leaned away from him. Maybe his mother had insisted on the shirt, the tennis racquet, knowing he'd be walking alone at midnight. Gwen and John hadn't mentioned the boy to each other. His gait appeared casual. Had they stopped they might have frightened him. He was only nine or ten, the age Johnny had been when Gwen and John first allowed him to boat to the island at night. What had they been thinking? There was nobody else on the sidewalk. The boy's tennis racquet threw a latticed shadow whenever the boy passed under a lamp. Had this happened before Johnny's death, or after? Where was the boy now? Had he reached the destination he had in mind? Or had he ended his adventure prematurely, in some way or place he hadn't intended? What was included in the End of Summer Basket awarded the winner of the jelly bean contest? one of the prisoners had asked her when he put in his bid. Gwen hadn't known the answer. What a relief, not to know the answer to such a superfluous question instead of not knowing the answers to the important ones. But had she thought this then, or after? What had Johnny been thinking when he flew off the dock? How many jelly beans were layered in the jar? Which prisoner would nearly lose his bathing suit tonight and get his thumb stuck in the drawstring when he tried to hoist the knot? What was a mother when her child was dead? And what was a lifeguard when the life most carefully guarded swam away?

Despite their ill-fitting bodies, their sloppy caps of damp hair, the prisoners were somehow more appealing to Gwen than were the more fashionably Lycraed swimmers, who snapped their neon-hued headgear into place and dove in already refreshed from what they had done before, sleek with whatever they might do after. For there was something grateful about the prisoners. They were grateful to be *out*. They were grateful for the hot tub, the chlorine, the slippery tiles, the view of a tree through Thermopane. Under fluorescent lights, their tattoos were as ornamental as needlepoint.

There were close to eleven hundred jelly beans in the jar, Gwen guessed, and looked up to see another of the lifeguards coming toward her, extending a small piece of paper. The seven prisoners climbed from the shallow end, wrapping their transparent suits in insufficient towels. The slip of paper fluttered ragged as a moth between the approaching lifeguard's fingers. Looking back at this moment, or perhaps even as it was happening, Gwen regarded the lifeguard, Val, as a messenger, the slip of paper a reply to all the questions Gwen couldn't clear out of her head.

"Thank you, ma'am."

"Thank you, ma'am."

"Ma'am."

"Ma'am."

The prisoners filed past her in their towels no larger than dinner napkins. Gwen reached for Val's tatter of paper. Whatever might be written on it was hidden by the fold. Why did Val insist on cramming every message into as few words, as few gestures as possible? Even Val's name was short for something more lovely. But so was *Gwen* short for *Gwendolyn*. Why had no one ever called her Gwendolyn? Because of her freckles. *Lap Swimmers! Guess how many Freckles! The Lucky Winner takes home—* but what was included in an End of Summer Basket? Gwen wondered. What would someone want at summer's end that they wouldn't have cared for at its beginning?

To Val's apparent surprise, Gwen unfolded the sloppy creases of Val's message and spread it flat on her knee. Was this the moment John's golfing partner, on call in the hospital emergency room, had started working so hard to resuscitate Johnny? So desperately did he work that he collapsed when he was done. Or not done, depending on one's point of view. Like John, the golfing partner was an anesthesiologist. His duty was to put patients to sleep. Maybe he had succeeded. Maybe Johnny wasn't drowned, only dreaming. What about? Gwen read on Val's note: *3,902.* How could two bids be so far apart? Gwen wondered, recalling her own. Not that it mattered, for if a lifeguard won the bid, the End of Summer Basket, with its box of colored pencils, the fallen-leaf-shaped pad of Post-its, the can of powdered cocoa, the apple-picking coupon for Sunset Farms, would go to the closest contender. But what would a prisoner do with colored pencils? Bore holes in the wall and escape to pick apples. But to where might Gwen escape, when apples weren't what she needed? She no longer could tell if she'd asked this then, or later. She'd slipped Val's bid past the slot in the bid box, climbed off her chair, and approached the empty pool, where the lane dividers needed to be reeled in.

Gwen wasn't lifeguarding, these autumn days, or drawing her salary, such as it was. On top of John's, her salary was extra, the few dollars that, had she earned them when he was just out of medical school, would have boosted them into the next-higher tax bracket. John never pointed that out, as other husbands Gwen knew about did. She would still love him if she could. He didn't know she wasn't working anymore, or how much she was swimming. Three hours in the mornings. Four in the afternoons. Her hair lightened from chlorine. Her heartbeat relaxed from all of her kicking. In striped racing suit and square rubber cap, she blended in so well with the refreshed-looking, sleek-looking lap swimmers that not even the other lifeguards appeared to recognize her. What did a mother become when her child was dead? What did a lifeguard become when she had positioned herself at the edge of the wrong body of water? John himself seemed to be grappling with this problem, seemed to be trying to flip his wife upside down or backward in some way that might allow him to see what should become of them.

When she was least hungry, that's when he tried to get her to eat, when she was least tired, that's when he led her to bed, and when morning revealed how she'd folded her body under a blanket of numbing dreamlessness, that's when John woke her, as if she might be a person who believed there was reason for starting another day. Last week she spotted a coin at the bottom of the lap lane in the pool, and dived to get it, then just as quickly let the insensible rescued object drop back to the sloped tiles, its fall slowed by the water. Then she couldn't get it out of her mind. All night the quarter stayed in the bottom of the pool, not rusting, not drowning, while Gwen lay in bed, not sleeping. Maybe one of the prisoners would find it, and trade it for a cigarette.

"You're thinking too much again, Gwen," John coaxed very gently from his side of the bed. Once, before a trip they made to Mexico, he'd had to give her a gamma globulin shot, but his handling of the syringe was so skillful she hadn't felt the needle. That was what she remembered, these days, whenever he spoke in his cautious beside manner—him putting in the needle and her not feeling a thing.

"Then I'll go downstairs," she answered without sitting up. "Too much for what?"

"For falling asleep."

"I don't want to fall asleep. If I go to sleep, I'll have to wake up."

"Someday we'll wake up feeling a little better than we do now," John said. From what reservoir did he dip his wobbling teaspoonfuls of comfort? From his little black bag, Gwen answered, the bag doctors no longer carried on house calls they no longer made, packed with bottles, vials, hoses, needles. No wonder John was able to work these days. He fueled up at lunch. His coffee breaks were sugared with other confections. Gwen didn't begrudge him his drug use as long as he continued keeping it to himself.

"I don't want to feel better," she answered.

"Neither do I," John admitted. "But I do want *you* to feel better, and you do want *me* to feel better. So if we only switch sides . . ." His voice drifted about, delivering its palliative to the bed, the striped curtains, the closet full of unfashionable clothes, the chirping of squirrels in the trees outside, the murmur of dreams Gwen heard tonight from her dead son's bedroom below her own.

Gwen flexed her muscles as if swimming between the sheets, wishing there were more natural violence in a swimmer's kick. Even the most forceful butterfly stroke was beneficent. The really unbearable thing was that talking to John, after Johnny was dead, wasn't terribly different from talking to John when Johnny had been alive. Between themselves they'd often remarked how like Johnny were their conversations. Mazes of battling logic, the pleat in Johnny's forehead as deep at age two as it might have been at sixty. Maybe Johnny wasn't drowned, only dreaming, hence the murmurs and thunks from his bedroom. But Gwen didn't mention this desperate idea to her husband.

"Gwen. Sleep."

"You have no right to tell me to sleep."

"Yes, I do. I'm the doctor."

Pump drugs in me, then, Gwen was hardly able to refrain from begging. She climbed out of bed, slid from her nightgown, pulled on a flannel shirt and sweatpants without any underpants so she wouldn't need to look at them hanging from the hook in the YMCA like a failed parachute, and went downstairs thinking she'd make coffee.

Instead she sat at the sponged kitchen table and laid her cheek on the Formica, like the way she sometimes pressed her face against the rim of the pool between miles of laps, to rest. Her grief was whole miles and miles of laps, barely begun to be kicked through or counted. Gwen would keep it inside her, where sorrow belonged, where it could be nurtured, birthed, sheltered, raised. *Raise the grief when you can't raise the child,* Polly might say. Gwen and Polly had made such good friends, between the time Gwen and John moved into the neighborhood and the time Tip and Johnny were born.

How do I know when I've swum away enough grief? Is it *swam* or *swum?* Gwen might ask Polly.

Hell with which one it is, just do it till you don't need to do it

anymore, pardon my Tasmanian, Polly might say, arranging photos in an album she'd spread open on Gwen's kitchen table. She
used to slide all the photos of Jack to one side, find a pencil in
her purse, and try out mustaches and sideburns on Jack to see if
she liked them. *Nope.* Even Polly's maternity dresses were sharp
as kites, her wrist slender in its watchband, her smile playful
under its fresh allotment of color.

Gwen pressed her cheek against the gleam of Formica and
allowed it to commandeer her. To the lake it led her, and in a
moment, to the purple bicycle that had sped off with her son.
The purple paint flecked with sparkles. Gwen had seen the
bike—its cocked wheels, its too adventurous posture. Maybe
Johnny was dreaming of an adventure. There were people in
the world who claimed belief in a thing was enough to make it
happen. Framed by the window, above the dishes in the sink,
the moon was a lamp on a tall post. Where the light struck the
tabletop, the salt and pepper shakers loomed like nuclear power
plant towers. In his room down the hall from the kitchen,
Johnny lay dreaming. Why shouldn't Gwen believe? For there
was something in the air, some ghostly scent, some nameless
intuition. Gwen finally got up to shut off the lights on the
porch. But the lights weren't on. And neither was the broiler,
when she thought she heard the ticking of the gas. Some
substance her husband the anesthesiologist had rigged up,
maybe, was disorienting her. Laughing gas from a hose in the
ceiling. She was lolling like a whale. Geese grieved for lost
mates. Doves mourned for everyone around them. Sorrow was
an obstinate form of affection, the only love that might halluci-
nate vividly enough to follow the crooked passageways from the
living to the dead. Not to grieve for a person who was dead . . .
*well then, you might as well not smother with kisses the ones who
are alive,* Polly Baymiller might say, with a dismissive shrug of
her slender shoulder.

The doctor did come downstairs to see Gwen after a while,
his hand fluted like a cup to hold the prescription for sleep.
Tylenol. Gwen supposed she should be grateful; him making his
rounds past midnight and not calling her to task for indulging

her insomnia. For a minute John only stood looking at her, though not in his time-honored way. Over the years he'd perfected a way of peering straight through her plainness at the details that stirred and excited him—her freckles running together, her eyelashes too short but so red, her chest flushed as if she'd been raking leaves. But this time he was turning her over abstractly, trying to figure out which way he and she might still be fitted together. What a pair they made, the lifeguard and the doctor. He was peering beyond her freckles, into the very core of her determination to resist him. At last he tried to coax her from the table with a pot of—warm milk! Who was he fooling? Did he think she didn't know how *he* was coping? And the nurses at work, they didn't know, either! The doctors, same! He poured the milk into the mug, lowered his face to the soothing aroma as if there weren't some concoction far more inviting in the floor stock at the hospital. Gwen knew enough to guess it might be Fentanyl. Class 2. Butt injected. Short acting. Addictive. John's casual ease with the mug of warm milk gave his awkward deception grace. For as long as Gwen and John had known each other, the ice-skating rink had been his Saturday-morning pastime, his Thursday-night exercise. He was endlessly, hopelessly novice, his figure eights more clumsy than prepossessing, his arabesques flailing, his turns marked by stutters and stops. Now he carried the warm milk close to his pudgy chest, the spoon in one hand, the mug in the other, arms crossed at the wrists where they met above his sternum. A skater's gesture. Gwen was the ice, she supposed. So cold. When she turned her nose away from the not quite mesmerizing steam of the milk, John only sighed and went upstairs without her, and drew her a bath before he got back in bed. A bath! He did this so cautiously, so like some other worried, slightly overweight, red-haired husband, instead of a doctor married to a lifeguard, neither of whom had succeeded in rescuing their son, that Gwen nearly relented. Had she grieved enough? No. But should she really crawl under the table? No. But why shouldn't they blame each other, him and her? But she could hear the water cooling in the tub, could hear the steamy droplets slide down the mirror. Perhaps she should join him upstairs. She would bury herself in percale, accept the offer of sleep from the warm sheets her husband tucked around her.

Gwen rose from the table and started down the hallway to Johnny's room. She would wash his dirty T-shirts. She would open the things that he had left closed, close the things he'd left open.

The door to the room was slightly ajar.

On his desk in a circle of lamplight, his math book lay open to a picture of parallelograms. Gwen shut it. If eternity was such a logical concept, why couldn't she grasp it? She and Johnny were two lines that would go on forever, never, anymore, to intersect. But they had been so very close to each other. Not like most teenage boys with their mothers. He'd even told her she smelled good, one day, "not like chlorine." He wasn't bashful with her as with other people. That morning she'd been flipping through a magazine she'd found under a bench in the locker room at the Y. Affixed to an ad was a tiny metal envelope filled with perfume. She'd clipped it open with a nail scissors and, not the perfume-wearing type, touched a drop to the skeptical tip of her nose. Maybe tomorrow she'd drive to the library and search the back issues of magazines for an identical crimped envelope whose contents she might ration molecule by molecule, reminding Johnny to dream himself back to her so he could tell her she smelled good. There'd be the unwashed men in their untied shoes dozing in the armchairs they'd appropriated in the circulation room, and there'd be Gwen flipping through the stacks of women's magazines, touching her fingertip to her nose like a drunk driver stopped by the cops.

If she believed she could hear her son sleeping, then it would be true. Of course, she had watched him in sleep, as all mothers watch their children. Even in sleep Johnny's brow would be furrowed, tense with the thoughtful effort of unconsciousness. His dreams were one math problem after another; he'd be calculating the circumference of a telephone call or calibrating lemonade. These were real dreams he'd told her about over breakfast.

Gwen pressed the switch on the desk lamp. She couldn't bear for the lamp to remain as he'd left it, the dumb circle of light going on and on without him above the pages of parallel lines. Funny he'd left the light on, for he was always so frugal with electricity, always the one to make sure the light in the closet was off, and the light in the bathroom, too. He was equally conservative of any of the ninety percent of brain cells said to go to waste in ordinary people. He made use of his own extra brain cells by worrying. Even as a toddler he worried he had allergies to dust, goose droppings, citrus, and down pillows.

They took him in to be pinpricked and examined. On the day he was told he wasn't allergic to anything, he came down with an actual head cold. When he got older, he worried he was hypochondriac, instead.

Or obsessive, he said once. Like Becka.

Like who? What? Gwen asked.

Never mind, Johnny answered.

Most mothers wouldn't close the math book, she was aware. Most mothers would rather dress themselves in their dead child's dirty underwear than wash it and give it away. But to leave the child's room the way the child had left it—that seemed the most insulting thing. Of course, Gwen didn't wish to forget her son. She only wished to kill off all the terrible things that didn't remember him, that went on and on without him. In the bedroom above, John was already getting ready for work. She heard him pause at the tie rack, his fingers outstretched but empty as if they'd forgotten what they were supposed to be doing. She used to love that about her husband. The lapses into which his serenity plunged him, the hush that fell around him when he did the most purposeful things.

She wouldn't see him to the door this morning.

She reached to strip the sheets off Johnny's bed, the pad from the mattress. She'd make the bed up fresh. Only then would she lay herself down on the cool, taut linens and be as close to him as the difference between the living and the dead might allow.

But the sheets wouldn't come off.

Johnny wouldn't release them.

He tugged and twisted. He grunted and fought.

For he was right there in bed, just as Gwen hadn't quite allowed herself to believe he would be.

3

Yes, Jack was charitable but not all the time. Were other women nude under their nightgowns? The answer depended on what a person—Jack, to be exact—considered *nude* to be. Polly had been nude every minute, nude under her dresses, nude under her coats, her stockings, her blouses, her skirts, her jackets, her scarves, her robes, her three-button suits, her bath towels, her blankets, the sweaters she borrowed from Jack's shelves in the closet. No matter what girdled Polly, her slender, soft body was always underneath it ready to be both yielding and confrontational, the puckered belly to be fiercely, unresistingly kneaded, the stretch marks thirsty for Jack's saliva. Her thighs and breasts, her laughter, her perspicacity, her mixture of slyness and modesty. Her pulse, her sex, her practical jokes. The backs of her knees, the tease of her fingers, her most sudden and patient of kisses—all nude under her belted, flared, ardent yet virginal clothing, and when the clothing was removed, then—Jack still needed to shut his eyes tight when he remembered. His black hair trembling, but not a speck of gray.

In bed, Jack watched from over his book as a woman on TV cleansed her pores with a cotton ball dipped in skin cream. The scent of the cream would be pleasant, even alluring. Her wrists in the mirror, as she swiveled to pin back her hair, were certainly female if not womanly, tapered if not graceful. Soon she twisted the wedding ring from her finger. The broad straps of her night-gown were colorfully embroidered, like delicate versions of the straps that held Jack's camera and binoculars. The actress wouldn't be nude under her nightgown even if she did pull it over her head. Even were the nightgown to be discarded, the robe flung from the set, the dressing table lamp bright or dark, it didn't matter, she would not, would never, be nude.

Naked, maybe.

Bare assed.

In spite of himself, Jack felt his sex quicken under the folds of the bedclothes, observed the sheet's undisguised accommodation. Funny. Some nights it seemed the whole room knelt over him, the bare ceiling white as the nape of a neck, bending to him.

4

Tip wrapped his arms around the girl who had snuck in Johnny's bed with him and with his tongue found the open flap of the collar of her flannel shirt. He pressed his lips against the button, holding his breath.

He'd been sleeping.

But he'd been awakened by girls often enough to know what was expected of him.

Foremost, he wasn't supposed to be surprised.

Instead he was supposed to behave as if he'd been waiting for her. Not *expecting* her, really, for it didn't reflect well on a girl to imagine she might sneak into the bed of someone who might not even know her name. But he was supposed to have been *wanting* her, his body if not his more considerate mind poised with anticipation of her appearance, and yet, poised as well with incredulity when she finally did appear.

Still, he felt he shouldn't reveal to her the truth about his fantasies—that the more extravagant they were, the more likely they'd come true. No matter how much a girl appreciated being the object of a man's imagination, still, when she drummed up the courage to sneak into his bedroom, she meant to reveal herself to him in darkness more than in light, so he would discover the fault lines in her nature, the vulnerabilities, the apprehensive hunger or sadness she might at other moments disguise, but which tonight allowed her to be so brazen.

Which meant it was polite of him to examine her vulnerabilities while at the same time breathlessly not allowing them to get in the actual way. How did Tip know all this, at age seventeen?

Simple. He'd learned it from his brothers. But then he shrugged off that answer as being inadequate as well as untrue. He knew it better than his brothers. Besides, any man who hadn't figured out certain things by the time he turned twenty would probably never figure them out at all. Tip was just one of the lucky ones.

That answer, too.

Inadequate.

They never took off all their clothing before getting unexpectedly into bed, the girls.

Pretending to be nearly as surprised as he was, they always left something on as a gesture of submission in the face of their own boldness, or maybe only because they liked him to peel the clothing off them—the lace undershirt, the too tight blue jeans, the panties of which the clusters of floral nosegays couldn't be seen in the dark. But this one was cocooned—a flannel shirt over sweatpants and scratchy socks. Her mothy dishevelment presented a challenge. Who was she? In what other ways might she be unlike the others? It was a game of blind man's bluff, Tip unhesitatingly touching her broad back, her generous collarbone, through the flannel. Had she sat upright and still, he could have drunk from the hollows inside her collarbone, could have filled the scooped-out places with crème de menthe and lapped it like springwater from cupped palms.

But she was neither still nor quiet.

Crying, she told him again and again that she loved him.

Her voice sobbed and broke.

Tip was terribly embarrassed.

And frankly, put off.

But when a girl told you she loved you when you were in bed with her, it was only polite to kiss her. There would be time for remonstrance later.

Besides, a kiss stopped her from saying she loved you, while your tongue in her mouth excused you from needing to say it yourself, compensating at least a little for the knowledge that the real reason you weren't telling her you loved her was because you didn't.

Still, Tip didn't kiss her.

He was too surprised, even if he wasn't supposed to be. And shocked and confused. And aware that all at once he had a past, made of everything that had brought him to this peculiar giddy moment. He was like someone who'd parked his car too casually at the top of a steep hill and now stood watching the car roll backward, the driver's seat empty, the rear wheels not having been correctly angled to the curb. He felt at once unburdened and yet neither flexible nor strong enough for the maneuvers that might be required of him. His family sometimes skied in Colorado, and for a moment the idea of becoming a ski bum presented a plausible mode of escape. He might open a Jack of Steaks in Denver, where one Sunday at Red Rocks Amphitheater he would come upon the same three girls he'd once glimpsed near the fountain while on a visit with his family, but now that he was living in Colorado by himself, the three girls would lead him home and want to fuck him all at once. Was this a fantasy? Did that mean it was going to happen? He hadn't intended to get a hard-on. He made the girls disappear. The car rushed down the hill and whipped around a noisy corner, the three longhaired girls allowed their six breasts to flop against his face before they dressed and went home. Then, when the excitement was over, certainty took its place. Years from now, on a visit to another city, Tip would watch a man nearly die in a drive-by shooting on the sidewalk in front of a supper club where Tip had mistaken chopped liver for chocolate pudding at the salad bar, and though he didn't foresee this or even surmise it, he understood that from now on it would be best to continue to see the humor in things even while he took them more seriously than before. Already he'd figured out, from the sound of her voice and the muscular definition of her body under her sloppy clothing, who had climbed into bed with him. He didn't know what he would do about it except take it seriously and think it was kind of funny at the same time, especially because he already did love her, in a way. For years he'd admired Gwen without thinking about it, the way any boy might become loyal to his best friend's mother because of the granulated brown sugar she replenished in the bowl on the kitchen table where he was so welcome for breakfast. Except for Pepsi, Tip wasn't fond of sweets, but he always sprinkled some of the strange hard beads of sugar on his cereal, because she offered it to him.

For the moment, it was only a white lie not to tell her who he was. He wasn't hurting anyone by pretending to be Johnny, the way she wanted him to be. She hugged him, she planted him with motherly kisses, trembling, too frightened not to be frantic, for if she let herself be calm she might need to admit her mistake. The darkness made it easy not to take a good look at each other. As did the twisting sheets and blankets make it easier to go on wringing incoherent declarations out of each other, as did the flavor of crème de menthe make it simpler for Tip to imagine he really did like sweets, because Johnny had liked them. He scrunched his eyebrows. He made himself too nervous to press his tongue anymore against the button on her collar the way the flannel seemed to invite him to do. He pretended the sheets were the cool lake, and that he'd pulled himself free of it limb by Johnny's limb, and that here he was, halfway between gruesome and a joke, but neither one nor the other as long as she kept saying how glad she was to see him.

The next night and the next, their groping gave way to embrace. Each day, Gwen's fingers ached simply to graze the idea of Johnny, while Tip found himself itching to be, just for a moment, somebody's son. In the darkness each night after he'd climbed down the ladder and made his way through the window over the desk, Gwen's hands slid maternally just to the back of his neck, while his own hands filially avoided the comfortable sweep of her hips. For sixteen nights this went on. On the nights Tip wore his bathrobe, a piece of paper crackled faintly between them in the pocket, and on the nights he wore his blue jeans, the denim drew a fine lint from the nap of her sweats. But both of them knew Tip couldn't be Johnny forever. He couldn't stand being undrowned night after night, and not making noise, and not making trouble, and not playing, just playing, with the top button of Gwen's shirt, because it was a shirt, with the acquiescence of any girl's shirt even though she was a woman.

Once he brought himself to say to her, "We can't kiss on the lips, but that doesn't mean we can't—"

"Shhh," she interrupted, not wanting to hear his voice.

"We can't even touch each other's bare skin, but that doesn't—"

"Shhh," Gwen scolded.

She forgives me, he thought, for having sat on the dock on the pyramid of careless teenagers, joking around while Johnny was stuck underwater. Indeed she lay very close to him, pressing up. No longer did he smell of crème de menthe. His breath was sharp with the odor of Pepsi. Johnny, who worried all sodas would make him jittery, caffeine or not, had never drunk Pepsi. He drank malted milk, iced milk, and Carnation Instant Breakfasts. None of these things smelled of Pepsi. Tip always did. It was the only sweet he liked except for a little brown granulated sugar, Gwen knew. She pressed her nose to his face as if to prove to herself that Tip wasn't Johnny. Sadness was to be expected. Grief there was nothing to be done about. On the other hand, love, Gwen remembered Polly Baymiller once having told her, was not a state of mind but a method of being, you have to act on the feeling in order to make it count.

Relieved that Johnny's best friend forgave her for lifeguarding the wrong body of water, Gwen pressed her knee against Tip's knee, hard and flush. Tip pressed his knee against hers in return. For a moment they were like two people holding open the same door for each other, each urging the other to be first to step through. Were they going to make love? Being so patient, so eager, so ashamed, so defiant, their uncertainties converged in a ticklish, perplexing way, until Gwen felt a sneeze coming on. No one could kiss with a sneeze in her nose, a horsy arch in her neck, a ridiculous grimace of teeth.

Tip climbed out of bed and made for the window over the desk, where the night sky was a high round pale green, like the rind of a scooped-out melon. If he and Gwen became lovers, he realized, then she would never touch him like a mother again. If Gwen and he became lovers, then Tip wouldn't scrunch up his eyebrows like Johnny's again, Gwen warned herself, stifling her sneeze by pinching her nose with her fingers.

The gesture shocked her by reminding her of her husband, whose shouts were nasal when he came. Orgasming, John brayed. She wondered if he might do it still. She hoped he would; she could practically hear it, could feel the high vibration in the wings of her pelvis.

Tip climbed through Johnny's window onto the lawn but managed not to indulge in the familiar, shoutable fact of having left another woman behind on a bed, as if Gwen were just another of the whole Taoist universe of girls. Collective blame, collective forgiveness would be Tip's outlook on sexual love, he understood at that moment. You make up to one girl by pleasing the next. You punish one by shortchanging her successor. He crossed the lawn to the ladder, let his moccasins slip off his feet to the grass as he climbed to his room, found some money in his dresser for a night out at Harry's. Harry's was a bar he liked to go to, a hole in the wall, or maybe two holes in two walls for there was a back room also, with two dartboards facing opposite directions, one higher than the other to make up for the slanted floor. The bar stools had never been properly bolted to the linoleum and the pool table was pushed so close to the bathroom that often players found it necessary to open the bathroom door in order to line up a shoot. Every Tuesday Harry's held a lottery. The winner bought rounds for everyone else.

Tip had won seven of Harry's lotteries since he'd turned seventeen, too young to be legal. Three hundred and fifty dollars' winnings, though Tip had fantasized more like five hundred.

Everyone knew he was lucky, but Harry couldn't forbid him from playing and still let him buy drinks.

Leaving his bedroom with a couple of dollars for beer in his pocket, Tip finally did climb out the wrong window just as he'd imagined he would sixteen nights ago, and no Florida grapefruits cushioned his fall as they'd cushioned his father's.

But all he got was a grassy thump on the ass. Ignore the pain and it will go away. Tip pulled himself off the jolt of the ground and, forgetting to look for his fallen moccasins, was still swearing amiably when he reached Harry's.

5

With a dry clap of thunder, autumn would someday come to a close. Impending snow would cast its cold light over the landscape before it fell, would freeze the mud white in the fields and bury icicles of dew in the funneled leaves of corn plants. Soon the drifts of the bodies of the second hatch of lake flies, which had swarmed around the telephone wires all through August before turning to fish-stinking dust on the roads and sidewalks, would be swept out of sight on the backs of the raked-up leaves. The birds would dress less flashily, the rabbits turn subtle with camouflage, the pine cones fall like dud grenades to their first dormant season. Over a single two-day period in mid-September approximately twenty thousand frogs attempted crossing a half-mile stretch of Highway D west of town, in search of squishable mud in which to hibernate come winter. "Name what part I am for, and proceed," declared the same Fisheries biologist who'd discovered the wrecked wing of Tom Bane's biplane eight years before. Now she knelt on the berm of the highway among the collage of squashed and hopping amphibians, only mildly chagrined to find herself unable to identify the living from among the green-yellow muck of the dead. What was the species? Too big for peepers, too numerous for leopard, was her private, beleaguered assessment. She'd never memorized her amphibians. They jumped every which way, though there was plenty of not yet frozen mud for every single one of them on either side of the treacherous asphalt, acres and acres of placid cold brown muck for the webfooted creatures, with their matter-of-fact grins, to hide out in.

"If I were you I'd just stay where the hell I already was," warned the Fisheries biologist, ducking the gust of a passing, smacking auto, the thump of frog on fender echoing behind as it continued on the highway. At least they weren't midwife toads,

Alytes obstetricans, her favorite of all surviving animals, the legs of the postmating males garlanded in strands of gelatinous eggs.

"Yeah, I'd stay put if I were a frog," the biologist repeated ironically, too self-aware to miss the self-directed wit. She'd already stayed put, for longer than any frog would likely tolerate. She'd stayed where the hell she already was for years, had chosen this long, dormant season, draped herself in dull plumage, hibernated in her cluttered living room and between the cinder-block basement walls of her office, protecting herself not from cold, exactly, but from coldheartedness. Her own, not to mention anybody else's. In spring she'd give it up, climb out of the ground, make herself eminently woundable again. Fall in love again, maybe, and though she shuddered at the notion, would not let herself cowardly relinquish it. If life was too short, this coming winter would feel like eternity. Why wait until spring? she asked herself suddenly. Why not do the foolhardy, masochistic thing now?

Because, she reasoned, spring mating was part of the natural order, the time everyone large and small makes asses of themselves. She might even get her ears pierced, come spring, she decided, more resolute than ever to hold off until then and stay safe and unadorned through the final months of her self-imposed years-long winter. She would earn those pierced ears. She would earn her next mistake by being too careful too long.

Soon she rose from her crouch to head for the sawhorses in the back of the DNR four-wheel. The highway department wouldn't care enough about frogs to close the highway, so she erected the barriers herself. ROAD CLOSED TO THROUGH TRAFFIC, two on either end of the half-mile stretch of frog crossing. On reflection she pulled out two DETOUR signs fitted with reflectors and set them up with the arrows pointing backward up the road, away from the trilling frogs. She might have stood a while longer just watching, but when a shotgun was fired in the distance where a footbridge crossed the marsh, she had a duty to check it out. Duck hunting season was past. Quickly the biologist put the four-wheel in drive and wondered how many frogs she'd find glued to the treads of her boots when she finished work for the day. She pulled away just casually enough to watch the first motorist stymied by the frog crossing detour. In her rearview she made sure he stopped as ordered. Many teenagers, not to mention a few grown men, would give their you-know-whats for a chance to nail down a hopping carpet of frogs.

John pushed his sunglasses high on the crown of his head, then repositioned them squarely on the bridge of his nose and stared past the sawhorse at the spectacle it had saved him from being too much a part of. No matter how he looked at them, the frogs were just frogs, thousands upon thousands upon thousands. If a single frog was in itself unextraordinary, half a million shouldn't be so spectacular. But a single frog wasn't unextraordinary, really, at least John wouldn't once have thought so. When he was in medical school, any living thing had seemed a galaxy. A grasshopper had evolved its own natural laws, a mollusk its own imperturbable center of gravity, a slime mold its own predictable cycles, a lamprey its own mysterious but insurmountable reason for being.

John had been in Steven's Point ten hours that day and still hadn't got his chance on the witness stand for the defense. Was it true that the anesthesiologist on trial had failed to apprehend the oxygen deprivation during surgery? Apparently. Had the deprivation caused the patient's epilepsy? Certainly. But should the doctor be held to blame for his own failing? No. Why not? Because he was human. So by that account no one anywhere should be blamed for anything ever? John laid the sunglasses on the dashboard, pulled a box of Jordan almonds out of his briefcase, and sat back to watch the frogs' migration. Now and then, other motorists turned around on the road behind him in search of another route home. John could have driven through Omro, been ticketed for speeding at twenty-eight miles an hour, and bought a slice of soggy pizza at the Kwik Trip. Gwen wouldn't even get close to a pizza, not to mention Jordan almonds, unless she made the crust herself out of grated zucchini. But Omro was out of the question, as was all turning back. He would wait where he was, as stopped by the sawhorse as if he'd been stopped in time. Not with lethargy but with his usual multidose of serenity he would wait for nature to take its course. From what reservoir did he draw such a measure of peace? He didn't know. Tranquillity descended upon him as if plain air were a soporific. For a while after Johnny's death, he'd imagined rage to be his narcotic. But rage might make him floor the gas and aim for the detour sign. The sawhorse would gallop into a ditch. The dead frogs would skid under the speed of his tires, would splatter even as they trilled.

"Someday you'll wake up feeling a little better than you do now," he would lie to the frogs as they turned into Rorschach prints on his windshield, just as he'd lied to himself and Gwen, because so far it hadn't turned out to be true.

For two hours he sat. The sun sank directly into a silo but the frogs were like marbles tossed on asphalt. The three most unbearable questions became: Why did the frogs remain on their side of the detour sign? Were the same frogs hopping back and forth, or did those north of the highway hop endlessly south, and those south, hop north? Of what grand design of nature, of which of so-called God's incorrigible plans, were the frogs a small, multiplied part?

Because there wasn't an answer, John forgave them all. The frogs weren't to blame for anything anywhere ever. The sun was too far away to be blamed, the frogs only four legs and a leftover stub of tail. The moon came up. Maybe the evening sky—a sky like a scooped-out, split-open melon—was responsible, somehow, for his suddenly unquenchable thirst for Gwen, who for sixteen nights had hidden behind Johnny's door. If only John got close to her, he might forgive her, too. Absently, he stepped from his car, pulled the sawhorse to the berm, drove slowly the half mile to the next sawhorse. The frogs turned to pudding under the wheels, bounced like Superballs off the fender. He wasn't killing them, exactly. They were only dying. Like everything died, sooner or later, as was natural.

By the time John reached home and made his awkward way to Gwen in Johnny's room, he'd missed Tip's fortunate exit over the math book and through the window, missed even Tip's lucky jump from Tip's second-floor window bearing money for Harry's Bar. John had no plans to sleep. All the nights Gwen had left him in their bed upstairs, he'd slept like the mouse he once found in a woodpile, snug in its nest of clippings. He'd thought it was from rage that he was able to sleep, pinned to the bed like a chloroformed specimen. But when he woke, it was never with rage. He could see that now. Every dawn he lit a stick of pine-smelling incense that reminded him of tennis, and when the incense turned to ash, he got up to wash his face. The ash was beautiful the way it clung to the stick in a fragile, looping thread that when he brushed clumsily against it would disintegrate, as did all ash, as did all things that ever turned to ash, as was natural.

When he opened Johnny's door and spoke his wife's name, Gwen lifted a freckled leg from under the sheets. John undid his necktie. Such a stupid fashion, neckties, and his woven belt too tight, and his socks slack around weak ankles. He threw the tie over a chair, kicked the chair farther under the desk than Johnny ever had. No matter what emotions roiled inside it, Gwen's body was as temperate as before, their lovemaking the same comfort to them as when they'd been ignorant of the need for comfort. Her breasts still as freckled, the valley between them still deep enough for him to lay his head.

7

Polly and the Fat Girl

Nursery rhymes nearly undid me, first time I saw the fat-girl policewoman. She believed she had all the time in the universe, but really, being human, she didn't have a second to spare for either nonsense or unrequited love. So I whispered to her, Whatever you would do if Tip wanted you to do it, he doesn't, so don't do it, sweet cop. Listen to me.

But she kept repeating the same nonsense anyway. Even unspoken, even having only just pushed their way to the surface of all the never-to-be-uttered declarations anyone carries inside them, the fat-girl policewoman believed her words to be tough enough to chew on till the dish ran away with—

"No I didn't, but if you want me to I will," she planned on saying to Tip when he caught up with her. She'd catch him off guard the way he caught her a few hours before, when she came into Harry's. She showed up at Harry's so often she was one of the things Tip expected to see when he went there, only not like a girl but one of the fixtures, gaudy but usual, like one of the beer ads lit up with neon. She wore a dark bead on a ring in her nose. She had a fresh, new perm with a smatter of henna that flashed a double take when Tip said what he said to her, loud enough for everyone to hear.

I will if you want it, she answered, only deep down where no one would catch it. How much private property can one girl hide behind a leather jacket? At Harry's, no one knew she was a cop. And they wouldn't have guessed she wanted a baby, either, though that was their blind spot, not mine. I could see it right away in the way she eyed the room when she sat on the tuffet— bar stool, I mean—like all she needed was a reason not to visit Harry's anymore as long as it was something she could rock in her arms.

Her unspoken words' delicate pinging would have surprised her, a sound like a ladybug clicking its wings on a sill. I didn't understand what she meant by them. She didn't what? If Tip wanted what, what would she do? But that didn't matter because he wouldn't want it anyway. Not from someone as clutchy as she was. Ladybug, get lost, I whispered to the fat girl, but that was only the beginning. There was an old pig sat down on a clover, thirty-seven patty-cakes baked in a shoo fly don't hoodwink my son, I whispered to her.

Her drink matched her fingernail polish. What the bartender mixed in to make it that color, I'd rather not have to know. But what plump forearms the fat girl had. The wrists pinched small as if by two corsets. Her hands like the quick, pointed swoop of two swallows, her finest feature, thus the black lace gloves designed to show them off. A new idea, these gloves, to be left on the bar near her barely sipped drink before she set off on her walk. Her idea, not mine. She meant for Tip to pick the gloves up, then come running after her to satisfy her fantasy the same time she satisfied his. But he was biding his time on the thresh-old of the dart room and didn't see her go. There must have been a nursery rhyme with corsets, and one with lace gloves as well, from the stack of yellow records I used to play for the twins whenever I was dressing to go out with Jack. Soon it was like opening a can of dog food and in march the puppies. No sooner had I switched on the twilight on my dressing table mirror than in toddled Jenna and Drew dragging their record player by the thick plastic handle, a box heavier than all the king's hatboxes, I always remarked, unbuckling the lid and sliding the whole thing into the big walk-in closet, where they liked to sit and listen among the clothes bags and coats. From where I sat at the mirror choosing lipstick and earrings, I never could quite follow those nursery rhymes, a shoe bag full of mismatched slippers, laces, boots, buttons, and buckles. But it was pleasant enough to tune in and out of. Housekeeping was never my boldest enterprise when I was alive, but the messes I kept had a certain pizzazz. I remember the wet towels heaped on the bathroom tiles, the curtains awry so the weather roared in through the windows, the towels all sifting snowily on top of one another under the soles of our feet. I remember the soaps cracking slowly down the middle, the fresh bars too large for the twins' squeezed bottoms. I remember when Handi Wipes came on the market, how ugly they looked all scrunched in the bucket instead of the bleached recollections of rags. The kids' undies were my favorite kind of rags, all the stained-up torn cotton crotches that couldn't be properly mended or bleached. I knew a lady once who scrubbed them with Ivory Snow on spare toothbrushes forgotten by houseguests, but me, I threw them in the rag bin—Looney Tunes, comic book heroes, days of the week, and little nosegays of posies. On the other hand I never could walk on a rag rug dressed in any shoes worth crossing from one side of a room to the other in, and now that I'm a ghost, I'm all bare floors and hallways, anyway. Skid marks and dead leaves. Waltzes and thunks. Sun motes, muddy hems, cheek to cheek, and dust, dust, dust.

What didn't you do but you will if Tip wants you to? I couldn't stop myself from asking yet again, but the unmindful fat girl only continued down the sidewalk away from Harry's Bar. I'd missed what Tip said when she sat at the bar with the ring in her nose and patted her lace gloves to sleep on the counter. Now I heard it in her mind like a kink in the plumbing, but still I didn't understand; didn't know what he meant, and couldn't make sense of her answer.

"Did you pierce your clit, too?"

Tip had shouted the question. Not even he could believe he had done such a thing, but he knew he'd get used to it, fast. Not many men could get away with what he got away with, he was happy to remind himself. His forthrightness turned women on. The more forward he was on the outside, the more gentlemanly he was on the inside, they all understood. But the fat girl was incensed, as she had a right to be. She took a final few sips—like sucking the fingernails off her own fingers, that drink—and gave a fond backward glance at the black napping gloves on the bar. Harry's was so flimsy the front stoop quaked from the music she left on the jukebox, a song meant for Tip although Tip had been snookered into a game of darts. He thought she would come up behind him to play. He pressed a dart to his nose, wondering how many parts of his fantasy might be rescinded before its attainment. The woman he'd imagined in his fantasy of gloves was . . . well . . . not fat. But he found he wasn't burdened by the discrepancy. He threw a hard triple nine. Too much of a good thing wouldn't hurt him. Besides, asking his question the way he had, he'd wounded her a little—the dark bead quivering against the cleft of her nose, the delicate sips she took of her drink as if to camouflage the sucking hole he'd made in her demeanor. He hadn't meant to be crude. He only meant to take hold of crudeness, per se, and establish it as one of the possible routes to the fulfillment of all curiosity. Or something like that. He might explain that to her. Then she'd breathe her answer in his ear, or at least tell him he was a jerk, the least he could do was buy her another green drink.

As for sweet cop, she was trying not to mind that Tip wasn't following her yet along the night-dappled sidewalk. Her footsteps impressed me; they were as ladylike as the boots she pretended to strut in; pointy-toed, spike-heeled lace-ups with the folded-over cuffs that keep going out of fashion in order to come back in. A person could crochet doilies with those heels, so precisely did they click click on the sidewalk, but she couldn't strut to save a ladybug's life. She was too eagerly maternal to strut, the boots so agleam with hopefulness I searched for my reflection in the points of the toes to find out which of us would be more ladylike if only I could be seen.

I couldn't be.

Which is always a terrible insult, no matter how many times I try catching a casual glimpse of myself but see no one glancing back at me at all.

I would have been, though.

The more ladylike. Of the two of us.

Jack would have thought so, by far.

Jack wasn't big on big, he used to say.

He was big on slender.

Then he'd take his big and press it up against my slender to prove he meant what he said. If only I had the fat girl's live shimmer, I could wrap my invisible fingers more tightly around the memory. Jealousy's a ladylike emotion, so for the moment I was content to be jealous of the fat girl. The slender ankles of her stretch pants under the swing of the rest of her made me long to be the next one to topple under a man's slightest push. One night, Jack waltzed us right off the edge of the pontoon, not into the lake but onto an inflatable raft on a double bed of algae so phosphorescent the face in the moon could have seen us, but we did it anyway. The slosh of the raft I could almost remember. The murky puddles under my elbows I almost remembered, the sting of a mosquito bite on the sole of my foot and the oily heat of citronella in every breath we shared I could nearly reimagine before the memory shuddered and flipped inside out, turning voices and pictures to the Night's stern hands on my shoulders, although I had no shoulders.

A dish and a cow. A spoon jumping over a flame. I still didn't know *clit* from a nursery rhyme. Whatever Tip doesn't want but he would if you did it, don't, I reminded the fat girl. When she swiveled her chin past the leather shoulder of her jacket, that's when she caught sight of the person who'd followed her out of the bar. Not Tip but a tall man with shoulders as knobby as Grandma's bedposts, still better than no man's shoulders at all, we agreed. It was the man with the hairy knuckles who tended the bar, tended it like it was something needing taking care of. My doing, his laying eyes on the black lace gloves. Thinking they were bra and panties, he lifted them as tremblingly as if someone were still inside them. A swizzle stick clung to a seam. He let it fall on the floor in his rush to lurch after her, moved like a dust ball under the dresser when somebody opened a window, nervous the broom might sweep him away. Pretending not to have noticed, the girl zipped her jacket and walked past her car. I had to crinkle my nose at that jacket, though I had no nose. Jack wasn't fond of leather on women. Like being naked on top of her clothes, a woman in leather. The girl was twenty-two going on forever was how she felt every morning when she slung on her holster, Madame in a Western movie. Every day at least once, she wished cops still rode horses so she could gallop and get paid at the same time. The saddle bucking underneath her as she wrote out traffic tickets, the vampy spurs a perfect match for the dark accessory of fingernails. *Vampy* was her word, not mine. It made me think of sad clowns, and of the tears of the cowboys on velvet paintings, the paintings so lonesome they came in pairs. I didn't want her to be a lonesome cowgirl. Nor did I want her digging her spurs into Tip, reigning him in with my grandchild. Suddenly all that was my purpose. I'd never thought about purpose when I was alive, I just went ahead and fulfilled it. But now I needed to recite it, like prayers. Please, dear ghost, let Tip grow up healthy and happy, was always the first and the last, no matter what came between. I hate to see a mother so lonely for her son, was one of the others, whispered to Gwen as she sat up nights after Johnny was drowned, her wet cheek lathering the flecks in the cool Formica.

You're making creases in your face, if you lie that way much longer your skin'll get stuck in that position and never smooth out, I teased my old friend that first night I quit my sightseeing trip through Iola and dusted my way to her darkened kitchen. Get up, Gwen. Is that the broiler still going? The back door unlocked? A sparrow in the back porch batting the screen and the porch lights left on?

Gwennnnn . . .

Hey, Gwen! I called, not a prayer anymore but a plea, knowing something was terribly wrong the second I knew what it was. Johnny's drowning was as horrible to me as if I weren't dead myself, as if I were still more mother than ghost.

I placed my hand on Gwen's shoulder. She made a move to shut them off, the lights on the porch.

Except, they weren't on.

Nor was the broiler.

She could see both of those perplexing facts the second she nearly stood up, but still she didn't suspect me. She was only a little put out when she plunked herself back in her chair. Do some chores, Gwen, they'll make you less desperate, I whispered, or just open every bottle in the house and smell the insides, for that's what I used to do when I was feeling low and there was no havoc in sight. The shampoos, the bath gels, the extracts, vinegars, and juice bottles, the body oils and cooking oils and every perfume decanter and nail polish remover and Vicks VapoRub bottles and bottles of mustard and Worcestershire sauce and plastic screw-top limes and lemons and Jack's aftershave, margarita mix and Tabasco. I said, Just a whiff of that health food soy milk, Gwen, and you'll be dizzy as a bride on a flagpole.

She wasn't wearing a brassiere.

Me, I'd have sooner spent a week without my underpants on. But to each her own.

Otherwise I might have told her to wash her lingerie. Really I only wanted her to perform some healingly ordinary task upon some daily object. There really was a sparrow trapped in Gwen's screened porch. The bottle of milk in the refrigerator was going south. The jar of shoe polish on the shelf in Johnny's closet had never once been opened. Only this last remark, about the jar of shoe polish being unopened the way Johnny had left it, on the shelf where he'd left it, was enough to make his mother get out of her chair.

Gwen was shaking like a china cabinet when she reached for Johnny's fingerprints still scrolled against his doorknob. Her pulse echoed against the hollow-core door that swung back from her touch as if ushering her toward the desk, where she found his well-thumbed math book open to a sketch of parallelograms, which looked like what happens to cakes if you open the oven too soon. The cake sinks in the pan, you have to cut it into shapes and make a tugboat like that was the plan all along. The things they had us housewives do! Mr. Clean was really Yul Brynner, I used to speculate. And guess what was cooking under the Jolly Green Giant's spinach leaf? Gwen tittered inside me. We were standing pulse to pulse when she turned off the desk light. But I couldn't comfort her myself. It takes practice, being a ghost, and I didn't know how to help her. I was nothing but the static in the flannel of her shirt and how the posters seemed to quiver on the wall. How dusky it was in the Night's house inside me, where every breath Gwen held made my stairs creak under the carpet. She was thinking about the laundry unwashed in the closet, where Johnny must have left it, and how curious it was that his bed smelled of mint. The sharp, soothing blade of a butter knife was the closest I came to recalling the smell. Jack used to wear not the perfume but the color, so I knew it wasn't Jack we heard rustling under the covers. I hoped it was Johnny, back from the dead like I was, so quickly he still smelled of toothpaste.

I was more surprised than Gwen was when she pulled back the covers, climbed into bed, and discovered through her sobs that it was . . .

I didn't let her quite see it was Tip, of course. I let her think Tip was Johnny, at least for a minute, an hour, a week. I was pleased with myself, having made up my mind that the way to help Gwen, and Tip as well, was for the two of them to comfort each other.

I remembered I'd been in Johnny's room before it was completed, long before the first family moved out and Gwen's moved in, when all the houses started going up around us in our new neighborhood. Let's trespass, we'd say, and Jack would give me a boost where the steps would soon be. Being tight with the developer, Jack kept the blueprints scrolled in his head. He knew all the bedrooms when there was nothing but ductwork. We had a picnic in this one, me and Jack among the knots on the subfloors. I was happily distracted. No food at that picnic but the flavor of untreated pine and the rich, male shouts of construction workers up and down our corner of the street.

We can't do this here, I remember Jack argued, so I excused myself a minute, stepped outside with a bullhorn, made my voice deep as coffee, and gave all the workers the whole short rest of the gorgeous day off, with pay.

They took my booming word for it, to my surprise. Hoots and hollers filled the air and then only the chatter of birds.

No bra, Tip discovered, snapping me out of my reverie.

No brassiere, I corrected.

No bra, he retorted, running his hand along the back of Gwen's shirt. He still didn't know it was Gwen, but that wasn't my doing. He still believed it was a classmate but not for long. The very first of many arguments I was to win with my son come hell or boiling water, I realized. He argued just like his father. It's Gwen. No, it isn't. No bra. No brassiere. No underpants. Panties. Underpants. Panties. Brassiere. Bra. Gwen. No, it isn't. If she's not wearing it anyway, what does it matter? It does. Doesn't. Underpants. Panties. I confess I took some pleasure in the warmth they stirred up those first couple of minutes not wanting to know who each other was.

The moonlighting bartender, Fuzzy Knuckles, who worked the day shift at Miles Kimball, trailed the fat girl past the cars. Ten or eleven were parked at the curb between Harry's and the bar with the Halloween decorations next corner over, and three pickup trucks crowded the dead end sign where the road sloped so abruptly into the lake that when the fat girl approached it she felt cocky with dread and bravery like someone walking a plank. The bartender planned to follow her overboard. She was fatter than she looked in those stretch pants and that tight shine of blouse she wore under her jacket, he surmised. Such toothpick legs, but such colossal olives on top of them. Undressing her would be like biting into the ice cube and finding the inside already melted, he imagined inside me, his tongue mopping the thirst from his own mouth as he noted the yellowing pillars adorning the Legion Hall. In the town he'd grown up in, the Legion Hall was nothing but an out-of-business Chinese restaurant paneled in cheap veneer still tacky with MSG, but here the hall was like a classy hotel gone to seed, where he and she might honeymoon together before setting up house somewhere, he was already thinking, already taking a third job to tide them over in hard times that they probably wouldn't run into, but still there was Fuzzy Knuckles Junior to think of.

On the *portico,* he grandly decided. Near the heap of lawn

chairs under the big tree, left over from somebody else's sloshed wedding. That's where they'd welcome Junior into the state of Wisconsin.

"Slow down," he said to the unmindful girl, who liked to watch her pointy boots bisect the cold wind off the lakeshore. "Give it up," she said over her shoulder, still craning her neck for Tip's late appearance, then gasping at the sight of a ball of black fur being blown out from under the chairs. Like a toy on my steps, that cat, kicked by the wind every which way but home. White skin showed between the ripples in its fur.

Poor cat, I thought.

Kitten, she corrected. Needing to be delivered to the pound.

A small cyclone of wind began turning the kitten in circles. It had to step on its own paws in order not to get swept into the seethe of the lake like its lost tabby sister, whom it remembered just enough for me to get a glimpse of the memory—drenched fluff perching tamely on a rock near the jetty's outer shore, transfixed by lapping water and fits of spray. Brushfires, burning on the opposite shore of the lake, enlightened it. As if in response to a high-pitch summons, the tabby's ears were aimed like fitful arrows toward the foam, into which it stretched its paw and was lassoed by its flea collar into the surf, where for a moment the animal whirled like a shirt in a clothes dryer before sinking from its black sibling's view. The fat girl finally caught the frightened black kitten and scooped it up eye to eye. Forget the pound. She'd keep the vagabond. How shivery it was! It weighed hardly more than a fresh tube of lipstick. Tip would scratch the kitten with his pinkie between its ears, she imagined, having noticed in Harry's the way Tip's little finger curled away from the mug whenever he drank his beer. He'd be mortified if he realized he did that. Too swishy, he'd say. She was smarter than I'd thought. And sweeter of heart. She gave a brush of her lips along one kittenish whisker, kissing away the few clinging drops of moisture. One whisker after another she cleaned this way, then plucked a blown leaf from the nape of the kitten's tail. The bartender gaped from a distance. He was stiff as a drink, his words, not mine, watching her gaudy fingernails turn so achingly gentle under the kitten's arms. Torture, he thought, a bed of those nails. The kitten batted a sopped paw at the ring in her nose. "No, I didn't, but if you want me to I will," she had to stop herself from saying, imagining the kitten was Tip. But she was well turned and stylish under all of that cheek, the fat-girl policewoman. She gave a pleasant, shy laugh when the kitten curled its tongue, wondering how she'd managed to be a cop for so long without ever having rescued a feline before.

"Truant," she scolded the kitten. "Are you stray, or abandoned?"

Abandoned, thought the bartender dismally, as the girl removed her jacket and slid the shivering kitten into a sleekly lined sleeve. The kitten slid to the cuff and clung there, glad to be free of the wind and the terrible magnet of water. The girl cradled the sleeve, crooning, "Rock-a-bye, baby." Demanding its sibling, the kitten mewed. Through his resoled shoes, the bartender felt the wind grow more fiercely persistent. Around the foot of the dead end signpost on the boat ramp lay a drift of broken mussel shells and bone-colored spirals, but across the lawn the yellowed porch of the Legion Hall flapped its striped awning in welcome.

Don't be such a lonesome cowboy, I whispered to the bartender. Neither I nor the fat girl had ever seen a man who'd nicked himself so often shaving. He'll be awful in bed, the fat girl supposed. But she was just midcycle—the first twinge of an egg just beginning to squeeze—and so optimistic she could practically feel it quicken. Besides, he'd look cute pushing a stroller, she noticed, stifling the ticklish start of a sneeze.

Fuzzy Knuckles had a vision of a toddler wearing Dad's barbecue apron, stuffing the pockets with the scavenged shells.

Anyway, what's one night? the girl realized. Maybe an hour or two. If we do it on the porch, I can get away easy. Thing is, it helps to lie down awhile after so he doesn't spill out of me.

"You're under arrest. Anything you say might be used against you," she announced to the bartender. He heard her even through the wind. The white bulk of the Legion Hall unrolled a carpet of grass.

He put up his hands, palms open, then leaned forward against a tree to be properly searched. The fat girl spread the jacket like a baby blanket under the chairs, and set to work obliging him with her trained fingers. Up one leg and down the other. Then up again and up again. For the moment neither one of them was lonesome, but the kitten forgot why it was hunkered in the sleeve. No one but me heard the pop of its claws as they pulled themselves free of the rayon lining, or watched the rear legs emerge from the ribs of the cuff. Despite my mute pleading, the kitten rolled straight for the lake all over again, drew its feet together on a rock, and dared the next wave to knock it into the current after its drowned sister. The ringing in its ears was high and piercing. All the jelly glasses splintered on the shelves in my cupboard when I realized what was making that sound. Tom Bane. And though it took me that long to realize he'd done the same thing to Johnny, when I knew it, I knew it for certain.

I had never been frightened of the lake before, had never objected to getting my feet wet, as we housewives used to say no matter how far out we swam. I remembered the petals, the fringes, the scalloped domes of our bathing caps, the rubber thongs left behind on the dock in ballet positions, the empty chaise lounges gossiping on the lawns, the wedges of lemon in half-empty pitchers of melting tea. I remembered my headstrong dives off the dock, after I'd properly stuck in my big toe and squealed.

But I couldn't dive now. I was frightened of the water, frightened by the ringing in the drowning kitten's ears, frightened of Tom Bane trapped in his sand bed, meek as he was and a nincompoop to boot but still a father I'd snatched out of fatherhood and sent caterwauling into an eternity of yearning.

Poor Johnny, I said to myself. Poor Gwen. Submerged, the kitten resembled a clot of wet fabric, a wet rag swirling in a vat of muddied dye.

The unmindful fat girl opened her eyes, watched some blustery branches swaying above her, and thought how wrong she had been when she'd surmised the bartender would be lousy in bed. They hadn't made it to the porch. She lay naked near the tree, her corpulence rather lovely under the cloudy moonlight. Fuzzy Knuckles agreed, and gave her what she was clutching at, gladly. She buried her cries in the crook of his knobby shoulder. How could she have missed him all these long months in Harry's, her eyes crossing the bar as if on tightrope to Tip when all along right before her was her kid's rightful dad? In an hour she'd be pregnant. A daughter, I hoped, fat like her mother, named Glinda for her resemblance to the Good Witch of the East floating toward Oz in a bubble.

Congratulations, sweet cop, I whispered. And to you, too, Fuzzy Knuckles, I added, matchmaker that I was.

But I was only a fledgling broom of a mother, wanting to sweep up Tip's regrets before they happened. Sweep sweep in too many directions. I needed a compass. I needed someone to help me navigate. What a time to feel nostalgia for my shoes, my bare feet steering clear of the undone housework around me, dropping the dust rag into the bucket. Never sordid, shoes. Innocent, even, compared to the places my barefooted ghostliness took me. The patents, the pumps, how solid the ground used to feel underneath them. The narrow gold straps of my cocktail sandals, six buckles per foot, and if I didn't buckle them quickly enough, the twins lined up to do them. The buckles as narrow as Jack's paper clips poking David and Dennis's smudgy noses when they rested their chins on my toenail polish. I missed the polish as well, all the orange, rosy things we women did to our feet. Lotions and pumice. Emery sticks. I used to sit straight legged on the floor in the kitchen and practice my arches, toes up, toes down, my feet like curved bridges that Drew and Douggie's toy train could pass under on its way to the toy post office. No one but Tip could arch his toes all the way to the linoleum like I could, but it's a talent he doesn't know he possesses and wouldn't like if he did. Too swishy, he'd say. The kitten sank in the lake. John soothed Gwen's wits with a back rub. Tom sang to his lake full of drownings. Tip headed for a Pepsi on the overgrown boardwalk in Butte des Morts. Where has love gone for the night? I whispered to my son, but the question I'd stolen from Sid wasn't enough to give Tip pause on his way out onto the quavering marsh. The Night must have known how impatient I was with my aimlessly balletic mopping, for It crooked Its elbow in mine with unexpected gallantry and led me off on my search for help.

8

The Traversable World

After she and her mother settled near the lake where the plane
had gone down, Honey no longer expected Angie to make
household decisions. So it was Honey who decided to carpet
their attached garage and hang curtains across the row of wobbly
glass windows. She secured the loose rungs of the ladder,
climbed with a broom to the rafters, swept the cobwebs full of
corpses of lake flies from the joists, covered the bulbs with bar-
gain fixtures, and informed her mother they would rent the
garage for living space "to a relaxed person who won't complain
if I use the driveway for my manicure stand." Already she'd
painted a *For Sale* sign for the boat, which needed to be wheeled
from the garage and towed to where it could be seen from
County Trunk A. She traded a college student a haircut and a set
of Ping-Pong paddles for him to hook the trailer to the back of
his truck and pull the boat twenty feet or so into the yard, since
he needed to pump the tires and resecure the bowsprit, after
which she inquired if he was interested in renting the garage and
if he knew any women who might go for a two-for-one intro-
ductory manicure deal.

"The apartment's got baseboard heating," she made sure he
knew. "Also the sink in the laundry room is for your conven-
ience. My mother grades papers upstairs, so you can't play music
unless it's something she likes." Honey indicated an enclosed
whitewashed stairway leading to Angie's attic.

"What does she like?" the student wondered.

"Rickie Lee Jones and Emmylou Harris," said Honey, making an apologetic face. She had planned on her mother's limited tastes being a problem, for Angie had strong opinions and blamed an occasional ringing in her ears on an unintended disharmony in the music Honey tried on her at dinner. Until recently, Angie hadn't listened to music at all. But Rickie Lee Jones's voice was like a flock of seagulls circling the nearby inlet, and Emmylou Harris's was like the moan and clang of a train so far down the tracks it couldn't be seen.

The student said he'd think about the apartment and that he'd tell his girlfriend about the manicure. Watching him go, Honey reconsidered another turnoff to potential tenants, which was that County Trunk A passed only steps from the door. But somehow the sailboat looked bigger outside the garage than in, and when glimpsed from between the boat and Angie's beat-up car in the driveway, the two-lane highway seemed less intrusive than before. The boat gave the house a secluded air, especially when the grass grew wispy and tall around it. Swallows fluttered where the tip of the mast would be, were the mast up instead of down, so Honey hired another couple of students to raise it in hopes the birds might nest there. The sails were missing, the rigging slack and frayed. Despite her fondness for the shipwrecked look of the vessel, Honey placed classifieds in all three valley papers, because she needed the money to buy and care for her puppies. In exchange for the first month's rent, maybe the garage tenant would build a pen. There was space in the backyard under a willow, around which fanned a cozy sprawl of other single-storey houses on adjoining swaths of grass. The boat had come with the house when her mother bought it upon selling the farm. Not including the bathroom and Angie's whitewashed attic study wedged in a corner above the garage, the house was just four small rooms. Angie had found a job teaching English composition at the local university and spent most of her time in her overstuffed chair in the attic, making notes, brackets, and arrows along the margins of her students' papers before returning them Mondays, Wednesdays, and Fridays to her office at school.

On the day Honey finally rented the garage, to a retired machinist who seemed glad to keep to himself and needed no kitchen because he ate at the senior citizens' center, Honey, wearing her knapsack, rode her bike to the animal shelter, where she purchased the first of the puppies. She and Angie had already filled out the paperwork and submitted to the required interview and visit, during which they kept to their agreement not to mention the pets that had come and gone before. Six hamsters, six kittens, two full-grown cats, one mouse, a ferret, a garter snake, a horned lizard, and two rabbits; during the first year in the new house, the pets had vanished week by week, except for the black-and-white rabbit, who caught his head in the gutter downspout and drowned. Honey and her mother had combed the culverts and shoulders of County Trunk A for miles along the railroad tracks, and stuck hand-lettered signs on the telephone poles, and driven out every night before dinner calling various names and stopping to check with neighbors, to no avail. Other than a shedded snake skin that turned up between the couch cushions, all that remained was a stray flea collar and a rubber ball stuck in the mirrored tunnel of the Hamster Haven.

Nevertheless, Honey wasn't sad about her pets' disappearance. Instead she was so relieved when she got home from school to discover that her pet was still waiting for her, that those days made up for the days when it wasn't. She thought of her pets the way people think of their grown children who've left home, missing them especially on holidays but viewing their left-behind water bowls as part of a natural order, thus sufferable. That they might be dead made no difference to Honey. What stung was that they no longer climbed onto her shoulder when she balanced the checkbook or made phone calls. The reason she planned on six dogs was that so many large animals all in a friendly tangle would be less likely to wander away without anybody seeing them go. Also, dogs responded to their names more than other animals were likely to do. Honey would name them after the lost kittens, her favorites among the pets. The first of the puppies, a yellow Lab, was named Happy, and appeared fully prepared to live up to her designation. She often smiled while chewing the strap of Angie's book bag or tumbling off the front step, and if not in sight was usually visiting Mr. Nichols, the tenant, who'd found an old telephone cord among his possessions and liked to time on his pocket watch the number of seconds it took Happy to disentangle her nose from the coils. He tended to confuse Happy's and Honey's names, but kept the garage carpet clean with a sweeper and remembered to unplug his hot pot when he wasn't heating water for a bouillon cube. He owned no TV and wore a headset for talk radio, so Angie was never disturbed by his presence. It was Honey who collected his rent on the fifth of every month and who calculated his share of the utility bills. Angie steered clear of the tenant. Their first month in town she'd seen the boy with the bicycle drown in the lake, or rather, had just missed seeing it happen, had turned away from the lake as if to save herself from seeing. However fleeting Angie's attachments to men, they were bound to lead to tragedy, Angie understood. Like the bewitched farmers' daughters in some of the weathered fairy tales on the egg crate shelves in her attic study, Angie was doom to all males who laid eyes on her for longer than a second. Some nights, Angie read the fairy tales to Honey while Honey painted Angie's toenails or fixed her cuticles. One of these nights, Angie decided that the topic that interested her most about fairy tales, and about which she'd write her dissertation if she ever got around to it, was that no matter how sad, the tales were comforting to read. They had a soothing vocabulary that might be put to good use in modern times. Angie might remind herself, "Once upon a time my husband failed to return home for supper," or "Once upon a time I saw a boy drown in a lake," and it didn't sound so terrible. At the grocery store, while putting back a two-dollar head of lettuce or choosing from among the pints of strawberries, Angie said to herself, "Thomas Bane, the farmer, had once found no greater enjoyment than to stack the fallen apples in their bins," and believed that if she turned around and saw her husband at that moment, she would forgive him even for dying.

Honey, whose view of the world was of a flexible continuum between what was offered and what was taken away, what was lost and what found, what attainable and what out of reach, had no need for the solace of fairy tales, and let her mother read them to her because she knew it helped Angie to do so. Honey's occasional bursts of regret for her father only strengthened her gratitude that he'd taken the trouble to put her on the planet before disappearing off the face of it. And it was a more than passable planet. The Rollerbladers drifting past in their fluorescent knee and elbow pads, the Thursday-night bands at Riverside Park within sight of where the drawbridge keeper stacked a pyramid of Dr Peppers in the window of his booth, the aisles of tropical fish tanks in the pet store where she purchased the crickets to feed her lizard—all affirmed her idea that nothing was more exotic than the ordinary, and nothing more ordinary than the exotic. The long Wisconsin winters, to which she was thoroughly accustomed, were tropical in their extremes. Lily pads froze harder than dessert plates atop their breakable stems. Along the lakefront, ice shoves erected themselves into jagged sunset-hued cliffs, and when the boat in the front yard became blanketed in drifts of snow, what more proof could Honey need that no place was more extraordinary than anyplace else? To Honey, the world seemed an infinitely traversable place, in which one rare object gave way to the next the minute she rounded a corner. Her vanishing pets were simply eager to find this out for themselves, as who wouldn't be, she asked, setting off along the railroad track with Happy on a leash and Mr. Nichols walking beside them swinging his Geiger counter between the ties. He had started making pop-top necklaces to sell at Honey's manicure stand, and though Honey didn't agree that her typical customers—women in bathing suits accompanying impatient boyfriends on fishing trips off Asylum Point Park nearby, or pairs of women driving to lunch at George's Gaslight Inn on Harrison Street—were likely to buy a pop-top necklace, she'd be glad to be surprised. Mr. Nichols only nodded, listening to the accelerated click of the Geiger counter before squatting to pry something loose from the gravel. Attached to his belt was a twisted handkerchief into which he dropped the pop-tops, but what he pulled from the gravel this time was a button with an anchor on it, the kind of button Honey often lost off the front of her pea jacket and needed to replace. He zipped it in the pocket of his parka. Like many old men, he was more self-absorbed than selfish, Honey saw, and he turned out to have been canny when he'd hit on the idea of the pop-top necklaces. Over the next couple of years, more and more women who got their nails done by Honey hung them from their rearview mirrors. Honey had a certain cachet, being so young and so freshly, naturally gorgeous, not to mention convenient and affordable. On Saturday mornings she set up her stand near the bleachers in the gyms and on the playing fields where the mothers came to watch their kids' basketball and soccer teams, and way before she got her driver's licence, used the car for weekly house calls to women whose fingers were puckered from warm baths. At high school she traded pedicures for term papers and social studies projects, and for copies of last year's algebra tests. Honey's boyfriends, none of whom interested her very much, felt more welcomed by the dogs than by Honey, so she took advantage of their visits by asking them to please hold the dogs in the tub for shampooing, then ushered the boys toward the garage so they could chat with Mr. Nichols about his gadgets while Honey scrubbed the tub and washed her own thick tendrils of hair in peace, and shaved her legs, and toweled herself clean with a few drops of baby oil. She liked her boyfriends but didn't see the point in going out with them to movies when she was more satisfied riding her bike along the railroad track or making house calls to women who wanted to tell her about things that had happened to them when they were Honey's age. Honey rarely had sex with her boyfriends, not because she thought sex was wrong, or because she worried about getting pregnant or sick. Sex just hadn't set itself apart from other activities yet, for her, and because she knew it might someday, she didn't want to take even kissing for granted. In bed with a boy, she felt she was in training for some more-authentic adventure, and when she tired of him, she relied on two methods of breaking up that wouldn't make the boy feel too diminished. One was to offer a puppy. Pedigreed or not, yellow Labs made smart, enthusiastic bird dogs, and since so many Wisconsin boys hunted, they longed to get their hands on one of those retrievers. Honey's favorites among the dogs had a slight brindle cast to the tips of their golden fur, like a souvenir of Honey's own coppery hair, but Honey kept those puppies for breeding. They were the smartest and the friskiest.

Honey's other method of breaking up was to send the boy up the whitewashed stairs to Angie's attic on the pretext of showing him the Eskimo tale in which the mother turns herself into a man by affixing to her body a penis made of bone and whale blubber, then sleeps with her daughter-in-law. Many of the boys thought Honey was joking when she told them about these stories, or asked, "Why are you telling me this?" with an embarrassed flap of their arms, to which Honey replied, "It's just a shape-changing story. Get over it," and led the boys to the tunnel of stairs like those in a lighthouse, in which a set of broken windows let in watery light from over the stretches of wetlands leading to Asylum Point Park. None of the boys had met Honey's mother. They'd been told she was at work, at all hours, in some office somewhere. The case of beer in the refrigerator in the kitchen was hers. No one else was permitted to drink it. That, and that Angie's and Honey's hair was the same unusual color, was all the boys knew of Angie except for her infrequent voice on the phone. None expected her to be sitting in an overstuffed chair in the attic amid stacks of papers—a beautiful, swan-necked woman wearing stylish eyeglasses that never quite turned fully in the boy's direction, even when she said, "You must be Robert Mill. How's your elbow feeling?" always getting his name exactly right along with whatever minor injury he'd recently suffered in sports.

"Fine," he would answer, startled.

"Did you finally get the money for that camera?"

"Not yet. Almost. I mean—"

"I have to say I don't agree with you about the Oneida fishing rights," Angie would go on, the elegant tilt of her eyeglasses still trained away from him even as she recalled everything Honey must have told her about him. Angie slid her marking pen behind her ear, teasing free a corona of hair. "But since when do mothers and their daughters' boyfriends have to be in agreement, especially about politics and that outrageous thing you said to the cafeteria lady about what to do with the gravy?" she concluded, removing her eyeglasses and squeezing her eyes shut while the boy found his way nervously out of the room.

Over the years, none of the yellow Labs vanished like the pets before them. If they wandered off the property, singly or in groups, it was only to explore the scrappy fields along the railroad tracks, though sometimes Honey got a call from one of the security guards at the Winnebago Mental Health Institute, who told her in his friendly manner that the dogs were being decommitted, so it was time to sign them out. Then she biked over to get them. On the way home—Honey always took the winding back lanes instead of County Trunk A when the dogs were with her—the dogs ranged ahead and seemed to pull the bike like sled dogs on invisible reins. She liked to see how long she could keep her eyes closed as she glided on the gravel, the tops of the cattails rasping as she pedaled, and often took the dogs on a detour to the weedy banks of Asylum Point Park, where they sniffed among roots and mossy rocks, barking furiously at the changeable water. In early winter when the giant chunks of the ice shoves began clambering up on the banks, or at winter's end when the lake turned to slush, Honey ushered the dogs into the car and drove them there to tease them. They pretended not to fear the groans and clatters of the ice, or the bony fissures straining to break past the surface. But Honey never let the dogs wander far on the ice, and if their legs splayed in four slippery directions beneath them, she stepped onto the ice herself to wrap her arms around their bellies and boot-skate them to shore, her coarse wool sweater tickling their gratefully folded back ears. What she wished was for her dogs to have as much common sense as she had, so they'd know what was good for them and stick around. At home, after she counted the dogs to make sure they were all there, had checked their paws for frost, and wiped the melted ice off the car seats, she set off to make house calls. One Wednesday, when Honey, eighteen, visited one of her clients, a stoical widow who wore her gray hair in spikes to match the triangular cut of her nails, Honey was introduced to the widow's son, just a year or two younger than Angie. Matt turned out to have been a member of the coast guard Search and Rescue team that had discovered the wrecked fuselage of Honey's father's biplane.

"That must be nearly a decade ago, that we found that plane. And they still haven't found a body?!" Matt half asked, half told Honey. "Your father's whereabouts—"

"Even my mother knows he's dead," Honey interrupted.

"No one could have survived that crash," Matt agreed.

Honey coaxed an excess of pewter nail polish back over the lip of the bottle. "She hasn't been on a date since I was born."

"I've seen her in the grocery store," Matt said. She looks like . . . some actress. Every time she leaned over the cooler, another red ballpoint pen fell out of her shirt pocket."

"Who she looks like is Mia Farrow," interjected the widow.

Matt asked to come over later that week, but Angie, knowing he was coming, stayed late at her college office sorting through files. Matt had no trouble finding the house. Everyone knew the place on County Trunk A with the boat that hadn't sold for so long no one would dream of buying it. "I'm not surprised she's not here," he admitted to Honey when she told him her mother was late coming home. "But you're disappointed."

"Not exactly," Honey answered. Until Matt showed up at the door, she hadn't realized how glad she was her mother wasn't home. Even Mr. Nichols was off somewhere, trying out his recently repaired snowshoes. The dogs, which Honey counted to be sure they were all there, were occupied with the soup bones he'd brought home from the senior citizens' center and scattered on the snow around the boat. They made a grisly spectacle, tonguing the crunched, blood-specked marrow onto the white drifts.

"I figured out who your mother looks like, anyway," Matt began, following Honey into the house.

"Mia Farrow," said Honey. "Your own mother told you that."

"Thing is," said Matt, "your mother looks like Mia Farrow,

and you look like your mother, but you *don't* look like Mia Farrow."

"No," agreed Honey.

"You're sturdier than you're mother," Matt went on. "You look like—"

"I look like you could use a beer," said Honey, who wrongly imagined she'd inherited her sturdiness from her father.

"Have you ever drunk hot beer on a cold day?" she asked, emptying the cans into a saucepan on the stove, then turning the gas up high underneath. She'd never heard of anybody doing this, but the tawny foam turned darkly sweeter as it climbed the curved walls of the pot, and the steam from their mugs, when she'd ladled the hot froth in, smelled like strawberries fermenting in a sunny field. Nothing forbidden had ever been forbidden to Honey, Matt could tell just by watching her tip the foam onto her tongue. It made him think of waterspouts. Anyone in the coast guard knew there was no way anyone in a boat might escape an approaching waterspout except to speed off at a right-degree angle before dropping onto their knees to pray. But it was Honey who turned her Philadelphia Phillies cap backward on her head and dropped to her knees before he did, and not for God. The warm head of the beer popped faintly on her tongue as she unzipped his fly. By the time they'd spent forty minutes in Honey's bedroom, Matt had made peace with what he was doing. No one could say he was taking advantage, for no person could take advantage of Honey even if he wanted. Anyway, she'd have clobbered him if he got off the bed before she was finished with him.

But while all her prior petting with her boyfriends had seemed in preparation for real adventure, like a path she needed to practice following before setting off for her true destination, still, now, having made love to a mature man who knew what he was doing, she felt only that she'd reached the edge of a yet more tempting landscape. She closed her eyes and fell asleep, "Fully dressed," she murmured, though she wore nothing but a new set of skin, more supple and tingly than the skin she'd grown up in. Matt had gone home to pack for a business trip; she hoped not to see him again. She dreamt of green fields turning to ocean, ocean to river, river to sky, her smile alight with the same embarrassed mischief that appeared on Mr. Nichols's face whenever he confused her name with Happy's. In the morning she stacked the Phillies cap atop the others in the trunk, checked it off on her father's list, and looked out the window to discover that the dogs had left the soup bone marrow staining the snow around the hull of the boat, and were gone.

The plan behind Mr. Nichols's snowshoe repair was that by following rabbit tracks beyond the railroad, he might come to the tracks of a fox and be led to its den. He'd always wanted a shot of a fox, to keep in his index card file along with his pictures of deer, possum, bats, owls, starflowers, and trillium. He wasn't a good photographer. The pictures of the bat resembled dead leaves clumped in a gutter, while the deer, foreshortened, looked like an eohippus, but Mr. Nichols and Honey were alike, they'd long since agreed. Humdrum things were miraculous in their eyes. Years ago, Mr. Nichols had parachuted with his friends, and designed and raced a solar-powered car, but exhilarating as these experiences were, he had to admit that just to look out the window while taking a bite of seven-grain bread was equally satisfying. If he couldn't get a picture of a fox, he wanted at least to glimpse the wild animal. If all else failed, what with the telephoto and the snowshoes, he was treating himself to a solid aerobic workout. The first set of rabbit tracks led to the grounds of an apartment complex going up near County Trunk A, but the second led to a tussle with the catlike prints of a fox. So eagerly did Mr. Nichols follow the prints, across the railroad and the highway to the edge of Asylum Point Park, that he needed to take off his parka, remove his woolen sweater, put the parka back on, and knot the sleeves of the sweater around a stop sign so he wouldn't need to carry it. Dusk was approaching. He wore wool socks and gloves, but only earmuffs under a thatch of hair. He ate some handfuls of snow, attaching the flash to his camera before continuing. The cold and his impatience to catch up with the fox combined to make a fierce, high ringing in his ears, but he was careful to pace himself in this weather; with the fox so near he might stumble upon it and frighten it off. Soon he grew worried, watching the footprints turn stale in the snow until at last he found a marking of skunk-smelling urine around which the snow was still melting. Don't touch the droppings, Mr. Nichols remembered. Fox droppings swarmed with parasites highly contagious to humans. Yet foxes were so graceful, leaving only a single ribbon of prints.

The prints veered onto the parking lot and down a boat ramp to the lake, to be lost among the tire tracks of ice fishermen. Mr. Nichols lay flat on the frosty dock, to see if the fox was beneath. His earmuffs toppled off his head but he retrieved them, peering ahead as he followed the mishmash of tire treads on the frozen bay. Night had stealthily fallen around the defunct lighthouse, and the ice held a lackluster cast of tin. If only he'd carried a flashlight. But there was not even a match in his zippered pocket, only a small round object. It was the button with the anchor on it he'd found with his Geiger counter, exactly like the buttons that fell off Happy's peacoat. Not Happy. Honey. He wished he'd given his friend the button. In retrospect his lack of consideration for other people often made him ashamed . . . but then the fox trotted casually across a ribbon of ice shoves, before his eyes.

His ears rang with excitement, his camera thumped against his parka. Ice shoves were difficult to maneuver in snowshoes. To Tom Bane, whose loosely hammering ear bones knocked against the knotted fishing line at the bottom of the lake, the sound of Honey's coat button skidding from the fuzz of Mr. Nichols's pocket when Mr. Nichols fell was like the ticking of buds splitting secretively open on fruit trees, a sound unquestionably Honey's own.

Honey packed Mr. Nichols's personal belongings in a couple of large boxes and drove them to the senior citizens' center so his friends might select mementos of him or at least make use of his gadgets and books. The things that seemed private—the papers arranged neatly in accordion files, the slippers that still held imprints of his unusually large toes—she burned discreetly in piles on top of the grill, saving the earmuffs the dogs had brought back to her not long after she'd realized her pets were missing in the first place. Just as she'd begun her search, they appeared in a jubilant pack. She counted them three times before noticing the puppies fighting over the earmuffs. After the police discovered Mr. Nichols's frozen body, she hung the muffs on a nail in the garage, and shampooed the carpet even though he had kept it scrupulously clean. She didn't feel sad about his sudden, unalterable absence, any more than she grieved for the lizard or ferret. What mattered wasn't that he was dead, but that among all the doorways, thresholds, stairways, invisible bridges, and tunnels that seemed everywhere at once in the world, there was suddenly yet another, newly devised passage. Also what mattered was that she found she cared about him more than she'd known before, as if his death had made an opening in her as well, one she resolved not to close. From now on if she cared about someone, she intended to know it.

Honey took special care in telling her mother Mr. Nichols was dead, suspecting Angie would be inclined to blame herself for the tenant's death even if the ice had broken underneath him. It hadn't. The ice was seven feet thick in the center of the lake this year. He'd simply suffered respiratory failure, Honey explained. For a short while she deliberated about whether the film should be rewound and delivered along with the camera to the senior citizens' center, or whether the undeveloped pictures were private and should therefore be burned. She solved this problem by deliberately opening the camera and exposing the film.

"The earmuffs stay," she said to potential tenants who stopped to look at the garage. "Utilities run about thirty-five dollars a month but if you do yard work and shoveling, I give you a break on rent."

Several months passed before, on a Saturday, some calls came from people interested in the garage. Honey was at her table in the sidelines of a grade school soccer game, doing nails, plucking eyebrows, making her favorite joke. "*Ladies first!*" she called to her customers, then tipped back her head for a sip from her water bottle. Reclusive as Angie preferred to be when in her attic study, she was willing to answer the door or phone if Honey wasn't home. If it was one of Angie's students, she told them to see her next morning at school, and if the call was for Honey, she jotted a message in her filigreed handwriting and placed it on the kitchen table. Then she opened a beer before heading upstairs or maybe stepping out to sunbathe on the boat if it was summer, reminding herself she was no longer upset it hadn't been Tom on the phone. Angie had often heard how difficult it was for survivors to lay a loved one to rest when there was no body to bury, but now that she no longer had trouble accepting Tom's death, she found that her notion of death itself had changed, as if to accommodate the feeling she sometimes had that Tom was still nearby. Tom had been an early riser, and even now, no matter how late she'd graded papers the night before, Angie still woke before five every morning as if to keep him company, for he couldn't stand being the only one up. It upset his sense of symmetry.

"Helplessly righteous dunderpate," Angie said aloud, thinking what a humbug Tom had been. "Imperious martinet." She reached for the Montreal Expos cap she could have sworn she'd left on her desk, but found it was gone. Her baseball caps often disappeared from where she swore she had left them, which was one of the things she liked best about them, the way they allowed her to indulge Tom's greed. But there were despots and there were despots. Never once had Tom done her a speck of harm. Or done a speck of harm to anything aside from the natural predators he ordered from catalogues, which he sicced on other natural predators disturbing the crops. Tom had been a gentle despot, a smugly intolerant, anal-retentive pushover. She had that to be thankful for, all these years later, she reminded herself, beer in hand, whenever she answered the door and found some live person standing there.

When Honey came home from the soccer game to find three Post-it notes affixed to the saltshaker next to the phone, her first hope was to keep herself from giving in and calling Matt back. Ever since their hour together, whenever she felt the echoes of their pleasure, she'd been able to lie back as if in scenic reverie, holding out for the views beyond the horizon, views that would only grow further away if she stepped off the path and called him.

On the first Post-it note was a name Honey didn't recognize, of a man wanting to rent the garage if he could sublease it June through September when he went to Italy.

"I didn't ask why anybody who cared to spend a third of each year luxuriating in a restored seventeenth-century villa might choose to endure the rest of the year in a converted garage," Angie had appended in her gracious calligraphy.

On the second Post-it note was the phone number of a girl Honey had never liked at school, and on the third the number of a Realtor looking for new listings.

Honey didn't trouble to file these notes, and as she crumpled them up, she hoped instead for a call from two men she remembered had come to look at the apartment a month or two earlier on the way back from skeet shooting. She especially remembered one of them, a shirtless man whose gun, at rest on his naked shoulder, made him look like a lopsided letter X.

"Don't mind the weapon," he'd joked recklessly to Honey as his friend preceded them into the garage. "I'm trying to teach him to watch his back. He's gonna get in a lot of trouble if he doesn't. A *lotta* trouble." He laughed, then, blushing, laid the gun on the carpet. His buff-colored hair was dusted with gray, like the sprinkling of talc a mother might give a child after a bath. The dark shadows under his eyes had already been there too long, Honey remembered thinking.

"Bang bang, I'm living to a hundred," the man insisted to his friend when he picked up the gun on their way out, then gave a shout of laughter that Honey felt all over again in the balls of her feet when she dropped the three Post-it notes into the garbage. She would do her best to live to a hundred also, she decided.

9

A Few Notes from
a Violinist Do Polly's Bidding

Gem wasn't eating his supper, was the next thing I knew.

A small thing to know, in the face of all I didn't. Tip's world was a spiral of blown cherry petals, yet Gem's aunt Carol's trailor was clear as day despite the rainwater stains on the walls and the scattered bouquets of fake flowers, dust caught in the scooped-out petals. I had to hold my hands close at my sides, although I had no sides, to keep myself from doing yet another person's housework. The dinette chairs needed taping. A fan wobbled in the ceiling. Lysle slurped as he ate, not a giant surprise in the face of all surprises yet to come.

I wondered, Why Lysle of all landlocked, blubber-eared types, when it was Sid I needed to help me sound out my way? Lysle was more beached ship than sailor, more lost than at sea.

If ghosts could sigh, my sigh would have blown the alphabet out of his soup. From far, far away, in that eddy of unstuck petals, the fat girl asked, "How 'bout the striped?" She and Fuzzy Knuckles were at Kmart shopping for plates. Also pot holders and Pyrex. He was the one who knew how to cook, but she'd be the one to put meat on his bones.

What's a clit? I asked her for the twentieth time, only louder than before.

Lysle jerked his head so fast, the ABCs splashed on his lap. Campbell's was Lysle's substitute for sending Gem to school. Gem had had his sixth birthday but couldn't tell his numbers from his name, and wasn't enrolled. He and Lysle were staying at

Gem's aunt Carol's, and there wasn't a school within walking distance of Carol's house in the pinewoods north of Iola. Three days out of four, Lysle trucked poppers and produce in the semi, and sometimes Gem went along, even though he wasn't legal, in the passenger seat. Carol left for work too early to drive her nephew to school, and Uncle Sid had bad feelings about Gem and school, period. Thought Gem would get cloned. Thought he'd be like other kids instead of special, like now. Besides, the VW was missing all seat belts. Also, Violet was dead, so wouldn't be there to pack Gem's lunches or make sure he buttoned his fly. Gem couldn't care less about missing kindergarten. The letters at home tasted better than the letters at school, he guessed, and the very idea of the flavor of chalk made him thirsty every time he tried not to think about it. Now he stared with such longing at the squiggles in his soup, he thought he might burst from hunger. Lunchtime. His nostrils flared with his thirst for the salty steam, and his dimpled chin quivered, but Violet had raised him well enough to teach him never to stick his head in a bowl and slobber like a dog.

He wanted to, though. He almost did, then he didn't, then he almost did again. Lysle lifted his own bowl, tipped his head back, and gulped. His Adam's apple ricocheted. The last wisp of Gem's steam floated backward so close to Gem's ears he believed he could hear it, but that didn't mean he could taste it, too. A yellow glob drifted among the squiggles, fat and nutritious looking. The cubes of potato were pink in the broth, so Gem didn't know what food it was, but he would've eaten the pink squares gladly if only he could. In the distance, from the woods outside the kitchen, came the echo and thunk of Uncle Sid building steps to his trailer. He promised to teach Gem to be a backwoodsman, too, if Gem got strong enough to hit a nail all the way in with three strikes of a hammer, like baseball. But Gem wouldn't get strong with no lunch on his bones. He was scared of his own brown eyes staring hungrily back at him out of the spoon where it lay untouched on the table. He didn't know to bite his lip to keep from crying. One tear slid under the neck of his shirt but the other plopped in his soup bowl.

"Why aren't you—for shit's sake, why didn't you say you wasn't hungry? I could've eaten it myself if you weren't practically blowing your nose in it," Lysle exclaimed, pausing to lick the last of the day's lesson from the lip of his own bowl.

"I *am* hungry," Gem answered between gulps of tears.

"Then eat!" said Lysle.

"I can't." Gem sniffled. The reason no music came through the trees was because the radio kept playing songs that reminded Uncle Sid of his second ex-wife packing candy boxes in Australia, but none of the boxes were shaped like hearts, so Uncle Sid didn't turn on the radio anymore. Funny, how small facts consoled Gem. The middle fingers of both of his hands were trapped in two holes in the crate he was sitting on. Two plastic holes, one on each side, and in went Gem's fingers, and now they were stuck. He thought of one caramel in every box of candy, and how there's always one flavor nobody liked, to make the others taste better, Uncle Sid had explained. "Like chocolate-covered boogers, only judging from what I keep seeing you doing, that must be one of your favorites," Uncle Sid always added. More tears welled up. Gem's cowlick trembled. Lysle didn't know what to do with a crying child, but since his anger was always good humored, he said, "If you don't want to eat that soup, what the hell are you salting it for?"

He rose to clear the table. Lysle always stood as if he'd sat on a tack, so sudden the spoon jumped in the bowl he was holding. Gem shook his head no. "I do want to eat it," he managed to disagree.

Lysle found a glass and filled it with milk. Milk's what he had forgotten. Where are you when I need you, Violet? he wondered. Just because I need you all the time doesn't mean you can't be here when I need you the most.

Look under the table, I whispered to him.

Lysle obliged. Gem's feet weren't touching the floor. There was blood on the crate round the holes where Gem's fingers were jammed in the pinch of the plastic.

"Well, I'll be a witch's patoutie," Lysle exclaimed. "Why aren't you yelling?"

"'Cause I'm brave," Gem answered.

"Braver than who?" asked Sid from the doorway, rattling his tool belt. His hair had come undone from its slim poke of braid. It was wispier than cigarette smoke, but his face wasn't an old man's, yet. It would stay as it was for a long time, weathered as rock but ferocious with chips of mica. I'm young, geologically speaking, Uncle Sid liked to say ever since he'd turned fifty. However long ago that was, nobody was telling. It was Sid's idea to flip Gem and the plastic crate gently backward on the floor, to take Gem's scant weight off the squeeze Gem was in. For weeks afterward, Gem had scabs on the joints of his middle fingers, but somehow all that gazing into his soup had caused him to learn his alphabet. *A* for *always, B* for *bafflement, C* for *celestial contemplation,* Uncle Sid drilled into him. Sid had replaced all the words of the military alphabet with words of his own. *L* for *lovelorn* and *last laughs. W* for *watching, wanting,* and *wandering,* not to mention the *whitewall* haircuts they used to force on recruits. But never *W* for Susie Wong, the wealthy lady who owned half of Hong Kong harbor. If the boat needed painting, Susie Wong assembled workers, got them on board, slipped the money in her pocketbook sharp as a hatchet, and made sure the painters were amply paid with leftovers from the sailors' dinner plates slopped in a trash can lined with a lawn bag.

H for *hibernation* except on *holidays. P* for *Purple Heart* in the long-ago *photo* Sid had sent home from the war. People first meeting Sid found him standoffish. He was like a man posing for a portrait while gazing at something different he'd rather be doing. Soon they'd catch on he was missing some of his far ear. His posture favored the negative space the wound had created. All of this was written in the Book of Sid, whose chapters fanned apart whenever I got within whispering distance of their tissue-thin pages, the red ribbon marker sewn to the binding. Reader or not when I was alive, I couldn't help but make myself cozy with that book when I was dead—snuggle into a chair in the parlor inside me and read. How a mishap in a ship's gunner turret could blow off part of an ear, leaving the rest of a person intact, the book answered right away so I wouldn't have to doubt it. Sid was the gunner. The bullets were antitank but they used them as antipersonnel when "the opportunity was unavoidable," Sid remembered someone saying. When, rarely, Sid witnessed a man struck by one of those weapons and not exactly die but just disappear in a poof of pink vapor, he reassured himself by thinking, It's only war, the way a person on the edge of their seat might say, It's only a movie. He'd been raised to go to war, Sid, the way Tip, Douggie, Drew, Dennis, and David were raised to be smalltown tycoons like their father. Sid's dead dad had been to war, his granddad and granduncles, too. Before Sid and Lysle, the men in that family had won every war they'd fought, and it passed no one's notice that the only Purple Heart among them had been earned as a result a U.S. naval mishap in the only war they'd lost. "Did you get that medal for losing your ear, or losing the war?" was their sole congratulation. Sid had been climbing down from the turret, picking some wax from his ear, when the bullet prematurely exploded. His hand escaped the shrapnel, but the ear was the emblem of both of Sid's marriages falling to pieces when he wasn't listening, he liked to explain. Sid's second ex-wife had been mysteriously slender for someone always smelling of chocolate, and the white smock she wore in her candy shop kitchen looked distinctly not virginal. On the counter sat a polished grocer's scale on which Sid felt compelled to lay his head to be sure he still measured up to her recipe for treats. But he always did seem to. Her approval of him, along with the amazing sensations accompanying it, greeted him whenever he opened the red service door off the back parking lot. She liked to trace his bad ear with the lip of a wooden spoon while they both leaned forward to kiss, a kiss like a macaroon star atop a candy tree. He was shocked on the day it was no longer offered. *I'm sorry, sir, your service is no longer required,* he said to himself whenever he saw another red door anywhere. He was like a man seeking solace in his favorite stretch of forest, only to find his favorite tree chopped down and the star an unattainable glitter in an empty stretch of sky. Had there been illustrations in the Book of Sid, that would be the one he turned to when he was high in his trailer at night, a woodcut with the caption *One evening he was met with a terri-*

ble surprise. Since the time his second marriage ended, after the Mekong River trip and before the brief stint in jail in Honolulu, he hadn't touched another woman. All the willy-nilly sparks of his crazy whoring war years had ended in the sudden bright bomb of his second marriage, and now he was more neutral than Switzerland. No woman even turned his head these days unless she was safe in the centerfold of one of his magazines stacked at the foot of his bed in the trailer. He liked the women with the chiseled features, the women who'd looked backward too often like he did, and were turned to stone.

It was Sid's alphabet I craved, not bothering to worry how I'd make Tip sit still long enough to teach it to him; the letters and all they stood for, all the trials he must first recognize in order to dig himself out. I forgot Tip was a man, imagined him a sturdy-legged toddler I might sing letters to off-key, his plump fingers in mine, imagined him eager to learn from his mother, as small children are. Sid's alphabet reminded me of David and Dennis's toy piano. In the dining room where they'd left it, under the table, it used to play scales by itself sometimes, over and over, the notes' insistent climb and tumble proclaiming a fond forgiveness, a declaration of composure in the face of what befalls. Tip's composure, that is. What befalls Tip, that is. *G* is for contentment with what is *given* rather than *gall* at what is withheld, Gem recited at most children's bedtime. Gem didn't have a bedtime, but Sid made him sit quietly in his pajamas and practice his letters every night at eight o'clock. *R* for *regret,* *S* for *solitude,* *T* for *today's titillation* is *tomorrow's trouble.* Gem always stumbled on that one, but someday he'd get it right even if he didn't know what it meant. Uncle Sid would teach him, when Gem was old enough to understand. Never counting to ten before acting rash, Sid recites the emotions *A* to *Z* only after they've wreaked their havoc, then breathes deeply of the disarray as if to soothe it as well as himself, sucking reconciliation from the small pipe he keeps in his tool kit like the stake of a tent in the hands of a nomad, building each new home when the last has failed him. Sid was living his ghostliness here on earth, wandering life as I wander death, shelter to shelter, loved one to loved one, until coming to rest. It wasn't just his alphabet I needed, I understood. Sid would be my compass, my companion, strong enough to whisk me from the waltz of the Night, guide me out of the ball-room onto a mountaintop, and court a few stolen moments of serenity in the midst of *Z* for *zenith,* the domed sky glowing above his tent, all his bygone shenanigans turned to gold-leafed pages.

Of course, just because I had my alphabet didn't mean Sid would just get up and go. The Night seemed to find this amusing, a matchmaker's joke, me and Sid, and in a way it *was* funny, because of how much I liked Sid's company. Despite my terrible urge for us to get moving, Sid had a reassuring way of staying put awhile, trusting the rest of the world to wait for his tardy deci-sion to join up with it again. Gem turned eight through eleven in that trailer with Sid and me, and never did exactly get the point of his ABCs. In the meantime it was Sid who dozed off on Carol's couch before Gem reached the *Z*'s. No matter when Sid awoke, way before morning, he stepped outside to pee, then crossed the crackly woods to his own trailer on its eddies of dropped pine needles. "Cool," he'd say, then sit on the slingback chair under the trailer awning to smoke a bowl, which it took me a long time to realize was marijuana. The trailer was one room with a deck just as tiny, and the smoke drifted backward and gathered at the doorway as if to be let inside. So inside we all went, Sid and the smoke and me, no matter how much I knew I needed him to take me back to Tip. Another year passed in that fashion, me steeped in the bath of Sid's solitude within reach of Sid's necklaces hung on nails on the wall. Jack would never wear a necklace even if his masculinity depended on it, but I liked them on Sid—the heavy coil of copper and thick black twine, the buffalo nickel caught on its lasso of beads. There was one cup in the trailer, one bowl, one griddle, one shelf of true spy tales, one model of a Viking ship, and one toy rubber shark with a real shark's tooth nested inside its grin. The shark's name was Bill. Nights, Sid thought Bill was his only companion. There was a box of instant mashed potatoes in the corner of the pantry Sid

didn't know about, and in the folds of the checked curtains lived
a walking twig Sid didn't know about, but other than that, the
only thing he didn't know about was me. Sometimes we went to
the Pit Stop, a bar in Wild Rose, where I helped win stuffed toys
from inside a glass case, but I was glad to be invisible even
though I'd finally got out of the appliquéd dress and the charm
bracelet dangling with all the children's names but Tip's. Jack
really must have been a true believer in heaven when he dressed
me for burial, otherwise there's no explanation for the cardigan
sweater buttoned just at my neck the way I wore it summer
evenings, with the sleeves hanging empty like wings. Jack must
have thought heaven was golden cobbles. He never guessed I'd
find myself in the Pit Stop dressed in only my slip, swaying like a
breeze on a clothespin at another man's shoulder.

Serenity's cool but we can't stay here forever, I whispered to
Sid. Give the stuffed elephant to the lady kicking the pinball
machine and let's please get out of here and go save Tip once and
for all.

But Sid was in limbo, those years, and I had to learn to be
patient and cool as cotton. He had so much behind him, he
didn't want to look ahead. Gem was the closest he got to the
future. Sometimes Sid turned the trailer over to Gem's fidgety
barefootedness. It was Gem who found the corpse of the walking
twig still clinging to the curtain, and Gem who made me more
and more homesick for Tip just by being Violet's son. Poor Violet's ghost never arrived. She'd always been shy as soap bubbles,
Violet, her soft laughter popping on the tips of her fingers. Gem
turned twelve the day after Sid took the stuffed elephant home
from the Pit Stop but not for Gem's birthday. Instead, Sid
brought the elephant with him to work and propped it on the
kitchen sink of a house he was building west of Iola. The sink
wasn't hooked up. The house was wide open to the scent of
thawing mud. Around the cleared land scarred by the treads of
the cement mixers, the deciduous trees divulged only the tightest
of buds, but from the roof where he squatted working, Sid could
see the bright swaths of conifers climbing the slopes above the
same rickety ski jump that made me miss Johnny's drowning.

Still, the mountains were molehills here in Wisconsin, he thought, squelching the Westward Ho! feeling as soon as it had its say. It wouldn't do to give in to the old urge to travel, when his face was a map of all the left-behind places he'd already done his best to tidy up in his wake. It was time to stay still, he said to himself in spite of all my urge to get us both moving again. Probably it was the vantage point, him up on the roof, that reminded him of the game he'd once played on the ship in the harbor. Where has love settled today? Not on the chairlift, not in the ski lodge, not in the cars on the road. But there was one spot too bright to look at. Too blond. Too lovely not to be where love had settled. Too married, too indefeasibly the wife-half of the couple for whom Sid was putting a roof on their master bedroom. She had been here yesterday, she was here again today, she'd be here again tomorrow. Apparently the sight of a construction worker straddling a roof beam made the woman think it wasn't mere earthly adultery but something spectral she was proposing. She was a violinist. She raised her bow in the direction of the elephant, tapped a foot, and began tuning up. Sid had been born and raised in Iola, but he couldn't recall any local legs wrapped in leggings and hiking boots like hers.

"Anything special you'd like me to play?" she asked, peering up through her tendrils of ropy hair to where he and his hammer were perched on a truss. It was chilly outside, so why had he taken his shirt off and stuck it in his back pocket? she looked like she wanted to know.

"How 'bout, play harder to get?" he answered, twitching his poke of white braid like the tail of a fly-swatting stallion. The way some construction workers imagined women without their clothes on, Sid imagined her stripped of her wedding ring and divested of her chummy husband, but still she was a woman and bound to draw blood.

"I don't know that one," said the pretty violinist, bending her injured expression to a new set of scales. Her body suit was opalescent. A lock of her straw-colored hair appeared to have been snipped off her head and fitted to the bow. It was hair Sid imagined he might scale a cliff on, hair he might traverse a rapids on, but that didn't mean she wouldn't let go of her end the second his life depended on it. Sid grunted deep in his belly, recalling too late that that was the sound he used to make when he used to make love. He grunted again. The violinist appeared not to hear him, but she wasn't as innocent as she pretended. Why would anyone practice her violin to the beat of his hammer unless it was the other kind of music she wanted them to make together? Sid could hardly remember the notes anymore, let alone the lyrics. He could only remember the dissonant endings and the promises he'd made himself never to sing along again with the beginnings. Even after he'd torn his eyes from her elaborate musical posture and got back to work, she kept diddling with him. His word, not mine. Sid imagined that if he lifted his eyes from the truss he straddled, he would see she straddled it, too, within reach of a flick of his tape measure, her snugly clothed thighs open to the raw pink friction of wood.

We can't stay here forever. Tip's in more danger than you are unless you diddle with the violinist, after which you'll be lonelier than all the empty seats on the chairlift smashed together, I interjected in the silence, seeing how Sid needed a good reason to get out of there. Tip was lonely, too, only luckily he didn't quite know it yet, I understood from what little I'd seen of my son—the Night's breezy entry, the flick of the radio dial, and then Tip in some girl's mirror, shaving. Mary Anne's lighted mirror. Susan's in the knotty pine frame. Marcia's antique looking glass that never quite reflected back at her the joy she believed she was feeling. The names of Tip's girlfriends rhymed in my head like a lesson I could have taught him had I been near enough to teach him anything a mother might manage to teach a son. He had thought he had his reasons for holing up in Johnny's basement as long as he did, just as Gwen and John had their reasons for wanting him there, so I had mixed feelings about seeing him go. He was more a son in their house than he ever was in Jack's, and they were more parents when on their visits downstairs they found some greased-apart motor Tip knew he couldn't fix. Also, of course, there was the memory of Johnny between them the way I once saw a full moon balanced on a crisscross of telephone wires. They held Johnny's memory white and aloft as if they thought he might hurt himself if they let go.

Still, I wouldn't yearn so much for Tip to let himself be happy if I wasn't scared he'd keep himself from doing it. I still hadn't whispered so much as Honey's name to him because I knew that's what Tom Bane wanted—Honey, and Tip's happiness to boot, and I intended to be there to look out for them when it happened. Besides, a mother doesn't foist herself on a son in his twenties. A mother picks and chooses her words of advice. Choose your bridges. Count your battles. Tip needs to learn the value of devotion. Find yourself a dog, is what I'd tell my son if only he would listen.

Sid finally did lift his eyes from the truss. How many years had it been since a woman slid her hands along his shoulders and fell backward at his touch? She wasn't there on the beam, the girl with the violin. He breathed a sigh of relief. The floor was too far below. They would have hit the floor fucking. He drove a nail into the wood. Something tapped at the small of his naked back. She had climbed up the ladder behind him and reached with the bow to startle him. Then she laid the bow across the strings of her violin and played a brief portion of a familiar melody. Sid drew a blank. She played it again.

It's the "How old are you now?" part of "Happy Birthday," I whispered to him. Tell her you're old enough to be her grandpa and you'd better get home and sleep off your arthritis. Then we get in the car and—

"Too old to be your old man," Sid interrupted.

The girl laughed, hurt but hopeful. The violin trapped a piece of her laughter and held on to it a moment with a merry sigh as she and Sid assessed each other to see how uneven a trade they were gearing up to make.

"You're married," Sid stated at last.

The girl positioned her instrument under her chin, lifted her bow, and drew out a flat. I don't know music but I can tell when it's sharply attired and when it's letting itself go. This note was trailing all sorts of loose threads and limp excuses.

"Then again, I was married once or twice, too," Sid said.

"Maybe I'm better off speaking with my hammer instead of with words. I'm an alien when it comes to talking, unless you count saying good-bye."

Sid mimed his own violin with his hammer, having said such a terribly sentimental thing. It's at least customary to say hello before good-bye, he wanted to add, but he didn't know how with the hammer. A hammer was for hitting. No matter what a man says to a woman and she says back, someone gets slammed. He slid the hammer in his pocket. "I'm going skiing," he concluded with a wave at the sodden, distant slope.

"Have a good one." The actual sound of the girl's voice startled him. Earlier, he'd caught on it was Southern. Now he understood it was Tennessee. A smoky blue drawl like mist in a valley. "See you Tuesday or Wednesday," she added. "I'll bring us a thermos of coffee."

"Why not Monday?" Sid couldn't stop himself asking.

If not for Gem, the intervening weekend would have been too long to bear, the coldest memories of winter still hulking in the trailer while Sid stacked boxes of Hamburger Helper and soup beans. Gem was learning backwoods cooking, watching Sid light the Sterno night after night. Sid ate like the backpacker he'd trained himself to be, a one-pot life he could carry around on his shoulders.

Quit playing with your uncle Sid's shark's tooth. He prefers it in Bill's mouth, where it belongs, I whispered to Gem.

Gem slid the shark's tooth into one of Sid's hiking boots hanging from the ceiling. He wasn't being disobedient, Gem. He only forgot the second idea as soon as the third popped into his head. At twelve, he craved a certain custom Harley he'd noticed on a poster in a music store. The bike was crusted with rhinestones like the sunglasses I used to wear when Jack took me riding in the convertible. Whole seasons had passed without my thinking of things like that. He liked me in curlers and a kerchief, Jack. He thought it made me look like Jackie Kennedy. He liked darts in a starched summer dress, Jack, and he liked when I took the wheel so he could pretend to be the fire hydrant when I drove too close to the curb. "Don't hit me!" he'd yell.

"I'll knock your socks off if you don't stop telling me not to," I shouted through the chiffon whip of my scarf, swerving so close to the hydrant I couldn't see it past the fender. We missed it, much to Jack's short-lived relief, but to get back at him for being a backseat driver, I skidded into a mail drop. We never wore seat belts, Jack and me. We liked to grip each other's knuckles on the dashboard if the road spun out of control. This time Jack's hat and my glasses struck the windshield with a clatter as the cigarette lighter popped out of the socket. The mail drop crumpled against the impact, drizzled with oil. Somebody's cocktail party invitations are going to smell like the time I spilled the nail polish remover on the telephone book, I remember I commented, and pulled a tweezers from my bag and set to work plucking my eyebrows, to Jack's utter astonishment. I'll show him a lady driver, I said to myself, remarking how the steering wheel was perfect for propping a compact. Never did I realize how much I'd someday miss it, that pinch and pull of the tweezers we take for granted when we're alive. Pale lunar eclipses like whole seasons passing, the plucked arch under each brow. *E* for nearly *everything* might at least be recollected, I planned to whisper to my son when I was close enough again. *S* for *savor* what you've lost as much as you *skipped* over what you had.

"What are we cooking?" Gem asked Sid.

Sid said to learn by watching and tasting. He imagined the violinist's low notes turning high as a fiddle under his plucking. Tomorrow was coffee day, but Sid would have none of another man's percolator, he decided then and there. Which meant he'd have to quit work and spend the mud season searching for someplace new to lay down his pillow. Before he knew it, he'd clamped off the camp stove and started packing. He shoved long johns and shorts into one backpack pocket and shirts and socks in another and all his toiletries in a Ziploc bag and folded his few dollars in the silver money clip he'd discovered sewn into his hand-me-down overalls when he was a boy. He found the mantles for his lamp, rolled his sleeping bag right off the bed, an old hand at quick getaways, Sid. He'd nearly forgotten how exhilarating it felt, to steal a quick minute to fasten his braid with two elastics, one at the top and one at the bottom, ensuring a stream-lined escape.

Ask where we're going, I whispered to Gem.

"Where are we going?" Gem asked, watching an icicle melt outside the trailer. The tall pines were a minefield of daggers. There was even a dead squirrel trapped in an icicle where it clung to a power line, and when it dropped to the thicket below, Gem intended to be the proud owner of it.

"Where am I going, you mean. Not you," Sid groused. "You weigh too much to carry. Anyway, your dad has big plans. He wants you to handle the eighteen-wheeler."

"Get outta Dodge," said Gem, although the thing about his father must be true, he trusted, because Sid's word was gold. Gem guessed if the giant truck's brakes gave out on a pass, that would be enough of a thrill to last him till he was sixteen, and if the brakes didn't give, he'd get his thrills other ways, like watching football games on the mini TV Lysle kept on the dash that smelled of the chunk of pressed mulberry wood clipped to the rearview mirror. Everything Sid said was true. Just like everything Sid touched was spanking clean. Even the oven mitt Sid slid into the backpack was velvety with the powdery fragrance of fabric softener squares. If Sid said Sid was leaving, Sid and I were as good as on our way at last.

"Take this," Gem said as his mother had taught him, handing Sid a tissue.

"Don't bother," said Sid, whose sneeze didn't come. He didn't let himself wipe his watery eyes on the captain's flag he'd stolen off the gunner overseas, either. The silk trophy had lain folded for years in his duffel of sweats, too big to display in the trailer without being smeared with pine resin or plucked at by stray cats that snuck out of the woods. Sid had got the brig for stealing that flag, but when he got out, he stole it again. Now maybe he'd end up somewhere worthy of its maritime flourish, and with this hope, he grabbed the stolen two-inch casing he used as an ash-tray. Finally he found the powdered potatoes in the cupboard, zipped me up with some spare coins he dumped out of a jar, took his hiking boots off their hook on the ceiling, and stepped into them quick without hearing the rattling tooth Gem had dropped in the toe, just like I'd intended.

"Yaoow!" Sid yelled.

Thus it was that he was bitten by a shark upon departing his dear trailer, tonight's caption might read if there were woodcuts in the Book of Sid. Life still held a few surprises here and there after all, he wasn't entirely sorry to know.

Part Three

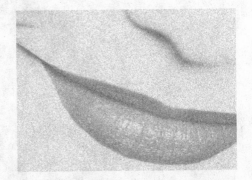

10

Doc

I

Despite the fact that nearly everything Becka wrote in her diary
arose from more private, less utterable thoughts than those
that she finally put into words, nothing she wrote was really a
secret, aside from some of the parts about Tip and maybe even
the parts about Becka's dream, the dream of black shapes moving
in loops and spirals against the white background. The dream
dismayed Becka because it made no sense, although since no one
who snuck a look in her diary would be inclined to interpret the
meaning of the black, moving shapes, she supposed there was no
reason to feel self-conscious about the fact that they had none.
At the end of the dream, the way the whirling black shapes simply darted out of sight, flick flick flick flick, leaving nothing but
the stark fluorescent background, was the most dismaying, the
most satisfying part. It thrilled her, then woke her so quickly
even the thrill disappeared.

Becka no longer lived in the house she'd grown up in. She'd
purchased one of the duplexes north of town, close to the recreation trail after the river swung away between tracts of woodland
and farmland not yet parceled for development. Every month or
so another freshly turned road appeared in view of Becka's door,
and overnight the rows of duplexes sprouted up along it with the
stereos and televisions already murmuring behind the curtains,
as if there were all sorts of people inside being sociable, like Tip,

or romantic, like Tip, or smart and ornery, like Tip, or assertive, poised, and professional, like Jenna, or even self-conscious, like Becka, but if there were, she hardly saw them. After the pavement had been laid and the shrubbery planted around the utilities boxes, still the view appeared strangely unpopulated, because the unassuming vastness of the terrain prevailed over the ornate roof lines. Except for the cottonwood trees that had spread their branches for half a century, the fuzz drooping off them like dollops of wax, everything Becka saw from her doorway looked like it could be peeled from the land with a fingernail, and the sparrow hawks hunting from the power lines seemed willing to wait another century for that to happen.

But the inside of Becka's half of the duplex was comfortable and familiar, for she had filled the cleanly ordinary rooms with some furnishings her father had left behind when he pretended to retire in North Carolina. Really Jack wasn't any more retired than he'd ever been, was right this minute scouting the Southern markets for seafood and produce to be shipped weekly to the chefs at all the Jack of Steaks in Wisconsin. To Becka's surprise, she felt less solitary now that her father had left than when she'd shared the big house with him after her brothers and sister moved to their own places. All the twins growing up side by side in their rooms always coming and going, and the mirror on the medicine chest in the bathroom beaded with moisture from somebody's shower, and the telephone busy or ringing, and the clarinet case instead of the lunch box by accident in the refrigerator, and the T-shirts the boys intentionally crumpled in the freezer to be cracked loose and worn frozen on sweltering days, and the matching sets of voices rising from the basement, where Douggie and Drew stuffed shotgun casings, or from the dock, where Tip and Dennis shouted, "Take me to your leader!" at a UFO, and the smugness of Jenna's voice winning another argument about whether or not it was nasty for a girl to hang her bras on the clothesline to dry—all of that had been over and done for a decade. Even the housekeepers donning rubber gloves to scrape the scales off the fish were history, since Jack preferred to clean his own fish now, and anyway, most women didn't walk around the house wearing rubber gloves anymore, *period,* said one of the housekeepers, embarrassing Becka by saying *period* in front of a man. Becka was shocked when Jack cashed in half of his shares of the company and retired, but not as shocked as when Jenna had sold her shares to her siblings and opened a travel agency in Green Bay. Not long ago when Becka phoned Jenna, the phone rang less than once before who answered it but Tip.

"Jenna's," he said.

"Oh sorry. Wrong number," Becka had said, so taken aback by her brother's voice on her sister's phone that she said this as flatly as she might to a stranger, ready to hang up rather than find out what he was doing there. It wasn't possible she'd dialed Tip's by mistake. Tip's number was 426-3333, which he'd chosen himself to look like four naked women. Tip had two responses to a ringing phone, Becka knew. Either he lunged for it because he wanted to find out who it was and what they wanted him to do with them, or he let it ring unanswered and made disparaging but maybe affectionate comments about the person he guessed was calling.

"No problem," Tip said to Becka, and hung up, not having recognized his own sister's voice.

Still, his voice pressed closer to her ear on the phone than in person. Even when they hunkered side by side in the restaurants, consulting over a patio blueprint or debating whether chefs' hats should be required, Becka often felt Tip was talking not to her but to the day itself, as if the day were a shower and Tip was singing inside it, responding to its deluge of possibilities. To Becka he still looked like the baby in the cherry bucket who didn't know she existed no matter how she tried to entertain him. He was famous for that cherry bucket photo, the only baby picture there was of Tip. His wide, toothless smile smeared purple and his dimpled shoulders straining with the effort of standing on his toes.

Whenever Tip had stumbled home late from high school

dances with his shirt buttoned wrong, Doug and Drew used to joke, "We know what you were doing. Picking another cherry to drop in your bucket."

"Can't argue with you there," Tip used to reply.

The reason he'd answered Jenna's phone was that he was dating one of Jenna's apartment mates, Becka soon learned. Jenna had had to offer Tip a ski lodge voucher and a free lift ticket before he finally accepted the trade: broke up with the girl who'd succeeded the girl who'd followed him home from Colorado, and agreed to have dinner with Patty, Jenna's roommate. The whole year he was in Colorado, Becka knew he'd be back. No matter what he believed he was doing out there and not writing home about—jobs, girls, the usual scrapes—Becka knew he belonged in Wisconsin, and of course she was right, though she didn't lord it over him when he came home or even tell him how glad she was to see him.

Patty turned out to be one of the elegantly unflustered people who helped track down lost bags in airports. She was taller than Tip but according to Jenna had the grace necessary for a tall woman to complement a shorter man. "She gives him *line*," Jenna said, impressing Becka so much that Becka copied the words in her diary. "How does my twin sister see things I can't, and say things I can't, and do things I can't?" were the words Becka didn't write, the ones hidden under that day's entry. *Jenna said an interesting thing today. She said it doesn't matter that Patty is taller than Tip because she gives Tip line,* Becka wrote, and felt the loops of the more pungent, unwritten sentiments snagging the ball of her pen as it tried to skim over them. *Jenna's always so smart,* Becka wrote, her pen tangling itself on the unprintworthy "smarter than me." But, as had happened before, Jenna turned out to be off the mark when she said Patty gave Tip line. It was Becka who saw, when she met Tip's new girlfriend one day, that while Patty did have the kind of grace that might complement a short man, like a tree growing next to a boulder, the grace was wasted on Tip. He didn't need another person's line. He had his own, unself-consciously superior grace. X-shaped, he didn't suffer from being shorter than other men. Rather he drew strength from his nearness to the center of the earth. He was compact, elemental, though the ornery imbalance he reserved for his mind saved him from doggedness. When he was sitting still, his blend of self-possession and reflexivity reminded Becka of that of the boulder in a filmstrip the nuns used to show at school. Even motionless the boulder was filled with static energy. When the boulder was pushed, stasis turned to kinesis. The difference between Tip and the boulder was that no matter how long the boulder sat still, its share of static energy remained the same. In the kitchen at Jack of Steaks, where Tip was showing Patty the new graphics he planned to adopt for the menu, the longer Tip stood unmoving, the more pent-up energy he acquired. Even Tip's bottle of Pepsi drew light inside it like a firefly trapped in a jar, Becka noticed, but in her diary she wrote only, *Jenna doesn't know what she's talking about.*

If one of the waiters were to find Becka's diary and read it to the kitchen, he'd be impressed by all the things that happened to people she knew and that seemed, once she'd written them down, to have happened to her as well. The girl who followed Tip from Colorado had been misdiagnosed with lupus in the ninth grade. Most lost baggage spent time in Chicago. By the time Tip moved out of Gwen and John's house, Gwen bench-pressed fifty pounds and ran ten miles daily, which John thought might be the reason she couldn't seem to have another baby. Becka had written all this in her diary as if, having done so, she was part of the pattern it might someday become, just as she was part of the patterns that already had happened and that had been dispersed. Before Jack moved to North Carolina, sometimes Becka still snowmobiled onto the lake with her father, who seemed to view their frozen nighttime excursions as a chance to say things he no longer allowed himself even to think about else-where. With Becka on board, Jack drove slower than the moon rose, he always promised, joking but not quite, and never sped up to jump the cracks in the ice, or made fake cracking sounds with a beer can scrunched in a glove. Instead, Jack angled the snowmobile to face the shore and stopped the motor, so he and Becka shared a quiet view of their house against the neighbor-

212 ◇ ABBY FRUCHT

hood of other snow-covered houses. In theirs only a single window would be lit up, because the housekeeper turned the lights
off behind her wherever she went. *"When your mother was alive,
that place glittered like a diamond on a ring,"* Becka wrote in her
diary that Jack once said, aware of no other meaning beneath the
words, for Jack meant what he said out there on the ice.

Becka usually worked mornings at one of the Jack of Steaks,
then came home for the afternoon before driving out to another
Jack of Steaks in the evenings. Mainly her job was keeping the
various books, and along with her brothers, each of whom managed one of the restaurants, maintaining inventory and supplies,
helping see that the food shipments came in fresh on schedule,
and overseeing personnel. Two frowzy nurses, whom Becka had
difficulty telling apart and who both resembled Becka in their
fondness for reading and bicycle riding, had rented, from Becka,
the other half of the duplex, and had got in the habit of inviting
Becka to join them Saturday mornings for the role-playing sessions that they and some other nurses ran at the women's peni-
tentiary in Fond du Lac on the southern perimeter of the lake.
Only once did Becka agree to go. The passage leading to the
gymnasium in which the role-playing sessions took place passed
through so many sets of security doors that the echoes of the
clanging locks shook the carpeted halls, the carpet so slick with
age, like oilcloth, that some of the prisoners bowled on it during
rec hour.

"Wrecked hour?" Becka wondered aloud.

"Recreation!" laughed the nurses.

"You can play any role you want," the nurses told her when
the session was about to begin. "You could be a husband, a
dealer, a pimp, or one of the women."

I'd like to be one of the women, Becka said to herself precisely, but as if she were covering up in her diary, she said only,
"Thanks. I think I'll just watch awhile."

After the role-playing session was done, all the prisoners,
guards, and nurses gathered in a corner of the gym for pretzels
and paper Dixie cups of Kool-Aid, and it was then that Becka
offered a few of the prisoners use of the Jack of Steaks telephone

calling card so they could call up their mothers, children, and boyfriends. On a paper napkin, she printed out the Jack of Steaks telephone number, then put the PIN number in parentheses. On further reflection, Becka included the Jack of Steaks Visa card number, too, along with its expiration date.

"Uh . . . Becka," warned one of the nurses.

"It's just to help these ladies get a new start," interrupted another.

"Yeah, we're gonna hit the ground running with this credit card and purchase us all some new drugs," declared one of the inmates.

"And gas for the getaway car," said another.

Becka stood calmly back, feeling as she did when, on the rare occasions out with Tip and his friends in a bar, she lit up a cigarette. She didn't look like a smoker, and when she drew in the smoke it seemed there really was some mystery about her that people couldn't put their finger on. Now there'd be another thing Tip couldn't fathom, because aside from Becka, he was the person who scanned the telephone and credit card bills for the restaurants, and would notice right away if the figures weren't as expected. How did her younger brother make his way so naturally, so purposefully from one moment to the next? Becka wondered. How could such a casually lit-up man even *be* the younger brother she had promised to take care of?

I can cancel the card in couple of days, she wrote later that night in her diary, back in her room, her head nestled against the same pillows on which she'd slept as a girl. Tip doesn't often think about me, she reflected, as suddenly as if she'd never had the thought before, which was how it always came to her, like something breaking when no one had dropped it, no one was near. Tip thinks about me only when I'm right in front of him and sometimes not even then, Becka remarked, recalling the way he used to climb the ladder within sight of her bedroom window. If anyone asked him, he would even admit he hardly knows me, she thought, reaching for her water glass. Tip was always honest, no matter how the truth might hurt another's feelings. Tomorrow at Jack of Steaks, were she to say to her brother outright, "You don't think about me as being a person you can count on," he'd answer, "Can't argue with you there, sweetheart."

She reached for the lamp, staring under the shade at the bulb before turning the switch so when she closed her eyes, she might see just the barest beginnings of the black, spiraling shapes darting freely against the white background. Maybe she'd have the dream, maybe not. Sometimes, waking from it and looking out the window at the low sky over the bike trail, she could see what one of the nuns at school had long ago referred to as the brush strokes of God—the broad, lustrous strokes against the steel-colored sky with the trees dabbed on top of it in hard knobs of color. When in the dream she watched the black shapes disappear—flick flick flick flick—there was always a suspenseful moment when she seemed on the verge of figuring out what the shapes must be, and what they must mean. But she never could, and that was the most thrilling, most satisfying part.

2

Tip's fantasy vision of three girls trysting (with him! simultaneously!) at Red Rocks Amphitheater wasn't the only reason he had loaded Johnny's car with his things and made his failed journey away from Wisconsin, but when over the years he explained how he'd ended up "lost in Angeles," although he'd never even made it that far west, the three girls played a potent role. As well they should. What man on earth whose fantasies always happened pretty much as imagined wouldn't follow that trihued rainbow to its glorious destination? Often he thought, I have a magnet inside me! Picture any woman and a week later there she'd be at the gas station next pump over, holding the tip of her long braid between her teeth as she overfilled the tank. The woman who could bite her own hair and still look all grown-up was the same woman who could make spilled gasoline smell like something other women dabbed behind their knees on purpose. Yes, she was smart in the eyes, she was dressed down-to-earth, she was as he'd imagined except for the surprise of the gasoline perfume. The day, years past, he loaded Johnny's car and waved good-bye to Gwen and John, the idea of the three waitresses (they were waitresses, he'd already decided) had been inside his head too long. So it was time to make it happen. Why Red Rocks of all places, Tip couldn't fathom, but somehow he could practically taste the three suntanned waitresses ready for action at one of the weekend concerts, their bare thighs in short shorts warmed by the sun-drenched lip of the wall on which they were arrayed like parts of a menu from which he might make his selection. Skip the entrée this evening, I'll take the sauce, the soufflé, and the peaches, he ordered as he drove. As the fantasy progressed and the glitter of the freeway dissolved into the cool, sweaty silver of three bare necks bobbing over his cock, his nuts, his nipples, he'd shouted, "Three at once and six tits!" a phrase he never repeated to the women to whom he told this story, knowing there was so much more to a person than what her body along with its ingenuity had to offer. But while driving Johnny's car to Colorado, he'd gone out of his way not to have to believe that, because what man with three female bodies all climbing on top of him swaying and bucking and sucking and opening and clasping and shouting and licking and clutching—what man on earth would take the time to get to know them for their minds?

Not that he *minded* women's minds, Tip had said to himself in the car on the outskirts of Chicago. But certainly there was no reason to complicate matters by imagining their minds in advance, he declared, releasing himself to the pull of the car as the road swung centrifugally past Chicago, the car like water in a bucket, the whole state of Illinois a single taut, swinging rope keeping Tip trapped in motion all the way to St. Louis. But even at its most breathtaking moments, Tip's vision of the three waitresses serving their needs at his table wasn't the only thing making him hot for adventure.

Add to that the indefatigable thirst for momentum of any man in his early twenties, only Tip had more than most because he had Johnny's, too. Johnny's road itch. Johnny's lust. Morbid but funny. Johnny would have thought so, would have liked the way his parents looked waving good-bye, both of them smart enough to know what they were doing. Letting Johnny go by letting go of Tip, only not so simple. Tip was the kite, Johnny the sky they were watching him glide off into. Something like that. Johnny could have written a top forty hit about it. Gwen and John didn't need Tip anymore to fill the third chair at the dinner table, would be the refrain, sometimes they piled sweat suits and medical books on the chair before Tip had a chance to sit down. They did this with vehemence, not against Tip but against Johnny's absence—the more stuff on the chair, the less no one was on it. Tip ate standing up anyway half the time, as Johnny would have done, more at home in Johnny's kitchen than in any room in Jack's house, not including Tip's own. Before his trip to Colorado, all those years ago, Tip had still slept in his own room lots of the time, always climbing the ladder to get there instead of being so generic as to use the door. He couldn't decide which made him feel better: his own bed, for the way it bade him trespass in his father's domain, or Johnny's bed, for the comfort it gave him to be a guest in Johnny's room. Some nights when Tip was working, Johnny's parents used to show up at the restaurant, Gwen in a tank top, no makeup, no hairstyle to speak of except combed to look damp on the nape of her neck. Gwen's muscles had acquired so much definition that the absence of sweat was moving to look at; the freckled skin frosty as if with a blend of talcum powder and whatever pure reckoning her exercise brought to bear on her. Grief had made her indefatigable. She had run the entire more-than-hundred mile perimeter of the lake. John had driven at intervals to meet her so she could nap in the parked car. There, John unwrapped the Band-Aids she needed for blisters, unscrewed her bottles of drinks, and soothed dollops of sunscreen onto her ears. When at last they reached the docks in the harbor near the hospital, local television cameras and a party of paper-horn-tooting well-wishers waited to greet them. Tip had watched it all on TV in their finished basement, where he was learning for the hundredth time that no matter how much he *should* be the kind of man able to dismantle a corroded outboard motor, clean it, and put it back together so it worked, he wasn't. He would someday run a chain of restaurants more energetically than anyone in the business, and on the other hand would shoot his brother's dog in the head so gently the dog was grinning—yes, grinning— when it fell into the hole his brother had dug in the woods, but ten years later when he told about his trip to Colorado, he still could not repair motors. The parts were too oily, too small, too grimy, too suggestive of things that might bring out the embarrassing squeamishness in him. Had he been blindfolded, he'd be unable to identify the parts by touch, the way he was able to align his fingers without looking at the computer keyboard or undo a girl's bra strap simply by breathing into the crease of her thigh the words, "You're gonna be just as beautiful with your clothes off as you are with them on." When Gwen appeared on TV in her faded T-shirt, Tip was unjamming a hose from a washer. He finally pulled the washer free but dropped it by mistake into a soup can full of hardware. In the words of the TV announcer, Gwen and John's shared odyssey had "lassoed the very waters that once claimed the life of their teenage son." Tip paused with his fingers in the soup can. "Yeah, and I'm the guy who sneaks out the window five nights a week so I won't have to eavesdrop on them trying to make me another best friend," he said to the TV.

But not even that was the last straw he'd needed to pull himself free of their welcoming basement, pocket the vacation pay he'd amassed at Jack of Steaks, and set off for Red Rocks.

No. It was the letter that had finally released him, the letter he'd pulled from his father's bookshelf and slipped unread into his bathrobe pocket the night he first spent at Johnny's after Johnny had drowned.

For a long time the letter remained in the lint-flecked pocket, until one of the girls Tip snuck up the ladder to his bedroom, the girl who perfumed her jeans with gasoline, come to think of it, asked what he would do to her if she read it.

"Same thing I'm going to do to you if you don't read it, only maybe a few seconds later," Tip shrugged. "All it is is my father begging my mother to join him in Indianapolis for a second honeymoon. What woman wants a honeymoon in Indianapolis!" he repeated, feeling the scorn in the pit of his stomach, along with his elation at being his mother's witness and confidant.

The girl, whose name he still remembered, Elizabeth, had run the serrated hem of the envelope up one of her arms and down the other before pulling out the letter and reading in silence. She was ticklish on her arms, but her smile had disappeared by the time she said to him, "No, it's not. That's not what it says. It's not her telling him she doesn't want to go to Indianapolis. It's her telling him she's gonna have the baby anyway no matter what he—well, I think maybe you better read it yourself."

She laid the letter on the bed. Against Tip's childhood bedspread, the pinked edges looked sullied and frayed. Tip considered ignoring what she had told him and doing instead the thing they'd come here to do. Those days, as now, his orgasms sounded more innocent to him than did his normal speaking voice. The whole golf course shook with the pitch of that voice when he made love in a sandpit, the flag rattled on the pole when he made love under the bleachers at the baseball diamond. That night was the first night he and Elizabeth were going to make it indoors, where he would need to be quiet unless he decided to let his father hear him. Tip had been looking forward to this, to the way the curtains would shiver at the window with his effort at keeping his cries to a whisper, to the way Elizabeth's inner silence might seem to flow backward in time. The primitive rush of sap if he laid his palm down on the bark of a tree, that was what a girl's pulse felt like inside her, although he didn't tell that part, either, when he told this story over the years to women, because the silence was theirs, not his to talk about, at least they'd want it to be if he told them about it.

The seam on which the letter had been folded was yellowed. Elizabeth had been right, it wasn't the usual letter. And she'd been right, too, in not having read it aloud to Tip, but that didn't mean he forgave her for reading it first. No. He didn't make love to Elizabeth that night or after, or even kiss her goodbye. He'd felt enough compassion only to lead her to the stairway rather than to the window, so she might go out the front door rather than climb the ladder alone to the lawn. She was crying. He knew he wasn't being fair, but fairness wouldn't matter to him anymore, he'd said to himself. He hadn't known, before he read the letter, that the doctors had told his mother she'd die in childbirth with him, or that the priest had advised she give birth to him anyway. His father's letter pleaded with her not to do the church's bidding, but Jack's vehemence was no surprise and therefore not the thing, either, that had caused Tip to pack his bags for Colorado. Tip's feelings about the church had never been ambiguous. Until the night he'd read the letter he'd been content to take for granted the strict fondness of its upbringing, its unforgiving stake in his character, the restraints as well as the blandishments it aimed at him no matter how he ducked them. But after that night, if the church were a living thing, he'd skin it first and shoot it later, let it see what it felt like to bleed itself dry. Tip was alive because of what the church had had the audacity to ask of his mother. It had valued his life above hers, had left his father too stubborn, had left his brothers and sisters no one to tuck them in past their bedtimes or change their prayers into rhymes or sneak caramels into their pencil cases. The church had traded a saint for a sinner. Tip was unworthy. That had been the thing that made him pack his bags for Colorado, so he could go there and be even more unworthy than had been bargained for, so gleeful a sinner there'd be no such thing as sin when he was finished. What's more, Tip began to have the feeling it wasn't the church alone he should hold accountable but the fidgety priest, a man with a voice like a no-nuts'. Tip would castrate the eunuch again if he could, grant the priest what he'd bargained for by telling Polly to die.

For the trip, Tip had packed only his barest necessities along with his tapes, his barbells, and one of the beeswax cylinder candles the bank sent the restaurants for Christmas. The bank had sent the same candles a year before, only a different color, so Tip knew how very quickly this one would burn, the rolled honeycomb dissolving in far less time than it took him from start to finish with the two college girls he ended up meeting at Red Rocks his first night there. Close enough. Not three waitresses but two college girls wearing ankle bracelets made of each other's coiled hair, the formulas for the previous day's chemistry test still printed on the insides of their thighs. Exam day was too chilly for miniskirts, but they'd worn their shortest anyway, knowing no professor would risk losing tenure to see what they'd scribbled underneath them. Tip had been the beaker, that night in bed. The two college girls turned a whole new flavor of soft drink when he mixed them together and allowed them to quench their own thirst. He'd had more fun that night than seemed fair in light of the amount of fun most people had in their entire lives, was what he said in lieu of the actual details when he told this story, although a lot of women to whom he told it didn't like the idea of sex as fun. They demanded more-important-sounding terminology.

"What does that mean, *fun?*" demanded one of his girl-friends, Mary Anne, tilting her moon face at him like a bowl of something he was about to get too big a mouthful of.

"*Fun* maybe isn't the word I would choose," another girl-friend, Ellen, had said, her familiar smile along with her cousinly affection for Tip eclipsed by disappointment. The house in which Ellen had still lived with her parents was across the river on a dead end street with no dead end sign and cars parked every which way along the narrow, potholed ribbon of pavement. Rear fenders stuck out of the too small driveways, and remnants of sidewalk buckled over the encroaching roots of trees, so anyone who drove into that street had to back out so painstakingly that by the time they reached the exit, someone else drove in at the last second, blocking it. Tip had felt as trapped by the shadow that crossed Ellen's face as he'd felt the night her father's car was the one to block his midnight escape from her driveway. So he'd done the equivalent of driving over the lawn, circling the house, and cutting through another lawn to the neighboring street. Which is to say, he got the hell out of there.

"What can I say? I'm fucked up!" he'd said to Ellen by way of apology when she called to ask why he hadn't been to see her. "You're better off without me."

"I'll call you at two in the morning," she warned.

Two in the morning was shorthand for Tip's being drunk,

Tip recognized. Girls tended to enjoy his occasional drunkenness, the way his straight lust turned yeasty. "This one's for you," he'd whisper into her mouth, his beer breath like a tide rolling into her body. Ellen in particular liked to smell beer on a man. The first boy she'd ever slept with had been drinking. "This one's for you, not me," Tip would say, and not come, and not come, and not come, and not come. Each time he didn't come, she came twice. Then he'd sleep in her bed until time to get up, something he never did when he was sober. He got homesick if he wasn't in his bachelor bed by dawn, in the messy apartment building where he lived. Mornings, he liked to hear his friends lurch for the toilet in the next apartment over, drop soap in the shower, yell when they cut themselves shaving.

Even so, it turned out to be a gentle rampage Tip went on, in retaliation to the church for having advised his mother to bleed to death in order to bring him into the world and wreak havoc on it. In the eyes of an outsider, Tip's variety of havoc was genuine but low budget. Sometimes it was all stuff waiting to happen, like ketchup in a bottle, not dripping out. You lift the empty mouth of the bottle to your eye for a look, and that's when every glop and sticky thunk of red goop douses the eyeball. Not life's blood, just red goop, Tip said to himself. Still, he meant every drop of it. Every heart he broke, he broke on purpose.

Ellen must have known this. She never did call back. A point or two or three in her favor. That proved it. She deserved better than someone like him. He was unworthy of Patty, too, only Patty didn't know it yet. The morning he told her about his trip to Colorado and the two girls waiting to show him the chemistry equations scribbled on the insides of their thighs, he braced himself for her to take issue with his vocabulary. Only, he wasn't ready yet for her to say something he wouldn't like. He liked her too much to have to start building resentments against her already. She was graceful, intelligent, regal. She had carriage, where most people merely had posture. Also, she comforted the freaked-out pets who occasionally showed up in lost baggage. Behind her office door she let them out of their cages and fed them frozen yogurt from the stand in the terminal. Tip found these womanly displays of affection encouraging as to character but unthreatening to him. If she loved him, let her feed him frozen yogurt, he could live with that as long as it wasn't pineapple banana. The thing he couldn't live with was yet another woman who got insulted when he told her fucking her was the best new toy on the market. There he'd be, too liquid to move, his bones sweeter than jelly, making every effort to lift his face away from the pulse in her neck to say, "Whew. That's the slinkiest Slinky I ever had," and before he knew it he'd be expected to soothe her hurt feelings.

But instead, when he was done with the Colorado story, Patty only said, "I thought you said fairness didn't matter to you anymore."

Tip was confused. "So, what are you saying?" he asked against his better judgment. A man who asks a woman for explanations in bed is asking for trouble.

"I'm saying maybe you do have more fun than most people and maybe that *isn't* fair. But that's their problem, not yours. Let's make breakfast. But first, say you love me," Patty bullied.

"I don't yet," Tip answered. "Even if I did, I wouldn't say it."

"You said it on New Year's."

"I was drunk," he explained.

"So get drunk again."

She mixed him a Tom Collins, just as on their first date. That first night, before they'd even touched each other, when she'd stood with her back to him in her dark skirt and heels, mixing the drink, he found himself wishing as never before that women still wore garter belts and stockings. "Death to the creator of panty hose," he said aloud to the slit in the back of Patty's skirt. She poured lemon juice through a strainer, then did a vigorous up-and-down with the shaker that made everything just quiver under her clothes. Tip nearly slid out of his chair, moaning. Most men didn't broadcast their ardor like that, first thing in a relationship. Patty poured their drinks, carried them toward him. He didn't hide his erection, couldn't even if he wanted to, he said to her. She put the drinks on the table, reached for the zipper on the side of her skirt. The skirt tumbled slow motion, her legs were so long. She did wear a garter belt. No panties. Her clit was moist inside the tuft of hair. Over the weeks, Tip had come to anticipate the whisper of the straps of her garter belt against his ears, but he was genuinely perplexed and even insulted when he discovered, on an evening when he stopped by unannounced, that she was as likely to wear a garter belt when she didn't expect him as when she did. Even to work, under her double-breasted, airline-approved suits, she wore one. And never any panties. He was jealous. Of what? Her chair? She had slightly tilted eyes, slightly tilted sunglasses to match. She was often amused but never coy. When she sat beside him in the passenger seat of his new truck, he reminded himself of his father alongside his mother. Something tickling his missing rib, as Jack might say. The road their only chaperone. Already Tip's truck could practically drive itself the sixty miles to the hunting cabin, which was where Tip and Patty would spend Saturday night. The weekend was a compromise waiting to happen, Patty was thinking. She wanted a hiking trail, a log overlooking a creek, that kind of thing. But Tip wasn't a hiker. "Too swishy," he'd say, even with a woman on his elbow. A man didn't walk in the woods without a gun on his arm, dressed in camouflage or hunter's orange, depending on the season. Thank God there were no wildflowers blooming yet this year he'd have to stop and admire the speckled petals of with her, he was thinking. Or songbirds. As if to get back at all the men who lugged binoculars and bird books into the woods, Tip sped up instead of slowing down at the *Reduced Speed Ahead* sign just outside Auroraville. The old feed mill sped by. Tip and his brothers planned to buy it and convert it to a Jack of Steaks if the foundation could be brought up to code. Tip meant to preserve the weathered authority of the exposed, refinished rafters, the stone floor sprinkled with sawdust and strands of corn silk when the restoration was complete. The feed mill said Jack of Steaks even in ruins, the river gushing behind it, the whitewash flaking off the planks atop the crumbling foundation. Wary field mice cowered there, beneath the hungry owl that perched in the rafters. Restoration or not, they were doomed, like the crows stealing corn from the deer feeders Tip and his brothers filled on the hunting land. Squirrels, too. That afternoon, Tip shot one squirrel and missed two crows. He was accustomed to missing the black-cassocked crows, but he liked the squawking when the bullet whizzed past them, the brief rain of torn leaves, the single feather floating to the ground as if the air weren't still ringing with the blast. Patty walked behind him. Why did he want her to watch this? she restlessly wondered. Her brothers hunted, her father, her uncles. More than once as a child she had ridden the bed of a pickup astride a gutted deer, stroking its long neck, marveling over the stiff density of fur and the necklace of burrs underneath it. Some men closed the eyelids of the dead animal, others left them open so the eyeballs glazed. But the squirrel was a matted clot of paws where it lay at the base of a tree, and what was the point of shooting at crows?

But she was tolerant. That was good, Tip acknowledged as he stepped across the gully where he'd once lost an arrow, resuming his search among the camouflage of weeds. Patty stood at the lip of the gully, yearning for a pond with a footbridge, or a creek with rocks for crossing. No one could ever claim Tip pretended to be unselfish. Except in bed. But in bed his unselfishness wasn't pretense. It was natural. She would put up with him the way most women everywhere put up with men. And he knew it. Which meant he'd keep doing his thing, with her tagging along, and when she finally insisted on doing her thing, he said fine as long as he could stay in the cabin to watch basketball on TV. Then she took her own kind of walk, along a lane that dipped between some fields in waning sunlight, and wondered, if Tip ever had a baby, not necessarily with her but with any woman, would he push the stroller, or would that be too swishy, too?

She wasn't angry to be taking her walk alone. To the contrary she felt her heart grow yet softer for him. His masculinity was shielded by such a complicated, vulnerable ego. For instance he would not eat just salad, even in private. If she asked him to hold her purse for a moment, he would, but with embarrassed impatience for her to rescue him from the humiliating possibility there might be tampons in it. He wouldn't in a million years accompany her to a theater, but he watched his friends get titty-whipped at topless clubs at bachelor parties every third weekend in summer. Right and left, his friends were getting married. That scared him nearly as much as the idea of getting married himself. Unworthy, he thought. Himself. Of marriage. Besides, you had to do it in front of a priest. Patty knew the broad shape of his fears without needing to know their particulars, and was wary of his temptation to blame them on her. Walking back along the road to where the rutted drive entered the family woods, she set her mind to expect this of him. He would blame her, for what had happened to his mother and to Johnny and for what might happen to her, too, if he didn't get packing before it did. But she would neither beg nor follow. Alone, she would not be quite alone, for there was something beside her, urging patience and pride upon her. Don't wimp out, it whispered. Not a voice. Not God. Only a womanly, old-fashioned knowledge, from which she might draw if she needed. Womanly? Old-fashioned? Yes, for there was something long skirted about this knowledge that seemed to stroll beside her trailing a weary hem. Weary because of all there was to tell a person that couldn't be put into words, that needed simply to be walked beside in order to be understood. Lesson number one: solitude need not equal loneliness. But wasn't that beside the point? Already Patty had come to depend on the slumberously possessive weight of Tip's cock on her thigh after lovemaking, and on the way, if he and she lay reading in bed, he grew secretly annoyed, thinking she was reading his book over his shoulder when really she was reading her own. What a complicated ego. He never got sick. He was breathless—awestruck—at the sight of a wild turkey. He had exactly his own way of scrunching a blanket into a ball before tossing it dismissively away when he rose from the couch, Patty remembered, and quickened her step.

He wasn't in the cabin when Patty got back. She checked the bunks with their smell of clean mice, and the back deck from where one of the feeders could be fired at if a high-voiced robber crow was stealing corn, and the truck, safe in the muddy tread of the road. There was an outhouse, too, but the door had rusted open as if to remind her of the genuine bathroom inside the cabin. If Tip ever found Patty missing from the cabin, certainly *he* wouldn't go looking for *her*, except maybe to see if she was sunbathing nude in the scratchy grass clearing. Which is where she headed next, for Patty would rather be the one gone than the one left behind. It occurred to her they might pass the whole evening this way, each returning from their outing to find the other gone off again. Then, passing a stretch of tall spruce trees too evenly planted, she caught sight of Tip at the end of a row where the woods turned scraggly again. The sun on its way down, the dim rays at a slant, him swiping the ground with the rubbery sole of his wader, sweeping debris off of something he wished to examine. Probably his brother's dog's grave. Patty knew the whole story. He shrugged it off when he told it, but the shrug wasn't as casual as he pretended. If it was such a usual occurrence for a man to shoot a sick dog, then why had he told her every minute of it in such breathless detail she knew there was hardly a speck of blood, "just a little spot of gunpowder right at the side of the base of the neck"? He'd found a penny wedged in the dog's dead ear, before he shoveled on the dirt. Heads for doggie heaven, tails for doggie hell. Tip flipped doggie heaven twice in a row, then put the coin back where he'd found it. The dog hadn't walked in months, her hips were displaced, her legs stank of urine, but she was grinning when she died, she expected to keep getting the pink underside of her belly scratched.

Don't romanticize everything the man does just because you're in love with him, Patty was reminded, setting off between the columnar trunks of the spruce. It wasn't the trees that reminded her. Nor the sun's tilting rays. It was her usual pride, strolling womanly beside her. He didn't ask you to get all gaga over him, Patty heard herself think. Don't slather it on, it's not *his* fault you want to kneel down and light a candle to the man.

Patty pulled herself taller, aware of her glossy black curtain of hair—how precisely it fell to just an inch above her bra strap. Funny she wore a bra but no panties, men said, but she didn't see the dilemma. She didn't like panties; too confining. She didn't like to go braless; too loose. She was a neatly made woman, tall with straight hips, a long neck, and fine, sturdy arches. Tip said she looked like a Virginia Slims girl, especially in pinstripes, her hair pulled glossily up, her collar crisp under a few stray wisps, her eyebrows plucked severely, offsetting the affectionate lines of her face. Tip couldn't name her taut blend of aloof devotion. He only knew it made him nervous, whatever it was. And her bedroom walls caught Tip off guard every time he saw them. Emerald green, they were hung all over with sepia portraits she bought in antique shops.

"Every one of these suckers is dead!" Tip occasionally remarked, not to Patty but not just to himself, either, because when Tip talked to himself he addressed all things close enough to feel the vibrations. "Worm food," he said in awe to the clusters of framed portraits, the men in overalls or coats, their mustaches groomed or bushy, men unfortunate enough to have discovered the joys of fucking prior to the availability of birth control. "Isn't it kind of weird, having all these pictures of giant dead families you don't even know the names of? Besides, not one of the hundred and one kids are smiling."

"Some of them have the genealogy written on back," Patty explained. "One of them's a postcard to somebody's sister recuperating in a hospital in New Orleans. And they're not unhappy. The exposures took minutes. They had to hold their faces entirely still. What I wonder is how a mother got nine barefooted children to stand so quiet."

Tip shuddered. Patty had noticed he was oddly, unpredictably squeamish. He would level a gun against the silky, combed ear of a dog, but wouldn't touch the postcard that had been in the hospital. And despite all the times he'd ever planned to lay himself down on Johnny's grave, he hadn't once set foot near his dead mother's headstone, a confession he'd made on Mother's Day when Patty asked if he wanted to go. He felt he didn't have the right. The spot was his father's, his brothers' and sisters'—let them go there to remember the face he'd never laid eyes on, the voice he'd never heard. Unworthy, he thought. Himself. Of the polished red granite, the bed of flowers Johnny's mother surely had planted, the cut elm tree a ghost too big to believe in. If he was wrong about the fact that she forgave him being born, the grave would tell him that. If he was right that she forgave him, the grave itself would still rebuke him. "Too creepy," he sometimes said with a shudder, and then, "Too sad, anyway. I don't know if I could fucking stand it. But I have other ways of remembering her. Well, not remembering, exactly, but . . ."

"Honoring her." Patty had made the error of filling in the missing words, making Tip blush so hard she'd needed to pretend not to notice.

As Patty approached Tip along the raised bed of needles between the spruce, she could hear he was singing under his breath, not to the dead dog and not to himself, but just . . . just singing. Once, making love, he sang an entire Eric Clapton song directly into her throat without seeming to be singing to *her*. Instead the song roamed and settled of its own drifting volition. He sang the way people prayed who no longer believed God listened. But he was only a man dressed in a hunter's attire crouched in the woods, Patty was reminded, a man stroking the ground with his fingers. As she came closer she saw it wasn't the site of the shooting he tended but the print of her own boot. He'd cleared the loose dirt from the imprint of the tapered heel. Tip blushed. If he'd been writing a love letter and Patty had snuck a look at it over his shoulder, he wouldn't have been more embarrassed. Or more incensed. Patty said to herself, *Oh well,* the way she might comfort herself in the second between falling and hitting the ground, not knowing how bad it was going to be.

"It's like a deer in high heels," Tip said to her, relenting. "I thought it was a buck, then I realized it was you."

"Is that a compliment, or are you disappointed?" Patty inquired.

"How am I supposed to know?" Tip answered with indignation. Patty's skin turned to pinpricks of anger. Knowing how anger covered for hurt, still she allowed the anger to shore her up against him. Tip witnessed the transformation. Hurt to anger, like straw to gold. Not every woman could complete such alchemy. He couldn't decide which kind of woman he wanted.

One who could, or one who couldn't. Life was too like a ball he had to catch, sometimes. Tip had witnessed the doctor closing Johnny's eyes. Thirty-three times Tip had rewound the movie *Crow* and stared at the sequence where Brandon Lee got shot for real on the set. He knew the difference between a live body and a dead one. Anything alive deserved enough anger to punish it for someday dying. Even Patty's slender, determined footprint gave him reason to think of this. Precise as it was, the print was only a trace, the pine needles quivering at the margins. I'm doomed, Tip thought. The second I almost give in to someone, I despise them. But when he rose from his crouch, he smelled the bison in the game preserve a mile away, the breeze riffling the grass around their giant fringed heads. He'd take Patty there to show her, later on. She wore panties today to protect against ticks. The flimsy cotton would be a novelty between his teeth. He nearly forgot to pick up his gun before following her to the cabin. What made him act as he did, whatever he did, whenever he did it? Was it will? Digestion? Sometimes he resisted, did the opposite of what he was inclined. If he believed in his dead mother's forgiveness of him, then he believed in her commandments, too, but that didn't mean he had to let her gentle urging push him around, at least not all the time. And if his own mother couldn't tell him what to do, what could? Polar magnetism? Sex? Patty swiveled on one foot to smile at him.

"I love that. Slanty eyes on a Lutheran girl!" the breeze made him say when they crossed the swath of dry grass combed under the power lines.

He pushed open the creaking door to the cabin. The double doors to the deck had already swung open. A scrap of paper, a feather, and a ball of dust had gathered on the thickly varnished table. From elsewhere in the cabin came a skittering sound. Tip and Patty were undressed before reaching the ugly couch and threw themselves onto the stiff, plaid upholstery. The same gentle odor of field mice that dusted the beds burrowed deep in the springs of the cushions. Patty had a way of opening her thighs very slowly around Tip as he kissed her, her long legs parting wider than other women's could go, her smooth panties gone before he'd fully appreciated them. Soon Tip was so excited he seemed to have forgotten what to do next, he was too taut, he could only hover, even as he realized what the faint skitter was in the other part of the cabin. It was loose nails rolling from their cardboard box on a set of hanging shelves on the side door blowing in the light wind. He slid his face past the funk of his own armpit to kiss Patty's breast. He didn't want to come before she did. He'd left the remote control on the couch from when he'd been watching basketball, and now his knuckles brushed against it when he reached between her legs. But a man never mixes television with sex, even if sex is supposed to be fun.

He wedged her legs behind his shoulders. A woman doesn't change the channels in her lover's house, he said to himself. Most women didn't know this. Patty never laid a hand on his television, a courtesy between lovers he somehow hadn't thought about before he'd met her.

"Tell me how hot you are," he whispered into her ear.

Better than fun, he concluded.

3

Once there was a couple walking on a beach. Just sightseeing as usual. On vacation. In Maine. So there they were strolling along when they came to a man walking in the other direction. There was nothing weird about him except his tiny head, which was really, really small. So the couple and him start talking, and he tells them his house overlooks the beach, and how do they like their vacation and stuff, and finally when they're about to keep walking the couple says, Well, mister, it's been really nice talking to you, but there's one thing we're dying to ask you. You seem like a nice guy and everything. So what happened to your head? Why's it so tiny?

So the man says, Well, a long time ago I was walking on this very same beach and I saw a beautiful woman lying in the sand. She was really sexy, and I thought, You know, this is just the kind of sightseeing I've been waiting for, but when I got closer I saw she was a mermaid washed up on the sand. She was stuck. So, much as I hated to see her go, I picked her up and set her free in the water. But she turned around and asked me what were my three wishes she would grant me in return for carrying her into the sea. So my first wish was, The first thing I want is a million dollars. So, bingo, I had a million dollars. The second thing was, I want a beautiful house up on that hill. So you see that house up on the hill with the windows and the towers? That's mine. And the third wish, I didn't know what to ask for because I already had a million dollars and a house. So I said, Okay, my third wish is, because she was so beautiful, she was the sexiest woman in the world and I couldn't take my eyes off her, and I said, The third wish is for you make love to me. But she said, How can I do that? Don't be silly. I'm a mermaid. That's one wish I can't grant. So I said, Okay then how about a little head?

Lawrence tipped back his head and laughed as if someone else was telling him the joke for the first time. He'd told it to people twice already before now, and each time, he was satisfied. But no joke was good enough until he told it to Tip, whose laughter constituted the strictest form of approval. Though Lawrence couldn't imagine how laughter might heal other people, he believed Tip's laughter healed him, Lawrence, whenever Lawrence was depressed or things weren't exactly going right. Tip even laughed when he balanced Lawrence's checkbook, and when he scrutinized Lawrence's version of tax returns, but while laughing at Lawrence's errors, Tip fixed them, too.

"Anyone who can get nine thousand dollars out of twenty-eight bucks and seventeen cents, I'm gonna switch you to book-keeper," Tip said.

Also, Tip was the one who convinced Lawrence not to take the bus to Superior to get the free microwave oven for touring an A-frame.

"I'll buy you a microwave wholesale if you want one that bad," Tip said. "But if you bake a potato in it, Lawrence, prick it with a fork. Not the oven, the potato."

"But I like fries," was Lawrence's reply. Then Tip told him he'd read in the paper about a telephone scam. Someone called you up and said your dad or your brother had been rushed to the hospital in a foreign country, and then they gave you a 900 number to reach the hospital, and you ended up talking forever with a person with a heavy foreign accent who didn't understand you no matter how many times you begged them to tell you what was wrong with your dad or your kid or whatever, and then finally you had to pay a hundred dollars for the phone call and then you remember you don't even have a relative in a foreign country.

"But I *don't*," Lawrence answered. A muscle twitched in his neck. That same muscle always twitched when he was confused.

"It's a nine hundred number," Tip explained. "They get money when you call it."

"But what about the hospital?"

"Listen. If someone calls and says your dad's sick, don't call the number."

"My dad's already dead."

"Don't call any nine hundred number at any time, Lawrence. You can't afford it."

"Not on what *you* pay me," said Lawrence.

Over the years, Tip had employed Lawrence as dishwasher, then waiter, now busboy. "The waiter thing," as the two friends referred to it, hadn't worked out. Lawrence had an easy talent for ambling into conversations in bars or at outdoor concerts, which was how he always managed to meet new people, but the kinds of people who chose Jack of Steaks over any other restaurant for dinner didn't want a waiter who told them what he thought of the movie they were planning to see or whether they should settle out of court with the hotel chain for the time another guest's key opened their door by mistake. The money Lawrence made as busboy, which was even less than the scant tips he took in as waiter, was made up for by the cocktail shrimp and jars full of chowder Tip sent home with him the end of every week. It wasn't only the sound of Tip's laughter that made a good joke better, or a bad joke excusable. It was the loyalty included in the throaty declaration of it. No matter how many scrapes Tip got Lawrence out of, no matter how many hours Tip spent helping Lawrence fill out his loan application even if Tip didn't think Lawrence should be taking out loans in the first place—no matter what, when Tip laughed, Lawrence felt he'd earned every minute of Tip's help just by being his usual blockheaded self.

"When are you going to ask her?" Tip had been asking Lawrence, ever since Lawrence confided he wanted to ask a girl to Tip's brothers' birthday party.

"I don't know."

"She'll say yes. I know she will."

"She doesn't even know I exist. You don't even know who she is. I'm not telling."

"She'll say yes, anyway. A lot of girls'll say yes to anyone."

"Thanks a lot," said Lawrence.

"See, I never know what you'll get and what you won't get," Tip apologized. "I was just testing your improved IQ."

"A lot of women appreciate me on and off for the short term," Lawrence reassured himself.

Tip nodded, knowing Lawrence was right. Women showed up on Lawrence's doorstep for months after the first night he took them home from a bar or a party, but when it came to him wanting a real, steady girlfriend, they tended to skitter away.

After telling himself the mermaid joke and wishing Tip were there to hear it, Lawrence paused on his morning walk home from the Laundromat, straddled the bike rack in South Park, and tilted his face in the spring sun. Clean laundry was bunched in his gym bag like a pillow, but he knew not to try to catnap on a workday. He could fall asleep anywhere and miss the bus to work. He didn't drive. Maybe deep down he knew how to handle a car. Driving a car was like riding a bicycle; once you'd done it, you could do it again. But Lawrence didn't know how to ride bikes either, and though he'd squeaked through drivers' ed, he hadn't exactly aced the motor vehicle bureau test. He just wasn't the coordinated type, and truth be told, he preferred the endless drift of being driven by somebody else, watching the world go by. He liked working at Jack of Steaks, liked the clink of the glasses, the forward-leaning postures of the waitresses sponging the tables, the leftover din after closing when the customers cleared out and left behind the nightly scarf or glove to be stored on the shelf near where Becka hid her diary under stacks of paper napkins like a neatly tucked bed.

Not even on the bus to work that afternoon did Lawrence dare close his eyes, but it was pleasant to wonder if he'd get up the nerve to ask Becka, or at least tell Tip it was Becka he was thinking of, get Tip's take on the probabilities. It was true she didn't look like she'd turn him down, but that didn't mean she was desperate. Instead, there was something willing about her that Lawrence admired and found reassuring. For instance, she was always the first to taste from the big pot of soup and instruct, "More dill." What's dill? Lawrence wondered. And she always looked up, never down. Even when a waitress dropped a tray of entrées coming out of the kitchen, Becka looked up at the high ceiling with its constellations of string lights, not at the mess on the floor. Her long neck, broad shoulders, short haircut, and thick eyelashes made Lawrence think of a llama. Also, she was *that* strong, famous for the piggyback rides she gave her older brothers at company picnics. Not Tip, however. Tip was too respectful of the enormity of sex to straddle any part of his own sisters, and though with Jenna he was brotherly in a shoulder-hugging way, with Becka he kept a certain chummy distance. Which was too bad, thought Lawrence, because Becka had something to offer Tip. She cared for him, was the long and the short of it, whatever that was supposed to mean. When Lawrence arrived at Jack of Steaks for work that day, he found Tip and Becka at the bar debating the pros and cons of live music, Patty's idea. Tip had doubts but was willing to be converted. Becka was entirely against it. "People prefer to have conversations at dinner," she argued, then opened the trapdoor leading to the basement and started down.

"There was this couple walking on a beach. Just sightseeing and—"

"They come upon a woman with no legs or arms," Tip interrupted Lawrence.

"No. They come upon a mermaid. I mean, no, they come upon a man with a tiny head," said Lawrence, frustrated to be moving through the joke so very quickly, including none of the dallying parts, like it being in Maine, and like when the man says how sexy the mermaid was. But he hadn't even got to that part when Tip said, "You know what you're doing, bonehead. Procrastinating. My brothers' birthday's tonight and you're talking about optical illusions when you should be dialing that girl's number. It's only a party at Harry's. It's not like you're inviting the lady to move in with you."

"I should call that garage apartment on County Trunk A," Lawrence said, off kilter. He'd been thrown by the word *procrastinating*. Just because he didn't know what it meant didn't mean he wasn't doing it, he supposed.

"I think I heard that one already, too, Lawrence." Tip was patient with Lawrence as always. Lawrence had been renting the apartment on South Park Street for more than a month, but sometimes he slipped into the still-looking-for-an-apartment mode. Tip had helped move Lawrence out of his previous apartment when the rent went up.

"No. I mean, remember that little place on County Trunk A? The garage."

"The place with the yellow Labs," said Tip. "That was a beauty bitch, the one with the red collar. I keep saying I should get a dog, but I want a noble one like her. *She* was a high stepper." Tip laughed emphatically. It wasn't necessary for Tip to find something funny in order to laugh. It was only necessary that he feel extra certain. Also, laughing, Tip refrained from remarking on what a blockhead Lawrence was for forgetting he already had an apartment, he didn't need to keep hunting.

But the garage was nicer, Lawrence regretted. He could open it on warm days, and live inside and outside at the same time.

"You twisted my arm. I'm getting one of those dogs. Maybe tomorrow," said Tip, popping open the cash register and doling change into the slots.

"Yeah," said Lawrence. "But let me tell you about this couple on the beach, they say to the man, 'Why do you have such a tiny—'"

"I am. I'm getting a dog. I'm going over there today. Soon, anyway."

The trapdoor in the floor behind the bar was still strapped open. That meant Becka was in the cellar either taking liquor inventory, restocking glasses, or writing in her diary. Lawrence had once witnessed the impossible. Becka, climbing down to the cellar, had slipped and fallen, but came to rest somehow closer to the top than when she'd lost her footing, as if she'd fallen up instead of down. Despite the simple explanation—she'd lunged backward for the step behind her and pulled herself toward it— Lawrence felt this could only have happened to Becka, who hadn't even dropped the pepper mills she was carrying. Her jeans were ill fitting, not like those of the waitresses. Her sweaters were smaller than they should have been, but not body conscious, only cinched in the exact wrong places. Her diary was so small that when she rested it on her lap and curled over it like a giant fishhook to write, she appeared to be striking matches one after another in an attempt to get warm. She was taller than Lawrence. But she was taller than her brothers, too. The reason she was awkward was that her twin sister, Jenna, was sophisticated as if in opposition. Twins must need to be as different as possible from each other, Lawrence supposed, though this truth didn't hold for Tip's brothers, who Lawrence couldn't tell apart except that Dennis kept his golf clubs in the backseat of his car, and David had two children. Becka always looked like she had to run out to the grocery store. Her twin sister dressed as if for a cruise. Being Becka's twin, Jenna wasn't Becka even more fervently than other people weren't. Jenna would never choose as her place of retreat a lopsided bar stool in the Jack of Steaks cellar amid a trio of gooseknecked lamps that appeared intent on mimicking the worst aspects of her posture. Nor, if Jenna were to write even a postcard, would she choose a red-inked pen that made her appear to be correcting her own grammar. What did Becka put in that diary? Lawrence was surprised not to really want to know. He only wanted to be the one she returned to after her round at darts at her brothers' birthday party. The way a girl reached for her drink at her boyfriend's elbow, ducking her head or giving a high five—Becka wouldn't do it like most people, but she'd do something Lawrence liked.

"Hey, Becka," he said, careful not to trip on the cords of the three gooseneck lamps. None were plugged in; the light for her diary came from the ceiling.

She seemed not to have heard him.

"Becka," Lawrence tried again.

"The new label's on the dock," she murmured in response, barely glancing from the furious sparks of her pen.

She was referring to the freshly delivered crates of house wine, which Lawrence was to shelve. He didn't take personally her assumption that what he wanted was the evening's work assignments. What reason had she to imagine he was going to ask her out? He certainly hadn't given her one. He was conscious of his dark hair falling in front of his eyes the way women liked, and conscious also of Tip's assertion that rather than being put off by Lawrence not having a car, a lot of dates would be flattered to be taken to a party in a cab. Lawrence only hoped the cab wasn't driven by the same lady who'd once taken him and his date to a concert, and who chatted the whole time about water filtration systems.

Becka's foot jiggled. The back of her sock had slipped into the heel of her loafer, which used to make Lawrence squirm when girls' socks used to do it in grade school. To fill the small amount of time that still felt natural enough between now and the moment he'd ask Becka to be his date for the party, Lawrence lifted one of the gooseneck lamps and began coiling the cord around the wobbly base. The metal lamp shade slid off the stem and thunked Becka hard on her bent-over head, knocking her off the stool. For a moment Lawrence managed to convince himself this needn't make a difference in his plans. In South Park, he often saw children falter on their skateboards, tumble off the arched bridge onto a skid of pavement, play dead, then jump up and continue as if nothing had happened.

But Becka didn't get up right away. Her eyes were closed, her mouth unconsciously open. Lawrence knelt beside her, wondering if to touch her head where the lamp had struck it would be to take advantage of her. He kept his hands on his knees, deciding not to run for help but to wait a few moments in hopes she'd wake up. It would be like in the movies, her wondering where she was and him kneeling worriedly above her. In the meantime, he found himself stealing a glimpse at her diary, which lay open on the floor. He wasn't a good reader. He tended to have to read even dollar bills twice to make sure it was a one and not a five he was handing over. Despite the neat, regular loops of Becka's handwriting, he didn't immediately comprehend that what he was reading was an account of how Becka had given the restaurant's PIN number and credit card number to a woman in prison who wanted to call up a boyfriend in Finland.

Where's Finland? Lawrence wondered, turning a page.

"Didn't anyone ever teach you you're not supposed to read another person's private diary?" Becka said with her eyes still closed.

That was exactly what the girl whose socks fell into the backs of her loafers might have done on the playground—pretended to be knocked out, then made fun of him for doing something he wasn't supposed to. Lawrence ran his fingertips over his own head, as if he were the one who'd been bonkered. Becka's head wasn't bleeding, but he could tell it was sore by the way she sat doubtfully up.

"You should have someone call you in the middle of the night to make sure you don't have a. . . . a *coma*," he said, in lieu of inviting her to the party. To invite himself to wake her at four in the morning and ask her to tell him her name seemed a safer approach. "I could make sure you still know who you are," he suggested.

"Sure, Lawrence. Who's going to wake you up to make sure you wake me up? Your mother?" asked Becka with a turned-up-nose air. Though Becka seemed to realize this wasn't her usual way of talking, instead of apologizing she settled smugly into it as if into the last ill-gotten swing at recess.

It was only when she tried to stand up that she noticed her feet still tangled among the legs of the bar stool. As she pulled them free, a lopsided leg came loose from the seat, clattered to the cement floor, and rolled with a knocking sound to the base of the steps. Just then, one of the waitresses appeared in search of

Lawrence, who was expected upstairs with a case of the new house wine for chilling. Before Lawrence could stop the waitress, she stepped on the bar stool leg. She was wearing wood-soled clogs, and when her legs kicked out from under her, one of the clogs flew off her foot and landed in a bucket of soapy mop water. The mop flipped out of the bucket, spraying pine-scented bubbles. To save the pages of her diary from being splattered, Becka slammed it closed, startling Lawrence backward into the dim cubicle of the dysfunctional bathroom used only for the storage of cartons of fancy ceiling bulbs. There was no clatter of glass, no dusty funnel sound of smashed frosted bulbs, but in the silence, Becka leveled on Lawrence a look of superiority that made him recall the chafed skin of the snooty grade school girl's ankle where the back of her loafer had rubbed against it. The same girl also often had a milk thread caught elastically between her upper and lower teeth, he recalled, pulling himself onto his elbows. A box of Frosteds tumbled toward him off the top tier, but he caught it one-handed. Still, Lawrence couldn't have imagined a loopier chain of bad luck if someone had paid him; all this mess and he still didn't have a date. Besides, he had the guilt-stricken feeling of having lied to Tip, even though he hadn't told Tip it was Becka he'd wanted to take to the birthday party. Maybe Tip knew all along. Maybe Lawrence taking Becka to the party was a favor Lawrence owed Tip, which neither of them had had the heart to name.

Careful of the sink, he pulled himself up from the floor of the bathroom, noticed, in the mirror, that his hair was still fallen in front of his eye the way girls liked, and crossed the floor to help the stunned waitress to a seated position. Her clog resembled a toy boat floating in the mop bucket. Lawrence blew on it to see if he could make it sail, then, aware that the waitress was watching, retrieved her shoe from the water to dry it on one of the chef's aprons hanging from a nail. The wood sole turned a dark, burnished color under his polishing, and the red leather practically glowed. That was something, for a waitress to get away with such bright, tock-y shoes and not scare off the customers. Her eyeshadow was the crisp green of lettuce. She was new here, he realized with a twinge of worry; she hadn't mastered the subtle, wild-horse-taming gaze of the other waitresses.

"Ask me tonight's specials," she said to him when Becka had gone upstairs.

"Sure," Lawrence answered.

"But no. Do it the way the customers do. Say, '*Can you tell me the daily specials?*'"

"They're not supposed to have to ask," said Lawrence. "You're just supposed to tell them."

"You're kidding," said the waitress, shaking her head. "I don't know if I can do this. We do have a few specials we can offer you tonight. Would you like to hear them?"

"Not really. But thanks. I usually get the extra bread, and Tip lets me take home the shrimp at the end of the week. Oh. Wait. Yes. Go ahead. I would like to hear the specials. Please," said Lawrence.

"I'm so glad this isn't the kind of place that has cracked-pepper sauce, like the last place I worked," said the waitress. "I once said 'packed kipper sauce.' But guess what? The person ordered it. Can you imagine?"

Lawrence shook his head no. He couldn't imagine. What were packed kippers? He urged the waitress to her clogs and didn't hesitate to reach forward and pluck a loose thread from the front of her shirt.

"Loose threads on girls' clothes drive me crazy," he told her. "Don't let me go upstairs without the wine."

"Grilled salmon with new potatoes on a nest of creamed spinach. Artichokes stuffed with herbed crabmeat with a side of lemon butter. Our soup for tonight is broccoli cheese, made with Wisconsin white cheddar. Whew. That's over with. I hate that," she said, wrinkling her nose.

"What I hate is Manhattan clam chowder," said Lawrence, placing his slow, gentle hand on the small of her back as they headed for the loading dock of wine.

4

In the wire-fenced dog pen behind the house on County Trunk A, the most recent litter of puppies, newly weaned, passed their spring days lolling in floating, shifting lozenges of sun and shade. Beneath them, the earth was swept clean as a floor in a kitchen, then laid out with straw mats shaken free every evening of beetles and ants. The puppies' new flea collars still made them uncomfortable, and to their dismay their drinking water, shared from a single mixing bowl, was rinsed and freshened every evening and morning, so accumulated no brothy flavor of food and spit. Bath time was Mondays, walk time noon and just before dark. Sometimes, the puppies were leashed to the handrails of the boat and given bones to gnaw, the leads so long the dogs circled the boat as they chewed, finding all the best places for burying and digging up. The litter was small; of three puppies the biggest had already been claimed and was due to be picked up that day. He didn't know it yet. Only the smallest puppy knew something was going to happen, though she didn't know exactly what. But she'd already learned that everything she managed to understand about the world was never going to be quite the whole story. Things changed every minute. In the stretch of unmown grass between the pen and the adjacent backyards, the grass was never utterly still unless preparing to rustle, and never rustled without some new thing emerging from among the stems—a nervous squirrel, a bit of colorful litter, or best of all the smell of diaper from the house next door along with some other, unfamiliar, invigorating smell that made her prick up her ears and train her gaze on the distance, where the laundry that had been flapping on a line had disappeared, and where once an entire willow tree had been chopped down since the last time she'd looked. From the side door of the neighbor's house there often came a toddler waving a feather duster of a bright pink hue that the puppy couldn't discern, but she could tell that the toddler shouldn't be escaping down the driveway without his suede-vested baby-sitter, who careened down the steps, fringes swinging, the instant the

toddler stepped into the dust of the lane. But the lane was ordi-
narily quiet, for the real traffic passed on County Trunk A out of
sight of the puppies unless they were led around to the boat and
permitted to slide on the deck, or even jump through the hatch
onto the cushions of the V berth, which smelled of fishy,
squashed lake flies even though they'd been wiped with Lysol.
The boat still smelled of years-ago lake water, too, though not as
lively and inviting as the lake smell that wafted from across the
lawns and lanes and the roofs of the houses. Unlike her siblings,
the puppy knew the lake was close by, though she hadn't yet been
taken to it on one of their walks or managed to strike out toward
it on her own. She wondered what it looked like, and what it felt
like and smelled like up close, and what it was made of, and what
would happen to whoever wandered into it. She could tell the
lake was different from solid ground or drifting sky, and different
also from the clear bland disk of water in the metal mixing bowl.
Was the lake a living thing? Yes, the puppy believed. The toddler
thought so, too, though he had never been there, either. He was
in the same predicament as the puppy, wishing to know more
about the secret of the lake, which often called him from his nap
in a high, ringing voice. Every time the toddler stepped without
his baby-sitter into the dust of the lane, the lake was where the
feather duster eagerly pointed.

Close to noon, a four-wheel pulled off County Trunk A and
with a crunching of gravel parked close to the garage attached to
the puppy's house. From her lacework of shade and sun in the
pen, the puppy could hear the music being shut off on the truck
radio when the engine was cut, and then the radio being flipped
back on just as the truck door swung open and someone stepped
onto the gravel, singing along with the music.

"*And it's been the ruin of many a tall man—*"

"Poor man, not tall man," laughed a lady's voice.

The lady stepped from the truck as well. She was wearing
high heels. Along the concrete footpath around the garage, her
footsteps were like ice cream being spooned into a bowl, and the
air from her direction smelled of Woolite and lipstick, so the

puppy wasn't surprised to see someone leggy in a short beige skirt being led toward the pen. The man was still singing, more softly this time, as he followed along. Honey had come out of the house to greet them. The man was shorter than the woman but was the one in charge of looking at the dogs, who had sat up glossily inside their pen. Not including the smallest, the puppies started slobbering and thumping their tails.

"The biggest one's already claimed. And now I thought you were them, coming to pick him up," said Honey.

Honey was disappointed, though she didn't let herself know it. Nobody knew but the smallest puppy, who could hear the disappointment in her voice, which held a faintly noncommittal note beneath Honey's usual enthusiasm. The note caused the hairs on the puppy's tail to stiffen, especially at the sight of the tall woman wearing the skirt, for that was the person against whom Honey's disappointment would have been aimed, had Honey gone whole hog and aimed it.

The woman, whose name was Patty, was unaware of Honey's disappointment, too. People usually were. Unaware of what other people felt about them. Close to the pen, Patty knelt in such a way that her knees wouldn't come in contact with the ground. She wasn't wearing any underpants; the fragrant spot between her legs gleamed dark under the fabric of the skirt. One of the puppies lunged for her fingers, stupidly expecting her to give him something to eat. Why should she? Patty wasn't thinking of the puppies, really. She was thinking of Tip and of how her approach to the pen might reveal to him her interest in the puppies, and that whichever dog he chose, she would love it nearly as much as if she were its mother. She had mother love in her; that's what Patty wanted Tip to recognize. But she was patient with the idea, willing to practice on the fortunate puppy her blend of affectionate scolding.

Tip didn't recognize any of this, of course. He watched how very quietly the smallest puppy sat, and how she went suddenly cross eyed over a droplet of moisture forming on the oblong end of her nose. All of the inside corners of each of the puppies' eyes had been cleaned that morning as on others, with a triangle of sponge soaked in contact lens saline solution, but the drop from her nose was more salty than that.

The adjacent house was always quiet this hour, but only for as long as the wayward toddler settled into his nap. He wheezed as he slept, so in the eyes of the puppy it seemed to be his sleep and not the breeze that made the printed curtains shimmer in the upstairs window. But the uncut lawn between the houses was shimmering, too, the puppy noted, and so was a piece of paper wrapping that came unsnagged from a thistle and bobbed placidly away. The season was new, the air gusty today, and chillier than it would be tomorrow. A taste of icicles remained in the damp ground.

"Which is smartest?" Tip asked. "The high-stepping one I've been dreaming about is gone."

"Not gone. She's the mother. Tell me which one *you* think is smartest," said Honey. "I already know. Did you know their fur is nearly impervious to water? That's one reason yellows make such good bird dogs."

"Not the biggest one, for sure. You look retarded, buddy. My brothers say females make better hunters than males. This one's the smartest, by far," Tip concluded, indicating the only puppy who hadn't slobbered on his fingers. The others kept wagging their tails and pressing their noses insistently into the mesh, but the gaze of the smallest was still firmly trained on the spot where the littered paper had disappeared between the wheels of a parked car. She didn't mean for the firmness of her gaze to be misleading, but it was. The more strictly she appeared to be looking in any particular direction, the more disparate was the actual range of her senses. She heard the toddler crossing the floor of his room, and she heard a delivery truck slam over the railroad tracks onto Snell Road, where a disoriented possum, still awake from the night before, gave off a fiercely resentful odor, and she noted the first few of the season's early lake flies swarming at the tops of some telephone poles. But when Tip said, "Come 'ere girl," the puppy walked somewhat daintily over to where he squatted. Patiently, she waited for the other puppies to finish their sloppy jumping around, before giving his fingers a tentative, experimental lick. He hadn't eaten lunch yet. His arms were shorter than most men's. His knuckles smarted a little; they always did. His eyelids were hung slightly unevenly, the puppy noticed, but then she decided they weren't, that was only the way he made up for holding his head so straight. He didn't like when Patty's beige skirt brushed too close to his arm, but he didn't move away, only stored the affront along with the other resentments he'd recently begun keeping hidden from her. Patty hadn't yet figured out he never liked talking at Sunday breakfast, he only wanted to read the newspaper. The other evening she'd asked him to pull off the road so abruptly he thought she needed to throw up, when all she wanted was to check the date for an estate sale posted on a flyer where there was less than a one-in-a-million chance they'd be selling old photographs no one except Patty in their right mind would buy. Also she sprinkled on so much talcum powder, his bathroom smelled like a woman's when his friends came for cribbage. Unworthy. Tip's bathroom. Of the scent of a woman's talc. Though the puppy couldn't know the particulars of Tip's wordless, untranslatable complaints, the stored-up resentments made a stew in Tip's kettle simmering so gently Tip hardly even knew they were there himself. But someday they'd all boil over. The puppy wanted to be there when it happened, so she could keep him company when Patty was gone.

Between Tip's pectorals and the strong, squared thrust of his shoulders, the hollow in his chest stayed deep and triangular. No shirt would ever fit him just right, but even Honey saw the way the buttons quivered with his pulse so the Jack of Steaks logo on his pocket appeared to be breathing, too. Honey wondered if Tip's name was appropriate for him, if he was upright but just off balance. She decided if the name wasn't appropriate, she would make it so. Just then the toddler, attracted by the high-pitched call of the lake, pressed both moist palms flush against the screened kitchen door. The door knocked open just long enough for the boy to set one tiny sneakered foot on the concrete step and stand still a minute blinking at the gravel driveway before turning and climbing down backward. The feather duster waited at the base of the steps, upright in the drainage hole of an upturned terra-cotta flowerpot.

"I want my puppy to have a strong will and not be jumpy," said Tip.

Honey kept her eyes shaded on the toddler, poised to cross the lawn and catch him before he lurched into the lane, but at the usual last minute the baby-sitter ricocheted on the step, pulling the phone cord too taut behind her. When she gasped and dropped the receiver, it skidded backward through the door like a wind-up toy. The puppy's paws flexed just as if she were pouncing on top of it. But she was still in thrall to Tip, who tried to catch the dog off guard by grabbing one of her ankles. He thought he'd make her lose her balance. The baby-sitter leapt into the driveway, swooped at the strap of the toddler's overall, and pulled him ardently against her. As for the puppy, she stood her ground. She didn't jump or grit her teeth, only pulled deliberately against the tug of Tip's hand before setting her paw firmly down once again.

"All she has to do is take his sneakers off before his nap and then he'll never make it barefoot across that driveway. Aren't those the cutest plaid sneakers?" Honey said to Patty, but what the puppy heard was more like, "You're not going to have this man's baby. I might, though." Patty nodded and rose, her eyes on Tip's wrist swiveling out of the puppy's way. Inside her skirt, lace garters flashed white against the triangle of shadow.

"Now I'm going to have to come up with a name for you before I take you home," said Tip to the puppy.

"She already has a name," Honey said.

The puppy cocked her ears. Her mother's name was Happy, she already knew.

"Doc," said Honey and Tip at once.

"What did you say?" they each asked the other.

"Doc," they both answered.

Honey slapped her hand against the fence. The oblongs of sunlight skidded across the gold weave of the mats on the floor of the pen and lay still again, like dice with the numbers already decided. Snake eyes, Patty noted from under her lashes. One on one. Pairs. Couples, she said to herself.

"You're kidding!" Honey was shouting.

"Nope. Doc it is, then," Tip agreed.

A short while later, as Tip and Honey reviewed the sale, signing it with a pen dangling from Honey's clipboard on one of Mr. Nichols's pop-top chains, Patty led the puppy into the truck and slid beside her to be pummeled by the noise from the radio, the beat so mesmerizing she and the puppy might have sat there for hours in the half-warm, half-chilly breeze that blew a few lake flies through the open truck windows. Patty, whose elbow yielded to the puppy's dozy slouch, was poised on the edge of already loving the dog. But she was waiting to be given the right to do so. By Tip, not by the puppy. Tip wouldn't grant it until he decided how he might eventually come to feel about his and Patty's whatever-you-wanna-call-it, as Tip would say. Stroking the puppy's square head under her long fingers, Patty smiled at the absurdity of using a dog as the fulcrum upon which Tip's feelings for her might at last strike a more encouraging balance. Patty's birthday was a week and a half away. She wondered what sort of present he might give her. Once, one of Patty's roommates had been given, by her boyfriend on her birthday, a fishing rod. Sitting in the living room later that night, the roommates had decided a fishing rod wasn't altogether a disaster of a gift. It meant he wouldn't object to her company on Thursday evenings on the bridge over the river at sunset, and that he found her relaxing to be around. But Patty didn't want to have to put a brave face on a popcorn popper, thinking they'd rent more movies together. She decided to get Tip a gutting knife for his birthday. Something with an etched handle and a tooled leather case, for disemboweling.

The puppy whimpered as her eyelids grew blissfully heavy. Tip and Honey were laughing, close to the boat on the lawn. The papers had all slid free of the clip and floated this way and that on the grass. Honey arched her back in pure, natural hilarity with no peer except for Tip's. Both were jealous of the other's ease, the other's arabesques and lunges. Papers danced past their grasp as if it were fun to do so. Tip yelled at the pedigree chart to sit and stay, suppressing his uneasy suspicion that the breeze was craftier than it appeared, the papers delighted with mischief, teasing the to-and-fro of some greater, more willful spirit while he and this girl locked eyes on a last scrap of paper. He wrote Honey the check and escaped. Honey, never uncomfortable accepting money from a stranger or even from a friend, flinched when she clamped the check between her teeth, as if Tip's money were a rose on a thorny stem.

Before Tip and Honey had so coincidentally agreed upon it, the puppy hadn't known her name was Doc. Now, to her ears, which twitched with oncoming slumber as she slobbered on Patty's steady wrist, Doc seemed a name to which a dog ought to bark in response, alert and excited, whenever Tip called it.

Satisfied with this vision of herself nosing down Tip's path, Doc's ears twitched into the rhythm of dreams, causing all four paws to tremble and the sharp blond tip of her tail to quiver. The familiar percussion of the baby-sitter punching the same number she often punched on the telephone made just a dent in a haze of sounds, as did the creaking hinges of the screened kitchen door and the scuffling of the toddler's plaid sneakers approaching the gravel driveway. A loose feather clung to the feather duster's round pink halo, and when the toddler pulled the duster from the flowerpot, the feather didn't let go, only gestured toward the lake. Already the toddler had learned to extract the duster as carefully as if it were the notched stick in a game of pick-up-sticks, his breath barely fluttering underneath his determination, his ears ringing, the chubby pinch of his diaper eclipsed by his enraptured concentration.

5

Edith Anne Alden Atwater VanCleve no longer remembered her girlhood name. But by the people who'd depended upon her when she was grown, she'd been referred to as Eddie, and she could remember that, and the incident with the frozen turtles, and the starched ironed smocks in which she was required to dress her brother, Jefferson's, three daughters each day before sending them over the footbridge to school, and the view of the ferns along the creek bed that Eddie could just steal a glimpse of on the way to gel plates in Jefferson's studio, and how she never wanted to hurt her brother's feelings by admitting how silly he looked while fiddling with the camera, his fat heart-shaped bottom in black trousers thrust behind him. Dawn or dusk, he set up his stereograph or some other experimental equipment, for he was an entrepreneur, Jefferson, and Eddie his currency—her smooth brow, her clear eyes, her delicate nostrils, high collar, and slender but broad-shouldered carriage gracing the walls of his studio. There she stood among the tourists in the paddleboat place mat series, or carrying her umbrella in the postcards of street scenes, or crossing the train platform carrying a basket of eggs that in the postcard might be mistaken for a newborn swaddled in flannel. In Jefferson's Welcome Wisconsin Dells calendar, there Eddie sat on an April lawn plaiting her niece's hair as if the niece were her own daughter and not her absent sister-in-law's, or snapping late-August beans in a bucket. For February was a picture of the long wooden table Eddie laid for supper more precisely than she'd have troubled to set the table were it her parents,' in Pittsburgh, rather than her brother's, in Wisconsin: the spoons horizontal to the chair backs, the milk pitchers at either end, the ladle upturned so precisely in the bare center that the time of day might be told from the shadow it cast on the wood. But never a vase of flowers, for Jefferson was troubled by the sight of picked flowers when he might just as easily level his camera at them in their natural, unbruised condition when he went off in the woods on one of his expeditions, during which Eddie looked after the shop and studio. He was so unflinching in his requests that she couldn't refuse him. Besides, she was better with the tourists than Jefferson was; more patient and more artistic, a hat here, a shawl there, the light directed on the image of a clump of wild white geranium blooming in a corner of the studio backdrop against which the tourists posed. Her parents' table in Pittsburgh had always held flowers clipped from the hothouse, where she had seen her last orchid and hibiscus. At age sixteen, in 1868, she'd made the trip to Wisconsin for tourist season to help finance Jefferson's wife's cure in Arizona. It hadn't been expected—had been entirely surprising, especially to poor Jefferson, not to mention the three growing daughters—that Jefferson's wife would remain in Phoenix once her cough subsided, leaving Eddie to bathe and feed the girls and send them daily to school before rushing uncomplainingly across the moss-laden bridge to the darkroom. In the hothouse in Pittsburgh, the air remained fragrant and moist, and all those years in Wisconsin Eddie never forgot it. If she bit her tongue to keep from begging Jefferson for a chance to walk in the woods, her tongue tasted the rust on her left-behind trowel in Pittsburgh, and when she lathered the slender necks of the nieces, she smelled the waxy bells of lily of the valley dangling above the hothouse goldfish pond. Not even Jefferson's darkroom stench of iodide and pyrogallic acid could make her forget that perfume.

But having been dead these last eighty years, Eddie had passed more time on her fragranceless, purposeless journey from one ghostly path to another than she'd passed of her life. Dead, wandering, she had believed—hoped!—that she might at last be making her ghostly way home to Pittsburgh. Why else would she have come back dead, if not to claim the thing she'd been denied, the place she'd been most sorry to leave so far behind? People with full plates never came back; they left satiated. Only those who'd left hungry still circled the table. How disappointed Eddie was now, to have circled and circled, hoping for Pittsburgh, then stumbled instead upon her face in a mirror in this small Wisconsin bedroom. The mirror was a shock. No mirror in the past had held Eddie's likeness, ever since she'd died. And for what reason was she carrying an umbrella? Ghosts didn't get wet. But here she was, a ghost in a mirror, more clear eyed and smooth browed than she'd felt for years, strolling under a canopy of damp forest in the unfamiliar bedroom. Eddie blinked at her reflection, which didn't blink back. A hat she vaguely remembered sat fashionably cocked on her head. She wore the dress she'd worn on the train from Pittsburgh, all her better dresses stolen along with her valise by one of the rowdy hops pickers. The hops pickers had come from the East Coast on the same train she had, four thousand girls over a two-day period, arriving in Wisconsin after the hops louse had ruined the crop in the Eastern states. The remaining dress, the one the pickers didn't steal because she wore it on the train, was the sturdiest of torments, brown as burlap. Its thick seams made bloody welts under her arms. She wouldn't have been sad to see it stolen along with the others, when she was a young woman, and once joked she'd travel naked to Chicago to buy a new one, but Jefferson never took her even clothed to Milwaukee, where he photographed the insides of mansions. He left Eddie in the studio, for she was so efficient in the darkroom, and anyway was needed with the girls.

It happened the mirror belonged to a woman named Patty, who shaved her long, modern legs smooth as butter, then polished the beveled frame of the mirror with a torn nylon stocking. While Patty rubbed, Eddie discovered it wasn't her actual face she saw in the glass. Nor was the mist actual, nor the forest. No, there was a photo hanging on the wall opposite the mirror in Patty's bedroom. The forest in the photo was only the studio backdrop with the clump of geraniums, against which Jefferson had once posed Eddie to try out a freshly ground lens. She remembered how she'd wished he'd take the picture along the creek bed instead, for how moist the creek bed was, and how alive with the shy calls of birds, yet how dry the studio, the planks creaking underfoot as Jefferson arranged his perspiring bulk at the camera. There they posed, Eddie and her nieces with their long, graceful necks, all carrying those silly umbrellas.

Every morning Patty, whose bedroom it was, took a shower, her legs like two glistening tallows relinquishing their smudged, nightly memory of flame. After a night with her lover, as after a rain, the smear of Patty's mascara made for a consumptive sight. But Patty never wept. That was something she and Eddie had in common. Among other things. Stubbornness. And not a speck of vanity between them. Also, patience. Four and a half months went by before Patty in a roundabout way informed Tip he had missed her birthday, even though Jenna had made certain he knew the date. Not *forgotten* it, but *missed* it was the term Patty used in her head, as if the birthday, like a train, had left without him, not having seen fit to wait. Him on the tracks with his suitcase in his hand, openmouthed with embarrassment for having put himself in such an unchivalrous position, the news of Patty's birthday like a small barbed pin she'd kept hidden behind her back until sticking him with it.

Eddie's parents had once sent, from Pittsburgh, a picnic cloth on her birthday, which afterward was stolen by two pigs who must have admired the bright colors as much as she had, only now she can't remember what colors they'd been. And every year, Jefferson gave her a silver dollar. For his friend Lawrence's birthday, Tip had given him two tickets to a Mellencamp concert, and for his brothers' had arranged the party at Harry's. Jack of Steaks patrons were given small oval cakes that resembled lacquered boxes, on their birthdays. On his own birthday, when Tip unwrapped the gutting knife Patty had chosen, he failed to recognize the retaliatory curve of the blade. Tip hated his birthday, because it was the day his mother had died. All the same he hung the knife in its tooled leather sheath on the fireplace in the hunting cabin, impatient to put it to good, masculine use. Bow season was Tip's favorite. Eddie sympathized with that, for autumn had been her favorite season, too, when she'd lived in Pittsburgh. The honking of geese was what had woken her when she was dead. Migrating, they seemed to mock her in Wisconsin, their flight a giant V pointing always in the wrong direction—never toward home. In Pittsburgh, autumn had meant moist leaves flopping against the glass outside the hothouse, and inside, plump goldfish asleep in their trough. In Wisconsin, autumn meant only the coming of too difficult a winter, the sacks of hideous frozen turtles carted home from beneath the ice of the lakes, their bodies hunkered in frosty shells, the sacks stored in the cellar until the time came for Eddie to pry the shells apart, eviscerate the scrawny reptiles, and plunk them in a soup pot. Thankfully she no longer remembered the flavor, only the viscous yellow froth that climbed the sides of the kettle.

When Patty began to reveal to Tip that he'd missed her birthday, the two of them were at one of the loft area tables in the Jack of Steaks Tip managed on Iowa Street, tasting forkfuls of food off each other's plates. Electric candles cast a blur amid the inky green torrents of ivy climbing the rafters—Patty's idea. The swizzle sticks were straws of blown-colored glass—Patty's idea. Tip thought they resembled thermometers. The loft was for smokers, also Patty's idea; between the ironwork railing and the view of the tables below, a veil of blue cigarette smoke stayed close to the ceiling. It had been Patty's idea to introduce Mexican nights, as well, although Tip had rejected her insistence on mole, relegating the notion of chicken in chocolate to a place alongside his other resentments of her. Lately, with discomfort, he more and more often found reasons not to capitulate to the things about Patty that made her as elegant as a Virginia Slims girl even though she hardly ever smoked. They'd seated themselves in the loft to see if the service was up to snuff up there.

"Do *what* to the elegant things?" Lawrence had asked him a day ago. Lawrence was folding tablecloths, careful to center the logo between the creases.

"Capitulate. Give in to her, I mean," Tip had answered.

"Give in to her what?" Lawrence had asked. Lawrence and Wendy, the waitress who'd tripped on the leg of the bar stool, had just spent their nineteenth night together. His previous record of nights with one woman was four and a half. Wendy knew Lawrence couldn't keep track of his banking. She knew he couldn't drive, that he had six times locked himself out of the house while taking out the garbage, and that he tended to confuse which were the hard-boiled eggs for lunch and which the uncooked eggs for breakfast in his own refrigerator. Even so, Wendy hadn't shown any of the usual signs of getting ready to skitter away. When Lawrence and Wendy were apart and he pictured her in his mind, he didn't see her the way he'd so often imagined the other girls, walking away atop the length of the giant black corrugated pipe near the golf course in Rainbow Park. The pipe had been aboveground so long, Lawrence still thought of it being in plain view with one of his numerous but intermittent girlfriends walking away from him on it. Why, he didn't know. The pipe was miles from his street. The girls just walked out the door and down the steps of his apartment. In his imagination, there was never a question of whether the girls might lose their balance on the pipe, which they followed like seasoned tightrope walkers slumming on a balance beam, notwithstanding the way the black plastic pleats caught the heels of their shoes. At the end of the pipe, they jumped to the ground with their arms outstretched in the sleeves of their casual sweaters, clumsy but freer than birds. But when Lawrence imagined Wendy, she was in his shower behind the clear plastic curtain beaded with water, a comforting, soapy, pink blur that made him sorry for Tip, who turned away from such comforting pictures, unnerved to think of himself in such a married way. Faced with such a picture—Tip's girlfriend's tits dripping shower water on his toilet seat when she leaned from the stall to borrow his razor from the medicine cabinet—Tip felt like one of the customers who always ordered the same lunch. The day you write down their order before they have a chance to say it out loud, that's the day they order something different, not liking to be pegged as creatures of habit. Tip was the same way. In Lawrence's eyes, Tip was already walking away from Patty along the top of the black pipe in Rainbow Park.

"I don't want to give in to *her*. What's wrong with that? Nothing," Tip blurted, before settling down for audition time, placing on the table the leftovers from a margarita pitcher and a saucer of assorted olives that Tip called "black olives," "green olives," and "weird olives." Lawrence, realizing he'd forgotten to replace the candles on the back rows of tables, reflected for a moment that the only thing he was really good for on earth was understanding Tip better than Tip understood himself. The knowledge wasn't a burden. Lawrence only wished he was smart enough to do something about it. The band had ended up being fine musically, but unhygienic looking. Jack of Steaks wouldn't hire a band whose members could have strung themselves together by the loose threads dangling from the holes in their T-shirts, even if the lady singer did have Irish eyes. Besides, it was true people wanted to talk at dinner, Tip decided. Who had said that to him? Patty, he supposed. He felt guilty toward her, knowing what Lawrence was thinking. If Tip couldn't stick with someone like Patty, who *could* he stick with?

Doc, Tip said to himself, already itching for the lucky independence of a weekend at the cabin. Last time, Doc had been chased by turkeys. Tip still feared she might choke on spilled corn feed, or hide under the truck where he wouldn't see her until after he'd backed out over her. There was so much Doc needed to learn, if she was to be his duck chaser, his *accompaniment*. Which was more than he'd ask of a woman, but exactly enough to expect of a dog. Johnny could have written a top forty hit about it. Only a dog could follow a man home but be waiting for him when he got to the door. And though it puzzled Tip to find that this was so, he felt a certain affection for Doc he believed he wouldn't feel if she were male. Solid and watchful as Doc was, she seemed in need of the kind of protection males give to females. Not to mention a good tease now and then. His favorite game was siccing her on toads. The toad jumped from between her paws and bopped Doc on the nose, or darted into the grass, or ended up in Doc's mouth to be chewed and released so gently the warty skin wasn't broken. Usually the game ended with the toad flopping into the culvert and Doc tumbling after. Rescued, the dog was still small enough to fit flush against Tip's forearm when he lifted her from the debris, her nose averting the crook of his elbow, for she resented having been coaxed into undignified behavior. Grasshoppers were almost as much fun as toads. One evening while Doc chased grasshoppers, Tip had noticed for the first time a certain slant of Patty's neck, a forward jutting so slight he had to look from just a certain angle to make sure it was there. She was wearing a snug-fitting crewneck, her hair in a clip. The jut of her neck irritated him as would a crooked picture on a wall. Tip wanted to reach out and straighten it. The slant of her neck made him see her as if she were old and he an old man still walking beside her, a circumstance Patty seemed suddenly to *expect* to happen, as if the notion of their growing old together were part of their arrangement. From the empty lot beside them came the firecracker pops of all the papery grasshoppers escaping from Doc. The sky had shone orange against the horizon, the houses square against the dusk on their new, treeless lots. The building in which he and a few of his friends rented apartments, a building they called "the zoo" in honor of the parties thrown in one or another apartment on weekends, was on one of the ramshackle lanes hugging the shore of Lake Butte des Morts, but Tip had had his eye on this other neighborhood as a place where he might someday like to buy a house. Just because he could practically see Patty stepping out of one of these houses in her crisp-hemmed miniskirt, bending to pick up the paper before heading for work, didn't mean she had a right to expect such a thing to happen. A wife with no panties, bending for the morning paper! A lot of men would give their arm for a future like that, but Tip's own mother had given her life in order for Tip's to begin. His mother had been a saint! No one but Tip seemed to care about that. Not even his own brothers, who still went to church sometimes. Tip didn't go, with a vengeance. Still, his future swung open and closed like a door leading to whatever he needed to do to repay his mother. Repay her for dying, one, and two, for forgiving him, blessing him, really, the lake and river like a necklace she'd draped on his unworthy shoulders.

That night in the restaurant over Mexican food, Patty didn't say straight out he'd forgotten her birthday. Instead, she said something roundabout about Tip's friend Johnny having been more sentimental than Tip. She'd never met Johnny, but she could tell from the things Tip told her about him, the names of his top forty hits, for instance. Maybe that was why Tip pretended *not* to be sentimental, Patty suggested, because he didn't want to dilute his memory of Johnny by being as nice as Johnny was.

"Repeat that, please. What do you mean, I pretend not to be sentimental?" Tip asked, avoiding a slice of jalapeño. He had no taste for spicy foods. His question, he knew, could be interpreted in two different ways. Was he implying that he *was* sentimental, or that he wasn't? He hoped the latter, feared the former, strove for a precarious, unpredictable balance. Other people were taught how to do this, but he had had to teach himself. Dare himself, really. Now he reached for Patty's hand, a rare gesture for him in his own place of business. He did like her, he decided. The tilt of her eyes, her poise, her clothing, her talents for business and professional decorum, her sexy sophistication in a variety of settings, the way she touched his body, the fact that she didn't appear to be after his money, her mixed drinks, the way she parted her long legs, her naked sex beneath the lacework of her garters, the way she wasn't unnerved if he banged on her door at two in the morning, the way she never called him on the phone to interrupt him with a need for reassurance when he was hanging with his friends, her style, her self-respect, her intelligence, her—

"From what you've told me, Johnny seems like a person who wouldn't let certain important things slip by just because they were more important to other people than they were to him." she went on.

"Johnny knows everything now, and *he* doesn't even know what you're trying to tell me," Tip said.

"You forgot something," Patty divulged, more gently than she'd intended. She lit a cigarette. Some nights she smoked, most she didn't. Tip, who never smoked, was reminded of another person he knew who sometimes smoked but didn't look the part, except he couldn't place who. To match her poised detachment, Tip held his drink to his mouth a moment before sipping. His little finger stuck out like a duchess's pinkie. He didn't notice how terribly ladylike this was, farcical almost, in someone so beholden to his own masculinity. Patty caught her breath each time she saw it, her hopes for him trapped in the base of her throat. A chimpanzee sniffing a rose; that's what she saw—the femininity of Tip's outstretched pinkie, and the brute, X-shaped, hairy remainder of him ignorant of the juxtaposition.

"I don't want to have to tell you what you forgot," she warned. "It wouldn't count, if I needed to tell you. Anyway, it was too long ago to matter anymore."

"Apparently not," Tip said.

On the one hand, Patty wished to retaliate, and on the other, she wished to put her missed birthday, which had hurt her terribly, gracefully behind her. She recalled how he'd phoned her at two that night, from a bar down the street, asking could he walk to her house to avoid driving home. The raucousness of other patrons was audible over the phone. It wasn't his occasional drinking that relaxed Tip, but the crazed noise of partying. He needed relaxation in this general, stupefied way. A certain near-bursting measure of grief was carried inside the impermeable compact shape of Tip's body, Patty said to herself as she geared herself up to let him make his oversight up to her. He needed his drunken dart games, the loudest, most desperate jukebox selections in order to release the pressure.

"I'll give you a hint," Patty offered, leaning closer over the table. "Do you find it fortunate that of all women on earth, your girlfriend is the only one not getting any older?" The waitress delivered dinner. She was Lawrence's waitress, the one with the green eyeshadow, already famous for having screamed in the kitchen when somebody opened a crate of artichokes, which she mistook for iguanas.

Tip's ears turned pink, but he still didn't get Patty's hint. Almost, almost, but he didn't want to. There always was something touching about a man's essential innocence around women, thought Eddie, the ghost, who'd lived long enough around her brother, Jefferson, and her nieces' husbands to know that that particular bafflement went with men to their graves, not because men couldn't help but be baffled by women but because they wished to be. A man's bafflement, she whispered to Patty, is his shelter, the insufficient lean-to he builds against the hailstorm of a woman's devotion to him. Jefferson, for instance, never imagined Eddie missed her Pittsburgh hothouse, her tendrils of orchids, the gloves of the house callers folded like buds when the talk went past midnight into the following morning. Had Jefferson asked, Eddie would have told the truth and that she wanted to be sent home. Never would she have lied outright to her brother, "Yes, Jefferson, I willingly consent to spend the whole of my womanly life raising your absent wife's trio of swan-necked daughters."

How hilariously stupid men allowed themselves to be, Eddie whispered to Patty, the men as stupid as the turtles in their sacks, frozen senseless in their shells. One funny warm February Sunday, Eddie had discovered the winter's catch of thawed reptiles thumping their way past the drawstrings of the sacs, their cumbersome claws painting streaks of red mud in the dirt. She picked them up two by two, lifted them over the cellar steps to the wet, snowy hill, then found a bucket of cranberries for a flapjack supper instead. She would never eat turtle soup again, she declared to the empty kitchen. Now, nearly a century later, it was amusement, not anger, that made Eddie cause Tip to drop his fork on his plate before she freed herself of her thick-seamed dress and joined Patty's cigarette smoke on its way to the tilted windows. You'll be fine, she gave a last whisper to Patty, you'll be alone for a while, but not without pride. As for me . . . how long will it take for a ghost to reach Pittsburgh? How many decades, how many wild geraniums, how many dropped stitches, missed trains, stolen dresses? However long, finally, Edith Ann Alden Atwater VanCleve was on her way home. Her name came to her like a path she might follow.

The fork fell from Tip's hand with an echoing clatter, and the words *I missed her birthday* slipped into Tip's head, as if, having dropped the fork, his mind created the reason for having done so.

He wanted, he really wanted, to slip from the table and vanish into the kitchen, where he might pretend to be needed on professional matters. The railing in this loft area wasn't quite right, was too decorated, too festooned with memorabilia. Had the cast iron skillets been Patty's idea? Certainly not. What might Patty suggest a man buy a woman four months late for her birthday? he was stammering to ask. That, and how old was she? If he was thirty, she was thirty-one, the age Tip's mother had been when she died. Tip weighed this vindictive fact in his head. Meanwhile a chip of wariness floated in each of Patty's brown eyes like small cameos in which he could see himself making a fool of himself. She seemed to know before he did what would come of this moment. An even greater embarrassment. No birthday present. Too embarrassing to have to buy and wrap a present after having been reminded to do so, as if he were obeying her. Besides, her next birthday would come in eight months, far enough away he might regain face by remembering it on his own. Unless, of course, he forgot it again. A man who loved a woman remembered her birthday, Patty saw him thinking. He must not love her, then, Tip said to himself, feeling tacky but rescued.

"I'll make it up to you at the cabin this weekend," he lamely offered. This was finally just another of those hemmed-in moments he'd come to expect with girls, women, whatever you called them these days.

Patty looked taller in the Jack of Steaks loft than on ordinary ground, when she rose from the table. The vaulted ceiling made way for her exit. Two sets of steps led from the loft to the main floor of the restaurant—service and public. Earlier, Patty and Tip had climbed the service steps up from the kitchen, but now it was the big, front, wooden, open-slat stairway for which she was headed. Funny that Tip should still be seated at the table, the dropped fork between his fingers, while Patty placed her hand upon the banister, and yet it seemed to be Tip who was walking away from Patty and not the other way around. Lawrence was right; if Tip couldn't stick with Patty, chances are there wasn't a girl in the world he'd stick with. Connie, Marissa, Jennifer, Laura, he could practically smell their shampoos on the pillow beside him, could see the lotions they swapped in his medicine cabinet, could imagine any one of them waiting too patiently for him to remember their birthdays and him camped at his table as if it were an island, the lit candle as susceptible to contemplation as a campfire. But Tip pulled his eyes from its doubtful flicker. He wouldn't steep himself in an examination of the ice cubes in his drink, the way other men might when they were left alone at tables. Nor would he leave without paying his bill. Unlike the rest of his family, Tip always paid at Jack of Steaks, to make sure he knew how it felt to be a customer hoping to get his money's worth. In return, he raided the bar after hours, buying drinks for the dishwasher up to his elbows in scraped-off plates. Dishwashing was the most physically taxing of all restaurant jobs. Valentine's Day was the worst day of the year to be in the business, for there were often arguments and spilled strawberry daiquiris and women knocking over the vases when they took their free carnations as if they knew they'd never get another thing out of the guy. Bread was the hardest food to keep fresh. If the rest rooms weren't stocked with paper and soap, you might as well shoot yourself in the head as try to keep the clientele you wanted. Ketchup bottles were not to be tipped lip to lip for refilling within view of the customers. Tablecloths were real linens, to be replaced with fresh ones between each and every seating. Milk was to be served in chilled glasses, beer in frosted mugs, salads on plates that had had time to cool after washing, potatoes and mushrooms thoroughly scrubbed, Bloody Marys garnished with one stalk of pickled asparagus, two olives, and a cocktail onion. No strips of masking tape were to be affixed to the coffeepots. All waiters and waitresses dressed in black jeans and a Jack of Steaks cotton knit polo adorned with the playing card logo. Not one of this litany of company rules could keep Tip from wondering if any man glanced from his T-bone in time to see up Patty's skirt as her high heels knocked on the wide-open stairway. Talk about skylights. Patty's North Pole could make any man witness whole constellations. Tip was jealous of anyone who would ever, from now on, for all time, get a glimpse of what glistened between those lace garters. His hard-on under the restaurant table broke the biggest rule of all.

6

"Name what part I am for and proceed," recited the Fisheries biologist, who had spent far more than the one dormant winter she'd forseen for herself on the day long ago she'd erected the sawhorses for the migrating frogs. Now that she was well into middle age, she was determined to spend this spring the way she'd originally planned—not dormant but open, her ears newly pierced, her body trembling with her own receptivity to the morning. Now she knelt on Birch Lane where it skirted the lake. A collage of hand-lettered *No Trespassing* signs marked the tree trunks of a nearby driveway, but the sky was vivid with fans of ivory sunlight breaking through a high pink tumble of cloud, and no one could hammer a *No Trespassing* sign up there. To the north, the marshy inlets of Asylum Bay rippled with tall yellow grasses, and above the defunct lighthouse, a blue heron faltered in a downdraft of wind.

The lake was just recently thawed, no longer clinking with slivers of left-behind ice. The fields to the south were flooded with runnels of dew. Blackbirds stirred on the broken-down fence posts. The time was seven o'clock on a late April morning, too early for the fishermen who later would gather on the same stretch of road used by lovers at night. Carp ponds. Car ponds. Nobody could tell her which was the real name, but both names made sense.

But the Fisheries biologist hadn't dropped to her knees in awe or stupefaction. With the earpiece of her sunglasses she traced the bulbous curve of a toddler's red plaid sneaker that stood alone on a mossy tree stump at lake's edge.

Like many women, she had a special fondness for baby shoes. When she'd first glimpsed it on the tree stump, she'd mistaken the shoe for a finch. Some teenagers were welcoming spring by drowning seagulls in Menominee Park, then tossing the dead birds onto the recreation trail, and for this reason the Fisheries biologist had stopped out of town on her way to work, driven into this shoreside neighborhood of mobile homes and cockeyed houses to see if the same thing was happening here. So, she kept her eye open for mangled birds—they were her *search image,* she said to herself in the jargon of her schooling—and since the sight of a murdered finch disturbed her far more than any mangled clump of seagull, her throat closed as she approached it. Truth was, she didn't much care about the screechy, nasty gulls. On the island where they nested in the harbor, they were drifts of sooty snow. Flying singly or in flocks, they were greedy and territorial, they smelled moldy and sour, their eyes were too small, they

showered the trail with slippery gobs of droppings. They sometimes attacked the swallows, and even inland from the lake they
crowded the tops of fast-food joints and outcompeted the
pigeons for spilled popcorn outside the movie theaters.

The next couple she knew who were having a baby, she'd buy
them a pair of smudgy plaid sneakers like this one, the biologist
decided, relieved to see it wasn't a drowned finch or even a gull.
A nugget of gravel was wedged in the scalloped tread of the sole,
but she felt she'd be presumptuous, a trespasser in the domain of
mothers and fathers, if she pried the pebble loose. She left the
sneaker on the stump for the parents to stumble upon, pulled
her hair through the ponytail band of her cap, and resolved to
walk around the whimsical neighborhood before climbing back
in the jeep.

On Cozy Lane the air smelled of bacon and eggs and clumps
of butter-and-eggs flowers. The houses were scattered like
blocks, decorated with cut-out silhouettes of zebras and cows.
The lanes went every which way or just stopped short. Around
here, any child small enough to fit in that sneaker must believe
he lives in Toyland. Two plywood geese wearing polka-dot bon-
nets carried a basket of apples between one kitchen door and
another, and on a broken-down flatbed were planted flags for a
vegetable garden. Pinwheels spun in the slightest of breezes. On
an actual caboose parked in one of the driveways, a silhouette of
a cowboy smoked a red pipe, and the multitiered swallow houses
were painted bright yellows and greens. Everywhere she turned
was another funhouse of mailboxes lined up in rows. Finally she
paused to listen in a willowy lot, where a tiger-striped rowboat
hung between posts of a swing set. The sound of the bike was far
off but approaching, her friend Shane's custom engine a mile or
so away on County Trunk A. In the week he'd been visiting her
from his home far north in Superior, he made a point of showing
up at her office bearing freshly packed lunch, his head bowed in
its bandanna so as not to hit the door frame. And one day when
he missed her at work, he caught her on her way home, appre-
hended her like a highway bandit, brandishing the faded bandanna. Most of the week, Shane slept through the mornings, his

full beard quaking where he lay on her couch, his head propped on one armrest, his bent knees on the other, his massive feet so pearly clean she laughed out loud when she first caught sight of them.

"You'd make a perfect milk mustache ad," she liked to say to him fondly instead of asking if he knew why the two of them were letting him sleep alone on her couch instead of in bed with her. He dressed like one of the biker gang the Sons of Silence, but when he wasn't on his bike there was always a tall glass of milk within reach of his clipped fingernails. The milk unveiled him. He'd be rolling a joint and there it would sit. Shane wasn't nearly as tough as he wanted to look. Her job was to remind him of that now and then over the years. They'd been friends a long time, too long, maybe, for anything romantic to transpire—through college, through graduate school, straight into her job at the Department of Natural Resources and Shane's belated escape from academia into the wild peace and bikerly rumble of his pizza place in the north woods. Mosquitoes big as dragonflies, he told her that first summer he phoned from Superior. Hats as big as pizzas, Mars so close in the sky sometime he could toss it in a wishing well just like a coin. What would he wish for? He wouldn't tell her if she asked, but she wouldn't, anyway, because she knew she'd be denied the chance to give it to him. Denied not by Shane, and not by herself, but by some pact they'd forged unwittingly between them, the same pact that kept him silent when he'd noticed her newly pierced ears, as if a mere compliment might be enough to suggest she had done it for him. Whatever he wanted of life, besides sleeping on her couch, shelling peanuts, and watching movies in her living room, skinny-dipping sometimes, going for beers—whatever besides that he wanted, he and she seemed to have arranged that he would need to get it from some other woman. She hoped he did someday, too. He was such a lamb, such a lion. His leather jacket was as cracked as a mudflat in August, but his jeans were mended with iron-ons instead of sewn-on patches. No thimble was big enough for his fingers and he didn't like pricking himself with the needle.

He must have caught sight of the DNR vehicle on Birch Lane, for now she heard the motorcycle turn the corner off A and slow to a throaty whisper as it made its respectful way to the water. Shane wasn't the type to stir up the blackbirds in Toyland. Christ, he didn't even like dogs barking in his direction. She felt the ripple of the engine in the ground underfoot as the bike crept closer along the twist of dead ends. But when she turned to greet Shane, she caught sight of the tiger-striped hull of the rowboat gently swinging where it hung from the swing set.

The moment she saw one bare foot poking past the gunwale, the Fisheries biologist knew it was the toddler with the missing plaid sneaker. Soon the other foot followed, still wearing its shoe, but barely, the strips of Velcro already undone. When the child poked his head up, the boat tipped just enough to let him flop easily onto the ground. A few crocuses bloomed near the posts but didn't claim his attention. Nor did the cuckoo clock mailbox nailed to a tree, the cuckoo bobbing on a rusty spring, a letter affixed to its clothespin beak. Even that did not distract him from whatever he seemed to be looking at, out on the lake. Except there was nothing out there. The few coots had flown off, an eddy of Kentucky Fried Chicken litter had floated past the elbow of the shore. The ground looked slippery where the toddler headed. Maybe he intended to dog-paddle to Chilton, imagined the biologist, recalling the tagged deer that once braved a summer alone on the seagull nesting island. At summer's close, the deer vanished, to be discovered weeks later munching melon rinds off a compost heap in Chilton, twelve miles away on the opposite shore of the lake.

"Hey," she called, humbled not to know what to say to a baby. She could beckon a field mouse right up to her palm, call an owl so close she could feel its gaze swivel to meet her own. She could lure a spawning salamander into her own cap, but she couldn't stop the baby from sliding his bare toes into the water.

Just then Shane rode up beside her with a flash of bandanna and chrome, like a bandaged knight. The toddler turned from the water and grinned like a pumpkin.

"They're looking for you on Y," Shane admonished the little

boy. "They flagged me down to ask if I had seen you. I tell you, if I had a baby-sitter cute as yours, I'd grow up *real* fast, get out of those stinky diapers, crawl into something more comfortable."

Already the toddler, having crossed the narrow stubble of yard, reached for the glint of the handlebars. Shane lifted the boy by his overalls and swung him onto the seat as easily as if he was used to a baby of his own. But Shane was one of those men who answered, "Not that I know of," whenever anyone asked him if he had kids.

"Do me your biggest favor," he said to the biologist. He pushed a lock of her hair out of her eyes and tucked it under her cap. She always was grateful for the way he touched her—no expectations, no disappointments attached.

"For you, anything," she answered. "But Shane, something's ringing in the lake, or else it's just in my ears. You hear it?"

"Only thing I hear is this kid's baby-sitter begging to wrap her legs around me in return for bringing him back," Shane said, raising one eyebrow. "How about I come to your office after lunch, tell you what flavor she served at the reunion?"

"That's fine," the biologist assented.

She lifted her hands to the ringing in her ears, shook the sound from her head, listened a moment until it crept back in, more persistent than before. When the bike spun away toward the windmills and the cutouts, Shane with one leather-jacketed arm close around the baby, she remembered the sneaker perched on the tree stump at the end of Birch Lane. Maybe a maple seed would take up residence in it, sprout through the spongy inner sole to the moss of the stump, grow a whole new maple right out of the shoe like a one-legged puppet, its nodding head a crown of yellow leaves. Wouldn't that be a fitting result of this morning? she asked herself, watching the scrim of Kentucky Fried Chicken litter float serenely into view again, just a bucket and a plate, some crinkled paper trailing a plastic fork. What Department of Natural Resources employee was worth her government paycheck if she didn't fish the garbage out of the lake when it was right there in front of her, practically begging her to come and get it, even if she didn't know how to swim.

7

Finally one Sunday when Tip had nothing better to do—the walleye weren't biting, and no game on TV, and he'd already finished mowing the lawn and chasing Doc's tail with the mower— he loaded Doc in the truck and headed for County Trunk A. Driving, he began to regret not having lain down for a nap, as he often napped on Sundays, the dimness of the day tangling itself in his deep blue sheets, and Tip chuckling in sleep, sighing, grunting, scratching, rolling over. When he was done napping, he often started the grill, for the restaurants closed on Sundays. He'd grill a venison steak, he decided now, as if lying naked in bed rather than following the road out of town. Her nose at rest on the dashboard, Doc tried not to show her excitement at the familiar stretch of road. She wouldn't let herself sit up or wag her tail or stick her face out the window, but when one paw slid off the seat, she was too rapt to pull herself upright again—too much in doggy suspense to move so much as a whisker.

"Where are we going, sweetheart?" Tip teased. "What road are we on? What do you smell? Who do you taste? What house is that? Who are we going to see?" he teased.

One of Doc's ears shifted backward, the other forward. That was all the response she allowed. When Tip pulled the truck into the gravel driveway and opened his door, she was already out the window, and when he shut the door behind him, Doc had already clambered up the dog ramp into the boat. There, she didn't slide down the tilted deck on her toenails as she remembered. She only sat at the bow and determined from which direction the smell of lake flies was blowing. All directions, she resolved. The two other puppies, her brother and sister, had been taken to distant towns, but her mother and the others were inside the house, lulled by the noise of the vacuum cleaner, whose wires Honey had recently repaired with a bread tie and rubber cement. Doc had once watched Tip attempt to vacuum under the stove without realizing the hose wasn't fastened to the machine. The vacuum cleaner whined in its usual fashion; Tip pushed the unattached hose along the floor; nothing came up; the clumps of dog hair and bread crumbs and stray pieces of breakfast cereal remained. Tip, annoyed, dragged the vacuum cleaner into the basement to be fooled around with long enough to satisfy himself he'd at least tried to fix it before he bought a new one. Even Tip's and Honey's vacuum cleaners, opposites, would attract, Doc understood, though not in so many words.

Honey didn't hear Tip's knock. When she had finished with the hallway and switched off the vacuum cleaner, there was still the radio playing while she rummaged in her work bag for the things she needed to bring out to the picnic table, where the baby-sitter had arrived for her manicure appointment. She, the baby-sitter, would be attending a funeral of a lady she'd never met, a lady in whose mouth a tadpole was swimming when she'd been pulled from the lake.

"I don't need to pretend to be sad," the baby-sitter explained to Honey when she'd made her appointment. "First of all I didn't know her. Second of all, I really am sad. For Shane. He was her friend for years. Besides, can you imagine whose funeral it would be if she hadn't found Robbie before Robbie went into the water? I could scream, thinking of that. Not because I'm responsible, either. I mean, that's not the only reason."

You're not responsible. But at least you mean to be, Honey had thought. Australian opal, she decided, would be a good polish to wear to the funeral of a person you'd never met. It had sparkle and depth, and planes of vanishing lavender buried amid black layers. Death wasn't entirely dark, Honey was certain, preferring to think of a multihued, flexible, traversable universe, just like this one. A tadpole swimming in the drowned woman's mouth! The papers hadn't included that part. The baby-sitter had heard it from Shane, who'd heard it from the dead woman's coworkers, who were raising the tadpole in a jar of lake water on the dead woman's office desk at the Department of Natural Resources. When the legs and arms had sprouted, they would let the frog go, with some kind of ceremony. Honey wondered what ceremony could be equal to the thing itself. Such an incubation seemed ceremony enough. In Honey's estimation, almost anything that happened happened in its own honor. Sex was a celebration of sex, food a celebration of food, spring its own welcome-home party. Today she wasn't downcast but conscious of sadness—her own, other people's, the world's in general. When a butterfly flitted past, Honey thought to herself it would die in two days, but that only made the flick of its wings all the more remarkable. It wasn't grief but polish that stung her eyes when she dipped the small brush past the lip of the bottle.

The baby-sitter was wearing six necklaces. Her hair was cut in bleached feathers. She wore nothing under the laced-up leather vest. When Tip arrived at the picnic table, she gave him only a twitch of a smile, keeping her eye on the kitchen door from which Shane might soon emerge. Honey set beers on the table, dwarfing the jar of nail polish. Then she clapped both hands on her hips and leveled on Tip a look of amusement.

"I take it we have some unfinished business," she said.

"I always was great at business," said Tip.

"But did you leave something behind, last time you were here?" Honey wondered.

"My checkbook's in the glove compartment like always," said Tip. "My sunglasses are at work, my other pair of sunglasses are on my kitchen counter, my other pair of sunglasses got stepped on by a friend of mine."

"That's something, to have your sunglasses go to work for you every morning," the baby-sitter remarked.

"Stepped on on purpose, or by mistake?" Honey asked, thinking he was built like a slingshot, Tip. All tension, yet absolute repose.

Tip hesitated. This opportunistic girl was weighing his pros and cons, he realized. Without even knowing she was doing it maybe, she leveled her clear eyes between his legs and enthusiastically took his measure.

"On purpose, but I deserved it," he said. He took a seat on the picnic table, where the baby-sitter was already peeling the label off one of the beers. The beer was Ko-oalan Lager, brewed in Honolulu. Please, not another fancy-drinks girl, Tip said to himself about Honey. But she's too young for me anyway. But there's something old about her. Not old old. Self-assured. Smart. Down to earth. But not entirely beholden to the constraints of ordinary mortality. A head of hair like it has its own generator in it, could power the entire neighborhood.

A tall glass of chocolate milk stood unattended at one end of the picnic table. It hadn't been there very long, Tip noticed; it was still cool; condensation clung all the way up the sides. Also, there was a baby in the dog pen, under the shade of a beach umbrella, stacking paper cups into a tower, then knocking them down with a kitchen scrub brush. The toddler's undershirt was stained pink, though the cup he lifted to his mouth was empty. The juice was in a baby bottle stuck in one of the fence links like a water bottle for a pet rodent. Outside the pen, the dogs, racing zigzags through the rivers of unmown grass between houses, paused now and then at their shared bowl of water snugly balanced on a coiled garden hose. Everywhere Tip looked was something to drink. He was suddenly terribly thirsty. Maybe that's what he'd missed, ever since he'd been here last—taking a long drink of anything. No matter how restful Sundays were supposed to be, he had things on his mind. It was Lawrence who'd stepped on Tip's sunglasses, after Tip had inquired of him if Lawrence was using the restaurant PIN and credit card number.

"The reason I wouldn't hold it against you is because I know you're not using the numbers for yourself," Tip had said firmly to Lawrence. "But I can imagine you wanting to help out someone else, and you planning to pay me back and everything, right?"

"This is to prove to you it wasn't me," Lawrence had responded after a moment. He plucked Tip's sunglasses off the crown of Tip's head, laid them evenly on the floor, and ground the rubbery toe of his running shoe into the lenses. One lens, then the other. Lawrence had once seen somebody do this in Harry's. "I would never crush anyone's sunglasses unless I meant it," he said, confused. Somehow the stunt had been more to the point, in Harry's. Tip's green-tinted wraparounds lay in two twisted pieces. Tip regarded them with fascination. Finally Lawrence had said, "I didn't take the credit card, and I have no use for a telephone card, and as far as I know I'm not helping anyone out with anything. I don't even know anybody in Finland, wherever the hell that place is."

Tip opened his beer with more force than necessary, requiring that he lick the foam off his fingers. Why was his proximity to Honey different from his proximity to other women in the past? he wondered. The usual magnetic laws didn't seem in operation. Usually Tip stayed in one place and the girls slid over in his direction. Even Patty, much as she maintained her composure, had effectively been handed him by his sister. Maybe Honey stayed cool because the picnic table was her place of business, Tip speculated, having already observed that nearly any place on earth might be Honey's place of business. Efficiently, she unscrewed a bottle of polish, clamping the lid between her teeth while taking the baby-sitter's fingers in her other hand and spreading them delicately apart. Her dexterity was mesmerizing. In comparison Tip felt only that he was fumbling with his purpose in being here. Since he'd never entertained any fantasies about Honey, how could they possibly come to pass? At last he forced himself to think of one, but it was too outlandish, and way too crude for Honey's standards. In the fantasy, Honey, weighing Tip's pros and cons, took his cock in her hand, just as she now held the baby-sitter's wrist, and said, "The pros are big and pressing. The cons inflexible. Let me chew on it awhile."

"Australian opal," Honey said to the baby-sitter. Those were her only words, as if in deliberate contrast to the ones Tip imagined her speaking. Tip pondered them as if they were a warning. Between her lips the words *Australian opal* sounded more substantial and longer lasting than any fantasy Tip had ever conjured into being.

"Shane fell asleep in the armchair," the baby-sitter divulged. "His feet stick so far out I can't make it to the phone without waking him. I think he's sleeping because he feels guilty. I think because of what's happening between him and me. I think he regrets the timing, him and me getting together . . . A lot of people are coming to the memorial service. Which might make him feel guilty, too. He thought she didn't know anyone except him.

There are people from her office, from her exercise club, folks she'd go for pizza with, that sort of thing. Is that my telephone? My mother wants me to call her."

Honey spread the polish in thick blunt strokes, in such measured fashion that even the baby-sitter began to understand the unusual need for silence, unusual because Honey was known for her easy conversation with customers. But this evening, Honey commanded silence in much the same way Tip often commanded hilarity. Every fingernail she painted—and when she finished with the baby-sitter's, she started in on the toddler, who cooed when Honey took him onto her lap—every chipped or perfect oval of Australian opal presented a warning to Tip that she was equal to the task of him. Her stick-to-itiveness was daunting in the extreme, all her pragmatism suffused with ardor. Interestingly, she appeared to have chosen not to look him in the eyes just yet, but there was urgency in her avoidance of the gaze.

Tip finished one beer, then another. Honey drank no beer at all, only ice water in which a lollipop was dissolving. The baby-sitter drank far more beer than she could handle, and fought Honey's decree of silence with more nervous chatter that ended only when Shane found them on the lawn and invited her to lean her agitated head on his shoulder. He drank a swallow of chocolate milk before proposing that the four of them—Honey and the baby-sitter, himself and Tip—promise to attend one another's funerals. Finally he swirled a finger inside his glass to even out the flavor, coaxing the baby-sitter's lips just wide enough apart to tilt the glass between them. She was quiet after that, her bleached hair aquiver on the biker's shoulder. Half an hour went by in which the only sound was the grunting of dogs. Evening started to fall. Shane would make a fine salad chef, Tip whispered to Honey. Guys like Shane could shred a cabbage with one swipe of a cleaver, then make a radish blossom into a rose just by squinting at it sideways.

"Tell me another time," Honey responded, refusing Tip's offer of beer, though her lips grew as moist as if she'd accepted. As often happened between Honey and her mother, the thing a normal mother might have said to her daughter became the thing Honey needed to say to herself, instead. Honey had been drinking too much beer, was what Angie hadn't said and never would say. So Honey filled in the gap. Drink beer only on alternate weeks, she scolded, and then, being Angie, reassured herself by saying, All mothers have their lapses. A mother who noticed her child drinking too much beer might not say a word about it, while a mother who'd be gung ho to talk about it probably wouldn't notice the guzzled beer in the first place. On the other hand, the mother who pretends to be everything to her child isn't kidding anyone. Honey took another sip of lollipop water, this week's nonalcoholic concoction, which didn't come close to quenching the thirst Tip seemed intent on creating in her.

"How old are you?" Tip whispered.

"Shhhh," Honey answered, as Tip had been poised for her to do.

"Nineteen," Tip guessed correctly.

Twilight gathered on the grass. Doc sat still with her eyes on the tennis ball the other dogs were passing around, chewing to shreds. Despite the wisps of the baby-sitter's hair commingling with his, the biker grieved more wrenchingly than anyone might console him, Doc noted right away. The toddler worried about his approaching bedtime, when he'd be expected to remain in his crib without anyone watching. According to Doc, those were the only glitches on this otherwise satisfying evening. The air smelled of four blustery workhorses being brushed in their stalls at the fairgrounds beyond the train tracks. Tip already smelled faintly of Honey, and Honey of Tip. Doc lunged for the tennis ball and closed her firm teeth around the savory concoction the other dogs had made of it, then snuck it under the table to finish it off. She wouldn't have traded being a dog for anything.

11

Polly Makes a Few Changes
in the Book of Sid

But of all that had happened, what I knew was only how much I didn't.

Even the tadpole swimming in the dead biologist's mouth, even the lake flies, even the toddler with the pink feather duster, even the ghost on her way to the hothouse. Even the wind, even the button with the anchor on it, even you know more than I do, I snarled at the Night, but the Night only folded Its darkness deep in Its big black pockets. You cad, I pleaded. You Hottentot. You ass. Tell me what to do. The Night raised Its eyebrows, like trees swelling with wind, and made the lamps flicker on the Book of Sid, which would be of little use to me, if any, or so I thought as I sat reading in spite of my worries.

Matt, Wheat, Freak, Titty, Foote, Cal, I read.

But what's that got to do with keeping the hungry ghost, Tom, away from Honey and my son? I asked, and turned another gold-leafed page so fiercely it tore, and beat some dust from the lamp shade, and held back my tears, and stanched my terror, and distracted my frenzy, and brushed back my hair although I had no hair. Sid was getting old, or so he kept telling himself, and that was why he could remember the names of his long-ago friends in no other order. Nothing demanded his allegiance to this order rather than to others, except that his old friends' faces, lined up that way in his mind's eye to begin with, beheld him.

Matt was always pushing to be first, I read. Cal was so mellow he was likely to forget he'd been handed the joint. Foote was the only person Sid had ever known to unfailingly say thank you in such a situation regardless of how many times the joint had completed the rounds of the living room. Titty snorted every time Foote said thanks, and Freak regarded every lull as an opportunity to introduce some philosophical quandary, such as whether cows were higher or lower than trees on the spectrum of self-awareness, "whatever that means," Wheat always said, but since Matt was so impatient, he was often out of the room by that time, as he was on the day in question, looking to play a trick on someone.

Sid had an album of photographs of his first wife posing naked for the camera in attitudes she and Sid selected from his stacks of magazines, except she wouldn't tilt her head back over one shoulder like some of the models, arguing she wasn't the coy type, now was she? Several poses depended on a ladder-back chair and a Stetson, but Sid found he preferred the simpler ones—a pillow for Mary to lean on, a fringed shawl they spread smooth on the floor underneath her, her body unadorned except by its own time-honored fleshly accessories. Thirty years later he can still remember what it felt like to kneel behind the steamed-up lens of the Polaroid camera, though thank God Mary didn't exactly have a pinup figure. Who needed one? The photos made him see her body's imperfections more clearly and therefore more indulgently than he saw them in the flesh—the lurid darkness of her crotch that turned imploring in the eye of the camera, the wobble of her thigh that never quite moved him in bed but on film caused the shadows to fall lumpy rather than smooth, making him want to tease and soothe them with his tongue. As for the physics of nude shots, angles presented a problem; Sid was trying to teach himself to aim for her pussy without foreshortening her legs or shortchanging her face, which to his regret looked more forgiving in these pictures than in person—regret because the face in the pictures was the one to whom he'd rather be married. Their little photo sessions—evenings after dinner, curtains drawn in the living room, Sid dressed in thermal long johns if it was winter, the heat blasting from the vents and then going quiet, blasting and then going quiet again, Mary with her fingers parting her labia—brought out, paradoxically, an innocence in her. And she was a difficult woman, Mary. Well, maybe she'd had a difficult life, would be a nicer way of putting it, though Sid sometimes wondered if that was nicer than required—what did it matter why she was a man-eating bitch as long as he was the one who got chewed up and swallowed? Still, during that second, not to mention last, winter of their marriage, the photos made him feel more generous toward her, as if instead of being merely scarred inside the way he supposed she was, she was also tenderhearted, the way he supposed she wasn't.

Sid had kept the photos in several white business envelopes in a plain manila envelope in a cardboard box containing ordinary photos, on the floor of the bedroom closet rather than in his strongbox or backpack or anything someone might borrow or steal. His life or marriage, whichever came within reach first, would be handed over to the great beyond if those pictures got out of his possession, Mary had warned him, and he'd have hell to pay if she found out he showed them to any horny sailor, no matter how long the ship was at sea. Sid had just enlisted in the navy. In a month he and Mary would be moving to Norfolk, Virginia, in preparation for his orders, but the photos would be the last thing Sid packed, meaning to keep his eye on them.

One day, by way of testing Sid's promise that he'd tell her if the photos were missing, Mary stole them herself and, after cutting into slivers the ones in which she wasn't her type, hid the rest in the kitchen, under the silverware divider, another thing that wouldn't be packed until last. Matt was the only person she told about the hidden nude portraits, when he came upon Mary dumping the slivers of rejected poses into a Chinese take-out carton to be dropped in the garbage, where they looked like leftover cellophane noodles. Maybe she thought it wasn't worth it to play a joke on Sid if none of his friends knew about it, or maybe she meant to tempt Matt into peeking at the photos under the silverware. But Matt was more loyal to Sid than Mary imagined, and anyway was tired of Mary flashing her knives and spoons in the direction of his appetite.

So on the day in question, when Wheat, Freak, Titty, Foote, Cal, and Sid were having one of their farewell parties in Sid's living room (Freak and Titty would join the marines just after Sid left for Florida, Freak would be wounded in an ambush, Titty's name ended up on one of these POW bracelets teenage girls wore, but no one knew it was him because they used his real name) and Mary was at her sister's house two streets away, Matt slipped the manila envelope from the silverware drawer, removed the white business envelopes of photos, and rehid them in a Betty Crocker file box of recipes without pausing to gape at the pictures. In the other room Freak went on about how cows were at the bottom of the spectrum of self-awareness among animate objects but trees were at the top of the spectrum of self-awareness among inanimate objects so maybe that meant cows and trees were equal though Freak didn't think so; Freak thought cows were empty-headed while trees were abstruse. It was possible boulders were more complexly self-aware than trees, Freak suggested, going on to affirm that just because cows were stupid didn't mean elk were, too. When crossing a river, a mother elk creates an eddy in which her offspring might cross in safety, Freak explained.

Matt rolled his eyes. He slid the empty manila envelope under the silverware again, and stood the Betty Crocker file box near the stove, where he'd found it. Once Mary discovered the photos were missing, Matt would tell Sid what he'd done. That way, the joke would be on her instead of on Sid.

Except as luck would have it Mary wasn't fond of cooking, and since the Betty Crocker recipes weren't something Mary wished to drag to Virginia, she included the file in a grab bag of cookbooks that sold for seventy-five cents at that week's moving sale. Among other items Mary sold was Sid's dead mother's Christmas cactus, which never bloomed on the day for which it was named. In the years that the cactus flowered too early, the pink crepey trumpets dropped from the plant and turned limp in the pot by the time Christmas Eve rolled around, and in the years it bloomed late, the first flower didn't open until after New Year's. Sid had built a shelf especially for it under the southwest window of his and Mary's apartment, and strung white bulbs around the edge to make up for the cactus being a Scrooge. Winter or summer, the plant didn't require much tending, but for a while it seemed every time he went near it, he caught sight of the neighbors' unruly kids doing something they shouldn't be— blackening the aluminum siding of their building with charcoal briquettes, for instance, or chopping raw green limbs off the maple, or attempting to pry up whole sections of driveway. Their names were Charmaine and Danny. Charmaine was a butterball with pierced ears, like her mother, and Danny was already a hood like his dad, and from the window Sid could see their futures spread out before them like there was a kitchen somewhere already filling up with dirty frying pans for Charmaine to leave the last fried egg to stick to if nobody ate it, and for Danny a rusting car with a saggy fender dragging the same sweater behind it all winter until one muddy day in April you'd hear someone yell, "Hey! Mom's sweater!"

But on the day in question the car was being loaded down with clothing still on its hangers and drawers yanked from dressers stacked three deep. Into the trunk went the TV, the sound system, some blankets, and a bread box stuffed with pairs of slippers, but the jack and spare tire lay forgotten on the sidewalk next to the kids' bicycles and a cage with the gerbil still in it.

"Where you going?" Sid called.

"Nebraska," said Charmaine.

"Nebraska's that way," said her dad, pointing west with a hair dryer. "We're going that way." He pointed south and set the hair dryer on the roof of the car. "We have twenty-three dollars, nineteen cents, and half a carton of cigarettes to get there with," he told Sid, who'd come outside to help.

"Here, kid," said Sid, and handed the children two cans of Mountain Dew.

"And some apples," said their mother, coming out of the house with a scrunched paper bag.

Thank God for apples, Sid thought. By five o'clock that evening the family was gone, and at five-thirty somebody knocked on Sid and Mary's door. It was a county social worker, whose visit with the children's parents had been requested by the school guidance counselors. She took the gerbil cage with her when Sid said they were gone, the pet shivering in the wood shavings when she carried it off. Later that evening when there was another knock on the door, Sid thought, *Mary.* She hadn't been home from work yet that day. Often if she got home late and didn't feel like digging in her purse for her keys, she knocked, even though he never locked up if he was the only one home.

But at the door was a man Sid recognized from when he'd worked years before at a printer's in Iola, a man who once lifted the copy machine straight off the floor so one of the girls could retrieve her heirloom ring.

"Where'd they go?" he asked Sid.

There seemed no need for explanation.

"Not a fifth of the way to Texas," Sid guessed.

"In what car? She still owes me six hundred dollars for that piece a shit."

"We're not likely to find a check sitting under the saltshaker on her tablecloth," Sid opined.

The two men crossed the darkened driveway and went upstairs to the abandoned apartment to see what they could find. Everything was as expected. Food still on the plates and a Cabbage Patch doll askew on a stripped-down mattress, schoolbooks and underwear scattered under chairs. But in a back room were twenty-eight microwave ovens still stapled in their boxes under a set of pink shower curtains.

"I'm not touching those," said the man, though in the end they each took one of the ovens and Sid took the shower curtain as a hymn to cleanliness. Unlike Mary, the shower curtain lasted all the way through to the end of Sid's second leave home from the navy with his friend Thomas, who was the first black person Sid ever really got to know. On the day in question, the woman tattoo artist, while giving Thomas a tattoo, advised Sid he ought to grow sideburns instead. Sid had the navy's requisite whitewall haircut; nothing but peach fuzz around his ears, including the one that'd been blown half off in the gunner's turret. He was twenty-two years old at that time, a baby, already married, divorced, maimed, healed, scared shitless some days, emboldened on others, and one of his shirtsleeves gnawed to tatters by its share of mysterious troubles. The sideburns would make Sid look like a Confederate soldier, advised the woman tattooing Thomas's arm. They would make him look like he had a Southern belle waiting for him in Chattanooga, and a mother who kept his letters in a drawer in a chifforobe. The artist bent closer to Thomas's arm, unaware of the pang she'd given Sid by having mentioned letters home. He hadn't written one to anyone but Mary, his wife, and look where that got him. Rope Yarn Sundays were the days set aside for writing letters home from ship. Also for sharpening knives, shining shoes, studying for rating exams, and sewing on buttons, but more than Rope Yarn Sundays, Sid preferred the two Sundays a year set aside for Holy Stoning. They used to do it like praying, dancing, or fucking; throw their bodies into the spirit of things. First, choose a brick, any brick. Then, chisel a dent the size of a quarter in the middle of the brick, unscrew a mop from its pole, and wedge the tip of the pole in the dent in the brick. The ship's deck was Sid's favorite of all blond woods. Between the wood and the brick went a mixture of sand and salt water pumped from the ocean, and then the grueling task began, the whole crew in shorts and T-shirts pushing the deafening bricks, the boat roaring with friction, the wood too hot to stand on and so clean at the end you had to shield your sunglasses against the snowy incandescence. Thirty years later Sid used this technique to sand the floors of the cabin he built in exchange for the trailer he kept in Carol's woods. On the day in question, he sold the trailer for thirty-five hundred dollars to a bartender in Green Bay, facilitating his escape from the amorous riffs of the married violinist, then surprised himself by being so careless as to test the money's sticking power by making a stop at the Oneida Casino. If all was lost at the casino, Sid was resigned to finding work in Green Bay. But if the money was doubled, he was destined to think of something much better to do. It didn't bother him to patronize the casino in spite of what so many die-hard Wisconsinites had to say about it, that the folks on the reservation had a lot of balls demanding their spearfishing heritage and tax-free hi-tech casinos at the same time. Can't have it both ways, the white fishermen along with rednecks like Lysle liked to rant and complain. The Oneida want to spearfish like their ancestors, they ought to live off their catch and forget about money and Western medicine and paved roads and TV sets and start dying of smallpox again, not that anyone wanted them dropping dead under the disco lights at the craps tables, but goddamn it, they gotta realize they lost the fucking war. Sid disagreed. There was nothing wrong with a person clinging to his past at the same time he courted the future. Who didn't? He stifled a sneeze, tickled by the idea of having a future again. He had a future every time he picked up and moved, but this future seemed different, as if it might really last, as if the calm that overtook him when he found a new place might really seem to have been waiting for him instead of being merely something he'd stumbled upon by default. Preposterous, but he imagined a place that might even *require* his presence. At least gambling made him feel like he wasn't alone in the world. Coins cascaded from the slot machine as if fortune itself condoned him. Quarters pooled around his hiking boots and swung in the hammock he made of his jacket to catch them. The attendant raised her eyebrows every time he almost sneezed when he stood at the counter changing the money to bills, the smell of the quarters twitching in his nostrils, the tiny colorful threads in the astonishing stack of hundreds bringing tears to his eyes not of sorrow or joy but of an abundance of regret that couldn't be reduced to its constituent parts no matter how carefully he named them. So close to his rightful future, he suddenly lamented all the futures he'd failed in the past. He wished he'd never left the navy, he wished he'd done his twenty years, he wished he'd earned his full pension, he wished he hadn't lost track of Thomas, he wished he hadn't lost track of his second wife, he wished he hadn't lost track of Mary, either. He wished the kayak he'd traded for the sword on the Mekong was still in his possession. He was glad he'd left the sword to his nephew, Gem—treat this mother-fucking weapon with the respect that the blood still probably on it deserves, he'd admonished the boy—but now he wished he'd taken Gem along with him, too.

On the other hand, it perplexed Sid, always, the Book of Sid confided, that the things he left behind were never abstract, once they were out of his reach. They made just as much clamor inside his head as if they were shelves overcrowded with tangible, throwable, breakable objects. He could still duplicate, for instance, the exact positioning of the upper and lower lips required for the smoking of every pot pipe he'd ever bought or borrowed. He could feel in his hand the heft of a mess hall soup-spoon, and in the small of his back the weight of each log he'd hefted while building the cabin. A tin clamor, a green din. Every loud report of every weapon he'd fired, every flat moan and sharp cry made by the violinist tuning her instrument, crowding him out of his trailer, now overwhelmed him. There were too many faces, too many scrapes, too many genialities for him ever to have enough peace and quiet. Some days all he wanted was to hammer a nail, but the nail always drummed up bygone stories and the hammer did, too. From now on, he resolved, he'd collect no new memories, no new mistakes or regrets. There'd be only him and the hour unfolding, him and the day like two of Freak's boulders sitting quietly in a blustery meadow passing their allot-ted millennia together. Sid wouldn't shine his shoes for anyone, he wouldn't cut off his silver braid for anyone, he wouldn't even write a letter home if anyone tried to make him unless the writing might unencumber his heart, which it wouldn't. What could? Home. But where was home if he was always loading it on his back and carrying it off again somewhere else? Sid nearly sneezed again. Some people left home only to have the pleasure of coming back to it. Some people traveled in order to return. But where was Sid's return? To where might he at last come back and rest? Not a place he'd ever been, his memories of which were lined up like tokens on tended graves, a Christmas cactus at one headstone, a can of Mountain Dew propped at the next, a vet-eran's medal, a case of beer, a camp stove, kayak, sword, box of chocolates, centerfold portrait. No, Sid wouldn't go back to those sentimental sites even if he could. He had in mind a clean berth no sooner than he was damn good and ready for one.

The casino attendant arched her penciled brows for the fifth or sixth time when at last Sid caught the sneeze and held it prisoner against the roof of his mouth. By the time it trickled meekly into his gut, he was ready to be off. He folded the bills into the silver money clip, slid the clip into his front jean pocket, started the car, picked a highway, any highway, and drove until he found the thing that looked like it needed him most.

12

Something's Burning

Knowing it would be impossible for her daughter and her three guests to attend one another's funerals as they were promising, Angie had nearly called out the window to tell them so. The window in her garage attic study was high and triangular like a tipped-up arrow, tilted open just enough on this spring evening that their balmy laughter swooshed gently past the glass to fall on Angie's shoulders, ruffling her sleeves. Already she'd climbed onto the arm of her chair to aim her voice at the lawn, but when her forehead grazed the window, the triangle swing shut and couldn't be knocked open again without the black rubber mallet, which was nestled in the junk drawer near the sink in the laundry room. Everything in Honey's house was where it belonged, Honey's mother reflected. Including Angie herself, she thought rather unhappily, still standing barefooted on the overstuffed arm of the chair.

"One of you is going to have to do your funeral alone unless two or more of you die at the same time," she said to the window, glad, finally, that no one could hear her. What good could come of correcting their fantasy, when all a fantasy was was an editing job—the splicing together of all unremarkable ways in which the material world and human inclinations failed routinely to coalesce? If the four people at the picnic table needed to believe they could somehow reconcile what they wanted with what was offered, then let them believe they could. Who would fault them for being hopeful on such a bounteous night—the picnic table a raft on a sea of grass, the darting figures of the dogs leaving wakes behind their tails, the twilight painting itself like water on cloth, deepening all the colors? Even here in the darkening attic, the bleached feathers of the wood duck decoy gleamed with small illusions of lost greens and faded blues, a few slashes of vermilion winking themselves into existence with neither paint nor brush in sight. The wood duck, come to think of it, wasn't where it belonged, for it would've looked perfect nestled in the patches of foxglove sprouting around the dog pen or in the shadow of the neighbor's voluminous willow. In the attic with Angie, the decoy was too lightweight to serve as a bookend, its delegation as paper-weight being more suited anyway to its bachelor identity. *SWD ISO someone to ruffle my feathers,* Angie had doodled on a yellow Post-it pad, composing personals for avian classifieds. *Single Male Wood Duck seeks nesting type. MD has lots of patience, in search of partner, no quacks.* Angie still liked that ad best, though it lacked a certain smoldering quality she frequently detected in the decoy itself. At the end of a long day, the bird looked ashen, dusty with cabin fever, while underneath their weathered stoicism the wings yearned for action, longed to take flight, even only as far as the picnic on the lawn.

Abandoned by DA but still no victim, Angie wrote, then filled in the words *Duck's Ass* before crossing them out desultorily.

Lately Angie felt restless, too, though she could barely admit the fact of this burgeoning eagerness even to herself. Maybe, just maybe, she'd have preferred to join in the picnic rather than remain a closet onlooker. It wasn't Honey who kept her locked in the attic, Angie sometimes needed to remember. Angie did it herself, the key a red Bic marking pen, the spares rattling in her pocket. If she'd ever known how to be sociable, she'd since for-gotten. More to the point, she felt forbidden to be sociable, as if under a spell in her tower above the garage, spinning bad student term papers into money in the bank and food in the cupboards. She liked the word *cupboards*—clung to it, really—because its unmodern quality mirrored her own and thus justified her seclusion. A board for cups—how naively old-fashioned a concept, like Angie herself. Her students at the university all recognized their instructor's vocabulary of attachment to a retreating past—the cobblestone doorstop she kept on the file cabinet instead of on the floor, where it might keep the door from closing in their faces, their graded papers stashed behind the mesh of the pie safe in the hall outside her office—so they visited only briefly and cordially even during office hours. In class she was fitful with industry. Their exams seemed to crackle when she handed them back, so busy with red ink that the ink seemed finally to be the thread that stitched their wrong answers together. Most of her students were as indifferent to language as if their mothers had banged cooking pots together instead of reading them nursery tales, she imagined complaining to her colleagues gathered in the hallway outside the main office, where the faculty and secretaries chatted. Maybe Angie would join them someday. Just maybe she had a "hankering" to chat, the old-fashioned word diluting, for a day or two, the immediacy of her longing. Lately they liked to joke about the memos sent by the chief of Campus Security, or by somebody forging his signature. The most recent warned that hairpins, carelessly dropped, might be picked up by suspicious persons who might use them to jimmy the office locks and make illegal use of the telephones. Prior memos forbade the inclusion of cans of tuna in any bagged lunches and the use of departmental petty cash for coin flipping during moments of curricular controversy.

When Angie was a child, she used to spy on her parents late at night through an open slot in the wall of a crammed linen closet. They'd be dressed in their socks and pajamas, playing hearts, smoking cigarettes, and talking about their meager investments. Surrounded by the bulging stacks of tablecloths and pillowcases, Angie pressed her face to the slot and dubiously eyed their dealing. In much the same manner she often stepped quietly across her cramped adjunct office and inched close enough to her open door to be able to see, and to wonder. If she was finally to exit her habit of seclusion and enter the real world again, was this really it? Or was it only another blanketed, murmuring closet?

Occasionally Angie caught sight of another figure standing in a doorway at the opposite end of the shiny hall, appearing to wonder the same thing. Once, when Angie just barely nodded her head, the figure eagerly nodded her own in return. This was all the exchange Angie had had so far with the recently hired poet in residence, whose name was Daphne. Aside from these few shadowy, eavesdropping glimpses (another old-fashioned word, *eavesdropping,* Angie comforted herself by thinking, someone slinking past the dowry trunk to press their ear against a knot in the wainscoting), Angie had caught sight of Daphne only once or twice, heading for lunch with the statuesque department chair, beside whom the tiny poet looked as bold as a stroke of calligraphy. Her first collection of poems was to be published in half a year by a small Boston press, and on the strength of this endorsement she'd been hired to teach poetry to the students who, having passed Angie's composition courses, became eligible for higher-level creative writing. Daphne's manuscript was included in her job application file, so early one Sunday evening Angie, who as an adjunct wasn't part of the hiring committee, had snuck in to look at it. The book was modeled on the *Physician's Desk Reference.* Each poem represented an ailment, and was far more playful, sly, and compassionate than Angie's colleagues appeared to believe poems could be. In the poem for diabetes, every adjective was *sweet* and every verb a form of *to needle.* But really the poem examined heredity along female lines, from the granddaughter's perspective. And the entry for renal failure included the same granddaughter lying supine on a patio chair while being cleansed of bitterness and bile but never—*across her dead body!*—of sorrow.

Close to the bubbling noise of the fish tank, in which the single fluted Chinese goldfish had fluttered in sleep like a submerged tiger lily (if the fish ever died, it was not to be flushed down the toilet, according to Security), Angie swiveled this way and that in the secretary's chair while unintentionally committing whole passages of her new colleague's poetry to memory. Bathed in the blue evening light of the fish tank, the manuscript of poems appeared to murmur in counterpoint to the bubbling filter, until the foursome, filter and paper, Angie and goldfish, seemed engaged in conversation. Despite her years-long habit of friendlessness, Angie recognized in this inanimate dialogue a frustrated facsimile of one she might have with Daphne, whose name was Daffy on the manuscript of poems. The two names made an appropriate enigma, for the poet resembled a boy in woman's clothing, his hawk nose casting shadows on a flat-chested tunic but his bottom peachy under drawstring pants. Angie imagined a field of stiff, sown grasses crackling under Daffy's delicate boots as she and Daffy walked across it talking and laughing, about subjects she couldn't likewise imagine, since she hadn't talked intimately with another grown woman since even before Tom had vanished. Whenever Angie's husband had approved of one of Angie's friends, he'd soon grown jealous of the friendship, and when the friendship didn't irk him, he grew disdainful of the friend. So Angie had lost the intuition for being on intimate terms with a woman. Besides, what visiting poet would glance twice at an adjunct composition instructor whose graduate thesis consisted of a binder carelessly swollen with random jottings, the pages a flurry, the never annotated tales an unhopeful mess of princes and wishes, dragons, mirrors, pricked fingers, and traded sows?

How ragged Angie's three-ring binder, compared to Daffy's sturdy sheaf of poems.

Saddened, Angie had distractedly laid the wonderful poems aside and gathered her things, meaning to make a necessary peace with her profession. If turning one brain-dead, marijuana-smoking simpleton into an essayist was no easier than spinning straw into gold, at least no king would order her beheading in the morning. If teaching English composition made her a peon in the eyes of a poet, so be it. How would she have managed to raise her daughter if, all those years of Honey's childhood, Angie had been a slave to the medieval rabble rousers of her thesis?

But had she really raised her daughter? Or had Honey raised

her? Though for years it was unclear exactly who was taking care of whom, only recently had this arrangement made Angie feel derelict. She felt blameworthy at having not been more motherly, censurable for not having incurred in her business-minded daughter the obligation to pay taxes on her earnings from the manicure jobs and the litters of puppies. Honey often went out (Angie rarely asked where) with one her friends (whose names and hobbies Angie overheard but whom she hardly cared to meet face to face) like a grown daughter was supposed to do. Had Honey actually graduated high school? Angie lamented not being sure. Was Honey using birth control? Did she need to? Angie sometimes guessed yes, sometimes no. Which of them earned more money? Which cooked a more nutritious dinner? Who would worry more if the other weren't home by bedtime? What was bedtime? Angie wished she knew the answers. Still, all mothers have their lapses, she reassured herself, unaware, as she'd forever remain, that these words were the same words Honey imagined her saying. Besides, Angie continued, any mother who pretends to be everything for her child makes a lousy model for an ordinary, fallible, absolvable human being, and isn't fooling anyone.

But if this was what was troubling Angie, something else was making Honey testy as well. Angie knew not to pressure her daughter for explanations. Having for so many years pretended that life was as she wanted, having less and less revealed to Honey her infrequent feelings of anger, confusion, and despair, having exercised such composure in the face of her welter of emotions toward Honey's decamped father that she no longer quite believed she ever had them, Angie couldn't very well turn to Honey and ask what's the matter.

"Nothing," Honey would undoubtedly answer, their talks less resilient, more perfunctory than ever before.

At Sunday dinner, Honey turned on the TV just when Angie was gathering the courage to ask if there was something they should be discussing. Angie's disappointment made her lethargic, though as the evening went on, the remembered phrases of Daffy's poems—the "too hurried transfusion," the "embryonic

miscalculations," the "unchaperoned square dance of genes"—
were like knocks on the door, trying to get her to let them in. Distractedly she wiped the table, climbed the whitewashed steps
from the garage to her study, and started grading student essays,
for which Angie's assigned topic this week was friendship. By
morning, the lines of Daffy's poems had slunk into a faintly echoing background, surrendered to dangling clauses and ambiguous
pronouns. Not until Angie went to work and heard the small faculty commotion outside the main office did she learn what the
lines must have been trying to tell her—that she had laid Daffy's
neat manila folder across a corner edge of the goldfish tank, and
that during the night the poems had fallen in.

"I saw a sort of a sea fan in there," the secretary was saying.
"So I—"

"But who would do that?" someone asked.

"Does Daphne know about it yet? Should we tell her?"

"Poor Daphne. Somebody's really . . ."

"Sick," said one of them.

And somebody else added, "Jealous. Even if it was by accident. You don't plunk someone's soon-to-be-published book in a
fish tank unless deep down you hate the jerk."

Angie backed silently up to her desk and tried to recall, from
the poem about meningitis, a line about the grown granddaughter being unable to swivel her head even painfully toward a
certain other person. But the words were indefinite, blurred, the
patient submerged, the sheets sodden around her. Maybe all
Daffy's poems would be watery now, with tentative rhythms and
uncertain edges, as if Angie *had* thrown them into the fish tank
on purpose in order to destroy them . . . out of envy or insanity,
as people speculated.

2

Now that winter was entirely, balmily over, seagulls flocked
everywhere in this broad, flat sprawl of a city, as likely to be
found in the sandpits of the golf course as on the flat roofs of the
gas stations. Now and then a gull made its perch on the boat on

Angie and Honey's lawn, not perplexed to find itself at such stationary mooring, for the moist lawn sloped like a wave just cresting. What remained of the chrome was peeling from the railing, and fell in silvery flakes when the gull took off. But no beautiful, remarkable, or ordinary thing that Angie saw in this city explained to her why she still felt she belonged here. Half a decade had passed since she'd given up wondering when and if the coast guard might stumble upon the remains of a body, and whole seasons went by when she felt no ghostly hint of Tom's presence—no clinking of coins being stacked on a dresser, no waking too early, and the San Diego Padres baseball cap remaining stuffed in her book bag, where she had left it. No longer did she always half expect to be flummoxed by her memories of his finicky ways, or miffed by the secret he'd kept of the plane, or shocked, all over again, by the thought of her tractor-driving husband knowing how to fly. Between one solstice and the next, the closest she came to remembering Tom might be a flicker of homesickness for the spreading cluster of mulberry trees that grew out of some buckling asphalt close to the farm outside Milwaukee. In season the mulberries ripened and fell, turning the crumbling pavement purple, staining even the leaves of the dandelions twisting up between the cracks. Evenings, Angie used to drive onto the asphalt, kick off her shoes, climb barefoot onto the sun-warmed hood, and pick the dangling berries for supper. At home, Tom plunked them in a colander, rinsed them ferociously with a nozzle, and baked them into pies or expertly risen muffins, but ate them only feeling vanquished, wishing he'd grown the berries himself or at the very least had picked them from some vine-laden corner of his own forty acres, the orchard of pear trees shamed by the flavor of the scavenged fruit. What a meddlesome contradiction, Tom. The sweeter the berries, the more destitutely he gazed at Angie from over the unfaultable muffins. In return, pretending to be unaware the perfect berries distressed him, she leveled her most accustomed expression, one of distracted happiness, in hopes he might pick up on it, start humming a tune while sanding the crested top of one of his decoys. For a moment, whenever Angie remembered the mulberries, she wished she had made Tom happier than he'd been, had taken the trouble to shake him free of his own shackles, somehow.

That same expression of absent-minded happiness she'd leveled on her surroundings for years, after he'd left her behind. If Tom's worrying affection for her remained in the air, if his anal personality still seemed to be fretting over one thing or another, Angie insisted on being too glad to be anything but vaguely conscious of that. And now that she'd begun to understand how wounded she'd been by Tom's defection, no matter if he'd deserted her on purpose or otherwise, and how grieved, finally, she'd been by his apparent, doubtless death, she was nearly healed. Time *was* a salve, but Angie knew her long seclusion had played a role in her healing, as had her reams of student papers with their lacerated confessions, her red ink blooming across the wounds, then stitching the rawest edges together.

She might not ever, she supposed, have anyone to talk to. Just once in a while would be enough. And maybe only by phone, Angie amended, unsure how she would fit another person in her study, where there was only the single, overstuffed chair, and the head-thumping slope of the rafters, and an entire rectangular section of floorboards missing between her desk and the vase of straggly peacock feathers. No one too tall or awkward, certainly not a man, would be comfortable in her study above the garage, but maybe, just maybe, someone would sit cross-legged on the rag rug quietly drinking tea.

On the evening Honey and her friends promised to attend one another's funerals, Angie was, as usual, astonished by her daughter's ease with other people. Once, she'd attributed Honey's friendliness to the natural social graces of childhood. But tonight, through the window, Angie observed her daughter more astutely than before, and saw that Honey appeared to have rescued all the spirit Angie and Tom must have packed away in mothballs and never nurtured between them. If there ever was a person to whom Angie might describe her daughter, she'd say, "Every good thing Honey does, something better spins out of it. Once, when Honey and I were walking near the softball dia-

mond where the Little Leaguers practice, a ball came over the
fence. Honey chased it along the bicycle trail where it rolled into
the hands of a little Hmong boy, bundled in red sweaters, out
fishing with his parents and aunts and uncles, so since Honey
couldn't bear to just take it away from him, she traded the boy a
friendship bracelet for the softball, ran the ball back to the fence
but tripped when she threw it over, so some of the dads came
running over from the softball diamond to—" and so on and so
on Angie would go, all the way to the part about the two dads
wanting to take Honey to dinner but instead Honey took the
walleye the Hmong had given her to the retirement home where
she does the ladies' pedicures, and where the old man who got to
clean the fish was so excited he forgot to take his medicine and
suffered a seizure that unlocked, in his mind, pictures of faces
he'd long since forgotten. "He described the faces, another old
lady drew them in a sketchbook, the sketches ended up not looking like the ones the man remembered but like faces some of the
other patients recognized, faces from *their* pasts, so everyone
rushed to tack them up in the cafeteria. That's what I'm talking
about. It's a kind of optimism or courage Honey brings to—"

Not having had a friend for so long, Angie would have forgotten the need to let the friend get a word in edgewise. Alone in
her upstairs study, realizing how boorishly her imagined friend
was being treated, Angie's speculation died on her lips, making
her prickly with embarrassment. Some people were lonely, others
simply alone, others meant to be loners. In a fairy tale, Angie
would be the willing hermit rather than the unwilling princess
locked in the tower miserably counting the leaves on the ivy
blocking daylight from the window. Solitude was to be her natural inclination, her niche in the cubbied tiers of society. The people hunkered in the chilly air around the picnic table—the
grieving biker with the black ribbon that remained tied around
the sleeve of his jacket even after he'd taken the jacket off, the
baby-sitter with the leather fringes swinging from her breasts,
and the X-shaped young man with the heartbreaking gray in his
hair—didn't know how good they had it. Honey would throw
flowers on all their coffins. She wouldn't cry, because she never

did, but she'd wear her high-top sneakers, whose treads would make designs of overlapping circles on the fresh-turned earth of their graves. To Honey, who all her life had been traversing ground that concealed every trace of her father, the ascendant yeasty sponginess of an actual grave must be like ordinary earth, Angie understood. And it occurred to her as well, for the very first time, that to Honey, whose father could be anywhere but was nowhere she looked, life and death must be equally elastic propositions, one no less impending or more elusive than the other. That was why Honey made her way so balanced between purposefulness and exhilaration. However sudden, fleeting, and accidental Honey's friendships, the friends she made were true.

Angie's unpracticed eye had seen this from as far away as the triangular window, but now, wishing to see it up close, she gathered her wits to step outside, pretending to admire the resounding blackness of the night. She carried her pen and one student paper so as not to make them think she might stay on the lawn all hours, lollygagging. She wanted a beer. How close might she come to the wine-red raft of the table and not seem to be clinging to it for dear life? Nobody saw her. The dogs had started barking on the side of the house facing County Trunk A, but Honey was being taken too seriously by the X-shaped man to care. Angie followed the concrete walkway around the garage, to find the dogs in a row like skidded cars honking at where the lawn met the road, where someone had paused on a bicycle. Against the insufficient glare from above the railroad tracks, the combination of rider and bike looked like some bizarre apparition of a giant insect. As Angie neared, the insect raised a human arm in greeting. The dogs went more wild but stood their ground. Angie discerned a diminutive figure in bicycle shorts. Man or woman, she couldn't tell.

"The lights on my bike are flickering," the figure shouted above the baying of the dogs. "I thought I'd walk instead of ride or at least get my bearings."

"I'll get the dogs out of your way," Angie replied.

Angie grabbed the dogs two at once by their collars and led them to the leads staked near the boat, both hoping and fearing her intuition was correct. She'd have been surprised to see how casually she moved in spite of her eyeglasses clenching sweat at the end of her nose, her hands tangled in ropes, her man's shirt open too many buttons, a bra cup showing. Finally the stranger came off her bike and grabbed the collars of the two remaining dogs, who licked her face apologetically.

"You're Angie," she realized when Angie had coaxed one of the dogs away.

"And you're Daffy," said Angie, even though that didn't sound like a very nice thing to say. But the poet only suffered more kisses from the last of the dogs, before asking if she could please use the bathroom.

3

Even before that first night began, as Angie plugged in her hot pot, filled it for two, and set two tea bags (oolong for Daffy, chamomile lemon for Angie) to steep in the unmatched mugs, Tom Bane had become aware of a slight permutation in the atmosphere. Aside from a few strands of grass and algae and the few souvenirs he'd coaxed through his harness of fishing line—the anchor coat button that had skidded out of Mr. Nichols's jacket pocket, a piece of fishing tackle resembling an earring, a sodden feather, and a contact lens—nothing but lake water inhabited him. Water sloshed in the spaces between his bones and made illusory pools in the dips and clavicles, soothing the swivel of ball from socket, or of one vertebra from the tenuous grasp of the next. Inside the rounded chamber of his rib cage, a restive current felt like nervousness to Tom, as if it were his heart and not the water that fluttered against his sternum, while any increase in barometric pressure made him feel heavyhearted. Thunder and lightning storms would already have shocked him into resuscitation and brought him back from the dead if they were ever going to, but shaken as he was by any crisis in the weather, the most that ever happened in a lasting way was that his chair fell apart where it had once bobbed against him and lay in rusted, spongy tatters around the bones of his pelvis.

Though it didn't amuse Tom to say to himself, I feel rather unnerved; the crash seems to have unhinged me; I can't even *lumbar* out of here, sometimes he did say it, because Angie liked puns and might have teased him in that fashion, the intentional irony of his wife's puns being that they would be speaking the truth; he *did* feel unnerved, unhinged, bloodless, breathless, blindsided. But scatterbrained, no. He was determined to take his death as seriously as it had taken him. Already one might say that he had managed to make something of his death, had not allowed it to drift away from him like seaweed clinging to a passing hull, or glisten on the wing of a darting mayfly before leaving him stranded in sludge. Mornings were spotlights hitting a mirror, evenings pellucid, nights penetrable if he made the effort to probe past the irrelevant stuff out there. Swallows, hornets, Jet Skis, paper cups, snowmobiles, snapping turtles, lost sandals . . . how irritating it all was, the lake a litter box of interference when all he intended was to fixate on the pure sky beyond it, and on the vision it might cast down to him. Where the top of the lake met the bottom of the sky was the zone upon which Angie walked with Honey, to and fro, toward Tom and then suddenly away from him and then gradually or all at once toward him again, hot, warm, cold, colder, warm hot hot cold. Sometimes when the water vibrated against the sky, that was Angie plunking a twelve-pack on the kitchen counter, and when the sky reared like a bedsheet hung on a line, that was Honey aiming the hose full force against the lake fly corpses clinging to the gutters.

How did Honey know how much her father liked a clean, neat, orderly house? Tom wondered. And how did she know Tom wanted her to break her boyfriends' hearts? The answer didn't matter as long as she kept doing it. Tom couldn't be bothered, anymore, with all the sent-away boyfriends he might once have been tempted to lure. Really, he preferred they suffer Honey's rejection than that they drown imagining she was going to miss them. Honey never missed anyone. Not even Tom. Didn't the boys know that? Twisted sweaters, Ray-Bans, an entire tub of diaper wipes—the disarray under the lake no longer aroused his interest so much, not even his souvenirs mattered anymore, as long as Honey and Angie behaved obediently as Tom was accustomed. They kept a sensible house, his devoted wife and somewhat wild but domesticated daughter, but still theirs was a house from which clearly the main man was missing. Around the central locus Tom might have occupied, the house swiveled like a mailbox loose on its post. He would've liked to be a plumber in that house for just three, four hours, or take a small, pointed trowel to a bucket of plaster. Still, Angie did the mowing the way Tom liked—the short, seamless rows overlapping, and no bag to catch the shorn ends of grass, so when she raked up the clippings, the lawn was combed softer than pasture.

She was up to something, Angie. He'd first felt it the evening she'd sat in the main office memorizing poems within sight of the Chinese goldfish. What was she trying to pull over on him?

Tom couldn't put the bleached bony knob of his finger on it, but there seemed to be something new happening that he wouldn't like if only he knew what it was. A maple pip skidded over the lake and broke the surface of the water with its papery blade. Some pips didn't do that. Some stayed on top. This one spun on a diagonal into the sand bed of grass. How arid this land was, under the water. How like a desert, a dune, the loose sand allowing Tom to see only a little more clearly the new thing that threatened him. When Daffy stirred sugar into her darkening tea, he felt a knocking in his skull, and when Tip bent his ear to Honey's description of the muscular legs of the retired dancer whose toenails she filed at the retirement home, Tom felt Tip's concentration travel along his snaggle of fishing line like a current along a wire.

The poet would be easy to lure past the margin of cattails, Tom considered, because she'd just recently moved to town and was therefore still exploring. Already she'd been to the bar with the Civil War memorabilia in Butte des Morts, and along the recreation trail, where, rounding a bend near sunset, she'd been mesmerized by the darkening silhouette of a grain elevator. Tom should have been reassured, but instead he felt weary, recalling the Fisheries biologist. Despite her willingness to wander into the water after the litter of fried chicken wrappings, the biologist had worn him out by being, after all, not what Tom wanted.

Didn't they always?

Wear him out?

After the exhilaration faded, wasn't he too often disappointed, bored even by the tadpole preparing to metamorphose in the mouth of one of the few women on earth who would have appreciated the gesture? Even the pink feather from the toddler's feather duster left Tom's ghost feeling gratified but spent, as if he really had wandered exhausted for years, searching, the way a ghost was supposed to. But it was difficult to roam when you were stuck in one place, confounded by tight knots of fishing line. That was why he had gotten into the habit of causing people and other animals to wander to him, instead. They did his wandering for him, as if ambling him closer to his destination. But really they didn't. Bring him closer. To his destination. Not even Honey's pets had brought him nearer to her, nor had his high-pitched keening ushered her closer to him in the lake. How deflating it was, not to be able to heave a disappointed sigh. But to have caused the poet's manuscript to fall into the goldfish tank—*that* was an accomplishment!—and now to cause the poet to forget she was holding a mug of tea . . . he found he could wring a modicum of pleasure from the way the mug tilted, the tea straining against the rim.

Too surprised by her visitor to be able to say or do much at all, Angie only watched the precarious tea, poised for the first hot spill.

Wincing, Daffy placed the mug on the rag rug and blotted her wet knee with the thermal sleeve of her Henley. Then she remarked, "It *was* you, Angie, wasn't it? Just tell me, so we can get it over with."

"Not out of jealousy, only by accident," Angie apologized, thinking sadly of the poems she'd plunged in the fish tank and left overnight for the goldfish to shit on.

"How do you do a thing like that by accident?" asked Daffy.

"You spend twenty years doing nothing but grading papers,"

Angie replied. "When you're done with each paper, you put your pen in your mouth and then with your left hand you reach for the next paper on the stack and with your right hand you drop the one you just finished into the yellow box."

Angie indicated a cardboard box on the desk. The yellow had faded; the toaster oven that had once been packaged inside the box had caught fire in the kitchen when Honey was three and had to be thrown out the door.

"Not Honey. The toaster oven," Angie said aloud.

Instead of making her blush, Angie's embarrassment at having completed her thought out loud revealed itself by fogging the tapered lenses of her elegant eyeglasses. If she concentrated hard enough, she might be able to correct her mistakes at least a split second before she made them, she considered hopefully, then dismissed the notion as impracticable. Not even the most accomplished composition instructor could edit her thoughts vigilantly enough to correct for twenty years of failing to want a friend, much less failing to make one. Since Angie and Honey, before they'd stopped talking, had been in the habit of doing most of their talking in the kitchen, it was possible that aside from scaring away Honey's disoriented boyfriends, Angie had never spoken aloud in this room to another human being.

Daffy appeared to sympathize. Angie wondered if Daffy wore a similar judicious expression when trying to figure out the next line in a poem—her head craned forward, her hawk nose jutting from under her shag of black hair. How plain she was. A squawk of a woman. Her head too large for such narrow shoulders. But her eyes were soulful and humorous under defiantly unplucked brows. "I don't think I know exactly what you're talking about," Daffy finally divulged, laying her palm across the top of her mug to catch the beaded-up steam.

"When Honey was three, there was a fire in the toaster oven," Angie explained. "She was buckled in her sling chair at the table. I was cooking eggs. She kept telling me there was a fire and I kept thinking she meant the one under the frying pan."

"Not that," Daffy interrupted.

"No. It was in the toaster oven. I didn't see it until I—"

"No, about dropping the papers into the yellow box. I don't know how you got onto that."

"Oh. I don't remember what we were talking about, either," Angie confessed.

"I asked if you were the one who did it and you said not on purpose."

"Oh. No. It wasn't on purpose. Unless I *am* jealous without knowing I am. You know that line, 'I'm a poet and I don't know it'? Well, I'm jealous of a poet but I don't know it," said Angie. "But really, I don't think so."

Daffy took a soothing swallow of tea. It was always an effort for her to keep herself from composing the lines of a new poem in her head when she was supposed to be focused on something else. Her friends in the town she had just moved away from all knew this about her, and were prepared for what they called her annoying fits of necessary reverie, the way she was likely to stare at a spiral of orange peel for a full two minutes without seeming to blink, and soon the orange peel appeared in one of her poems, slightly transformed, maybe a broken spiral instead of a whole one. It wasn't that her friends all accommodated themselves to her poetic distractions, her husband liked to remind her. It was only that the people who remained her friends were those who tolerated her lapses in attentiveness to them. The ones who couldn't got away. Survival of the Daffyest, in other words, said Gregory.

On certain nights in Angie's study the moon glinted on the railroad ties half a mile away. But tonight's sky remained opaque as velvet, and the murmur of voices from around the picnic table no longer seemed to reach through the window.

Angie had nearly forgotten them, anyway.

She supposed she was making too much of this visit. Daffy, caught on her bike on a moonless night, would have knocked on the door of the Winnebago Mental Health Institute if it wasn't obscured by that frowzy nest of willows. Shifting in her chair, Angie forced herself to recognize the intractability of her social ineptitude, as evidenced by the incontestable fact of her having overlooked the prerequisite of offering Daffy the chair instead of taking it herself. Even the tea was wrong. What did it matter that Daffy had chosen the oolong, when Angie had already snapped up the last bag of chamomile lemon? Angie sipped the oily tea with dismay, wondering if too much of the evening had elapsed for a sudden infusion of manners.

"How are you feeling about your new job? The boring department, the brain-dead students, the seagulls pooping on your books," Angie added, chagrined. Was this the kind of thing she'd have said all these years if she'd had someone to talk to?

"I don't think it's boring," Daffy answered. "Some of my students are smart, and the smartest ones are always most wary. Not of me, but of poetry per se. And then you start talking to them, and when you hear about the things they're going through . . . jailed sisters, lost food stamps . . . there's only so much travail a person can take and still agree to spend their spare three seconds diagramming a poem. But have you ever noticed how many really fine poets used to be stutterers? Dyslexics? Other than that . . . I get claustrophobic on all campuses. All the ornamental grasses, and brick and brick and brick, and meetings meetings meetings meetings meetings. How long have you been in the department for? Not that I don't like meetings," she added. "Some of my best friends are meetings."

"You talk to your students? About their *lives?*" Angie was agog. A sigh escaped from Angie's chair, and then a piece of white stuffing popped free of an upholstery seam and parachuted gently through the hole in the floorboards. "I used to wonder if my daughter would be a student here. But she gets claustrophobic if you even mention school. She once climbed out the window of her third-grade classroom."

"I didn't know you had a daughter."

"She'll be twenty, this year. Her father disappeared before she was born. His airplane's in the lake. Bits and pieces of the fuselage."

Daffy's hawk nose inched forward yet farther, her hair parting around it as if to afford a more decipherable view of the puzzle Angie presented. Angie was trembling, with general nervousness or with the import of what she'd just revealed, Daffy couldn't tell. Daffy had already observed that Angie wasn't used to spending time with other people. She seemed so very eager, and she kept making small, forgivable gaffs. For instance, she had offered Daffy no saucer or spoon on which to put her tea bag, the mug of tea by now so strong Daffy knew she'd have a hard time sleeping that night. Also, in plain sight beneath the desk lay a pair of ragged panties trailing a thread of elastic, probably kicked out from under a bathrobe some midnight a long time ago.

"I used to think he went to Hawaii, other times I used to think he hid at his brother's in Ohio. No effects in the lake, as they say; no pilot's license, driver's license, secret Kiwanis Club membership card. Which confused me for a while, because I preferred confusion to certainty. If a man fakes his death in order to set up a new life in Nevada or somewhere, why would he take his old wallet with him? And then I'd think, Yes, but if a man faked his death, wouldn't he think it would help to leave a body? So he couldn't have faked it, I used to say to myself, because there wasn't a body. Except he couldn't have died, either, because there wasn't a wallet. The whole thing never got any less hilarious. Now that he's dead—I mean he *has* to be dead, doesn't he?— now that he's dead I try not to laugh about it anymore," Angie concluded ironically.

"This lake?" Daffy asked. "Before Honey was born."

"The plane was found when she was eight. And he'd never even told me he could fly. So I learned he was a liar same time I learned he was dead. But it was only a lie of omission. He just didn't want me to know the most exciting thing about him, maybe so I wouldn't miss him so much when he was gone," Angie explained. Funny to be talking about this after so many years of keeping it to herself, and funny, too, how her feelings and thoughts, hitherto a dense fog of worries and hopes, might seem to be impressing themselves upon her in the act of being spoken, becoming animate, somehow, like a genie let out of a jar, who might let her in on yet another secret she didn't want to hear. A cigar-smoking genie, Angie amended, sniffing the air and catching a faint whiff of cigar smoke.

"You poor thing," Daffy comforted.

"No, I'm not," Angie countered.

"But anyone would say—"

"But anyone doesn't."

"But if you told them about it, they—"

"But I don't," Angie countered. "I haven't even really ever talked about it with—" She caught herself up. She'd been going to say she'd never talked about it even with Honey. Her own daughter. Who was nearly grown, nearly a woman, nearly as old as Angie herself had been when Tom had vanished. Except he hadn't quite thoroughly vanished, had he? Angie wondered, sniffing another trace of cigar smoke while yearning momentarily for the quiet midnight hours of the empty study, the graded papers piling up beside her, and no one making her say things or think things she'd never thought or said before. Words made things final. Or maybe finality found its expression in words.

Daffy raised her unkempt eyebrows. "Why did you say 'secret Kiwanis Club membership card'? Since when is membership in the Kiwanis Club a secret?" she inquired, goose-bumped, tugging at the hems of her bicycle shorts.

"Because if Tom was a member of the Kiwanis Club, he knew better than to tell me. What woman wants to have to look at a Kiwanis Club member in the shower every morning? Not me," Angie insisted.

The chair gave another sigh, and the same piece of stuffing that had vanished past the floorboards rose from the hole and was levitated over the desk. A second piece clung to a cushion, not having yet been released. It seemed to Daffy an act of supreme generosity that Angie had chosen to get through two decades alone rather than to burden any student or friend with her troubles, or even to write poems about them. Angie was like the toys in children's stories, the toys who came alive when the children left the room, and bravely sorted out their problems— their feuds, their discontentments, their popped springs and missed gears—only to snap stoically back into position when the children reappeared. Except now the big chair with its telltale loose seam threatened to give her away. Which Angie seemed to want it to, really. If no one could blame her for protecting her privacy so many years, surely no one could fault her wanting a coconspirator. Daffy would write the poems *for* her, then, hexed by the dandelion fluff of upholstery stuffing floating around in search of a poem to drift into and set seed. Maybe she'd start tonight, since she wouldn't be sleeping. The insomniac tea was gone, the bag seeping caffeine into the mug. But Daffy didn't set the mug down just yet, out of kindness for Angie, who seemed not to want the visit to end.

"Did you the leave the word *patient* out of all of your poems on purpose?" Angie asked. "So you have doctors and hospitals and nurses and examining table but no patients, pun intended? Or was that just how the poems turned out?"

"First it was by accident, then I noticed it and started doing it on purpose. Thanks for noticing. No one else did," said Daffy, conscious of Angie's pleasure on hearing this compliment. Had Daffy not been so aware of Angie's long habit of forbearance, she would already have risen from her getting-to-be-uncomfortable seat on the bumpy rag rug, bypassed the smeary underwear at the foot of the armchair, and offered Angie a shoulder to cry on, a luxury Angie had probably never been offered. Nor had the daughter most likely, wherever she was. Daffy wondered how closely the daughter resembled the mother—if with their shy confrontationalism, their resilient bodies that appeared to have been knocked over only to spring awkwardly up again, mother and daughter managed to be each other's ballast and support. If so, where was she, the bewildering daughter? She'd be wearing a man's shirt, too, a shirt that, like Angie's, was one the husband must have kept in the rear of the closet, because the shirts hung in front had all been worn threadbare since the night he didn't come home. *I can't tell if it's on purpose that you're so unhuggable,* Daffy imagined saying to Angie, turning Angie's question back in her direction, *or if that's just how you turned out.*

Instead she asked, "I still don't know exactly what you mean, when you said you didn't do it out of jealousy but by accident. Why would anyone think it was jealousy? And how could you do a thing like that by accident?"

"I *am* entirely sorry," said Angie, confusing Daffy even more. Daffy didn't know a thing about the poems in the fish tank. No one had told her the fate of her manuscript, which was in fact her only hard copy. The other copy along with the disc was in the hands of the press in Boston. The outdated computer over which she'd slaved through eight revisions of the manuscript had been donated, before the move, to Big Brother, Big Sister. When Daffy had asked Angie if Angie had been the one to do it, she wasn't talking about the blurred, lumpy poems that when not yet dry had been slipped back into her application file. She was talking about something else entirely, namely, the fake interoffice memos. It seemed fitting to Daffy that Angie had written them, though neither jealousy nor happenstance provided explanation. No matter, Daffy reasoned, recalling the chilly darkness and the dismal pedal home. What had she been thinking when she had set off, oh, hours ago? Gregory would be sleeping by now if he wasn't still in Madison. Could she borrow a flashlight, she asked as they made for the stairs, wondering how, of all her new colleagues at the university, she'd managed to be stranded at the home of the one too addled to offer a ride.

Disappointed at seeing Daffy place her mug on the kitchen counter and button the neck of her Henley, Angie neglected to switch on the outside light. In the back of the house, the screens flexed in the windows. Along Cozy Lane, the colorful pinwheels ticked as they spun while the maple leaves held their silvery insides hidden. Beyond shore in a dip past a sandbar, Tom Bane fussed on his mattress of silt. The tangle of fishing line pulled at its own knots when it wavered in a current. Among the rustling cattails dotting the marshy inlet behind the defunct lighthouse at Asylum Point, the season's first crickets had not yet stirred, but Tom's femur lay poised in its bracelet of seaweed, listening for them. Crickets brought luck. The Chinese once kept them in ornate cages. Alive, Tom had always disdained the notion of luck along with any superstition. Ladders were ladders, black cats were black cats, crickets were the farmer's thermometer: divide the number of chirps per minute by four, add forty, the answer accurately represented the ambient temperature in Fahrenheit.

One chirp per second meant the air was fifty-five degrees. Strange but true. No luck about it. But tonight he felt he could have used some luck, he'd have been relieved to hear the sawing of crickets and know there was a chorus egging him on, easing his disgruntlement. It wasn't fair that he should be so far from his daughter, so near and yet so distant she wouldn't know his face if he rose up before her, plucked the San Francisco Giants cap off her head, and plunked it on his own. And it wasn't fair that when Tip, at the picnic table in the backyard, felt the breeze playing against the zipper of his jeans, he confused the breeze gladly for the lust that was there all the time, anyway.

Always trusting his instincts about his companion's desire, Tip grasped Honey's hand the way he'd watched her grasp the baby-sitter's knuckles, and slid the tips of Honey's fingers under the half-inch flap of his tightly closed fly.

Honey didn't startle. She never did. She sat tantalizingly still. From their place on the opposite bench of the picnic table, the sitter and the biker observed the incremental change in Honey's posture and guessed the reason even though they couldn't see her hand. Despite next morning's funeral, they were taking the evening's romance in stride, Shane said to himself as if to ask the dead biologist for her permission. Permission to do what? she might ask. To be incautious, he'd answer, to pitch himself forward against this pungent new romance as if into an illusion, against the sitter's fringed vest as if testing its ability to keep him from hitting the floor. When the sitter took hold of his empty milk glass and rose from the table, he followed, the fringes of her vest barely swaying in the breeze as he rested his hand on the small of her back. Honey said to Tip, "They look like a man purchasing a Victorian lamp."

"Already turned on," Tip added, hoping the plan wasn't to leave Honey saddled with the toddler, who now lay asleep on a blanket in the pen. So, people keep their babies in dog pens these days, Tip noted, wanting to show Honey the picture of him in the cherry bucket. Women always got a soft spot when they looked at that photo and saw the essential gladness of him, as one girlfriend had too aristocratically put it, although Tip couldn't remember which one. Tonight, the distinctions Tip had once made among all his female companions held no meaning anymore. Even their names—EileenPattyMaryAnne-Catherine—ran together like the list of saints he'd been expected to memorize in school. Some were girlfriends, some lovers; tonight he couldn't remember the difference. Was Mary Anne one girl or two? What made one a lover and another a girlfriend? Probably had to do with the way they sucked cock, Tip decided, tense under Honey's smooth knuckles. When the door of the yellow house swung open so fast it made a dent in the siding, Tip flinched. Knotted only in a towel, her fringed vest gone, the sitter raced down the steps and made barefoot for the dog pen to collect the baby. No mother could make more primal a gesture than the way she unlatched the gate, squatted on her haunches, walked into the pen in that posture, scooped the toddler in his blanket, backed out of the pen still crab-walking, and raised his tousled blond head to her shoulder as she rose up again.

"I must have watched her perform that maneuver more than a hundred times, and the answer is no, for your information, the towel has never come undone," Honey firmly declared. Then she gave Tip's hard cock a squeeze of blue denim, traveled the length of the zipper with the crook of her knuckles, but didn't unzip it the way he desperately wished, and moved her hand onto her lap as if to state her hand's preference for laps for the moment. Her own, not Tip's. Possibly there was something even *prim* about her, Tip feared. But if there was, he wouldn't break it. It would be the piece of china remaining in the shop with the bull in it, the single item remaining on the shelf when every vase and cup around it had shattered apart. If he sang to her as they made love, she would splinter like a painted rose on porcelain. But there would still be the prim, untouchable part of her preserved on its shelf. The songs he sang off-key into the ears of his lovers while sliding into their bodies were often Eagles hits. But not this time, for Tip didn't want the song playing in his head already, couldn't stand the disparity between what he was certain would soon come to pass and what hadn't yet transpired. To Honey, the one he would sing would have to be one of his drowned friend, Johnny's. No music, no lyrics. A song not yet born, yet a ghost of a song. A song already buried yet never conceived. A song risen up yet part of the earth.

"If you were wearing a skirt, I'd slide my hand up it like this," Tip insisted, and pushed his finger inside the foamy lip of the beer bottle.

Honey considered a moment before responding. "No matter what you do, you're not disgusting. That's one of the first things I noticed about you."

Later Tip would say to Lawrence, "I can't tell if she's hitting me when I'm already flat on my back, or if she's knocking me off my feet."

"But she's got a good punch," Lawrence would add, as usual translating Tip's remark into its lowest common denominator.

Tip, who could already anticipate Honey's punches, wondered if there was anything she admired yet feared about him in return for the things he admired yet feared about her. Possibly he'd know before the night was over. But how long were the nights in these parts, he longed to know, toying with the label of his Ko-oalan beer.

"I don't mean to be crude," he finally said.

"No. The crude things you do aren't crude once you've done them," said Honey seriously, for their bantering quota had been fulfilled. Tip swallowed, bore up, tried to be brave. He felt haunted again by the environment at large and wondered what part of it, nosy or fond, might try to make his next decision for him. Make it a good one, he wanted to say. And then he wanted to add, None of your business, for as usual his self-sufficiency, ingrained in him since the days of the cherry bucket, seemed to butt up against some willful encroachment. In some places in the neighborhood, the blustery weather gained force, while in others it eased. The unmown grasses succumbed to a momentary calm, while the treetops rasped. The cable antennas swiveled on the rooftops. A moth alighted on the table. From the front lawn came the creak of the mast as if the boat had come unmoored.

"I'd like to sleep in the V berth tonight," Honey told him. A breeze knocked off her San Francisco Giants cap, but she didn't chase it. "I've never wanted to sleep there before because of the spiderwebs."

"We can sweep them away with my shirt," Tip offered.

He took off his muscle shirt and handed it, balled up, to Honey. Honey knelt and untied her own laces. Not his.

"Don't go into that boat with your shoes on," she made sure he knew. "It scuffs the scuffs."

Then she waited while he pushed off his shoes and socks. Not to be one-upped in the delicate matter of whether or not they were going to sleep together, he unbuckled his belt as well, a compromise between leaving it on and letting Honey undo it herself. He pulled it smoothly from the loops and rolled it tightly to be wedged in one of his sneakers. Doc darted between the legs of the picnic table to pause at Tip's crotch. She had radar for his erections. She didn't like to hang around when he had sex, but she always knew when it was starting and when it was over. Shirtless, shoeless, he let Honey lead him toward the boat and the answer to his question. Would he fuck her, or not? He couldn't stand *no*. Yet *yes* frightened him terribly. The silence he expected to hear in his lovers—like the primitive silence of trees, against which his shouts and even his whispers were so satisfyingly loud—was upside down and backward in Honey. He was the one who felt silenced as they neared the boat, which he'd examined earlier that evening when Doc jumped belowdeck. His impression had been unfavorable. No man worth his fishing reel, depth finder, and radar screen would dodder around in a moth-eaten sailboat when he might race a speedboat instead. But now Tip's own power boat, in the shop since the previous summer, suffering one repair or another, was nearly forgotten in his hopes for the renewal of the cramped little V berth, its moldering cushions, its view of the night through the propped-open hatch, the centerboard out of sight like the blade of a rusty pocketknife ready to cut from one side of the lake to the other if he and Honey were able to coax it free. Even the question of whether or not they'd have sex paled in light of the other things he wanted to happen. He welcomed the problem of the bilges steamy with melted snow and spring rains, and how together he and Honey would need to scoop out the years' detritus—the buckets of drowned spiders and slimy clots of vegetation—and toss it overboard.

But there in the front yard were two people saying good night to each other. The smaller wheeled her bicycle down the front walk, then bent to adjust its troublesome kickstand just as the porch light at last went on. Honey's mother, whom Tip recognized from the color of her hair and the dignified set of her shoulders, stood on the front stoop holding back a few dogs and being valiantly polite in the face of her guest's departure. Her awkwardness was the thing Tip marked in his mind as being the quality most different between mother and daughter. Meanwhile he already knew what he was going to be unable to stop himself from doing. His ears rang with the irreversibility of what had already been put into motion. Maybe the earth compelled him, maybe the sky. Maybe something he had eaten, maybe something he had left untouched on a plate. It wasn't Jack who had taught him to be this polite. Chivalrous, yes, but self-sacrificing, never. Still, Tip was going to offer the squirrely woman a ride home, so in her dark clothes she wouldn't be mistaken for a rodent by a ravenous hawk, or pushed off the side of the road by a trucker with a distaste for *I Break for Small Animals* bumper stickers.

Her bicycle fit in his truck bed. Her feet barely reached the floor when she took her place in the passenger seat. His dashboard compartment flipped open when they rounded a corner, spilling out his assortment of shotgun casings.

"What do you mean, she said she's a poet?" Lawrence asked when Tip told him the story of his stopped-short evening with Honey.

"I mean the lady writes poems, I guess," said Tip, keeping his mouth shut about the other thing Daffy had told him, that she was an atheist. Something to do with her being a poet, she'd tried to explain. Lawrence would screw up the table bussing if he knew. Atheism wasn't exactly a popular sport in this part of Wisconsin. And Tip could see why. It was one thing to renounce God for something He either had or hadn't done, Tip reasoned, but to deny His existence was too weird and existential, not to mention self-deceptive, when all you needed to do was look in the mirror to see what a mess the Guy had already made of you.

Daffy lived all the way over on Twelfth Street in a house with an impressive set of shortwave radio antennas, and by the time Tip had dropped her off, unloaded her bicycle, waited for Daffy to let herself in the door, and sped back to County Trunk A, hoping to be greeted by a citronella glow on the boat deck, Honey's house was dark and closed, accustomed to the slumber of mother and daughter inside it. The V berth was empty. Doc found Tip's sneakers somewhere near the picnic table, but Tip didn't put them on. Honey was probably wearing his muscle shirt, and the poet was wearing the flannel he kept in the truck. He had shirts all over town in dresser drawers and closets, unless women burned them. Once, a girl had returned to him some other old boyfriend's shirt by mistake. It was a good shirt, but Tip had long bypassed it when he went through his closet, until the time came to give it to another chilly lover needing something extra to cloak herself under. Probably that's why so many girlfriends gave their boyfriends presents of sweaters and shirts— to have enough to go around. But that didn't make it acceptable for half the women in town to be decked out in left-behind Jack of Steaks polos. Jack had laid down that law a long time ago, scolding Tip and his brothers with, "We don't need that kind of public relations."

Tip was chilly when he drove home, but didn't want to submit to the whim of the world around him by shutting the windows. Not very often did Tip become aware of having relinquished, to the capricious universe, control of his options. Maybe not ever before. Even when Johnny lay unbearably drowned on the roll of soaked white paper on the table in the emergency room, Tip had felt that to tear the EKG unit out of the wall and smash it in the sink was to follow his own inspiration, not somebody else's. At the same time, tonight as on others, he craved advice, guidance, succor from a voice far back in his memory, a sound like dishes being washed behind the closed door of a kitchen, but since he couldn't hear it now there was nothing to do but throw himself onto his couch in this zoo of an apartment complex where the usual late-night parties couldn't entice him. Nor could the boardwalk at Lake Butte des Morts, the rickety planks he still followed now and then to the lookout tower when there was nothing he'd rather do than throw bottles at cars too far away to hit, to get back at all mothers for not watching over their children. If his own was everywhere, she was nowhere, too, and Tip couldn't turn her head whatever he shouted tonight. All his slammed doors were muffled, frustrated echoes, his heartbeat a kid's snare drum barely annoying the neighborhood.

4

Tip's belt had been eaten by two of the dogs, who'd chewed their way toward each other like sunbathers digging a sand tunnel, then flung the stretched leather under the boat, where Honey found it while sweeping cobwebs from the hull. Angie watched her daughter balance a stepladder on top of the cockpit, batting sticky clumps of web that when they fell on Honey's hair turned to gossamer veils.

Angie, discouraged, feeling like Cinderella after the ball, idly dumped her and Daffy's tea bags into the garbage and wondered what might happen if she skipped work today. She had her freshman class scheduled, then office hours. So detailed were her comments in the margins of their papers that her students hardly needed to talk directly to her, but never had she missed an office hour. Neither had she skipped a departmental meeting, where her shyness caused her colleagues to take her few suggestions very seriously. The one time she'd skidded in twelve minutes late for class, having caught her sweater in the runner of her file cabinet, she'd felt unraveled all day, as if the snag in the rescued hem were really a loose thread in her entire moral fabric.

All morning while she was sweeping and scrubbing the boat, Honey's thoughts returned to her mother's funny-looking guest of the night before—returned to something fierce in the shag of the eyebrows and the beak of the nose, fierce, yet whimsical, a bird face on a totem pole, the hair sprouting like tender, dark ferns. Who was she? A Jehovah's Witness, maybe. But then Honey recalled the ungodly bicycle shorts. A traveler stopping for directions. But then Honey recalled how the stranger and Angie had bidden good night, as if intending to see each other again. Perhaps the woman was a neighbor borrowing last-minute eggs for a midnight omelet, but Honey knew the neighbors, had trimmed their hair and waxed their eyebrows, knew the shapes of their ears and knuckles—while Angie knew none of them, not even their names. Honey batted at the mast with the whispery broom. The stepladder wobbled but Honey's bare toes held, the mast rang with each swipe, a spider dropped onto Honey's tank top, swung like a pendant on a filamentous chain. How easy to look batty, Honey realized with a start. How accidental to appear eccentric in the world's eyes. A car passed along County Trunk A. The boat rocked, the spider clung to Honey's shirt like the brooch on a Halloween costume, the broom rang against the mast, a whole osprey nest might fall on her head any minute, if there was one there. She peered up to see. The driver of the next car saw nothing but a crazy girl shooing away an invisible pole sitter. Maybe last night's visitor had been a friend or, nearly as surprising, an acquaintance of Angie's. Maybe Angie wasn't as crazy as she'd looked all these years in her attic, but was really just a person at home in her chair, biding her time until the good began to make up for the bad and invited her into the world of the living again. Could be, Honey admitted, admitting also she hoped not, preferring her mother crazy the way she was used to, the chair stuffing clinging to Angie's sleeves when she descended from her attic to find out whose turn it was to fix dinner. Maybe it was only the chair stuffing, all these years, that made Angie look like her own seams had come undone. Maybe it was only the combination of high-society eyeglasses and cheap lace-up sandals that made her look like an ostrich who'd neglected to hide its head. If so, then Angie might just be a variant of any normal sane woman whose husband hadn't had the heart to leave a note. Honey could see it all clearly now: Angie pregnant in the farmhouse outside Milwaukee, gazing out the window at her husband adjusting the brim of his Atlanta Braves cap as he planted, and then, next time Angie looked, there was nothing but a sunflower nodding in the direction he might have taken. How cruel he had been, accidentally, of course, Honey conceded. At once she was full of understanding for her mother's shell-shocked air of aloof serenity, but that didn't mean she'd be glad to see the end of Angie's tenure in the attic. Like the moon in the sky, Angie belonged there, under the triangle window. Honey propped her broom beside the precarious stepladder on top of the beached, creaking roof of the cockpit, contemplating the possibility of finding herself under the wing of an ordinary mother. Thank God she was grown, too old to be raised in a conventional household.

But if Angie had made, or was making, a friend . . .

Honey didn't know if she could stand that. At least it shouldn't come as a huge surprise, not with the way Honey had to turn on the TV at dinner just to drown out the crackle of her mother's dawning restlessness, her mother's recent impatience with their accustomed way of life.

Honey jumped to the deck and was swabbing the hull with a solution of ammonia when Angie left the house for work. With relief, Honey noted that her mother looked as she did most mornings. Having spent the whole night in her chair and never got into bed in the first place, Angie always looked like she never exactly got *out* of bed, either. Her tote bag bulging with papers, her keys burrowing in the bottom so she had to pull the papers from the bag to find them, the papers jammed between her knees, her glasses sliding down her nose and landing plunk in the bag just as she fished out the keys. Yes, the real Angie had rematerialized, leaving behind the desperately poised sorority girl of the evening before.

"Bye," Honey called.

"Bye," said her mother. "Are you going to the supermarket? Could you pick me up a—but never mind if you're not."

"I could pedal over there, Mom," Honey interrupted, tapping her foot.

"Thanks, then," said Angie. She retrieved her eyeglasses,

crammed the papers back into the bag, and drove off without having told Honey what she wanted from the store. Honey figured if she bought things willy-nilly, one of them was bound to be the thing her crazy mother needed. Angie was herself again, a creature of her own invincible habits. The moon was where it belonged, therefore the world was traversable again. Probably the fierce, funny, tender-looking woman with the eyebrows like seven kittens chasing a ball of yarn had been only a student delivering a procrastinated paper, and would never return, except maybe to pick up her grade. An F, Honey hoped, then softened. Give her a C, she can't help it if she can't spell.

Honey dipped a toothbrush in the bucket of ammonia, taking extra care to scrub the decorative sash around the portholes. If half of her was proud of Tip for having offered to drive her mother's visitor home, the other half was furious, her memory flashing on her incredulity when he'd ushered the stranger into his truck instead of following Honey into the boat. He was like a dog snapping at its own tail, wanting to escape the inescapable. Proud or furious, Honey was amused. Now that she'd dispensed with her worries about Angie, she let Tip's image return to her, his X shape needing an O to play tic-tac-toe with.

If he would come . . .

He would.

If Honey had anything to say about it . . .

She was certain she did.

When the deck had been rinsed and the bilges scooped and drained, she rattled her bike lock in the garage, then waited for the dogs to gather their leashes and come running. As she pedaled the gravel berm of the road, scolding the dogs with a flick of her wrist, the spiders began reestablishing their territories from mast to bowsprit, unaware that the sailboat wasn't the same as before, and never would be again. Once unruly as a sunken ship, home to all the elements, now the vessel was becoming a downright creditable domicile, the cushions airing in the sun, the steps to the cabin swept of dead leaves, even the scratched portholes spritzed, swabbed, and polished.

*   *   *

No sooner had the poet's oolong tea bag stuck to the dry inside of the mug than she forgot the brief visit with the hermit and went about her days as if she had never once set foot in the tower room, Angie silently repeated all that following week at school.

Having spent that first morning wandering the house—the small living room with its lackluster carpet and fraying couch, and her bedroom in which she rarely slept, with the window so close to the ceiling that the ivy Honey tended on the sill hadn't yet reached the floor—and having felt put out because the customary shabbiness wasn't transformed by the impossibly glittery social engagement of the night before, Angie was trying out the efficacy of her fairy-tale-speak, the quaint phrases she'd once needed to invent in order to make, of Tom's disappearance, a tale that might comfort her rather than piss her off.

In the morning, when the songbirds woke the poet from a long night's sleep, all thoughts of the hermit had turned to dust, and drifted through the open casement when she shook out her nightdress. But the fairy-tale-speak didn't seem to be working in relation to Daffy, Angie reflected, disappointed when each day closed with no word from the poet, and no sign of her at school no matter how late Angie stayed in her office reorganizing her file cabinet. In the deep bottom drawer were no files at all, only some personal items she needed now and then at work—toothbrush, tampons, umbrella, spare car keys. The packets of tea she whisked out of sight, so she wouldn't need to see them every time she wanted a cough drop and be reminded of the fool she must have made of herself playing Martha Stewart in her attic study when all the while there was a pair of dirty underwear snagged near the yellow box of papers, and a hole in the planking as big as a trapdoor, which now seemed a blessing in case Angie ever felt so embarrassed again she needed to crawl through the floor. But Daffy would never sit cross legged in the attic again, Angie believed, and because of the campus layout—classrooms in one quad, offices in the other—it would be possible for Daffy to avoid Angie even at school, so as never to have to drink another bag of insomnia within sight of last month's menstrual stain, a stain so faint Angie practically needed to submit the snagged panties to DNA testing to know that it was there.

But even if Angie's transgression wasn't visible to the naked eye, the really embarrassing thing, if she was honest with herself as she forced herself to be, was that she'd known that the panties were there all along, ever since the night the elastic dug into her thighs so annoyingly she kicked them off, and just hadn't bothered to pick them up.

On Saturday morning it was indisputable that Daffy must have snuck into the office during the night, for she'd left a few letters in the secretary's outgoing basket. The sight of the neatly printed addresses sent a wave of confused hurt through Angie, who couldn't understand why Daffy hadn't left *her* a letter thanking her at least for the hospitality, or if nothing else a poem devoted to their failed tea party. Angie bristled, opened the canister of goldfish food, and sprinkled a pinch among the trailing leaves of the plastic plants. The goldfish ceased its incessant circling and began to kiss the surface of the water, its lumpy innards pulsating under translucent skin.

Angie gazed at the secretly ugly fish with such consternation that she failed to hear the footsteps approaching along the polished hallway, and glanced up just in time to see—

Not Daffy at the threshold, but David Bruhl, who taught the literature of the frontier. Angie had so absented herself from the social life of the department that David didn't hesitate to slide his handful of fake security memos one by one into the faculty boxes.

"You'll keep my secret." He winked gamely at Angie.

"Who would I tell?" Angie asked, reaching for her memo.

"It has come to my attention that certain members of the faculty have encouraged disregard of my requests by circulating rumors designed to raise doubts as to they're authenticity," she read.

"You used the wrong *they're*," she told David.

David nodded, winked, rubbed his eyes, blew his nose, checked his watch, and reached into his pocket for a pack of cold capsules. So that was where Daffy had been all this time. Home with a cold.

Still, it took Angie until that evening to sit herself down at the cleared kitchen table and pull the telephone toward her to ask Daffy if there was anything she needed—some chicken soup, maybe, or a heating pad. Honey was in the shower, which made the moment more propitious for the call—less of a spectacle. Still, Angie hesitated, aware of her vulnerabilities. If Daffy wasn't sick, Angie would be more hurt than she was already. Not having had a friend in so long, she pondered the illogic of preferring that her new friend have a fever instead of something more fun going on.

"Sorry, we can't come to the phone right now," said Daffy's voice on the answering machine.

The water quit running in Honey's shower, the shower curtain slid along the rod. *We? Who's we?* Angie wondered, stung, and laid the receiver back on the phone. Honey must have just bought this new zebra-striped tablecloth. If a lion escaped from the circus in town, it would head straight for their kitchen.

"Somebody called?" Honey poked her head in the kitchen, her hair frothy with mousse, her bath towel knotted in a rosette. Daintily attired, the sturdiness of Honey's body was the first thing people noticed about her. Then, when she put on hiking boots, shorts, and T-shirt, the thing people noticed was her soft skin and rosy femininity.

"No," said Angie.

"Then who did you call?"

"Whom," Angie corrected.

She took her hand off the phone and traced the curved white maze among the stripes of the zebra. Honey tapped her bare foot, drummed her toes on the floor. Just because she'd mastered this gesture as a child didn't mean she was being childish. Miffed, she gazed at her mother from under the flick of a comb, hating Angie for not telling the truth, and adoring her for the very same reason. Finally Honey moved the phone onto the counter—*where it belonged,* Angie could see her thinking.

Who's *we?* Angie wondered again, ashamed. Daffy hadn't

been avoiding her. Daffy simply had other people to do better things with than hang around the secretary's office making small talk Saturday mornings with David Bruhl. Even David Bruhl had another life in Milwaukee, where he and his brother owned an Irish pub. Daffy had a social life, David Bruhl had a pub, Angie had hyena bait splayed on her kitchen table.

Honey was dreamily wiping the phone with a corner of towel when it rang. Sometime, somewhere, she'd seem someone else dust a telephone in just this manner.

"Hello?" Honey raised her eyebrows and continued. "*Whom* may I say is calling, please?"

"It's Daffy. I star-sixty-nined it."

Star 69 were the buttons you pushed if you wanted to return a call you had just missed. Honey held the phone to her mother. "It's your student," she whispered.

"Tell them I'm not here."

"I'm afraid she's not in right this minute," Honey apologized.

When she had hung up, she said, "Next time it rings it'll be Tip trying to say he can't make it tonight like we planned. So nobody answer. If he gets the answering machine, he'll be so relieved not to be able to call off our date that he'll show up early. But I won't be ready. I won't be ready till eight."

When the phone rang a moment later, Honey wheeled away from it. The clean smell of strawberry kiwi spun through the kitchen. Angie lifted the tablecloth up by the seam and flipped it into a square small enough to slide into the drawer with the dish towels.

On the far side of town, Tip hung up the phone, delivered of having to back out of what might be a promising evening.

"She's too smart for me," he grumbled to Doc, who thumped her tail when he sat down beside her on the bare vacuumed carpet.

For a moment, both submitted their senses to the unfamiliarity of the house they were sitting in, surrounded by half an acre of whispering marsh grass along Lake Butte des Morts. The house wasn't Tip's yet, but he was certain he was going to buy it as soon as he could get some of his people over to check out the wiring and see if there were any structural features rotting under the floorboards. The Realtor waited in the car while Tip and Doc took a last look around. The boathouse needed repairs. The kitchen was dumpy, but there was a wood-burning stove in the bedroom. All faucets dripped. The whole thing had been papered by somebody's grandmother, but the neon Pabst sign above the wet bar in the living room was staying, and so were the pleated blinds on the sliding glass doors, blinds silk-screened with a scene of a hunter crouched behind a duck blind as ducks rose into his sites.

Tip made a last run into the basement to check for seepage. The pipes were copper, the insulation blown in, the furnace had to be older than the house itself, a stack of *Penthouse* magazines fanned open next to a new water heater. Tip was so relieved he was practically singing when he and Doc rejoined the Realtor in the driveway, but only Doc knew why.

Though she'd been showing up in class as required, and covering the movable blackboard with diagrams of sonnets and sestinas, Daffy hadn't really been teaching her classes the past week and a half. In truth she was absent, sequestered, the curtain drawn around the cot on which she felt supine inside her body, eyes open to the reproach of the ceiling. If she wasn't exactly sick, still she was the patient she never named in her poems, so ill, so wounded that she hadn't found the strength to tell even her husband what had happened to her.

"Villanelles, not fontanels," she corrected a student, the chalk making her jump when it snapped in two. Since her commalike posture endeared her to her students and camouflaged the patient staring at the ceiling inside her, she kept her hawk nose to the blackboard, which squeaked backward on its wheels across the classroom, forcing her to pursue it in her blousy dirndl trousers. Not even the most perceptive of her students would guess that something terrible had happened and that Daffy blamed poetry.

Not that the poems themselves were at fault, she needed to

remind herself, instead laying the culpability on her die-hard belief in them. Thirty years she had hunkered over notebooks, manual typewriter, correcting Selectric, first word processor, new PC. Two and a half years ago now, the small, reputable press in Boston had accepted for publication her manuscript of poetry ten years in the making. Two years she'd been revising in consultation with the editor. One year ago they'd mailed her a mock-up of the book's design, including layout, typeface, and decorative headings. Eight months ago they'd sent a copy of the three-color cover, seven months ago a less expensive, two-color version, three months ago she'd been offered this teaching job on the strength of the forthcoming publication of *Physician's Desk Reference* in the midst of the current bad market for poetry, and no more than one month ago, the press had faxed her some enviable endorsements by well-known poets all willing to be blurbed on the jacket of her book. And then . . . but then . . .

"There's nothing *wrong* with free verse. But this assignment calls for the completion of a fontanel, I mean a sonnet," she interrupted her thoughts by saying to one of her students, a politically minded girl who refused form on principle. A few of her students were awfully talented, in a brutally indifferent way, their really great lines mostly stumbled upon, but that was the way they still thought it was supposed to be—accidental, sudden, intuitive, indisputable—but most of her students, well, if Daffy couldn't teach them to write an excellent poem, at least she could teach them respect for the sheer discipline involved.

But then on Saturday a week ago, Daffy's editor had phoned her at home to say that she, the editor, was being let go, but that the book was still scheduled for October, so not to worry.

"I thought it was supposed to be August," said Daffy, before remembering to sympathize with her editor, who after all was out of a job.

And then on Sunday the publisher himself phoned Daffy to say sorry, the book was cut.

"What do you mean?" she had asked, confused. *Cut* meant the volume was bound and ready, didn't it, the folds between the pages sliced open for turning?

"We've run out of money for printing and distributing poetry," he explained. "Just like about everyone else did a long time ago. With our revised budget, if we brought out your book, no one would end up reading it."

"No one would have read it anyway," Daffy argued in desperation.

The extreme quiet of the house, once she'd put down the phone, began gradually to fill with the noise from outside, the shouts of the men dismantling the shortwave radio antennas left behind by the previous owners. Gregory had sold the apparatus for a small sum of money, which he and Daffy were planning on using for a road trip in November when Daffy's book was safely out and Gregory had a midterm break from law school. Proud that his wife was a poet, Gregory already quoted her poems on his Web site and was so pleased by the cover, he'd made a poster-sized copy to be framed in his law office someday. Daffy was helping pay for his schooling out of her teaching salary. She could lose her job now that she'd lost the credibility earned by this book. It didn't matter how finely honed her poems, how intelligent the emotion behind every counted syllable. What mattered to the university, and to herself as well, she needed to admit, was the binding, solid and sure, the rich, heady scent of the printer's ink, the bits of fiber and chaff pressed intentionally into the pulp. How many times had Daffy run her fingers along the rough-cut pages of other poetry books, practicing for when the pages would be her own, so substantial the paper fairly throbbed with the echoes of the lines she'd read aloud to make sure they said what she hoped they did? However slender, however overlooked, a book meant the poems might be picked up and admired, even read, one after the other, in order, in the tensed, quivering arc she had so painstakingly designed for them.

A flimsy lattice of antennas wobbled on Gregory's shoulders as he and the buyer loaded the shortwave apparatus onto the truck. Another man made a spool of a length of wire. The front yard was littered with small Eiffel towers of metal resembling the rubble of a bombed metropolis. Daffy buried her panic inside her, not wanting Gregory to hurt himself trying to rescue her. A plane roared overhead, the buyer drove off, and when Gregory came into the house, Daffy was in her study with the door closed, the computer on for camouflage. He never bothered her at work, never begged her to join him at bedtime if she was struggling or even toying with a poem.

"Excuse me, Susan." Daffy caught up with one of her students as they filed out of class. "Susan, I would prefer it if you didn't sit behind me in class. When I lecture, I like my students to be able to see me."

Daffy's boldness, because she'd put off saying this to Susan ever since the first day of classes, gave her the wherewithal to show her face at the office and call her publisher. She knew she should send her poems right away to other publishers, but first she needed her disc back from Boston.

"I can look for it," said the publisher dubiously. In the background was a listless tapping noise. "You're sure we didn't send it back . . . In any event, you do have your manuscript."

"The only one I have is the one I included in my application files here, but it was never revised when I went over the final copy with you. I sent the proofed manuscript back eight months ago. You said it was fine," Daffy reminded him.

"Yes it was fine. It was very, very fine. We've recycled some things, already," he added. "As for the disc . . . a lot's moved out already. I'll call you if I have a chance to—"

The line went dead, and when Daffy redialed, it had been disconnected.

The usual faculty were hanging around the hallway outside the main office when Daffy rushed past to pull her folder from the application files, but the group had dispersed by the time she'd reached the file cabinet.

THE PH   CIAN'S DESK *smudge*
PO MS by *blurrr*

"Please help me," Daffy whispered to the secretary when she saw the wrecked stanzas, the cheap ink awash on the stuck-together papers, all the readable phrases mixed with illegible smears.

"Get Angie, please," she added in a whisper when she heard Angie's familiar morning dash for the ladies' room, Angie's cheap sandals slapping against the linoleum.

"Angie, please," Daffy repeated, the patient sitting up in bed, pressing the nurse call button when the night seemed too scary. Angie—why Angie? Because Angie wasn't Gregory. Because Angie was there. Because Angie's attic study was proof of the value of retreat, proof that seclusion might seem to stop time while the rest of the world pressed on with its indifferent business. Because Angie seemed to know you had to break stride in order to take things *in* stride, Daffy answered herself.

Besides, Angie was the only person on whom Daffy could imagine falling apart.

Maybe Daffy's tears, or maybe the lunar glow of the goldfish tank, exerted on Angie some reverse pull of internal gravity that made her no longer as desperate to pee as she usually was, mornings she'd finished teaching. There was a rest room off the parking lot but not a minute to use it and still get to first class on time. There was a rest room one floor up in the classroom building, but if the elevator jammed in the basement and there were too many women already rushing for the stairs, Angie decided to brave the second half of class and use the rest room afterward. Today she'd let class out a minute early, ensuring that the stairs would be free and clear, but the rest room had been closed for cleaning and the one across the courtyard in the student union was blocked by a spilled cart of cafeteria trays. From the windows in the breezeway, as she scissored toward a third rest room, her book bag thumping against her leg, she had caught sight of Daffy making her way across campus outside. Angie had passed up the rest room and followed, driven not by Daffy's disappointing absence of the previous week but by her need to look Daffy in the eye and get it over with, this first step in the undoing of whatever misconceptions had crossed Angie's mind since that night in the attic. The friendship she'd strained toward so awkwardly appeared unable to receive her, and now she wanted to measure, in Daffy's face and manner, the degree of her own humiliation. So she headed outside, the tight hold of her posture not enough to keep a spurt of urine from escaping. When at last Angie edged past the students smoking cigarettes on the front stoop of the humanities building, they had to whisk their coffee cups out of the way so she wouldn't—oh well—knock them over. Coffee trickled down the steps. The front door was stuck closed, then swung vigorously open. The ladies' room was down the hall, so Angie made for it blindly, crashing into the soft, scented dress of the secretary, who caught her by the arm at what seemed to be the last possible fraction of an allowable dry second and said, "Daphne needs you right away."

Even the bruise on Angie's leg, caused by the rhythmic swing of her book bag, ceased its thumping the minute she extended her arms around Daffy's narrow shoulders and waited to know what to do next. Except for an occasional squeeze with Honey, Angie hadn't hugged another person in two decades. And Tom's embraces hadn't given her much to look back on, aside from a memory of his stiff wedge of shirt collar poking her in the nostril when it was time to pull away.

For a while she stroked Daffy's head, Daffy no longer quite weeping, Angie no longer cooing, only the fish tank tsk-tsking between them as if about Angie's lost eyeglasses, which weren't pinching the end of her nose as usual, and weren't tiaraed in her hair, where she sometimes discovered them after she'd yanked them out of her way. Nor were they sunk in the depths of her book bag, for they had lost their tight grip on her face when she'd rushed up the steps past the tipped cups of coffee, and now had entered the possession of one of her students, who would find them years later in the inside pocket of his green and gold Packers jacket, having been too shy to return them to her.

5

At night d   ms quiver on the por while the strob
light from t   ulled over cop car

> *huffles th   ts   ailing like cards in a*
> *deck of petals.*
> *For how long must I   ark bo   ss it all?*

"Why do the spaces look smaller than the words that used to fill them?" Daffy asked, her dark head trained on the paper before her, Daffy's office desk cleared, except of her and Angie's elbows and a second sheet of paper, a carton of Kleenex for emergency fits of tears, and two pears Daffy had pulled from her satchel and balanced side by side as if in mimicry of the two women knocking their heads together over the first blurred stanza of the eleventh ruined poem. "Hair Ball" was the title, ironically named for the CAT scan that would, by the end of the poem, reveal the tumor. Angie remembered how, when she'd first read the poem that night in the secretary's office, she'd known the tumor was coming but was shocked nonetheless by the revelation.

"Why do the spaces always look smaller than—what?" Angie asked, neatly copying the line on her fresh sheet of paper.

"What filled them. The *words*," Daffy answered.

"What filled them. The *words*," Angie printed, rereading the line in puzzlement until she realized it wasn't part of the poem at all, but only something Daffy was saying to her. True. The blurred smears didn't seem big enough for all the letters and words that would eventually take their places. By four o'clock in the morning, roughly two thirds of the blurred, smeared spaces in the ten poems preceding "Hair Ball" had been treated to the utmost scrutiny and finally restored. The other third would need to wait for the light of a clearer-headed day. By now the Mr. Coffee atop the mini refrigerator in the secretary's office had twice run dry, and there was no more real milk, only a few scraped spoonfuls of creamer. The moonlighting janitor sat in his easy chair in the broom closet watching a video. The fluorescent lights emitted faint, tinsely noises they never seemed to make in the daytime, but Daffy's gooseneck lamp shone like the light of an operating theater on the poem that lay in surgery beneath it.

Daffy's office smelled inexplicably of the same cigar smoke Angie had caught a whiff of that night in her study, Angie noticed.

During one of Daffy's forays out to the rest room, Angie peeked into a cookie jar on a shelf. No cigars, only a few tubs of hotel-style jelly and packages of crumbling melba toast.

No cigars in the desk drawers, either.

And not a single book of matches.

And on the bookshelves, no ashtray.

Still . . . Angie sniffed suspiciously. She knew the smell from years back, though she'd forgotten how she'd savored the burnt chocolate residue, the echo of brisk autumn leaves. Tom's occasional farm hand had smoked cigars in the shed where the two men were working together. For months, the complicated perfume of the cured tobacco had seemed to mock Angie's blend of agitation and relief whenever Tom emerged from a long, long day with the table saw. Glad he was safe? Yes. But just a whiff was enough before he turned cloying again.

She slid her hand into the pocket of Daffy's jacket, which was slung over the back of her chair, finding nothing inside but the pebbly texture of linen. What an uncomfortable power the mere fragrance imposed, evoking not merely the idea of Tom's presence but its incarnation. Angie might even attempt to speak to him, if only she knew what she wanted to say. Instead she forced her attention back to the ruined poem, and began reconstructing the opening lines—the geraniums, the porch slats, the claustrophobia of the CAT scan. In less than an hour she and Daffy had completed the stanza, eaten the pears, and started in on the crackers and jelly. When dawn had long since risen above the seagulls roosting on the flat roofs of campus, they set out of the building toward class.

The double glass doors of the library rattled as they passed. Two coins clinked through a parking lot meter. The blind chemistry professor paused with her cane at the crosswalk when the doughnut truck sped by. Every morning in all the twenty years Angie had ever taught at this campus began like this one, and yet today's familiar reel felt only provisional, as if the years of mornings had been nothing but a coming attraction for what might follow.

"Who's *we?*" Angie finally brought herself to ask, though in her breathless rush to keep up with Daffy, her question sounded more like, "Hooshweee?"

Daffy slowed her pace to regard Angie from over the determined jut of her nose, the way when considering a line in a poem, she might decode the utterance of an imagined gale.

"On your answering machine. '*We* can't come to the phone right now,'" panted Angie in explanation, ashamed to have phoned but left no message. "Leave it to me to take it personally that . . . but if you're married and don't want a—"

"I haven't told my husband my book was canceled," Daffy interrupted, bending to adjust a buckle on her sandal. "I haven't told him the press closed down. I haven't told him the manuscripts are either lost or ruined. I haven't told him I have no discs, and no copies of the poems. I haven't told him I feel like a ward full of hypochondriacs waiting for their bucket of placebos. Not that he and I don't talk. It's just better to leave certain things unsaid sometimes. Although, other things, it's better to say them. Like what I didn't say when you told me about your husband. If I weren't such a scared dipshit, I would have asked you if you ever had a really good cry, and if you wanted to finally, I would have told you, well, go ahead, do it, cry on my shoulder or at least scream a little. But I am. A scared dipshit. Look at that gull. Where did it come up with a clamshell on campus?"

Until they'd left the close scrutiny of Daffy's desk to step outside, Angie hadn't missed her eyeglasses for even a second, but now she marveled at the distinct clarity of Daffy's features while behind them the campus was appropriately erased. It seemed natural to Angie that the rest of the landscape should be whited out. Her attic study canceled. The ivy not reaching the floor in her un-slept-in bedroom canceled. Honey herself, if not canceled, postponed, so the sole claim on Angie's attention was Daffy's brown eyes, their humor and nimble focus. Not having had a friend in so long, Angie was taken aback to discover, in this one, qualities that discomfited her. If Daffy's face was the sole thing Angie chose to look at in this moment, Angie's face was to Daffy only one in a hundred things worthy of examination. But Daffy's gaze wasn't fickle. It was only, to all things, respectively sympathetic. And it was this very quality that rescued Angie from having to respond to Daffy's invitation. Crying was a way of saying good-bye, which wasn't the appropriate thing for a woman to say to her dead husband when he was trying so hard to greet her with the scent of cigars.

"Do you think all parents put aside thoughts of their children, sometimes?" Angie asked as she and Daffy started walking again, more slowly this time than before.

"Why shouldn't they? I would. Gregory wouldn't," Daffy replied, becoming quiet long enough for her gaze to shift inward. "Gregory would throw himself into every minute of being a father."

"And you?" asked Angie.

"I've begun to think fatherhood isn't for me," Daffy answered.

Across campus the harsh screech of the un-bell-like bells signaled imminent class time, but Daffy turned off the sidewalk to enter the featureless smudge of the parking garage, as if they'd agreed to skip out on their classes and have breakfast together. Angie's students riffling the empty pages of their notebooks, canceled. Their indiscriminate use of declarative phrases, canceled. Their honest, lusty sentimentality, canceled. Their rhapsody, their cynicism, their pierced noses and indiscreet snacking, canceled, canceled, canceled.

Driving, Daffy felt her dejection about the drowned poems grew, but she was bucking up, because what else was there to do? How could anyone have babies when even poems caused so much pain by getting lost or otherwise annihilated? At least she might reinvent the stanzas, hold a seance of sorts, the fluorescent light stepping in for the flickering candle, and Angie as substitute muse. Would the poems be the same? No. Better. More spirited, she encouraged herself, buoyed by the idea of breakfast with the muse, who interested her.

Did Angie believe in ghosts? Daffy ventured to ask. What was the last thing Angie's husband had said to her? Did Angie ever sense his presence nearby?

"Last words?" Angie reflected. "Probably, 'Okay, okay, okay, okay, okay,' when he left the house. Because Tom always ticked things off on his fingers if they were arranged to his liking. I was pregnant in the rocking chair reading a book when I last saw him, so one of the *okays* probably referred to me. Or maybe two, if I was wearing my slippers. As far as whether I feel his presence . . ." Maybe, just maybe, she would mention the clinking of coins on a dresser, the waking too early. But not the tendriling smell of tobacco, which had followed them into the car, the faint chocolately sweetness a husk with Tom's dry face inside it. Had it been with her all these years, hiding in the reaches of her desk drawers? Did Angie believe in ghosts? If so, might Tom be one of them? She wouldn't answer that question for now, she decided, too alarmed by what she might say.

The car swung onto the bridge across the sluggish river, from which could be seen the Jack of Steaks restaurant in a wing of sunlight cast aside by the shadow of a neighboring warehouse. Inside, the two friends shared a pot of coffee, a basket of glazed rolls, and an order of bacon. By the close of the meal, when Daffy opened the zippered flap of her satchel to pull out her wallet, she was comfortable enough with Angie to offer her one of her slender cigars.

Later that night, Daffy finally told Gregory about her book being cut by the doomed publisher, but not about her ruined manuscript, and not half of what there was to say about Angie. If she ever did muster enough courage to write another poem, she said to Gregory, the poem would be about Angie in the restaurant. Angie's dismay, Angie's terrible disappointment at the sight of the cigars, as if there were nothing on earth she would have wished less to see. Tears had flooded Angie's eyes, as if something were being taken away from her rather than offered.

"Did she get over it?" Gregory wondered.

"I put them back in the satchel." Daffy reached again for the zippered flap, for she would share the cigars with her husband while lying naked in bed. She might put the husbands in the new poem as well, but only in the background.

6

In all their years of shared dinners, Honey and Angie had never been to a restaurant. Their round kitchen table, their pepper mill and honey bear, the candle Honey sometimes lit in the top of an empty beer bottle, the radio on in some other part of the house—if all those things added up to the illusion that Honey and Angie had gone out to eat, still it was only their kitchen, their spaghetti and cheese on a plate with tossed salad. As a child, Honey would have liked a restaurant at least on birthdays, would have gotten a thrill when the waiters and waitresses lined up to sing. As Honey grew older, she baked shortbread on birthdays, with pinwheeling candles that didn't blow out, so it seemed to be by choice that they stayed in their kitchen, where the dogs could lick the plates and where Honey could climb over the counter instead of walking around it to refill the water glasses. Besides, now that the TV was so often on during dinner, Honey had taken to phoning her manicure clients over dinner as well, to schedule appointments.

Why, then, did it make Honey angry when Tip mentioned he'd seen her mother and the poet four times in a week and a half in Jack of Steaks for breakfast? They sat hunkered over countless typed pages. If Angie's napkin slipped under the table, her spare pens fell out of her shirt pocket when she bent to fetch it. Sometimes the women brought a dictionary and sat next to each other instead of across, so they could refer to it simultaneously. Other times they just talked, and rustled the pages, and drank so much coffee Lawrence joked he might as well set their table in the ladies' room. Texas toast was what they ordered if they were hungry, or a side order of glazed country ham served with two sets of silverware.

Honey told herself it must be the glazed ham that angered her, since she'd never tasted it herself. But soon enough she realized that just to know why she was feeling something didn't make the feeling go away, even when, that night with Tip sleeping beside her, she amended the anger to jealousy. It took Honey a great deal of honesty along with more humility than she was comfortable with, to admit to being jealous of her mother's new friendship, but neither the honesty nor the humility made the jealousy go away.

Tip's arm around Honey was of no solace. As on the previous several nights, they were lying in the V berth, their feet piled in the cusp of the V, the wide part still too narrow for them to lie side by side on their cushions. Their limbs knotted together, one of their heads always needed to be in the crook of the other's neck. Both Honey and Tip felt somewhat doomed, sleeping contentedly in this fashion when in the past they'd prided themselves on being able to sleep only if no one was touching. Tip had sometimes let a woman hold his hand as they dropped off to rest, but in the seconds before sleep he pulled his fingers away. Honey hadn't even spent whole nights with her previous boyfriends. In the confines of the V berth she and Tip hadn't yet made love, hadn't even come close, exactly, only lay in a patient tangle unusual for them both. For both, the reason for holding off was the same. To conjoin, through love or lust it didn't matter, would make them inextricable. Too much *will* was at stake; if they relinquished it, then they would each have only the other person to hold on to.

But tonight the weight of Tip's leg seemed to mock Honey's will, and the bulge of his biceps under her ear only affirmed her sense of her mother's betrayal. So little did Tip seem able to offer her in consolation at this moment—his sleep like the black inky water of the quarry, his half-nakedness a pale stone sinking to the bottom—that Honey wondered if perhaps their week-and-a-half-long cautious affair might better end unconsummated, their adventure abandoned under the same constellation of stars that had witnessed its beginning. Honey lay very still for a moment, to see if her stillness might seduce her into a reconciled sleep— her mother's breakfasts with Daffy excused—but all that happened was that it became clearer to her that since Tip couldn't help her, all the things she had so quickly learned about him might finally fail to bind her affections. The way he stopped his truck at the edges of fields to aim a spotlight over the darkness, illuminating the eyes of the wild animals, would finally fail to move her. The way he swallowed his voice at the sight of a flock of turkeys would fail even to puzzle her. His hatred of crows, as if they were demons, fail to interest her. His downright fatherliness with Doc, his superstitious distrust of Bloody Marys, the way he sang in his new kitchen while spicing fried potatoes, his delicate refusal to answer certain questions Honey might pose about his former lovers, his transparently feigned interest in the varieties of incandescence among Honey's shelves of nail polish—all of these things would add up to no more than her memory of his feet crowding her ankles, his always clean, always cotton, always white briefs swelling monumentally against her printed bikinis.

She slid Tip's foot from her ankle and sat up in the berth, remembering not to bang her head against the low ceiling. Unfastened, the hatch swung easily upward, and in a single practiced movement, she found herself crouched on the foredeck. Her cotton sheath lay coiled on the aft deck, moist with the night's first offering of dew, and when she jumped to the grass, there fell a showering of mist from the wings of the taller blades, as if the front lawn mimicked the weed-ridden inlets at Asylum Point Park. That was where Honey would embark, she decided. But what was taking her so long to get under way? Only these few nights of distraction by Tip, she concluded efficiently, making her way to the house with dual purpose—to find the lost sails, and to check her intuition about Angie. She entered the garage, pulling open the door leading to Angie's whitewashed stairway. At the top, as she expected, the study was empty, the bead board walls glossy with stillness. Angie wasn't in her chair. A book was wedged between the cushions. The light was off above the chair, but the triangle window had been closed so long that the few moths trying to reach the moon had beat themselves dead on the pane.

Honey crossed to the yellow box—empty of papers—and gripped the edges of the desk, which needed to be dismantled to be pulled from the wall. She laid the top of the desk on the hole in the floor and wheeled the supporting file cabinets out of the way. Six long narrow drawers had been forgotten on the wall behind the desk. Honey braced herself for sticking when she pulled on the first of the handles, but the drawer scraped open precipitously and nearly fell on her toes. It wasn't on runners. Inside lay the mainsail, blasting the room with the smell of mildew.

In the second of the drawers lay two nylon jib sails girdled neatly in their own rigging. In the third lay the missing boom, in the fourth, the flaked remains of a coat of varnish on the grip of the tiller.

The fifth drawer was empty, so Honey opened the sixth without expectation. A small anchor lay nestled in coils of rope, a sight that both irked and relieved her. What else was she forgetting if, novice sailor that she was, she would have forgotten the need for an anchor? Varnish, battery, motor oil, mast light; she recited the list while stacking the sails in preparation for sliding them downstairs for scrubbing. Compass, barometer, sailing lessons, she allowed.

Downstairs, her mother's bedroom door was open, the ivy trailing from window to baseboard. Angie lay peacefully asleep on one side of her bed. What daughter would be thrown for a loop by a sight like that? But Honey's mother slept in a chair in the attic, not in bed like normal mothers. Already the room smelled different than before, like cigars, Honey realized. Tip hadn't mentioned that her nonsmoking mother reeked of tobacco.

Soon Honey unfolded a corner of jib sail in the laundry room sink and donned rubber gloves. Camp stove, radio, kerosene lantern. The sailing lessons she would forgo, she decided, her eyes burning from detergent, her ears ringing with the indefatigability of her scrubbing. It made no difference which side was port and which starboard when what she wanted was that the world remain traversable, the lake so vast an enticement, so like a siren, singing her nearer and nearer still.

*   *   *

Doc had been to Tip's family's hunting land, had been led between rows of evergreen trees to the spot where Tip's brother's dog lay buried. She hadn't misunderstood Tip's flicker of nostalgia when he'd pointed his trigger finger at her ear and joked, "This is you, too, someday, sweetheart. This is where you bark your last bark. This is where you wag your last tale."

So on the day she wrenched her back while jumping out of the truck, Doc concealed the injury with as much ingenuity as any dog could muster, pretending to be too taken by the faltering buzz of a yellow jacket expiring under the coffee table to want to go outside, and later that afternoon, when she finally did need to go out, masking the pain by yipping at a killdeer swooping toward its nest near the boathouse.

The nest caught Tip's attention. Three brown speckled eggs lay in the grassy lap of a bowl scooped out of the gravel path. Tip was of two inclinations. One was to smash the eggs in the nest so the trespassers wouldn't wake him with all of their peeping, while the other was to steal one and hatch it under a heat lamp for Honey to raise when she decided to approve of him again. How he had lost her approval, he hadn't been able to figure out. But it was clear he'd been dismissed, more like a waiter than like a boyfriend, as if he'd served the courses out of order. But if he had, she'd seemed perfectly contented to eat them that way, and he believed she'd see her error and rehire him soon, he'd remarked to Lawrence the day before. Lawrence said be sure to get a raise if she did.

Tip reached for the egg with the fewest speckles. The killdeer feigned a broken wing, as killdeer do when their eggs are threatened, and hopped fitfully away across the lawn, screeching and mewing until Tip rose from the undamaged nest empty-handed.

Meanwhile Doc twisted backward on the grass to chew on her rump until the pain was spread thinner, making it easier for her to follow Tip back past the sliding door into the living room. There she lowered herself to a square of sun on the carpet, meaning to wait out the pain while Tip fussed with his stereo wires. The speakers hadn't worked exactly right since he'd moved, when he'd had to dismantle the whole system in his old apartment and set it up here in the new house. The feedback disgruntled Tip but provided a distraction from all his waiting for Honey to change her mind. He'd told Lawrence Honey didn't go for beggars, didn't even train the dogs to sit for treats, just threw them a Milk-Bone when she wanted to stir up some action. Besides, having read Jack's entreaties for Polly to join him in Indiana, he'd never groveled for a woman and didn't want to start now. Too humiliating, he told Lawrence.

"Yeah, I guess because she's the first girl who ever dumped you," Lawrence commiserated.

Tip was appalled. "She didn't dump me! She didn't do anything, really. She only told me she didn't want help with the boat."

"Same difference." Lawrence had shrugged. One by one, he slid the tray of clean water goblets into the overhead rack at the bar. Both ends of the rack were open. If he slid in more goblets than the rack could hold, the goblet on the far end would be pushed out and hit Tip on the head. Lawrence weighed the hunk of crystal in his hand, considering. It wasn't his own girlfriend's red clogs he imagined walking away along the black pipe in Rainbow Park. It was Honey's high-top sneakers, getting smaller in the distance.

"Did you send her some flowers?" he'd suggested. "Go over there? Serenade her or something?"

"Ordinary rules don't apply," Tip had answered. Honey confounded him, he admitted to Lawrence. She'd shown no interest in touching his scar, as even Patty liked to do first thing when they'd gotten together, and his motherlessness didn't faze her a bit, fatherless as she was.

Lawrence had upended the extra glass and slid it onto the rack. The glass at the far end fell in a beeline, missing Tip's head but landing smack on one of the ceramic tile samples he'd lined up on the bar so he could choose the floor for the new atrium. The water glass remained whole, the floor tile cracked clean down the middle. Tip moved the broken tile out of the way, handed Lawrence the unharmed glass, and shifted the next tile into position. This time, the falling glass did graze Tip's head before shattering on the floor, but the jolt had only caused Tip to sit awhile in uncharacteristic solemnity. If only his mother had joined Jack in Indiana. If only a woman could just do for once what a guy needed.

"If women are angels, I'd rather go to hell," he'd said.

Lawrence agreed. "Becka's the one who used the credit card and PIN," he divulged, feeling around on the shelf for Becka's diary. Which wasn't there. Lawrence had been disappointed. Not her interest in the PIN number but her interest in Tip was what Lawrence had wanted Tip to see.

Tip had barely blinked at this mention of his sister. "Becka has nothing to do with it. She does the buying. That's her job, Lawrence. I've been thinking maybe it was Patty. But that's a joke. Patty stealing! Really the only females worth half the slack we cut them are the four-legged ones," he remembered saying, and now patted the blanket beside him on the couch for Doc to join him. He'd reconnected the stereo wires, but when he dug in the blanket for the remote, meaning to blast himself into unconsciousness, the speakers gave no sound at all.

Doc only thumped her tail on the carpet, and when Tip patted the blanket a second time, she only thumped her tail harder. Tip pulled a cushion from under his head and threw it at her ear, a gentle throw, the soft cushion the thing that usually sent her scrambling, except that this time she didn't twitch a muscle, only shrieked so loud Tip thought it was the speaker feedback coming at him again.

From the corner of her eye the last couple of weeks, Angie had frequently caught sight of Honey at work on the boat—Honey patching the sails, sanding the rudder, varnishing the tiller, studying the rigging diagrams in a book she'd checked out of the library. And although the two of them had been avoiding each other for a couple of days, Angie was mollified—moved, really—by Honey's unspoken agreement with her that it was time to sell the boat. Honey must have intuited Angie's decision to take a leave from teaching next semester and work on her thesis, with

Daffy's advice. She must have reasoned that with the money they'd get for the boat, along with Tom's small life insurance policy, which Daffy's husband, Gregory, had convinced Angie to claim, they should be able to get through the rest of the year—passably, anyway. Any number of things might happen by the end of a year, and Angie had her suspicions, although Honey would bristle if she knew what they included. The X-shaped man was not in sight, but Honey had a high color about her, and Angie saw in her daughter's flushed cheeks and eager, inexhaustible industry a fiercely willed repose.

So, one weekend when Honey was off on her pre-Saturday-evening manicure rounds, and a man pulled off County Trunk A and knocked on the door with a money clip bursting with bills, Angie was ready.

The dogs weren't barking at this man the way they usually lost their marbles over strangers, so she let them nose around. In the driveway, the man's yellow Volkswagen Bug still purred even after the engine had been shut off. Angie could see that the car was well cared for but slipping with age, the few dents beginning to rust and the side mirror losing its finish, just like the driver himself. The genuine article. Grizzled at the edges but still going strong.

"Forty-two hundred," she said to him.

"Let me take a look at her," answered the man, removing his boots before climbing aboard. His wool socks were too warm for the season, but his bare legs were already bronzed and his face sun-bitten. On deck he looked as weathered as if he'd been there the whole time the boat had sat in the yard with weeds sprouting out of the bilges, waiting for the night stars to bode finer sailing.

"Can I go down below?" he called.

Angie heard, *Look out beloooow!* and was determined to sell the boat to this wayfarer as if her very humanitarianism depended upon it. An old-fashioned word for an old-fashioned man, *wayfarer*. He wore a single silver braid as if in place of the pirate's saber he might have worn had he been born to a century more conducive to his general demeanor. The boat seemed to need him as much as it needed water.

He handled the money clip with greater reverence than he handled the money, of which he counted out to Angie two of the thousands, kept the third for himself, and counted the remainder in hundreds and twenties, refusing Angie's offer of the guarantee she knew Honey would have insisted upon. The frayed sleeves of his sweatshirt were grayish with wear, but Angie could smell the detergent still trapped in the cuffs.

"Money back if it sinks," Angie insisted.

The pirate shrugged philosophically. "She sinks, you won't be hearing much from me," he said.

With chafed hands, he stacked the final bill on Angie's palm, then topped off the stack with his remaining laundry quarters. Honey would be pleased with the two thousand five hundred dollars and fifty cents on which Angie and the sailor had finally agreed. Besides, Angie would have traded him the boat for an eye patch if that's all he had. He was like a man with his hand lopped off by a shark, except in his case, it wasn't a hand he was missing, it was a boat. The boat clove to him like another weather-beaten part of his body as he stifled a long sneeze, thanked her, then stood for a moment with his hand on his mouth, shocked by what he'd just realized. No Volkswagen Bug in history had ever pulled a twenty-two-foot sailboat before. But that didn't mean this one wouldn't if he put his mind to it. In the time it took for him to stifle the second sneeze, he'd already purred off to the hardware store, telling Angie he'd be back in a minute and a half, maybe twenty. Angie was still sitting on the front stoop with the twenty-five hundred dollars warming her palm when he came back with a bundle of hardware and lined it up on the ground, naming the items aloud. Two angle irons, two U-clamps, a bag of bolts, the hitch, and a bag of aircraft nuts. He pulled a drill and a battered manual from his toolbox. "*How to Keep Your Volkswagen Alive*," he read aloud to Angie. "*A Manual of Step-by-Step Procedures for the Compleat Idiot.* What they mean is, car repair for leftover hippies. It's better than the *Whole Earth Catalogue.*"

He threw his head back and laughed, and nearly sneezed again but caught it, for he'd already put the manual to work, drumming his fingers along on the diagrams before crawling beneath the car with the drill in the crook of his arm. A Volkswagen has no frame, he called out to Angie. There's nothing keeping the back to the front but the pan the chassis sits on. You hook a trailer to that bumper, it'll pop like a kernel of corn. But he had a plan. He'd bolt the angle irons onto the torsion tube, then bolt the opposite ends to the bumper and connect the hitch. Easy as popcorn pie, he said. Besides, his wasn't an ordinary Bug, he added. It was a Baja High Performance, eighteen hundred cc's, bought at auction with the money he got from so long ago he could hardly remember the color of the shower tiles in the house he'd built for a wealthy executive, but they were gold, golden tiles, the prettiest shower ever made. When he had finished both his talking and his handiwork, he remembered to lower the mast of the boat before driving, a job that called for a trio of sailors, in his case apparently all rolled into one.

"I'd say good-bye if I was sure the bumper wasn't going to fall off anyway," he said.

"I would, too," said Angie.

The car nearly didn't make it, after all. It stalled on the gradual climb from the lawn to the highway, then continued so slowly that, fifteen minutes later, the cars lined up behind it still rolled past the house. Angie put the money in the checkbook Honey kept in a basket on the kitchen windowsill, and watched the tortuous parade. The dogs watched, too. When it had wound out of sight, they regrouped to sniff the ground where the boat had once stood on its trailer. Soon the dogs began turning up the soil with their noses and paws, dirt flying every which way, whole soup bones unearthed among clumps of foxglove and flying dandelions. Not long after, when Honey drove disbelievingly up in her car and sat dumbstruck in the driveway, utterly motionless with despair at the terrible sight of the missing boat, the dogs appeared to have dug a hole for her plans and all her future adventures and covered them up like one of their chewed-up treasures.

Much as a blind person might be unable to imagine color, or a glad person unhappiness, Honey had once imagined that a feeling of surprise must by nature come suddenly, precise as a slammed door. But as she sat in the car she felt the feeling steal over her so softly that she didn't know its object. Surprised, but by what, exactly? Not merely by the terrible disappearance of the boat, she didn't think, and not by her sudden shock of nostalgia for the missing anchor, which was painted a bright sea blue and whose purposeful, fixed weight would be more welcome to her now than the sails themselves. Not the sky, which was as much in flux as always—day becoming evening becoming fog instead of night—and not the fact that she'd agreed to play bingo at the retirement home next Wednesday, and not even, exactly, the sound of Tip's truck on the road behind her, for she had spoken with enough of her clients to know how love affairs yo-yoed and twisted and turned. Tip would always be a little suspicious of her just because she was a woman, she understood—suspicious that she might hurt or abandon or betray him—but that wasn't the thing that surprised her, either.

Honey insisted on being the one to drive to the veterinary clinic, because she knew the way and because Doc would be more comfortable in the dog bed in the rear of Honey's car than on the slippery passenger seat of Tip's truck. She backed the car easily around the truck, and in case her mother was watching, gave a brief wave in the direction of the house before driving off with Tip, the fog hovering over the bump of the railroad ties and Tip's hand nudging the crotch of her blue jeans, *where it belonged.* That's what surprised her, the way she felt like one half of a two-part puzzle, like the links you push apart and then pull back together, the logic of their entanglement no less mysterious than that of their apartness. Still the shock of the vanished boat was with her, making her tremble. In the dog bed behind her, Doc sensed Tip's recognition of Honey's sadness. Tip hadn't thought of Honey as being a person capable of feeling undone. Perhaps she hadn't been, before. Nor would Tip have put up with it, before, in any woman. Despite her own dose of pain, Doc gave an approving snort. Tip said, "Sweetheart, you'll feel better soon. We'll take such good care of each other."

7

Had it been Tip's idea to offer the poet a ride home? Tom Bane wondered.

Or had it been his own?

Unless Angie's new longing for friendship had been the poet's idea, just as it had been Honey's idea to sleep in the boat? Or was Tom the one who, not knowing how he had done it exactly, had anchored the boat in his daughter's imagination, only to have it so brazenly taken away?

Although Tom didn't know exactly what to make of the events of the season, he felt he ought to be contented with what had been stalled and with what had been put into motion. Even when he was alive it had been difficult to know, on a daily basis, what he had accomplished and what he had simply observed. He remembered the way he'd used to stand at the edge of his fields in his blue jeans, watching the crops poke out of the ridges of soil, the tiny bits of palest green just beginning to reveal the orderly rows in which they had been sown. He remembered shooing birds off the limbs of the pear trees, only to have the birds dart back again, and he remembered the flasher scarecrow he'd made of a flapping raincoat, which failed to keep the birds away for longer than a week. Today he could make those same blackbirds fly north ninety miles to plummet beakfirst past the lily pads if he wanted. And could, if he wanted, cause Honey's dogs to lose their stubborn bearings and swim too far out on their next splashing foray into the current, and drown.

But Tom found he was less interested than ever in overcoming the common sense of the dogs, and the idea of blackbirds was no more enticing than that of a gust of cigarette ashes from somebody's dumped-out ashtray. And when a small bubble rose from among some strands of algae tickling his ribs, the bubble felt like his remorse for the havoc he'd created in the lives of creatures he didn't really care about—the horse searching for apples in the flooded orchard in Fond du Lac, for instance, and the biker's drowned friend, the Fisheries biologist—in order to draw nearer the people he wanted. Angie, he sensed, was now out of his grasp, for which Tom was prepared to blame his own blundering lack of efficiency. But Honey was still within reach. Tom couldn't have said why he relished the idea of Honey bringing Tip Baymiller sorrow rather than joy. He only knew it was within his sphere of influence to make it happen, in a way that it wouldn't have been within Tom's influence if he were unlucky enough to be alive, one of the millions of flesh-and-blood fathers bemoaning their snooty, indifferent daughters who wouldn't give them the time of day.

Of one thing Tom was entirely certain. Love didn't come from the heart and never had and never would. He loved his wife as much now, in her escape, as before, in her persistent, solitary need of him, and yet he didn't have a heart at all any longer, did he? He loved his daughter even more than he loved his wife, and yet the love couldn't possibly come from his heart if he no longer had one.

What had once been his heart was now less than a handful of silt trapped in the gills of a hundred sturgeon.

What had once been his heart was now the mineral deposit that turned green on the pennies people tossed off the footbridge for wishes.

No, the heart had nothing to do with love. Nothing, nothing, nothing at all, Tom repeated.

Part *Four*

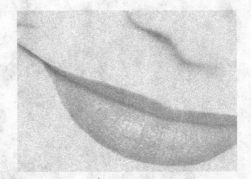

13

Just Because It's Sid Who Hears a Lullaby Doesn't Mean Polly Can't Finally Rest, Too

The story of Matt, Wheat, Freak, Titty, Foote, Cal was only one version of how Sid came to be the owner of the boat, if a boat could be owned, for the Book of Sid was never unmindful of the irony that in the process of unencumbering himself, Sid had collected yet another sentimental attachment.

The other stories of how he'd come to be the owner of the boat were neither lies nor imaginary. They only started in other places, other years, with other people and followed the same Sid through other experiences, but led always to the same yellow Volkswagen bucking and straining with the impossible weight of the sailboat, the headlights drooping like eyes when the journey was done. Sid might as well have strung up the sails, hitched the trailer on backward, and let the boat pull the car, instead, but the yellow Bug was dutiful in its struggle, if no longer purring, and never to purr again. Three miles Sid covered in two hours of driving, if driving was the word for the Volkswagen's drawl on the treadmill the road had become, the wheels catching and lurching, the hood buckling, a high popping and hissing, shaking the throatier sounds of the engine. Several times he overheated and needed to stop, along Snell Road's horizon of redwing blackbirds perched on the tops of cattails. Sid had already regaled me with what his psychedelically inspired Volkswagen manual advised when it came to the dipstick being too hot to touch. "You must wait . . . enjoy the scenery, take a little walk. If you have a bus, and a friend, it might be a good time to go in the back and ball."

Beyond the sea of chirping blackbirds there wasn't far to go. Which was a good thing, because the car wouldn't have made it otherwise. But the defunct lighthouse was a better place than most for embarkation even if Sid seemed to have no plans for us to sail anywhere, wanted only to moor within sight of the unblinking signals. Sid adored lighthouses, snuffed or otherwise. They made him think of votive candles flickering resolutely on altars, the lapping surf genuflecting on its way to safe harbor. This lighthouse stood on a knoll buttressed with chunks of concrete jutting into the horseshoe expanse of water. Its paint was pocked and battered, its stiff wooden doorway needed no lock, no hinges, just the tarry planks adhering. No grass in that jutting-out spot, just a single hasty fire pit ringed with bare earth. Funny that a breeze should be visible in such a place, I whispered to Sid when I finally got my voice, speaking of breezes. Sid didn't hear me, of course, except in the usual, unsatisfactory way. Why would wind be visible if there was no grass, no tree, nothing to blow? he wondered, as if the thought were entirely his own. If I pouted, Sid wouldn't see me. If I fretted, threw a hissy fit, slapped him, begged him, ordered him, he wouldn't comfort or console me, recoil, relent, or obey me. Which isn't to suggest I didn't enjoy his company. We may as well have been made for each other. Me a bucketful of yearning seething beneath the drape of an invisible nylon slip, and Sid a man who thought a thimbleful of yearning was too big to abide. He was just like any man sitting near me eating dinner unmindful of who had prepared it for him. Sometimes I scratched his neck. He thought my touch was the wool in his sweater. Sometimes I mussed his hair. He thought his hair was going wispy like an old person's did, and pulled off the elastics, and redid the white braid, and snapped on the elastics tighter than before. But we were together as close as was possible—no tree within two hundred yards of the lighthouse, and the tall marsh grass shrunken to stublets where the inlets gave way to the open lake, so we watched it together, that breeze—me stepping out of my nylon slip, for I was giving up even on lingerie, throwing my housewifely modesty to the birds, who couldn't see me anyway. If I were a scarecrow, I'd be nothing but the shadow of the top of the slanted pole, the ears of corn growing right through me so the birds had more kernels to steal—but still I was feminine, as they say, a single passageway all that remained of my house, and the dust swept outside past the perfumed threshold, and mossy quivering flowers clinging to the moisture on my walls. Sid passed that first evening at the lighthouse dreaming with his small head—his words, not mine—and slid his callused fingers past the flannel sheet with which he lined his nubbly sleeping bag, and supposing he still had some hormones left in him after all, gasped with my first glance under the covers, moaned with my second, moved his hand a little faster, and asked himself, Who didn't?

After midnight he got up and rekindled the fire in the blackened pit for supper. That's what Sid meant when he said he wouldn't shine his shoes for anyone. When hungry, he ate. Climbed out of the cottony lust of the sleeping bag and behaved as though the evening were just beginning.

Maybe it was the foam on the miniature crests of the whitecaps that made the air seem to tumble and spew that night, but Sid was warm in his sweatshirt and expert at starting the fire with bits of litter he collected along the lakeshore. Also some lengths of splintered planking he pulled off a wrecked dock wedged in the rocks. I sat naked beside him but pantomimed tucking my nightgown beneath me. A private joke: *What would Sid think, to know he was flanked by a naked woman, however illustriously resourceful he'd been in escaping us?* Naked, but dead. Dead, but not frigid, though what Sid didn't know wouldn't help me. How lustful I was, now that I was where I wanted to be, and how terribly untouchable. When I was alive, with the exception of my heels and my lipsticks and the playful swing of my pleats and the grand amount of hollering Jack loved the way I did while lovemaking, I was positively excruciatingly demure, as we housewives were expected to pretend to be, one hundred and one uses for Saran wrap notwithstanding, not to mention the year of the paper dresses. The dresses were fashioned of what felt like paper toweling printed with the same paisleys and checks decorating Gwen's shelf paper. Gwen and I supposed we were expected to roll to and fro on the floor if anything spilled, and let our husbands wipe their hands on us when they got done oiling the parts of the snowblowers. I bought a paper dress anyway, the idea that they were housedresses serving only as camouflage for certain more mischievous uses to which they might be put. I wore mine on the evening Jack accepted from one of his business associates two tickets to the symphony even though he knew how much I hated sitting still listening to music. Songs were for dancing, or driving cars. Raking leaves, I used to pipe my favorite radio station through the speakers outside, or playing hopscotch with Becka and Jenna when they were nothing more than two, their pebbles Parker House dinner rolls in case they picked them up and ate them. But to sit in a row of goggle-eyed concertgoers all hypnotized by the flicking cuffs of the conductor as if he were the person responsible for making the world go round just used to piss me off. Sid's words. Not mine. *Get my goat. Flip my lid. Get my gourd.* Jack didn't notice my dress was paper until intermission, when I steered us to a lady we knew from church. I was wearing proper underwear, tasteful jewelry, strappy shoes, a lacy shawl around my shoulders to soften the boxy cut of the sleeves. Worn in this fashion, the dress had a certain currency, I remember, an indolent droop at the neckline, an impertinent hem. The lady from church had an eye for such things, but no sense of humor. She said, "You're wearing one of those paper towel dresses! To the symphony! In the evening! Polly, you could get away with anything, couldn't she, Jack?"

Jack said he supposed that was true, Polly *did* get away with *almost* everything, and slipped the shawl off my shoulders to reveal where the stiff paper armholes jutted. In retaliation I stepped on his toe on the way up the carpeted ramp to the balcony, after which he scrunched his soft leather gloves on my seat so I sat on the squeaky fingers, in exchange for which I yanked on his belt when he rose to applaud, but we just couldn't get the better of each other that night, me and my husband. The dress tore in the car before we reached home, so we parked at the car ponds across the inlet from our lit-up neighborhood to tear at it far more effectively than it might manage on its own. Within minutes a policeman had knocked on the windshield, the yellow beacon of his flashlight sliding between Jack's bare chest and mine, but Jack told him go ahead and drag us to court, for there was no greater justice for a man than to be caught tearing party streamers off his own wife at the car ponds after the symphony, of all things. The policeman departed. The dress, once off, couldn't be patched on again. It was confetti. Rice at a wedding. Remnants of bits of tatters of pieces, like Jack's and my marriage is now. I remember our children playing in their sand box, throwing sand into the flour sifters, turning the crank, Dennis crying because he got some in his eyes, David patting him on the head with a plastic shovel, Drew burying Jack's watch, and Douggie thumping it with a stethoscope to see if it was ticking. Jack was at work, but that night in bed he had sand in his lashes, sand even in the pockets of his pajamas. I'd gone out and bought a new watch clean as a whistle, set it in the saucer where Jack had left it; turned out it was different from the watch the twins had glommed in the first place, but still I was the funnel through which they all came together, Jack and the piles of twins all reeking of the tanning lotion I'd smeared on their shoulders not knowing the harm it might cause. None of us mothers knew that, then.

Forgive us, I whispered to Sid, whose own mother had put no lotion on Sid's burnt shoulders at all.

But Sid didn't hear me. He was telling himself his own stories, as I intended. And as I intended, that first night on the lake at the defunct lighthouse, his stories had a way of falling in pieces, just like the paper dress. The gerbil left in its cage, the loyal Confederate sideburns, the ruckus raised by the blackbirds when the Volkswagen cooled and Sid banged shut the hood—I found I could pick them up, the parts of Sid's stories, and toss them over the waves like Jack used to skip flat stones with the boys, pieces of shale that bounced fifteen times if Jack threw them the best he was able, except mine didn't skip, my clamoring handfuls of stones, the gathered parts of the roiling stories plucked like nuggets of gold from the pages of the Book of Sid. The lake parted for them in a fistful of places, then closed hungrily over and let the stories shower the fields of tall, mirrored grasses waving at the margins of the sandpit where Tom Bane lay tangled in fishing line.

Because it wasn't the whitecaps making the night spew and tumble.

It was Tom and his ghostly plans.

Tom wanted his daughter. He was ablunder with need for Honey's admiration. Honey had taken to dreaming. At night in Tip's arms she dreamt of the lake and by dawn she'd be lacing her boots for a solitary walk, leaving even the dogs behind. My son didn't like her going, but he didn't like to say so. But when he woke from sleep and she wasn't by his side, it made him wonder if by mistake he'd broken up with her during the night. After some speculation it dawned on Tip that Honey'd left him simply because she wanted to take a walk, and he liked that even less, because no matter how many times a man said he admired independence in a woman, that didn't mean he should have to eat breakfast alone.

Also, Tip had heard a story on the news that scared him, although he didn't like to say so. Honey knew about it. She'd been sitting right by him when the news came on TV and felt how the story caused him to bear up and then to surrender. A man and a woman had been driving their truck along a four-lane. The newscaster said they were having a lovers' quarrel. The man slammed on the break and complained to his lover, "You go, then. Don't say I never told you to go." So she opened the truck door, stepping smack into speeding traffic, landed finally "on the hood of her own boyfriend's truck," Tip occasionally repeated out of the blue, while cooking their supper or sometimes just popping open a Pepsi.

Close to the cattails along Snell Road, Honey's walk led her this morning. So close she could taste the grains of pollen, her ears ringing with the peepers alert in the marsh, her socks soaking up with dew. She drew in a lemony fragrance of moss, thinking what a strange set of problems might occur simply as a result of her taking this enjoyable walk. For one thing, her morning walks made Tip unhappy, because they made of his and her nightly togetherness an uncertain thing, exactly as undependable as he once would have needed togetherness to be. Half asleep, he had said to her this morning, as she had set off, "You go, then. Don't say I never told you to go," as if she wouldn't do it otherwise, wouldn't follow the thoughtless twisting of corridors among the cattails just to see how much closer to the lake they led her now than yesterday, her ears ringing with the inevitability of the water. So far she'd steered clear of the pull of the water, the way she'd once steered clear of sex, wanting it to be there—pure, untouched—later on when she was ready for it. Besides, she had a funny feeling she'd see her lost boat out at some mooring, some other girl sunning herself on deck. She'd tell Tip about her walk when she got back, if it would make him feel better, if he wanted her to. Which he would, but he wouldn't say so.

Get away from that lake, I told her, but she didn't seem to hear me.

When she crouched at the car ponds to unlace her boots, I tossed in another handful of glittering pebbles, to distract Tom from her and from all of Tip's sorrows, which Tom kept in his larder like pickles in jars, the lids screwed on tight in preparation for the day he meant to open them and serve them up—the dills and the sours, the garlicky midgets seething in brine. Tom thought how lucky he was, and what a good plan he'd made, to pull Honey close and break Tip's heart at the same time. But Tip wouldn't eat Tom's bitter pickles if I had anything to say about it.

Wheat Freak Titty Matt Cal, Tom heard, bemused, his very jawbone unclenching molar by molar as if with a first sip of cocktail. *Matt Cal Wheat Foote Titty,* he heard, along with the part about the Betty Crocker file full of wide-open beaver, Matt's precise terminology rather than mine.

In spite of himself, Tom Bane was entertained by Sid's pebbly shower of memories. Tom became even a little relaxed, a little careless with eager sociability, this being the first party he'd dudded himself up for in he couldn't count how many years. An incisor fell out of his jawbone as if he'd chomped too trustingly on an olive. His ulna slipped free of the elbow. Honey paused with her fingers on the laces of her boots, deciding to visit her mother instead of taking a dip. Angie wouldn't be home, but at least there'd be the Post-it notes stuck on the kitchen table.

Meanwhile Sid greeted the morning embers of his campfire with well-aimed spit and regarded the pale doused fizzles of ash. A man like him—a man who'd just then forgotten the names of his friends—should empathize entirely with ashes, he thought, and did.

It took Sid nearly the whole next day to manage the job of putting the boat in the water.

He'd overlooked the boat ramps on his way to the lighthouse, and wouldn't dare make the Volkswagen struggle with the load another inch. The rear bumper was loose, and the chassis had settled during the night as if the car had been dropped from the crown of the lighthouse and bounced when it struck the ground. To what remained of the exhaust, the muffler barely clung. Sid could see the whole pan titled in the shadows between the misaligned wheels, but could find nothing leaking or oozing.

We strolled arm in arm to the boat ramps and hailed a man with a four-wheel, who agreed to tow the sailboat down the ramp in exchange for the pleasure of seeing Sid's home where his heart was. The boat gracefully took its place on the surface of the lake. Sid was tense with expectation—what if she sank?—and braced himself against the tiller, but if anything, the boat perched quite high on the hull, just so.

Behind the cabin of the boat, in the bilge where the water collected and sloshed, was a crank for lowering and raising the centerboard, which kept the boat stable. It wasn't easy to reach. Sid needed to twist around backward with his feet wedged against the ceiling and his head in the hole to see what he was doing. His shoulders became mired in the steamy dank grip of the bilge. He dropped his wrench in the water, held his flashlight between his teeth, managed to scoop up the wrench with the bucket, and cursed himself for enlisting in such a stinking excuse for a rattletrap die-hard navy.

The crank lock was broken. The centerboard wouldn't go down until Sid found his trusty WD 40, and then it wouldn't go up again until he twisted the kinks from the cable. Finally he untangled the extra line and rigging and coiled them loop over elbow, to be stashed near the backpack and cookstove in one of the latched deck benches. The stolen captain's flag he strung as a curtain for the makeshift head (the bathroom nothing more than an empty coffee can balanced on a roll of toilet paper), then took the flag down again, finding the arrangement disrespectful. But on the mast, in its element, the flag swayed with the current and made a puckering sound like somebody lipping a pipe. What was the name of the constellation Sid had stolen the flag out from under that night in the Philippines, he tried to remember, and *did* remember, but promptly forgot. Sid shrugged. What else was it he'd wanted? A brass clock and barometer. He hung his wristwatch on a hook above the plank he'd bolted in place for a table. If he was nodding in the lamplight and woke peering at the watch through a slitted eye, it would be like he was noting the phase of the moon, he said to himself, and forgot the ship's clock, and forgot the barometer, too.

The motor wouldn't start right away and the tiller came loose as Sid steered toward the mooring he'd picked out in the bay, but the anchor held fast when he lowered it down within sight of two cormorants fishing. Sailors recognized the long-necked, swivel-headed birds as emblems of gluttony and supplication, though to watch them Sid thought their hunger appeared only ordinary. The way they swiveled and peered, darted and dove, one fish in the throat and another in the gullet when they came up again for air, only to dive back under, headfirst as if in prayer, but greedily enough that the whole feathered body tipped in after, wasn't really so different from anyone else wanting some-thing and knowing how to get it, he thought. Like wanting lady-bugs to put in the potted plants and knowing all you had to do to get some was turn on the TV and they'd come flocking round. And Lysle's wife, Violet, used to stand at the desk at the trucking firm and not move an inch until they wrote Lysle's paycheck six days late and handed it sheepishly over. The fish-guzzling birds were no different, checking Sid out like someone spying on him through a periscope, wanting all his stories. Sid grinned, and wondered, *What* were they called? Of *what* were they emblems? then lay back against a cushion to light his small metal pipe. The seeds spat in the bowl like companions around a campfire. The afternoon passed. The birds could spy on him forever and discover only a man so mellow he'd forgotten a dinghy for paddling to and from the mooring, in order to purchase groceries and such. In a storm or if the motor on the sailboat conked out, he'd have to hail someone or swim. His boat was a peaceful island. The birds dove under it looking for fish. Toking, holding, coughing it out, Sid wondered if maybe fasting would be a fine way to celebrate the beginning of his ironical hunger for abstinence. He decided it would be, as long as he had enough stash. His word. Not mine. Evening neared. The marijuana was the thing that was making him forget things, he gratefully believed, never guessing it was me. At dusk while he sat smoking, flocks of seagulls rose into the sky to be silhouetted while feeding on clouds of lake flies, making a pattern like an Escher print, only more frenetic. Sid didn't want the crazy birds to stop darting, for it was pleasant to sit on the boat and smoke, and forget, and watch the white sky exploding in sharp, diving, black lunatic wedges. Still I didn't let him dream of the patterns when he dozed off to sleep, like Becka did, for that was her dream, not his, though she never made the connection, Becka, between the gulls and the dreams I encouraged her to have about them. The dream made Becka happier than she would otherwise have been, stood in for other freedoms she wouldn't let herself indulge. Sid never had any dreams, but whenever he woke, he believed he'd forgotten them. This morning he only needed to pee. The roar of his urine filling the coffee can wasn't as lonely as he'd imagined it might sound. From her place on shore around a wooded bend from where she couldn't see the boat, Honey could hear it in the ringing of her ears, and stepping closer, steadied herself on a moss-covered rock. She wondered what the girl had thought about in those last seconds between stepping from her boyfriend's truck and landing on the windshield—about a door that had opened too wide for her, maybe, and slammed behind her too loudly.

On some Rope Yarn Sundays, the navy requested that the enlisted men make Turk's head fancy work of all things. When Sid had put the lid back on the can and stood the can atop its roll of toilet paper, he tried to recall how Turk's head was done. Wrap the rope around a beam in one direction and another, then paint it white and haze gray. Simpler than it looked, unless he was forgetting the complicated parts. Sid always did like that color, what was it, again, *which* gray? The name vanished from his memory the second I tossed it overboard, sank past the grass stems translucent as glass. Still, Honey slid forward from mossy rock to willow bough, peering round the bend at a glimpse of boat that looked too familiar to bear. I tossed Tom the part about the sword on the Mekong not breaking the rind of the pumpkin. Obedient to its bladderful of air, Sid's memory of the pumpkin dove uncertainly and finally floated, but the sword struck the glassy green stems with a clatter that made Tom's bones vibrate with the sound of ice in tumblers at a cocktail party. How rollicking he felt. His ear bones slipped into the sand, along with the remainder of his teeth. He was burying the most sensitive parts of himself. I tossed him the name of a trail on which Sid had gone backpacking years ago. Sid recollected the sign atilt on a wooden two-by-four wedged behind a boulder at the trailhead, but the name was ablur under ferns and columbine.

That was the way the most hectic of our days proceeded, mine and Sid's. Doc smelled squashed lake flies on the soles of Honey's boots one afternoon, and then a day later on the hem of Honey's jeans, a bloom of red algae. She'd stuck her bare toe in the water, leaned out on a cushion of moss so spongy it barely held firm, but she still hadn't had a good enough look at that boat, for which she would have swum out in her clothing to try to buy it back again. In all her years of imagined swimming, she'd never once been submerged in a body of water, she realized with a start, then removed her hiking boots before dunking her feet to the ankles to compensate, her hands as well, the tips of her long hair skimming and dipping. I tossed Tom the stone about the menu for the gourmet freeze-dried meals Sid used to buy himself for backpacking over holidays, the whole potful of which a bear guzzled one Fourth of July when Sid was gathering kindling.

Sid sighed, unburdened, forgetting the menu, forgetting the bear, the dawn sky a page of fading stars with no stories to interfere with the slight mist they pulled from the lake. Honey, who wasn't the sighing type, positioned herself more matter-of-factly on the saddle of the willow while pulling from her pocket a bottle of sapphire blue.

The polish winked at the current as she smoothed it on her nails. Back away from the water, I begged, but Honey didn't want to listen. The brush slipped from her fingers, rolled the length of the log, and spun into thin air like a cottonwood seed.

I tossed Tom the stone about Sid's dead mother's Christmas cactus blooming on the wrong days.

Honey lunged for the dropped brush, felt a pang at the magnetic pull of the water, stronger than before, and clapped a quick, wet hand to her ear to quiet the ringing she heard in her head.

Sid forgot his first wife's sister-in-law's name and then how many times his second wife's father used to show up in the bakery wanting to buy cashew brittle just when Sid's wife was pulling Sid into the kitchen to trace her wooden spoon along the shrapneled lobe of Sid's ear. He tried to remember, were the wooden spoons clean when his second wife dangled them over his tongue, or had they held, in their grain, remnants of butterscotch, chocolate, coconut, cherries, raspberry cream, or praline?

Underwater, the glass stems splintered and rang until Tom's fishing line floated apart in two wavering tendrils, casting an opening wide enough for the rest of Tom's bones to escape him. The joints of the toes went first. How I wished I knew their names so I could bid them good-bye, scoot them more quickly away. This little piggy went to market. Nice seeing you. Drive safely, I bid them sweetly, averting my gaze from the sight of Tom's pelvis splitting into its proper oblivion, the femur slipping from the hip, the hip from the spine, until soon Tom's larder was left unguarded, the jars of Tip's sorrows untasted, their paraffin crumbling, their dates one by one expiring.

Honey, subdued, watched the dropped nail brush trace a sapphire ribbon of current away from her. That was me saying good-bye. I didn't know how else to say it, but I suppose it was enough because the ringing passed out of her ears. Squirrels clucked in the trees as she rose to go home, carrying her shoes by the laces. The morning was just beginning. Tip would still be in bed when she got there if he knew what was good for him. Hold him for me, I whispered to her. Give him a hundred kisses. Tell him you love him. And then, I said to her, pressing my luck, Make him say it back.

Time doesn't fly on this boat with Sid, but still the air begins smelling of autumn, geese gather in their V's as if in practice for flight, blown leaves drift to and fro. Every so often I allow myself to think about Jack.

What's *he* hunting this season? I wonder with a dash or two of sauce, half doubting he still misses me at all.

But if he does, what parts does he miss the most? Maybe the parts that are gone forever. Or maybe the parts I still have.

Then one day when Sid is mopping the aft deck, the Night fetches me away to see Jack in linen trousers on a lawn chair on a balcony watching the sun set over a golf course in one of the Carolinas.

On Saturday nights Jack often goes dancing, I learn, on Mondays and Tuesdays he likes to go camping, on Fridays he often charters a helicopter to take him and a date—a date!—along a coastline like gold coins trickling between his fingers, because what else is money good for? His date fastens her hair in a paper kerchief for one of those excursions. At the end of the evening the kerchief is still in one piece, a large paper triangle, which she folds into a smaller paper triangle before slipping it into her evening bag. Jack shudders, stunned. The children had been his permission to miss me. He didn't think in those terms, but still he knew it deep down in his gut, because that's where Jack knew things he didn't want to have to put into words. Every school play he'd ever attended had allowed him a pang twice over, one for watching the children remember their lines, and one for me because he couldn't keep from thinking I wasn't there watching it, too. When Jenna and Becka turned sweet sixteen, Jack, missing me, neglected to make them a party. And when Dennis got married, Jack barely danced with the bride. And when David and his wife were expecting the first of our grandchildren—whose names I don't know!—Jack opened a savings account in the newborn's name but never brought a stuffed toy or a ball. And back when the boys received identical report cards, the pairs of twin A's like a scaffolding upon which Jack felt more balanced than proud, he'd missed me, except that after a while it wasn't me he missed, really, but only some leftover fuzzy idea of me until even that was taboo. For he's a stubborn fellow, Jack, more stoical than Tip, if such a pointlessly courageous male feat is humanly possible. He still flips his lit cigarette backward inside his cupped palm.

But when the date refastens the clasp of her evening bag over the tight wedge of folded kerchief before taking Jack's hand to climb out of the helicopter, he recalls the paper dress we once shredded to streamers that night at the car ponds. For years, longing for me had been out of the question, but now he feels me so hard it makes him stand stock-still where he isn't supposed to, under the still-whirring blades of the copter. The pilot can't move him. The danger can't move him. I'd lead him out of it myself if his date weren't trying so valiantly to do so. She must have taken off the kerchief too soon. The propeller makes a terrible mess of her hair but gives her and Jack something to laugh about as she pulls him along on the tarmac.

My own hair is mussed, too, but Sid can't see it. I might comb it all night without him lifting a finger to part it. I might weep all I want to, buckets of tears although I have no tears, but Sid's bucket will still be hanging on the hook he's secured for it, the bilge water already dumped in the lake. Men, I whisper to Gwen, whom I find at the gym, at the weight machines. And now look at me getting all weepy, I whisper, weepy not for myself but for all us mothers, Freak's elk included, her baby paddling through the eddy she makes in the river, the elk bracing herself against the wildest current. Tip's never told Honey about the airplane he watched crash with Johnny, whose top forty hits he misses so much, I whisper to Gwen. Nor has Honey told Tip of her father's smashed biplane dredged from the lake years later, and that she doesn't miss her father at all. I don't know if their shyness about this event they have in common is a good idea or not, I say to Gwen, as if I have any say in the matter at all. Gwen sets the weight pin at sixty, and lying back on the cushioned contraption fits her elbows to the lifts. She'd disagree if she could hear me. A mother *has* to have say, she'd argue, in anything her child does or doesn't do, right or wrong. It's just that we can't know, then or later, how much they do was us and how much they do was them. Don't blame yourself for your child's antics, she'd tell me, but don't clap yourself too hard on the back, either. Tip'll do his own thing, at least that's how he'll see it, so you may as well look at it that way, too. Now get your ass back the hell to that boat where Sid's got something he wants to do for you and pardon my Tasmanian, she scolds, adjusting the headphones of her Walkman, content with the contradiction she and her husband, John, have agreed to uphold; their forgiveness of each other for Johnny's soaked, drowned khakis necessarily unspoken, because to speak it might undo their atonement of it.

Unmindful of my return, Sid lights the lamp with a wooden match, then fans out the sulfurous flame. When he throws the spent match to the water, it floats off like the parts of the raft the girl died on in Hong Kong harbor, but Sid doesn't remember that story. Instead the match puts him in mind of a child's diorama meant to depict bygone logging days. Before logging, before the lake had been damned, the fifty-mile expanse had been nothing but wild rice paddy. Why does Sid remember such a thing and yet forget . . . and yet forget . . . but what has he forgotten? he wonders. He's forgetting even what he's forgetting, he thinks, and slides out of his clothes to search the duffel for his sweats, the kerosene lantern casting its skittery glow against the walls of the cabin as he stifles another sneeze and strips to bare skin. Positively enfolded! That's how he feels. Something thunks against the bow. Two mallards, mates for life, knocking their beaks on our hull. Sid steps into the sweats, pulling the drawstring so loose around his hips he might slide his hand under if he gets in the mood. A funny couple we make, him in his sweats and me with no sweat at all. Soon he blows out the lamp and climbs into the V berth, resting his head on the laundry duffel within reach of a joint and his friend Thomas's cigarette lighter.

But after a moment, dismayed, he pulls himself up on an elbow, pulls his silver braid free of its bands, and combs it loose with a comb he finds in a duffel before gathering the hair into threes again. He remembers to pop open the hatch for fresh air, and for a moment watches the boarded-up window of the lighthouse, which really does seem to glint in the darkness. Something *is* bugging him. How is it that love has settled on *him* this evening? he wants to know. What has he done to deserve it? *H* is for *hermit,* but *S* is for not feeling as *solitary* as he had expected to feel. All the backpacking trips he's ever made by himself beat this journey by far in the loneliness quotient—the tree line visible below him, the bald, snowless slopes of the mountains so indifferent to his presence it was as if they were pretending to be asleep and would get up and be their usual, echoing selves once he stanched his puny fire and limped back to the trailhead. But the boat's another story, different from the one he thought he was telling. Perhaps it's a cop-out to imagine oneself a recluse on a boat, after all. A boat's a *she,* therefore a sailor can never be entirely a bachelor. With that, satisfied, he zips us both in his sleeping bag, takes another tasty sip of marijuana, snuggles against me, and closes his eyes.

G is for *gesundheit,* I whisper into his crumpled ear, and think a moment of my grave, the red granite marker uncluttered by memento, tended only by grasses and visited only by weather. Sid draws in a breath, arching his back. His sneeze blows me so far past the reach of the Night, I couldn't have stopped to put a flower on my grave even if I'd wished.

About the Author

Abby Frucht lives in Oshkosh, Wisconsin, with her two sons, Alex and Jess. The recipient of two National Endowment for the Arts Fellowships, she is the author of four prize-winning works of fiction, including the novels *Life Before Death, Snap, Licorice,* and *Are You Mine?* and the short-story collection *Fruit of the Month.* Ms. Frucht has written essays and reviews for the *New York Times,* the *Philadelphia Inquirer,* the *Chicago Tribune,* and other newspapers. She travels twice a year to Montpelier, Vermont, where she is a member of the faculty at the Vermont College MFA in Writing Program.